Prologue

As often happens to many authors when writing a story, the characters take on a life all their own. Such was the case of the first book in the Creed series of novels, *No Town for Outlaws*. In fact, the book even started out with a different title, and the Creed family was added as the story grew. Soon, they began to take over the story, with a multitude of twists and turns to their own stories that simply couldn't be told in *No Town for Outlaws*.

They began to haunt my mind as I started another story, one totally unrelated to the original book, or any of my other stories, until finally I put the others away to create a book dedicated to three of the Creed boys and their time in Arizona Territory before their father called them home in this prequel to *No Town for Outlaws*.

Ben, Todd and Zack Creed each begin to grow their own legends, as well as increasing the family legend, in this story of law and lawlessness in Arizona Territory. And if you like this tale of the Old West, there will be many more stories written about the Creed children, as well as their parents, in the future as I'm already inspired to write many more stories about the members of this family.

Cherokee Parks

Cherokee Parks

Silver, Gold And
Blood
In
Arizona

A Creed Novel

Cherokee Parks

Published by DS Productions

ISBN: 9781705479766

First Edition: August 2019

Book Cover Design: CowboyZone Enterprises

Printed in the United States of America

Dedication

This book is dedicated to all my friends and family who stood by me through thick and thin, and gave me support and encouragement throughout the years; to all the U.S. Military Forces at home and abroad, and their families, who are sacrificing so much so that we may remain safe, and free; and especially to every working cowboy the world over, for carrying on the traditions of a bygone era. They truly know the meaning of "The Code of the West," because, from Texas to Montana, California to Florida, including in Alaska and Hawaii, in places like Queensland, Alberta, Saskatchewan, and a thousand other places around the globe, they still live by it every day. God Bless you all.

Additionally, I'd like to include all the medical and hospital personnel who took care of me both before and after my surgery, and during the ensuing calamities that followed. Without them, I would still be living in horrific pain, and might not even be around as a result of the unrelated complications that popped up post-surgery.

"No man in the wrong can stand up against a fellow that's in the right and keeps on a-comin'."

Captain Bill McDonald - Texas Ranger

Chapter One

"I'm here ta take ya in, Thornton."

The big man standing at the plank bar didn't bother to look up before answering. "I ain't goin' no damned place 'til I get good an' by gawd ready. An' when I do, it ain't gonna be with you, whoever the hell ya are."

"Well, I reckon that's one way o' lookin' at it, 'cept that ain't the way it's gonna play out. You can ride with me peaceable like, 'r over your saddle. Your choice at this point. But one way 'r another, you're goin' back ta Prescott with me."

"Bob, you'd best just go on along with him. I'm not real anxious ta clean the blood off'n the floor again."

"Aw, shut the hell up an' pour me another whiskey, Stubs. The rest o' the boys'll be here shortly, an' I figure ta ride out with 'em when they go."

"Thornton, you'd best pay attention, 'cause I only got a warrant for you. But I reckon there's some what's wanted among your pals, an' I won't hesitate ta take them in with ya. An' I don't really care how I do it."

Finally, the big man stood to his full six foot seven inch height and three hundred pounds, and turned to face his accuser. The end of the makeshift bar was bright, and Thornton had to squint to see the man standing on the other end. "I reckon you don't have no idea how many men I've killed, do ya boy? It don't matter ta me who the hell they are, if they get in my way I just kill 'em."

"Yeah, like unarmed Indians, farmers, settlers, even women. But how good are ya when ya face somebody better'n you?"

"Sonny, I ain't met that feller yet, not in this territory."

"Bob, I'm tellin' ya, ya'd best go on along with this feller.

Don't you know who he is?"

"I told you ta shut up, Stubs. I flat don't give a damn who he is, he's as good as dead…" Thornton said as he made his move. He barely touched the butt of his Remington before the first slug entered his chest just above the second button of his shirt. The second slug ripped through Bad Bob Thornton's skull just below his left eye, and the big man fell, almost knocking over the plank bar.

"Sorry, Stubs, I gave him ever' chance. Any chance you got some fresh coffee 'fore I try ta load that pile o' shit on the back o' his horse? I figure I got near a two ride ta get back ta Prescott, an' I don't cotton ta my own cookin' 'r my brother's grub, let alone my camp coffee."

"It was fresh made an hour ago, Zack. Will that do ya?"

"Sure thing, Stubs. That ought ta give me a big 'nough jolt ta help me pick that big galoot up high 'enough ta get him over his saddle."

Both men chuckled, and then Stubs retrieved the coffee and a pair of cups. "Hope ya don't mind me joinin' ya, but I reckon I'd best fill ya in on somethin' I heard last night now that it's just you an' me in here."

"Sure, set down an' tell me what ya heard, an' who said it."

"Ya know, ya could cut off half a day if ya was to go over the top at Jerome."

"Yeah, hard ride though. 'Sides, I need ta try ta meet up with Todd west o' Fort Verde tomorrow afternoon. He should be comin' back up from a couple o' days o' scoutin' around Townsend for some rustlers workin' the area."

"Yeah, well that ties in with what I heard last night. There was a couple o' new riders come in, said they'd been workin' around

Townsend an' up an' down the Agua Fria an' Verde River basins, but when I asked 'em what outfit they was ridin' for they changed the subject. I got names, but I reckon they wasn't their real names. Carter Jackson an' Morton Forseth is what they give me."

"Believe it or not, Stubs, I think that's who Todd is lookin' for. An' you're right, their real names are s'posed ta be Jack Carter an' Seth Morton, so it doesn't appear they are very original in pickin' a name. Well, guess I'd best drag that hump out o' here an' see if I can get him loaded."

The young man polished off the dregs in his cup, stood and strode to the body, removed the gun belt and his money pouch, and then grabbed him by the heels and started dragging the three hundred pound carcass toward the door. When he stopped to catch his breath, Stubs asked, "Say, what was he wanted for this time?"

"Usin' Navajo an' Yavapai for target practice. Killed three men, two women and a baby last week outside o' Shong-a-pavi two weeks ago, an' a young Yavapai boy an' his mother ta the southwest o' Prescott last week."

"Damned fool thing ta do, even for a snake like he was. 'Course, nobody ever said Thornton was the sharpest tool in the shed. Zack, I'll help what I can, but my ol' back is all but done for. I got a spare plank in the back, an' maybe we can roll out one o' the empty barrels an' set one end o' that plank on it an' at least get him up ta where we can roll him onta the saddle."

"Yeah, that might work. Show me where that plank is, an' I'll grab it while you roll the barrel out. Fair 'nough?"

Twenty minutes later, they had tugged the body up the plank as far as they could, led the outlaw's horse alongside the end of the plank, and yanked and pulled until the corpse was bent over the saddle. Not wanting to take any chances on him slipping off, Zack tied Thornton as tight as he could to the saddle after covering him with his short tarp.

After carrying the plank back inside the saloon, Zack decided to sit down and rest for a moment before climbing aboard his blue roan for the trip south to Fort Verde, and then west to Prescott. Stubs had left their cups on the table, and brought the pot of now old coffee over, filling both cups, saying, "I s'pose I should be cleanin' up that blood 'fore it dries inta the floorboards, but I'm plumb winded."

"Ya think it'll discourage any o' your customers from drinkin' in here, Stubs?" Zack said with a smile.

"Naw, I don't reckon it will. In fact, it might even encourage a few more ta come in just ta see where Bad Bob Thornton bought it. Maybe I can even charge an admission," the saloonkeeper laughed.

Just then, three men came shuffling into the saloon, none to happy looking. "Stubs, that looks like Bob Thornton's horse outside with a body draped 'cross't the saddle. Is that Bob, an' who done it?"

"That would be me, mister. I'm carryin' a warrant for his arrest, an' he decided ta try not goin' along with me ta Prescott."

"An' just who the hell are you?"

"Yavapai County Deputy Sheriff Zack Creed."

"An' you outdrew Bob?"

"Yes, I did. What difference does that make, Callendar?"

"None, really. 'Cept that there's three of us now, not just one, an' ever'one o' us is as fast 'r faster'n Bob. It ain't lookin' real good for you ta leave here alive, boy."

"I don't have any current warrants on any o' ya, so my advice is that ya leave things be. As soon as I finish this coffee, I'm walkin' out o' here. Don't try ta stop me, 'r you'll just end up like your friend. Understand?"

The three men looked at each other, then one of the others said,

"Best stand up an' meet your maker, Creed. 'Less ya wanna go out settin' on your ass."

"Parker, I suggested real nice for you fellers ta let things be. Same goes for you, Nettles. Let it go. Ya see, here's the thing. I'll for sure get two o' ya, maybe all three o' ya. Yeah, ya might get me, but is it worth takin' the chance that you'll be one o' the two I get? Then there's also the chance that I get the third one winged sa bad he don't live long, 'r ends up crippled. I'll ask ya again, is it worth the chance? Now, I'm gonna stand up real slow like, then I'm walkin' out that door an' mountin' up ta ride. One move from any one o' the three o' ya an' I start shootin', got it?"

Zack rose slowly, moving to clear himself from the table and get as far from Stubs Allard as he could, not wanting to take any more chances than necessary that his friend might take a round accidentally. As he was moving, the three men separated by several more feet, obviously thinking the further apart they were the harder it would be for Zack to hit any of them. That was their first mistake. The second came before Zack was halfway to the door.

Even in the dimly lit room, Zack could see the first man make his move, and yanked his own Colt. He drilled the man while his hand was still in the air, then fired on the second man, who had grabbed the butt of his Remington, before firing on the third man, who had cleared leather but never got the chance to lift the barrel before the .44-40 slug lodged in his mouth. Walking to the only one who survived, the first man, it was apparent he wasn't going to last more than a few more minutes.

"Mister, I tried ta warn ya. Why'd ya think ya had ta try me?"

"Didn't believe nobody was that fast. Had ta see, I guess."

"Hate ta tell ya this, but I got a sister that's faster'n me, an' two brothers even faster'n her. You three wasn't even in my class. An' neither was your pal Thornton." Turning to Stubs, he continued.

7

"Stubs, I think I can load these three by myself, but now I'm gonna be late gettin' inta Camp Verde tonight. Any chance ya got somethin' I can gnaw on 'fore I get on my way south?"

"Not fixed, I don't. But if you'll wait a bit I can put on a slab o' fresh venison an' another pot o' coffee."

"Well, get it started while I make these three ready ta travel," Zack said as he grabbed the largest of the three and tossed him over a shoulder, and then walked outside. By the time he got to the survivor, the man had joined his friends in the afterlife.

As he walked back into the saloon after tying off the third man, Stubs was pouring a fresh cup of coffee after placing a plate full of steak and eggs on the table first. Hungrier than he realized, Zack wolfed it down in short order, washing it down with most of the pot of brew. Without asking how much he owed, he threw a double eagle onto the table, nodded and then started for the door. "See ya next time, Stubs. An' again, sorry for all the blood on the floor."

The saloonkeeper, coming out of the back room, just waved, and said, "No problem. Ya sure 'nough tried ta do it without any shootin'. Tell your brothers I said howdy next time ya see 'em, will ya?"

"Will do. I sure will," he said as he stepped into the mid-afternoon light and strode toward his horse, Blue. Stopping just long enough to reload, something he cussed himself for not having already done, he slipped the Colt back into its resting place, and then stepped into the stirrup and lifted himself into place. Leaving the lead rope tied to the horn, he started the nearly twenty mile trip south to meet his brother Todd west of Camp Verde. Hoping the Montezuma Café in the town surrounding Fort Verde would still be open when he got there late that night, he tapped Blue's flank and began his trip.

For the first mile, he caught quite a few looks, and decided that it must be a rare thing for the folks living in Cottonwood to see four dead bodies strapped to their horses and being led through town. Then again, he figured, that might be an eye catching sight about anyplace. But it wasn't long until he was alone with his thoughts.

Still a mile from Fort Verde, he could see the lights of several houses, the fort, and what he hoped was the café. He nudged Blue to a faster pace, but was a bit disappointed when just fifty feet from the Montezuma, the lights went out. Taking a chance that Sally might open up for him and fix him a decent meal, he pulled up out front, jumped down and ran to the door, tapping on it and calling Sally's name.

Sally Mercer was a widow woman from East Texas who had taken a liking to Zack and his brothers, sort of their second mother, and treated them accordingly. Seeing that it was Zack, she quickly unlocked the door and let him in, locking the door behind him. "Zack, what in the dickens are ya doin' out at this hour? You ought ta be fed an' bedded down by now. An' who are ya haulin' in dead this time? Set down while I have Chili put some coffee on. I just got a load o' Arbuckle's. Good thing, too, as all my customers was gettin' upset." Turning toward the kitchen, Sally called out, "Chili, Zack Creed's here! Put on a good steak, plenty o' taters, three 'r four eggs an' a fresh pot o' Arbuckle's!"

From the kitchen came a long, low moan. "But Sally, I was all but done cleanin' up the kitchen an' gettin' ready for mornin'."

"I know, but you can fix yourself somethin' an' come join us. That work?"

"Yes, ma'am," followed by more moans and groans, which elicited a smile from Sally.

"Well, ta answer your first question, I'm tryin' ta get ta where I can meet Todd tonight ta the west o' here. Them fellers is Bad Bob Thornton, Jim Callendar, Billy Parker an' Ted Nettles. I was up ta Cottonwood with a warrant for Thornton, but he decided ta put up

9

a fight. Time I got him loaded an' grabbed a snack his pals come ridin' in an' took offense ta my killin' their friend. So, they get a free buryin' in Prescott's Boot Hill with their friend."

"Serves 'em right. They was in here a few days back, give me all sorts o' grief 'til I brought out Cinderella an' threatened ta use her on 'em if'n they didn't start behavin'.'"

Zack couldn't help himself; he had to laugh at even the thought of Sally and her scattergun backing the four raucous outlaws down, especially with a shotgun named Cinderella. Sally let him have his laugh, as it seemed amusing to her as well.

"All right, pretty boy, that's about enough laughin'. Cinderella is liable ta take offense if ya keep it up, an' I like ya too much ta see ya get plugged by her," Sally said with a huge grin gracing her face.

"Coffee comin' up, Zack," came the call from the kitchen.

"Oh no, looks like I'd better get you some dishes and silver, young man, 'r we'll be pourin' that coffee on your lap." A minute later, Zach had a cup full of fresh coffee, a cloth napkin and dinnerware spread on the table in front of him, and not long after that a plate overflowing with good food.

"Where ya figure on beddin' down tonight, Zack?"

"Well considerin' I got four dead bodies out there, I reckon I'll head west from here, up Copper Canyon ta that little draw on the side o' Grassy Mountain. There was water an' decent grass last time I was through there, an' it's only another fifteen miles ta the Agua Fria, an' I should be able ta catch up with Todd there an' we can ride inta Prescott together."

"Well then, how about we put tagether a travel sack for ya. I got a pile o' corndodgers made up for tomorrow, an' ya can have some o' 'em ta share with Todd. You seen Ben lately?"

"Nope. Last we heard he was somewhere 'tween Prescott an' Wickenburg prospectin'. Reckon he'll surface 'fore long, either with a strike 'r another dead hole."

"Well, I'd sure like ta see him again. Tell him that, will ya?"

Chapter Two

After paying Sally and thanking her for reopening the café for him, Zack mounted up and started west. He was thankful for the full moon lighting the wagon road snaking up Copper Canyon, and for the reasonably easy climb, even though it was some twelve hundred feet in six miles. Still, it took him under an hour to get to the little spring-fed ribbon of water coming out of the short draw along the east side of Grassy Mountain.

Zack had just turned Blue into the draw when he caught the flicker of a campfire up ahead. Not knowing who might be where he had planned on settling in for the night, he quickly pulled up and tied off the horses on a good patch of grass. Digging into his saddlebags, he snaked out the high top moccasins his Yavapai friend, Grey Owl, had fashioned for him. They were still like new; yet as comfortable as anything he had ever put on his feet.

Working his way into the draw by staying in the trees and up on the slope, Zack finally came to a place where he could look down into the small camp. Though it was too dark to see their faces or hear what they were saying, their voices still carried up to him. One voice stood out, sounding all too familiar. Slowly he worked his way down closer to the camp, straining to hear what they were talking about. Finally, he could hear them clearly.

"Yeah, my brother an' I use this spot anytime we're near here. Fact is, I expected him ta be here when we got here this afternoon. Only thing I can figure is he ran inta trouble up in Cottonwood."

"You sure right, Todd, trouble four fold," Zack said as he stood and walked into the camp his brother Todd was sharing with two strangers.

"Took ya long enough, Zack. Where's your mount an'

12

prisoner?"

"Blue is down in the timber 'long with four more horses with bodies tied ta their saddles. You still got coffee on?"

"We just finished the last o' the pot, but I'll put on a fresh one while you fetch your critters."

Ten minutes later, Zack led the string of horses into the camp and tied the four with bodies off to a big tree in the middle of a sizeable stand of grass, not wanting to strip them and have to load them up again in a few hours. He led Blue to the rope corral with Morgan, Todd's horse, and the other's horses, stripped him and turned him into the corral, and then carried the saddle and bridle in closer to the fire.

Dropping them in a bare spot in between the saddles of the others, he shifted the saddle into a good position to sleep against, and then dropped down into the curvature to wait for the coffee, and find out who these other two men were. "So, Todd, who are your camp mates?"

"The very two fellers I was down south o' here to scout around an' find. Jack Carter an' Seth Morton, this here is my brother Zack. Zack, funny thing is, these fellers say they're Special Rangers with the Arizona Cattlemen's Association, not the rustlers we heard they was."

"Yeah, an' I knew they weren't cowboyin' anywhere, after Stubs talked to 'em last night at his place an' they couldn't name a ranch they was workin' on, but lawmen? That's pretty rich."

"Yeah, I thought so, too. Even went so far as ta try ta make sure they was on the level. Took me a hard ride ta Phoenix ta see if they was tellin' it straight, but I came back knowin' less 'n when I left."

"All right, so just what are two s'posed ta be Special Rangers for the Arizona Cattlemen's Association doin' up in this neck o' the woods?"

"I'm Seth Morton, Zack. We were told ta find out where the cattle were disappearin' to, no matter where it took us 'r what we had ta do ta find out. Cattle been missin' all the way from Cochise an' Santa Cruz Valley ta ever' spread in Maricopa County, an' from the looks of it they been comin' this direction. We haven't caught a single head yet, 'r even figured out where they're movin' 'em 'cause they ain't around here nowhere."

"Where ya looked 'sides 'round here?"

"We been as far as Strawberry an' Pine, but there wasn't a lick o' sign over that way, so we started workin' back south ta see if we could pick up any fresh sign. Todd here grabbed us just ta the west o' here, headin' toward the Agua Fria. Made us ride ta Phoenix with him just ta prove we was who we said we was. Then he made us stay with him ta set here an' wait for you. Said you'd wanna see to it your boss knew all about this, an' that he couldn't afford ta have us traipsin' around all over the place an' coverin' up the sign the two o' ya would need ta get ta the bottom of it."

"Well, he's right. I reckon the sheriff'll wanna know that stolen cattle are bein' run through Yavapai County for parts unknown. Fellers, I hate ta tell ya this, but you're goin' ta Prescott with us in the mornin'. I figure we need to roll out at least an hour for sunup, so we'd best shut it down for the night an' get some shuteye. Whattaya think, Todd?"

"Agreed, brother. See you fellers come mornin'."

***

By the time the sun started to peek over the horizon, the boys and their new traveling companions had crossed Oxtail Draw and were skirting Cienega Creek headed west. Even leading four horses carrying the dead, they made good time and rode up in front of the Yavapai County Sheriff's Office just after four that afternoon. Fortunately, the sheriff was in, and listened with great interest to Zack's explanation of events in Cottonwood before sending one of the jailers to fetch the coroner.

He didn't lose any interest once Todd introduced the two Special Rangers, and listened to their tale of rustling cattle and running them somewhere into Yavapai County, but they weren't please with how he handled it. "Gents, I don't care who you are, or that Todd has tried ta verify it, you aren't gonna run around MY county chasin' cow thieves. Now, ya can ride with Todd an' Zack while they chase down these rustlers, an' once they get 'em corralled ya can ride back an' tell your bosses you helped snag 'em, but they'll be tried here in MY county. Got that?!"

After several attempts to change the sheriff's mind, they gave up and agreed to work with Todd and Zack to track down the rustlers and see if they could put an end to their employer's miseries. Then it was Todd and Zack's turn to try to convince the sheriff that they already had enough on their plate. Giving up after a few minutes, they asked for one more thing.

"Boss, any chance we might get a day 'r two ta rest up an' rest our animals 'fore we go back out again?"

"Well, that I can let ya do, boys. After the way ya cleaned up Flagstaff when I sent ya up there an' the way you're takin' this bull by the horns, I reckon I owe ya some time off anyway. Ya can check with the other deputies an' see if they've seen any unusual movement o' cattle that don't look right. Oh, an' 'fore I forget it, Ben was by here a day 'r two ago askin' about ya. Said he'd be at the Hotel Congress 'r down on Whiskey Row, an' ta tell ya ta come find him."

"'Bout time he showed up here again. What say we go get our critters boarded an' go find him, brother?"

'Sure thing, Zack. Sheriff, we'll let ya know 'fore we decide ta ride out."

"What about us?" asked a puzzled Jack Carter.

15

"Well, I'd say you're on your own for now. Like ya heard, we'll be around a day 'r two 'fore we go on the hunt. 'Til then, I reckon ya can find somethin' ta do here in Prescott. See ya in a couple o' days," Todd offered them as an answer before grabbing Zack and heading for the door.

An hour later, after getting their horses put up, they made it to the Hotel Congress, but Ben wasn't in his room, having told the clerk that if his brothers came looking to send them to The Palace Bar on Whiskey Row. From force of habit, the brothers split once they stepped through the doors to the saloon, each stepping to an opposite side of the entrance and waiting for their eyes to adjust before walking into the depths of the building.

After a few minutes, they were able to see well enough to recognize Ben seated against the back wall with a bottle of whiskey on the table in front of him. Zack walked along the bar while Todd walked along the row of tables placed against the wall, meeting at Ben's table. "Ben, you payin' attention, 'r sleepin' with that drink?"

"Oh, I seen ya come in, boys. I just been focusin' on that feller standin' at the end o' the bar. Set down an' I'll have the barkeep bring a couple o' glasses."

Each brother taking a seat, Todd asked, "So why ya watchin' that character?"

"He picked up my trail 'bout halfway 'tween here an' Goodwin, an' he's been like a tick on a dog's ear ever' since. He thinks he's pretty sneaky, but I spotted him not a minute after he started doggin' me. An' I'll wager when I head back out he tries ta stay with me ta my claim."

"You hit somethin' somebody'd be interested in?"

"Too soon ta tell if it'll pay 'r play out, but I got good color. It assays out ta roughly ninety-five percent, real high grade ore. It's

16

been alluvial ta this point, an' I'm still lookin' for the source of it all."

"Damn, Ben. That's one o' the best assays I've ever heard of 'round here lately. 'R anyplace else for that matter."

"Yeah, well if it holds, I'm gonna need a lot o' help gettin' it out. Ya wanna come in, I'll give ya forty-nine percent ta split 'tween ya if nothin' else changes."

"Really? Well, how soon ya think you'll know that?"

"It may take me two, maybe three months 'fore I can find the real source an' see how it looks, but if it starts payin' big I'll either come get ya 'r send for ya."

"Where's this claim at?"

"I ain't tellin' nobody 'til I know if it'll pan out. 'Til then, not even the assayer knows for certain, 'cause I gave him one o' my old claims as the location for this last ore. I'm already drawin' flies like that one at the bar, so I'm gonna keep it hid 'til I'm ready ta start real production on it. You boys ate yet?"

"Nope, not yet."

"What say we chow down back at the Congress? My treat. Say, how long you boys gonna be in town?"

"Just a couple o' days, Ben. Seems there's some rustlers stealin' cattle south o' here an' movin' 'em north through here somewhere. Sheriff has sent us ta bring 'em in. You?"

"Pullin' out day after tomorrow. Just came up ta grab fresh supplies. My burro come up lame, so I'm buyin' a new one off o' Saltpeter Murphy. He's a tad on the high side, but he always has the best livestock, sure worth the money. Now let's get out o' here," Ben said standing. Yelling across the bar to the bartender, he said, "Petey, you can have the rest o' this bottle! I'll see ya again tomorrow afternoon!"

The barkeep waved as the three brothers strode through the door and out onto the boardwalk, chatting and laughing as they made their way down the street toward the Hotel Congress, Ben sobering up quickly on the three block walk to the Congress. Halfway there, Zack pointed out, "Ben, your shadow is back there. Want me ta see who he is an' if he's got any special plans?"

"Naw, not yet. 'Sides, I know who he is. Wait 'til we make the corner, an' then drop off an' wait for him. Me an' Todd'll step inside the lobby an' then out the side door an' catch ya back at the corner."

As they rounded the corner, Zack stepped behind a big bush and dropped down while Todd and Ben continued on across the street to the hotel. A few minutes later, the man rounded the corner and stopped on the boardwalk watching the hotel entrance.

"You lookin' for somebody special, mister?" Zack said as he stepped out from behind the bush, Colt in hand and pointed directly at the man.

The stranger jumped, and stuttered, "N-n-no, s-s-sir. J-j-just takin' a walk is all."

"Well, I'm not buyin' it. You was standin' in The Palace a few minutes ago, an' followed us when we left. Now tell me who the hell ya are an' why you're followin' my brother."

"I-I-I d-d-don't know what you're talkin' about, mister."

"Well, my brothers will be back here shortly, an' we'll be expectin' the truth when they do. If we don't get it, you'll be settin' in the county jail 'til ya decide ta talk."

"Jail? But I ain't done nothin'. How can ya put me in jail?"

"Suspicion."

"Suspicion o' what? Walkin'?"

"Ben, this critter ain't talkin'. Ya said ya know him?"

18

"Yeah, I do as a matter o' fact. Charlie, what the hell you followin' me for? Somebody put ya up to it?"

"Y-y-yessir, Mr. Creed. Mr. Meador sent me."

"Boys, Charlie here works at the general store in Wickenburg from time ta time. I went in ta Wickenburg for the last bunch o' supplies I needed, an' paid with gold nuggets 'cause I didn't have any ready cash. Charlie an' his boss, Pendleton, made a big deal outa my payin' with nuggets, an' this character callin' himself Simpson came in while I was gettin' loaded up ta leave. He overheard our conversation, 'r at least enough of it ta make himself some assumptions. He caught me outside the store, an' started pressin' me ta sell him a part o' my claim, askin' where it was an' such. I turned him down flat, an' now we got Charlie doggin' me, no doubt ta try ta find out where my claim is."

Turning back to the frail looking man surrounded by the Creed brothers, Ben continued. "Charlie, you head on back ta Wickenburg first thing tomorrow. Tell Simpson that you have no idea where my claim is, an' that I all but lost ya three 'r four times comin' ta Prescott. You can also tell him that ya checked the assayer's office, an' the claim is somewhere 'round French Gulch, ya think. Look, you don't tell him ya got caught, 'r that I told ya want ta say. Here's a double eagle for ya ta keep all this 'tween us. Fair 'nough?"

"Yessir, Mr. Creed. Sure thing! These fellers is your brothers? An' they work for the law?"

"Yup, deputy sheriff's, both o' 'em. Now g'won an' git. We're gonna go get us some grub. See ya next time I go ta Wickenburg, Charlie. An' remember what I told ya ta say, hear me?"

"I sure will, Mr. Creed. You have a real good night now. An' I'll be gone south by daylight. An' just so ya know, I don't like that Simpson feller, but my boss said ta do what he wanted. I think the two o' 'em come up with havin' me ta follow ya."

"Alright, Charlie. Thanks for lettin' me know. Tell ya what, I'm workin' on something, an' if it works out I'll give ya another double eagle next time I see ya. How's that sound?"

"Real good, Mr. Creed."

Chapter Three

Once Charlie had meandered down the block, the three Creed brothers crossed Gurley and stepped into the restaurant at the Hotel Congress, grabbed a table, much to the consternation of the maître d', and made themselves comfortable. A pretty waitress somewhere in her twenties hustled across the dining room, making certain that she was the one waiting on these three handsome men. Bringing a fresh pot of coffee with her, she apologized for not bringing cups with her, but promised to return with them as soon as she could.

"That's fine, Mitzi. I see ol' François is still givin' ya grief. Man, did he give us the stink eye for not lettin' him seat us, but I wanted ta sit in your area 'cause then I'm guaranteed ta get good service."

"Why, thank you, Ben. That's so sweet of you to say," the blonde with the twinkling eyes and smile said, pouring on the sweetness. "Do you handsome men know what you'd like to have for dinner tonight?"

"Me, I want the biggest steak in the house, plenty of taters, sautéed onions an' mushrooms smotherin' that steak, an' a big cold glass o' milk for starters," Ben said, obviously going off the menu for his order.

"You know what, I believe that'll do me, too," Todd said.

"Might as well make that three orders the same, Mitzi," Zack said rather sheepishly.

"Yes, sir! I'll turn in your orders, and be right back with your cups. Oh, the pastry chef made fresh apple tarts today, and I have just a few left, in case you'd like something sweet for dessert," the waitress said, smiling at Ben.

Ben nodded, and watched as Mitzi sashayed across the floor toward the kitchen door. Zack and Todd were soon teasing him about settling down and starting a family. "Now, fellers, you just have no idea. Mitzi an' me are just friends, an' I aim ta keep it that way."

"She might have different ideas about that, Ben, from that smile o' hers an' the way she struts for ya."

"Hah! She's all show, hopin' for a good tip is all. An' she always gets one from me. 'Sides, I think the local banker's son is the one she's really after. Girl has an eye for money, an' that damned sure ain't the kind o' gal I'd ever want ta hook up with."

They fell silent as she approached carrying their cups, and then made a big show of serving their coffee. "Benny, are these the brothers you talk about? The deputies?"

"Mitzi, if I've told you once I've told you a dozen times, it's Ben, not Benny, An' yes, these are two o' my brothers, an' yes they work for the Sheriff's Office."

"Sorry, Ben, but I like calling you Benny. It kind of makes you my fella, at least as long as you're at my table," Mitzi said with a big smile. "My, good looks must run in your family," she added, rubbing up against first Todd's shoulder, and then Zack's. "Oh, I forgot to ask how you boys wanted those steaks, so I told the chef to make them all the same, rare. Is that alright?"

Both Todd and Zack nodded that it was, so she continued. "They'll be out shortly. Shall I bring your milk now, or with your meal?"

"Anytime is fine, but one glass might not be enough, just like one pot of coffee won't be enough for us."

"I'll bring another pot out with your meal as well, then. Say, I almost forgot to tell you, Ben. There was a man in here looking for you earlier today. Said he was an old friend of yours. I sent him to

The Palace. Did he find you?"

"Can't say he did. He give you a name?"

"Sam Stoddard. He made real sure about that, that I knew his name."

"Stoddard, eh? Well, he ain't no friend o' mine, but he didn't show up ta The Palace either. I collected the bounty on him when I first come ta this territory, an' I s'pose he's just gettin' out o' prison now. Prob'ly figures ta settle a score," Ben said shaking his head.

"Anything we need ta know about him?" Zack asked.

"Naw. He's no backshooter. He'll want ta face me down. Nothin' ta worry about. He's quick, just not that quick. Here comes the grub. You boys hungry? You'd best be!"

As the huge platters of food were placed on the table, Mitzi had to make a second trip back to the kitchen to bring out the milk and a second pot of coffee, loading the table to the edges. The Creed's dug in, and were nearly halfway through their meal before any of them spoke again.

"Zack, what's the sheriff got ya doin' next?"

"Me an Todd is goin' huntin' for some cattle rustlers from down south a piece. We got ta work with a pair of rangers with the Arizona Cattlemen's Association what was hired ta find 'em, but the sheriff don't want anybody outside the county ta take down any criminals, no matter where they come from."

"They're movin' stolen cattle north instead o' down inta Mexico? That seems kind o' strange, don't it?"

"Yeah, that's what I thought, but I rode clear inta Phoenix ta get the lowdown on these rangers, an' the rustlin'. It's the straight of it, at least as far as I can tell. I run onto 'em over just east o' here," Todd filled in what he knew.

23

"Well, first off, why was they lookin' over this way? If it was me, the last thing I'd even think of was ta run stolen cattle up the Black Canyon. Nor would I take 'em up the Verde, either. If it was me, I'd run 'em up Sycamore Crick an' then over inta the Tonto Basin, then on up toward Green Valley. But here's the thing, they got ta have someplace ta stash 'em, 'r a buyer waitin' that can move 'em pronto so they don't get found. I wonder if there ain't somebody up 'round Winslow that's handlin' the cattle, sellin' 'em 'r loadin' up on the Sante Fe and shippin' 'em east from there. Yessir, if it was me I'd ride east a bit, see if I couldn't pick up a trail over in that direction."

"Ya know, that' makes a lot o' sense, Ben. Zack, whattaya think?"

"Well, I reckon early in the mornin' day after tomorrow, we'll be riding over ta the Tonto Basin an' see if we can't find some sign. Guess we'd best look up 'em two rangers an' let 'em know."

"Well, I ain't gonna spend too much time lookin', I'll tell ya that. I got a hunch, from what I've seen, them two are green as gourds. I just believe we can travel faster an' make less commotion goin' on without 'em. Might stand a better chance o' catchin' 'em picaroons if we was to set out alone."

"I think you're right, Todd. The way I see it, if they catch up with us tomorrow, we might let 'em in on it ta keep 'em from whinin' ta the sheriff, but that'd be the only reason."

"Well, it looks like you boys are about ready for dessert. Three apple tarts?"

"Yes, ma'am, and more milk an' coffee, if you'd be so kind," Ben said without asking either of his brothers if they wanted the sweets.

A few minutes later, they were each served an apple tart with a generous helping of whipped cream on top. But those tarts didn't

24

last long, disappearing in less time than it took to plate them and deliver them to their table. Pouring fresh cups of coffee, all three leaned back in their seats and took a deep breath, and then leaned back in to sip their brew.

"Ben, ya sure ya don't want ta go with us on this trip? We could sure use the backup…"

"Naw. As much as I'd like to, I need ta get back down ta my camp. I know the two o' ya can handle it just fine. Just keep your heads down, an' don't walk inta any traps an' you'll be back here in no time with them rustlers in tow. I don't know 'bout you two, but that meal made me plumb sleepy. I reckon I'll head up ta my room an' get some rest. You two stayin' here?"

"Naw, we keep rented rooms over ta Mose Brody's place. Needed someplace cheap ta store our stuff an' ta lay down when we're here in town. Maybelline made us a deal, an' Mose makes sure nobody bothers our gear."

"Sounds like you gonna get a chance ta walk off your supper, eh?"

"Yup, an' I s'pose we'd best start that direction. We'll need ta take care of a few things ta get ready in the mornin' so we can pull out the mornin' after. Where you gonna be so's we can catch up with ya tomorrow?"

"If I ain't here in the hotel, I'll be at The Palace 'r at Renner's Café. Ol' Jason is a good guy, an' me an' him like ta jaw from time ta time when I'm around. Ya know he's from Hitson, didn't ya? Kinda nice ta talk ta somebody from back home from time ta time. That an' his wife is a damned good cook."

"Shoot, he's never said a word the few times I been in there. There's quite a few Texas folks 'round, but none from too close ta Colorado City. Well, maybe we'll catch ya there tomorrow, an' ya can introduce us proper. Ben, see ya in the mornin'. Oh, you did say this was on you, right?" Zack said with a big grin.

"Yeah, I did. G'won get outa here. I'll see you boys tomorrow."

The brothers shook hands, Zack and Todd going their separate way while Ben sat at the table for a few more minutes, mostly waiting on Mitzi to let him know what he owed for their meal rather than chasing her down or dealing with the snooty François. It didn't take long before the waitress came prancing out of the kitchen and straight to where he sat.

"Anything else I can do for you, Ben? Oh, and I have a change of uniforms here, so I don't really need to go home to rest. That is if you want some company tonight…"

"Mitzi, like I've told ya before, I like ya, but not enough ta sleep with ya. You'd be better off flirtin' with some o' the local lads, 'cause ta tell ya the truth I'd tip well as long as the service is good, no matter how pretty and sexy you are. Now, how much I owe ya?"

"Twelve dollars, Ben," she answered, biting her lip slightly in a mock pout.

"All right. Here ya go," Ben said as he handed her an eagle and a double eagle. "Just make sure to take good care of my brothers when they come in, will ya?"

Smiling a toothy smile, she nodded, tucked the money into her apron pocket, and practically skipped to the cash register. Ben could only smile at the exuberance of youth, as his mother had once called it, and again at the sight of the sneer on the face of François. Ben couldn't help himself as he mocked the maître d' with a sneer of his own.

Ten minutes later, he had climbed the stairs, strolled down the long hall to his room, entered, dropped his clothes and was fast asleep, barely in the bed.

That was exactly where Ben was still laying when the sun trickled through the window the next morning. But the light no more than tickled his face and he was up, rummaging through his possibles looking for a fresh shirt. As he washed the sleep from his eyes, he decided that his first stop of the day would be Renner's. He quickly dressed and skipped down the steps, in a hurry to get that first cup of coffee of the day.

As he stepped out the lobby doors of the hotel, he suddenly remembered that Sam Stoddard was in town and looking for him. He stopped dead in his tracks, reversed course and retrieved his gun rigging, and then continued on his way to that cup of coffee. Fifteen minutes later, he and Jason Renner were sipping hot brew and chuckling at the latest joke Jason had been told by another customer. But the thought of Sam Stoddard never left Ben's mind for a second.

At the same time, Zack and Todd were sitting in Zack's room making a list of the items they would need to take with them, not knowing exactly how long they'd be gone, or where they'd be able to resupply once they were on the trail. Satisfied they had thought of everything they'd need, they split the list. Zack would line up all the ammunition they planned on taking, and Todd would arrange for the foodstuffs and other items. They had two packsaddles, but owned no packhorses. Besides the two regular mounts each normally rode, they each had a second mount. Fresh horses on a long ride would be a premium, so they were thankful for having the extra riding horses, even if they had to use them as packhorses for part of the trip.

After they left to assemble their supplies and extras, Zack remembered that he had left all his tarps with the coroner, wrapped around the dead bodies he'd brought in. Thinking about adding one more stop, the coroner's office, he wondered if the tarps were still good enough to use, or if he should just spring for new ones. Opting for new ones, he made a mental note to swing by the ice company; the only place one could buy tarps cheap.

By noon, the brothers had gathered all their supplies, or arranged to be able to pick them up that evening, and met at the sheriff's office to compare notes and check in with their boss. The sheriff was out on an investigation, leaving them to their own resources for the rest of the day. With a couple of hours to spare, they decided it was time to see what Ben was up to.

As they approached Renner's, Ben had just stepped outside and was standing on the boardwalk looking around when he spotted them. That's when the voice rang clear in the morning air.

"Creed! I'm here ta kill you! Grab that iron so I can call it a fair fight!"

"Sam, let it go. You served your time. It's over. I don't want ta kill you."

"Hah! You kill me? That's a laugh. The only reason you even took me is 'cause ya had the drop on me. Now we're startin' out even, an' you're the one dyin' here today. Now pull that pistol!"

"Not gonna do it 'less ya force me to, Sam. No need ta take any chance that some innocent will catch a slug."

"The hell with 'em. If they ain't got sense 'nough ta take cover, that ain't my fault."

"I still ain't gonna pull 'less ya don't give me any choice, Sam. Let it go, an' walk away while ya still can."

Ben had no more than gotten the words out when Stoddard started his draw. A draw he never finished as Ben's first bullet struck him in the right shoulder, forcing him to drop his pistol. Figuring it was over, Ben holstered, but Stoddard pulled another pistol from his belt with his left hand. Ben's second shot entered in the middle of Stoddard's face, permanently closing Stoddard's eyes and dropping him to the ground like a rock.

Chapter Four

"Ben, I'll need you to stop by the office and fill out a statement. No problem with the shooting, as I saw it all go down. You gave him every opportunity to walk away, and it was clearly self-defense. I'll handle it with the city attorney, though he may want to interview you," City Marshal Jim Dodson stated.

"Well, he'd best do it today if he does, as I'm pullin' out before daybreak tomorrow."

"I'd rather you delay that for a day, just in case."

"Not gonna happen. Like you said, it was self-defense, an' if he won't take my statement an' your word on it, he can go ta hell. Or he can see if he can find me yet today, 'cause I got a claim ta work an' it ain't gonna get done if I'm hung up here."

"Alright, Ben. Like I said, I'll handle it, as long as I get that written statement from you before you leave town."

"I'll come by an' fill out a witness statement as well," added Jason Renner.

"We will as well," Zack offered on behalf of himself and Todd. "Havin' two deputies ought ta carry some weight with that lame brained attorney."

"I doubt he'll accept your word, boys, since it was your brother involved, but you can give me a statement and I'll add it to the stack. Well, I was on my way to investigate somebody stealing Mrs. Bostwick's chickens, and you know how she can get if she thinks somebody doesn't drop everything at her beckoned call Still, now she's got to wait until I get the coroner to pick up this body."

"Now, there's a call I wouldn't wanna take, Jim. Good luck with that one!" Todd laughed. "I was sure glad when the city annexed Mrs. Bostwick's place, saved us havin' ta run out there for nothin' every week!"

Jim joined in the laughter, but hurried away to fetch the coroner, checking his pocket watch as he walked off. Ben turned to his brothers and asked, "Were you boys comin' ta find me?"

"Yup, but we'd hoped ta catch ya 'fore ya left, an' get some coffee here first," Zack said.

"Well, I'm plumb coffee'd out, fellers. I was headin' for The Palace when Stoddard showed up."

"Jason, I reckon that let's us out, an' we'll have ta settle for that gawd awful stuff they serve at The Palace. Shall we go?"

Ben responded by shaking Jason's hand and saying, "Jason, I'll see ya next time around. Boys, let's head out. I got something I wanna talk to ya about 'fore we all leave town again, but let's stop by the marshal's office an' get them statements filled out first." Without waiting for an answer, Ben started walking away.

After filling out their statements, the trio walked down Montezuma to the saloon, walked in, found a table and ordered beverages, Ben a bottle of whiskey and the boys ordering coffee. "Alright, Ben, what was it ya wanted to tell us?" Todd asked.

"You don't wanna have a drink with me first?"

"Naw, the sheriff don't like it when his deputies drink during the day, so we'll just stick with this goop they call coffee."

"Alright, then. While I was talkin' ta Jason, he told me Jake Bidwell was by ta see him. Jake an' me worked a claim tagether for a time, down by the Superstitions, an' since we was only pullin' a few dollars a day in dust, I pulled out. He stayed there ta work the claim 'til he plumb give up on it. I figure he really pulled

31

out the same reason for the same reason I did, a notion that we needed ta keep our hair. Them Apaches didn't take too kindly ta us snoopin' 'round. Well, sir, I ended up here in the Bradshaw's, an' Jake went ta huntin' in the Tonto Basin somewhere off o' Tonto Crick."

"Ben, that still ain't tellin' us anything."

"Zack, ya need ta learn a tad more patience, boy. I'm gettin' there, just needed ta let ya know I trust the source o' what I'm 'bout ta tell ya. Seems Jake was comin' down the Tonto late one afternoon, headin' down for supplies, when he seen a good sized herd o' cattle bein' pushed up the Basin. He hid out, not knowin' who they was, an' they pushed 'em right straight up Tonto Crick. They was still headin' up the last he seen o' 'em. Like I said last night, if I was lookin' ta move large numbers o' cattle without bein' seen 'r makin' sure they wasn't easy ta track, that's the way I'd go with 'em. Once ya get ta the Green Valley area, there's a hundred 'r more places a fella could hide five 'r six hundred head. An' from there it ain't but a three day push ta Winslow. If ya don't find what ya want there, look further east, toward Pleasant Valley. From there, if they don't take the herd north they could move 'em toward New Mexico. The Mormons won't do anything ta stop 'em 'less they start ta messin with what's theirs, includin' the women. That whole area, well, let's just say ya need ta tread lightly an' stay away from all the people ya can while you're up there."

"Thanks, Ben, for passin' that nugget along. Might save us a heap o' trouble 'fore we're done."

"That ain't all o' it, either, Todd. Seems them two sidewinders ya ruin into might o' been workin' for the Cattlemen's Association alright, an' scoutin' for the rustlers on the side, 'r just usin' the Cattlemen's Association as a cover up. Either way, it's highly likely they're in on the whole thing."

"How'd ya figure that out, Ben?"

"Jake again. Them two fellers was in ta eat while Jake was there, said he knowed 'em ta be no account."

"Ya sure it was the same pair?"

"From Jason passin' on Jake's descriptions, it had ta be the same critters. All I'm sayin' is if they ride out with ya, ride easy 'round 'em."

"Well, we ain't seen 'em since we rode inta town with 'em, an' I sure don't figure ta go lookin' for 'em, either. If they find us, so be it, but that's how it's gonna have ta be."

"I got it figured the say way, brother, 'less the Sheriff tells us otherwise when we make our last check in 'fore we pull out."

"Well, tell him what I found out when ya see him. If that don't do it, then you'll have ta figure out how ta handle if they show. You all lined out ta go?"

"Yessir, all we got ta do is load up, check our weapons, and get a good night's rest."

"Same here. But I do have one more thing other than that. If it works out, well, I'll tell ya 'bout it next time I see ya. Ya sure ya won't have a shot with me?"

"Naw, in fact I think we'd best see if we can find the boss an' start gatherin' up our gear an' gettin' loaded. It'll be dark time we get finished up."

"Me, I made a deal with Salty ta collect all my supplies and get the burro packed so all I got ta worry on is my possibles an' check my weapons. Clete put new shoes on Captain so he ought ta be ready ta ride. Got some pretty rough country ta cover, an' good shoes is a requirement where I'm goin'."

"At least you know where ya can go for supplies when ya need 'em. We won't know 'til we see a place."

"Now, Todd, that just ain't so. Guess I should o' told ya. Ya can always get supplies in Green Valley, but watch your step there as that's where most o' the renegades load up. Or down in Pleasant Valley there's a store the Mormon's set up where ya can reload. There's two 'r three little mercantile stops along the Mogollon Rim, one o' 'em is run by ranchers mostly for their own hands ta buy tobacco an' such an' the other two is run by scalawags tradin' with the Apaches 'r any Navajo that drift their way. Up toward Winslow, there's a couple o' little towns started by the Mormons that'll sell ya supplies as well, just no tobacco 'r liquor. Guess it all depends on where the trail takes ya, but there's plenty o' places dotted around that'll do ya for vittles an' such."

The clock across the street in the courthouse clock tower rang four, and on the last strike Ben polished off his drink and said, "That's my cue, fellers. Time for my meetin'. You boys keep your topknots on, hear? I'll see ya when I see ya." The elder brother nodded to the younger brothers, tipped his new Bowler and walked straight for the door. A moment later and he was gone again, leaving the boys with too many questions and not enough answers, but that was typical of Ben Creed.

"Todd, what say we head for the office, see if the boss is back in yet an' see if there's any new marchin' orders?"

"Sounds like a plan, Zack. Shall we?" Todd said, making a big show of bowing and pointing the way to the door.

Ten minutes later, they were standing in the lobby of the office asking Mrs. Bishop if Sheriff Walker was back. Told he was and directed back to his office, a moment later they were seated across from his desk waiting for him to finish writing. After filling him in on what they had learned from Ben, the sheriff leaned back in his chair for a moment, looking from one to the other before finally responding.

"Boys, you two are the handiest deputies I believe I've ever worked with. All right, play it your way, an' if them two show up try not ta tip 'em off that you know what's goin' on here. But you keep a real close eye on 'em. I found out some o' the same things as I was out an' about taday, but nothin' as detailed as what the two o' you learned. I'll send a wire ta the new sheriff over ta that new Apache County ta let him know you're workin' for me, an' that ya might be pickin' off some rustlers operatin' in his neck o' the woods. That should keep ya out o' trouble over that way. You tell Ben that if this new claim o' his don't work out, I got a badge here for him as well, if he'll take the job. Now g'won, get out o' here an' get ya a good meal an' a good night's rest, boys. An' be careful."

"Yes, sir, we will," they both responded as they rose from their chairs and walked outside. From the office, they did their best to lay low. An hour later, their packhorses were loaded with all but the last minute things they would load the next morning. The packhorses were stalled in the livery stable along with their mounts, and the boys were satisfied they had done all they could to be ready to ride before daylight. The only thing that remained that night was to get a good meal and plenty of coffee.

Stopping at Renner's, Jason said, "Decided ta stay open for a bit, as Ben said you'd be lookin' ta eat an' get some coffee in ya yet tanight. C'mon in an' grab a seat. Ya know, we're normally closed up by now, so if ya don't mind I'm gonna lock the door so's nobody else can get in. Margarite's all ready got the spuds cookin' an' a nice pair o' steaks set aside just for you two. Oh, an' Ben done paid for it, so enjoy!"

It didn't take long before Mrs. Renner delivered the food, and Jason sat down with a fresh pot of coffee and some conversation. "Ben tells me you boys showed up 'roun' here near two years after he did, an' though things don't change much back ta home I'd still like ta chat with ya 'bout the goin's on in our part o' Texas, if ya don't mind."

35

"Not at all, though I don't know what we could tell ya that's different since we pulled out two years ago."

They needn't have worried, as Jason asked plenty of questions and they answered the best they could, and it seemed to be enough for him. It was already getting dark outside by the time they finished eating and talking with Jason, and then stood up to leave. Tossing a half eagle on the table, they thanked Jason and Margarite for staying open and stepped out onto the boardwalk.

"Todd, quick. Beat it around the corner," Zack said in a harsh whisper.

Both men jumped to the corner of the building and slipped between it and the building next to it. "What's up?"

"Them two fake rangers ya drug in are down on the corner lookin' around. I figure they're lookin' for us."

"Let's slip out the through the alley an' head for the boardin' house real quick. I'd sooner not have ta drag them along with us if we can help it," Todd whispered back.

Zack nodded, and fifteen minutes later they had avoided the pair and made it to the boarding house. Zack let Mose and Maybelline know that they'd be gone for at least a few weeks, and paid them in advance for their rooms before joining Todd in his room.

"You remember ta tell 'em that ta say they hadn't seen us an' didn't know where we was, in case somebody come askin'?"

"I sure did, brother. Mose said he's always up 'round four an' would have us some coffee on 'fore we head out. I was wishin' we'd a figured out a way ta get some coffee, knowin' that we'd be ridin' on an empty belly 'til camp tomorrow night."

"Well, if it suits ya I picked up some hardtack an' pemmican ta gnaw on through the day tomorrow. Figured that'd hold us."

"Sounds good. Let's sack out, brother."

Fifteen minutes later, the gentle snores floated through the doors, and Mose just chuckled at the surprise he and Maybelline were preparing as a treat for their best boarders.

***

At ten until four, Mose tapped lightly on the boys' doors, and then tapped again when he got no response. He was ready to tap again when he heard Zack answer, "Yeah! I'm up! Be out for coffee shortly."

Mose poured the coffee and put out Maybelline's special delicacies, a heaping tray of bearclaws. Taking a seat himself, he grabbed one of the bearclaws, and thought about hiding one more for a snack later. His hand was almost to it when Maybelline walked in.

"Mose, whut the hell ya a doin' thar? 'Em's is fo' 'em boys."

"Yassum, but momma 'ey is sa goooood."

"Oh, ya ol' devil you, ah saved ya some fo' latah. Now po' me a cup o' 'et coffee 'fo' I lay a steer up ta the side o' yo' head," she said with a belly laugh.

"What's so funny, May?" Todd asked.

"Oh, nuttin'. Jus' is ol' knothead a bein' foolish again. Set on down, now, an he'p yo'se'f ta some o' 'em bea'claws. Ya knows ah wasn' gonna let mah boys gets outa heah wit'out somethin' in they's bellies. Mose, git on up now, an' fetch 'at sack outa the oven fo' 'em ta takes 'long."

Mose jumped up, stepped lively around the table, popped open the door to the oven and pulled out a flour sack full of something, and tightly tied with a loop at the top with a heavy string. Laying it on the table, Maybelline reached for it and double-checked the knot to make certain it was secure.

"Boys, 'is heah is a sackful o' corndodgers. Now ah knows ya ain't gonna be gettin' no reg'lar meals out thar on the trail, sa ah figuahed the bes' thang ah's could do was ta fix ya somethin' 'et'd hol' ya fo' a day 'r sa."

"Maybelline, you have no idea how we love 'em corndodgers o' yours. Shoot, a sack like that, we'll likely run out by tonight."

"Seriously? Maybelline, you are an angel!"

Chapter Five

With their bellies full from an unexpected breakfast, the boys made their way across the street from the boarding house to Cooper's Livery to retrieve their animals for their journey east. Crosstown, Ben was already mounting up at Murphy's Livery for his trip into the Bradshaw's and his claims. It would be several weeks before the Creed boys would cross paths again, and Ben wondered how his younger brothers would make out in their hunt for the rustlers. He trusted they were capable, and would come back in one piece, hopefully to find him as the owner of a profitable mining operation. But there were unseen adventures awaiting both he and his brothers as they each rode out that morning.

Todd and Zack were just topping the hill overlooking Prescott as the pre-dawn light began seeping onto the horizon, each also wondering about Ben and his trip south, and each wishing in a way that they had gone with him instead of heading out on another campaign in the name of the law, such as it was in Arizona Territory.

"If we hustle right along today, we might get ta make it ta the Montezuma Café an' some o' Sally's good cookin' 'fore full dark. An' she might even have a place we can lay up tonight that's warm an' dry."

"I don't see why we can't, as long as we don't encounter any problems. It'd be nice not ta have ta eat your cookin' tonight," Todd replied.

"Who said I was cookin'? As I recall, it's your turn ta do the cookin' on this trip out."

"Now that's a stretch, brother. I done the cookin' the last two times out."

"Then we'd best get a move on 'r you'll be goin' hungry 'cause I ain't doin' a lick o' cookin' tonight!"

The boys settled into a ground eating pace, pushing to cover the thirty-five mile distance to Fort Verde and the Montezuma Café before Sally closed for the evening, each quietly thinking about not only the good meal they'd get but the task in front them. Chasing rustlers was a dangerous job for a posse, let alone just two men, especially if the rustlers were well organized or just plain mean.

They spoke little as they pushed throughout the day, and with the sun just touching the horizon at their backs they started down Copper Canyon and the last half dozen miles into Fort Verde. It was well into twilight when they pulled up in front of the Montezuma and dismounted. Stepping into the café, they were surprised to see it was still nearly half full of people, mostly Army officers and their families, happily devouring platefuls of food. They made their way to one of the few empty tables and sat down virtually unnoticed.

After a few minutes, Sally spotted them, gave them a quick wave and stepped back into the kitchen. A moment later, she was carrying two cups and a pot of Arbuckle's to their table with a big smile. "Zack, I didn't expect ta see you again sa soon, an' you brought Todd with ya. An' I know just what you boys need to eat. Already got Chili workin' on it. You got a place ta lay down tonight, 'r are ya stayin' with me?"

"I reckon we'll be stayin' at your place, if ya don't mind, Sally. We got ta ride early, an' ya get up plenty early 'nough for us, so it ought ta work out good," Zack stated.

"Say, Sally, where'd all these folks come from tonight? I don't recall you ever bein' this busy this time o' day any time I ever been here," Todd asked.

"Well, ever since I started givin' away a free piece o' pie with a full evenin' meal I'm havin' ta beat 'em off with a stick, Todd. We

41

always been fairly busy from mornin' 'til mid-afternoon, but never had much business in the evenin'. I told Chili and Maude I was thinkin' 'bout shuttin' down 'round three in the afternoon, an' I'd have ta give each o' 'em just three days a week ta work 'stead of the way we been doin' it. Then Maude says why don't I do somethin' ta bring the Army folks out in the evenin', an' a free slice o' pie is what we come up with. Reckon it works, wouldn't ya say?" Sally finished with a big laugh.

"Well, I sure hope ya got plenty o' pie left for us, Sal."

"Yup, enough I can give ya a regular slice 'stead o' them little pieces I give the rest o' my customers," the heavy bosomed woman said, leaning in close and speaking softly so only the boys could hear. "Well, let me see if Chili's got your plates ready, boys. I'll be back shortly."

After a filling meal topped off with generous pieces of fresh apple pie and another pot of Arbuckle's coffee, the boys made their way out behind the café to Sally's home. Putting the animals and their saddles and packs in the barn, tossing them hay and pouring some oats on top, along with making sure the water trough was full, they headed back to the café to help Sally and Chili clean up from their evening servings.

An hour later, with the pots, pans and dishes all washed and put away, Chili said goodnight and Sally and the boys headed to her house. "Boys, I'd love ta stay up an' chat, but I'm plumb tuckered out. I'll call ya 'round five when I roll out, an' maybe we'll have some time ta chat in the mornin'."

"That's fine, Sally. We're tired as well. Get some rest," Zack said, patting her on the shoulder gently. "We'll see ya in the mornin'. An' thanks again for lettin' us camp out here tanight."

"Aw, think nothin' of it, boys. I'd be ashamed if'n I didn't offer. 'Til the 'morrow."

Sally woke them, but was already gone when they rolled out. As was their practice, the animals were cared for first, and then they headed for the café after loading up the packs and saddling their horses. The place was packed with Army personnel along with locals by the time they walked in, but Sally motioned them back to the kitchen where she and Chili had set up a small table for them in the corner by the back door.

Gulping down their Arbuckle's and a plateful of biscuits and gravy, the boys were more than ready to head out. Each grabbing Sally in a bear hug, they said their goodbyes and thanked her again for her hospitality, and then made their way out into the cool, Arizona morning air.

It was still dark as they rode past the fort, crossed the Verde River and rode southeast toward Sycamore Canyon, and by the time the sun was in mid-sky they had made it up the narrow canyon out onto Mud Tanks Mesa. An hour before sunset, they had ridden south, crossed Calf Pen Canyon and up onto Hardscrabble Mesa, calling camp on Hardscrabble Creek.

It was a quiet camp, as both men were tired from the two days of hard riding. They settled for coffee and what was left of the corndodgers for supper, and sacked out twenty minutes after the sun had disappeared.

Morning came all too soon, but by the time the sun started lighting up the sky they were already on the trail. Across the mesa, they dropped down into Oak Spring Canyon, and back up onto Buckhead Mesa, calling a halt at midday to rest the animals from the constant up and down of the terrain. By two that afternoon, they were back on the trail, and an hour before dark they had crossed the East Fork of the Verde River, crossed Birch Mesa and were in Green Valley, where they decided to camp for the night.

It was another quiet camp that night, but they did discuss future camping arrangements. Deciding that they should stop at the little

43

store the next morning, just to see what they could learn about the comings and goings of the Green Valley area, they also decided it wasn't a good idea to broadcast why they were here. Figuring that camping in a more secluded, hidden spot was the best idea, they planned on moving camp before settling in to do.

Checking one of the Army maps that Zack had managed to snag from a drunken soldier in a poker game one night several months before, they saw a nice spot to hide their camp about three miles east of where they were at the moment, which would leave them just under two miles back to where they thought the store was. Agreeing on the move and the site, it wasn't long before they were both sound asleep, at least for the moment.

With the cool night air of the mountains of Arizona came the sound of cows bawling in the distance. Not just a few cows, but a lot of cows. Both young men sat up, looking at each other in the fading firelight, their features barely discernable.

"'Less I miss my guess, it don't sound like them stolen cows are gonna be hard to find, Todd."

"How far off ya figure they are?"

"Ten, maybe twelve miles. Hard ta say up here in this valley. Could be closer, but the way that sound is driftin' in an' out I'd bet they're in the wide bottom of another valley east o' here a piece. Sounds like a couple hundred head, so I s'pose they won't be in one spot long 'r they'll have all the grass eat up, if they ain't already."

"Might be why they're causin' such a ruckus. Wonder what the local folks think o' that racket?" Zack asked.

"I'll bet most o' 'em is tucked nicely in their soft featherbeds an' don't hear a thing. What say we skip the store, an' that spot for the new camp, an' see what we can see without getting in too close?"

"Yessir, fine idea. We'll need ta be on the move 'fore daylight, so I'm goin' back ta sleep while I can."

"I'm with ya there, brother," Todd said.

Cherokee Parks

Chapter Six

It was fifteen minutes before the brothers got to the livery stable to retrieve their animals that Ben Creed mounted up and started south. Following the old trail toward Groom Creek, Ben hustled along until he made five miles, and then pulled his animals up into the junipers and tied them off. When the sun started lighting up the horizon with the pre-dawn, he was snugly settled into a crevice watching the trail for any followers.

The trail Ben traveled was routinely traversed by other miners heading into the Bradshaw Mountains, each seeking fame and fortune or working mines having already having struck gold. He knew all of the other miners in the area, and most of the men who worked for them, so it would be pretty easy for him to spot any interlopers or characters who shouldn't be there.

When no one appeared on his back trail, he climbed back to the animals, led them back down to the trail and mounted up. Weaving in and out along the twisting trail, Ben stopped near at his old friend's mine, the Davis Dunkirk Mine, and then repeated his check of his back trail. When no one showed that wasn't supposed to be there, he remounted again and started the next leg of his journey.

Winding through the rough terrain of the Bradshaw's was not only time consuming, it was tiring for both man and animal. It was nearing dark as Ben pulled up on the small spring he was looking for a quarter mile from the Bodie Mine. It was still a long, hard day's ride to his claim in the rough terrain, but the last thing he planned on doing was letting his guard down, not for an instant. If his strike was anything like he thought it would be, there would be a dozen miners surrounding him within days of word getting out. Not to mention the number of claim jumpers that would try to take over the site, and kill Ben to get to it.

As usual, Ben was up and on the move long before the sun broke the surface of the earth, planning on reaching his hidden camp while he still had enough light to unload and store his supplies and turn his horse and burro into the large grassy spot below that camp. By the time the sun was up full, he had already crossed Longfellow Ridge and was northeast of Pine Mountain.

Stopping at Gates Spring, avoiding the settlement of Goodwin, he made sure his stock was well watered and filled his canteens with the best water in the entire area, and then remounted and headed off almost due south toward the northwest base of Tuscambia Mountain. Stopping to check his back trail several times, he saw someone following his trail just after noon, and decided to wait on the rider. He had to wait almost an hour, making his plan of arriving at his base camp with some daylight left just a dream.

Ben was hidden in the junipers on the south side of Arrastra Creek, patiently waiting as the rider came to the spot where he had circled his animals and crossed and recrossed the trail, making following any tracks confusing. The tracker dismounted and walked around trying to get a sense of where Ben had tricked him when Ben spoke to him.

"Lookin' for me, stranger?"

"I ain't sure who I'm trackin' here. Boss said track that sign and see where it goes, so that's what I'm doin'. An' who might ya be?"

"Not 'til I get some answers from you first. Who's your boss, an' why is he so concerned about my tracks?"

"I work for Dandrea, an' we been losin' cattle ta some o' the miners what run out o' fresh meat from time ta time. He don't mind 'em takin' a steer from time ta time, long as they pay for it. An' when he seen somebody hit Gates Spring an' avoid Goodwin, well, he got kind o' suspicious. Most o' the miners don't try ta hide, sa when one does it just looks funny."

"Well, cowboy, as you can see, I'm well supplied an' ridin' on out o' here, so I reckon your job is done. Time for you ta mount back up an' head for home ta report that I ain't takin' none o' your beef. I will tell ya, though, that there's been some Apache an' a few Yavapai sneakin' round up here for the last several weeks. Could be they been helpin' themselves ta some easy to kill fresh meat. I leave a bag o' tobacco hangin' in the trees in my camp, so they can help themselves to it an' they leave me alone as a result. Now then, by dark I'll be well gone from this area, so if ya don't mind I'd rather ya head out 'fore I do. I got me a little spot I like ta camp in, an' I don't appreciate any company showin' up unexpected like. Get my drift?"

"Yessir, I sure do. But the boss is still gonna want a name, an' ya ain't give me one yet."

"Just tell him Creed. My little brothers work for the sheriff's office, an' if he needs ta know more'n that he can ask the sheriff."

"You're Ben Creed? Sure sorry, mister. I'll make sure the boss knows it was you. Sorry I bothered ya." A moment later, the cowboy was mounted and riding north at a steady gait.

Ben waited a half hour, just in case, and then continued on his way. He didn't stop again until he topped the ridge above Barrel Spring late that afternoon. From his vantage point, he carefully scoped the trail he had taken. Nothing was moving, except a few head of mother cows and calves, and a nice fat buck already sporting a growing rack of fuzz.

Dropping down to the spring, he left the animals have their fill of the cool water, and then headed to his camp. Wondering which of his two claims was going to pan out, he decided to work the one showing high-grade gold over the one with high-grade silver with abundant copper, since gold was bringing far more than silver at the time. The two were just under a mile apart, which made his camp all that more valuable to him as it sat almost an equal

49

distance from the two, just under a mile to each.

He neglected telling his brothers about the silver mine on purpose, knowing that gold is always what catches the ear. But they were neither one afraid of work, and no matter which mine worked out they would be all in once they finally gave up the law. It was just after dark when Ben finally made it to his hidden camp on the headwaters of Blind Indian Creek, too late to store his supplies, but not too late to start a small cooking fire.

As soon as he had stripped the animals and had the fire going, he led the animals the short distance to the fork of another small spring-fed rivulet that fed into Blind Indian Creek, hobbled them and let them loose on the lush grass. Hiking back up the small, intermittent feeder creek to his camp, he nourished the fire and put on a pot of coffee and a skillet full of sliced potatoes, and then sat back and waited until the potatoes were cooked before tossing in the steak he had saved from town, knowing it wouldn't last another day without being eaten.

While the spuds cooked, he shook out his sougan and made everything as comfortable as he could for the short night ahead. Devouring the steak and potatoes, along with drinking the entire pot of coffee, Ben was ready to catch some shuteye. With his eyelids heavy, he still took time to make a pot of coffee for morning so all he had to do was bank the fire and set the pot close enough to heat. He laid back in his bedroll with his head against the saddle, and was out like a light.

He allowed himself to sleep a bit later than normal the next morning, but between the forest birds and his animals he was wide awake just as the golden orb peeked over the slope of Tuscambia Mountain. Stirring up the coals and adding some small pieces of dry grass and stems to aid in it coming back to life, Ben was satisfied enough with the new fire to put on the pot of coffee before hauling out the oats from the pack and giving his critters a generous portion of the grain they loved.

Back to feeding himself, he decided coffee and some hardtack biscuits would suffice after two weeks of lounging around in Prescott and last night's heavy meal. Three biscuits and most of the coffee later, he decided he was just stalling the work he needed to get done today so he could get back to mining the next day. Pulling the pot away from the fire enough so that it didn't burn but would still stay hot, Ben rose and stretched out the kinks of two hard days in the saddle and a night back on the ground, and then finished opening up the pack. Looking around to ensure no one was in the vicinity, he grabbed the first armload of supplies to be stored and stepped to the other side of the rivulet.

Pushing the brush back to reveal the opening, Ben bent over slightly and stepped inside, and then waited for a moment until his eyes adjusted to the darkness. At the back of the small cave, Ben stacked the canned tomatoes, peaches and other canned goods on the natural shelf, and then picked up the candle and lit it, poured a bit of the wax onto the rock surface and placed the candle where it would light the area. Stepping back into the sunlight, he walked to the pack, grabbed another armload of supplies and re-entered the cave, placing the supplies in carefully designated spots. For the next two hours, he restocked his hidden supply depot before pulling the brush back over the opening.

Satisfied that he had managed to put away enough supplies to last the next three months, he sat back down to have another cup of brew. He had no intention of checking his claims until the next morning, and was going to take this day to nose around and make certain no one had been around during his two week absence. Stretching out his largest tarp and tying two corners off to a couple of trees selected for the task, he staked the other two corners to the ground with some stakes he chopped out of branches off of other trees. Then taking two of the smaller tarps, he closed in the sides of his lean-to, tying the top to the big tarp and staking down the opposite ends to the ground.

Satisfied that this was as close to what he'd done previously, he rearranged his bedroll and saddle along with the packsaddle under the lean-to, and poured himself a cup of coffee and then stood back to admire his handiwork. *This trip I reckon I need to make me some stools to sit on while I'm around camp, 'r in case I get comp'ny. Like the boys. Guess I'd best make three stools, an' I reckon a small table while I'm at it. Hell, why don't I just build me a cabin? HAHA!*

The sound of Captain whinnying downstream shook Ben out of his private reverie, and he instinctively grabbed his new Henry rifle. Reaching the small pasture and watching Captain's ears, Ben decided it must be animal, not human, as the burro, who he had started calling Clem, had taken a protective stance.

Ben hustled back to camp, leaned the rifle against the closest tree, stepped under the lean-to to grab his gun belt and strapped it on. Checking the position of his knives and then the pistol, he grabbed up his rifle again and started up the incline in the direction the animals had been looking. He hadn't seen any bears around last fall, but there had been a couple of big cats and several bobcat in the area, and although it had been a fairly mild winter they might still be hungry enough to try a horse or burro. Even though trying the burro might be biting off more than they wanted, they would also be in for a big surprise in trying Captain.

The horse had already stomped at least two cats to death in the seven years Ben had owned him, and he had severely worked over a small black bear up on Mt. Lemon three years back. Still, when it came time to go for supplies, or to ride out for anything else, Ben wanted to do it on Captain. He had grown to appreciate every nuance of the big palomino gelding, wishing the previous owner had not gelded him.

As he climbed the hillside and reached the top, he couldn't have been more surprised at what he would find. His animals had tricked him, as it wasn't animal. It was human. Indian to be exact, and female. And in pretty bad shape.

Chapter Seven

Todd and Zack packed their overnight camp and poured the leftover coffee over their small campfire, and then mounted up and headed in the general direction of the sounds from the night before. By midafternoon, they were overlooking Tonto Creek from below Derrick Canyon, but with not a single cow in sight.

"Reckon we're above where they were, 'r they've already moved out?" Zack asked.

"Ta tell ya the truth, I just don't know. I reckon we'll have ta ride into the canyon an' see if there's any sign, but I can tell ya this, there ain't much grass down there."

"That's what I was thinkin', Todd. Like it's been grazed down lately, like last night."

"I'm thinkin' we'd be better off ta ride on up the canyon several miles, but stay up on the ridges an' hid as best we can," Todd said.

Zack only nodded, and led out following the Tonto Creek canyon, taking the bend east until they reached the gentle inclines of Goswick Canyon, and the sign of over two hundred head of cows being driven north. Crossing the canyon, and then following Apache Ridge while staying in the heaviest trees and brush, it was getting close to dark when they finally saw the herd.

Breaking over the top of the ridge and down the east side until they came to a spring, they decided they were in a safe enough place to camp. Unloading all they could, they built a small fire and put on the coffee and rolled out their sougans.

"Todd, I'm gonna work my way over the ridge and see if I can spot their camp. Be nice ta know how many o' 'em we're dealin' with 'fore we have ta light into 'em."

"Alright. I'll put some grub together while you're duckin' your turn at cookin' again. I knew you'd figure out a way ta get out of it, one way 'r tother."

"Naw, I'll fix breakfast. I just kind o' wanna know what we've gotten ourselves into, brother."

"Yeah, alright. Don't be too long," Todd suggested.

Switching into his moccasins and grabbing his rifle and scope, Zack trotted up the gentle slope to the west, and then down to the edge of the tree line above the generous meadow below. In the growing darkness, it didn't take long to find out where the rustler's camp was located. *They aren't even tryin' to stay hid, prob'ly thinkin' they are in the clear up here in this rough country. Might serve us ta let 'em keep thinkin' that way.*

Pulling up the scope to get a better look into the camp, Zack had to chuckle to himself when he recognized the two men at the fire. He and Todd had hauled them in several months before on minor charges, and had talked about how these two were bound and determined to find a way to get hung.

Watching the camp for another half hour, no other riders came into view, even when he scoped the area while there was still a hint of daylight, so Zack decided he had done his due diligence and stood up to head back to camp. Taking one more look back into the rustler's camp, he was surprised to see a new man standing there chewing out the two hapless outlaws.

Wishing he could hear their conversation, though it looked to be pretty well one-sided, he thought he was getting the gist of it even from afar. Apparently they were a day or two late in showing up, and the boss wasn't happy with them. The big man kept his back to Zack, so seeing if he was one of the known ringleaders operating in the northern half of the state wasn't working out.

And then finally, the man walked around to the other side of the fire, giving Zack a good look at him. *I'd swear that's Ike Stockton, but why is he workin' so far west? Maybe it's gettin' too hot in New Mexico for him an' his bunch.*

Not able to do any more from where he was, Zack picked up his rifle and worked his way back to camp. Over the meal of beans and hard tack, he filled Todd in on what he had seen. "Todd, I'm tellin' ya, we were right about Earl Carson an' Micah Slate. They're sure lookin' for a way ta get hung. But it sure looked ta me like they was visited by none other than Ike Stockton, 'cept this is a long way from New Mexico Territory an' his usual stompin' grounds. If he's pullin' the same tricks as he does over yonder, them beef are goin' ta the Army. We just got ta find a way ta prove it, an' I reckon the only way ta do it is track this herd ta wherever they're headed."

"Stockton? Are you sure?"

"Well, not really, but it sure looked like him."

"As far as Earl an' Micah, no surprise there, but Stockton? That seems a real stretch. I reckon we'd best roll early so we don't lose track o' where they're goin'. No sense in wastin' time tryin' ta find their trail again if we hang back too far 'r wait a day."

"Pretty much the way I was thinkin', too. Oh, an' thanks for the grub. I swear, I'll cook breakfast, even clean up tonight."

"'Bout damned time ya took on some camp chores, Zack. I'm hittin' my bedroll. I'll make sure ya roll out in time to put together the grub in the mornin', even get the fire goin' for ya."

"Yeah, thanks, brother," Zack said with sarcasm dripping from his voice. Then, laughing, he continued. "Fair 'nough. See ya come mornin'."

Packed up the next morning, the two Creed boys made their way to the north side of the ridge, and then to the north edge of the meadow, staying hidden in the trees. It wasn't long before the two rustlers were up and moving, starting the cattle toward the northwest before turning them back to the north us a feeder canyon leading to Salt Lick Canyon.

There was no sign of the man Zack thought was Stockton, so they assumed that he had ridden back in the direction he had come from, probably toward where these men were pushing the cattle. They pushed on across the easiest terrain they could find, allowing the cattle time to graze as they traveled, with Zack and Todd following in the distance. By noon, they had turned back to the west and let the cattle settle in along Green Valley Creek in the Little Green Valley.

The boys walked their horses out onto a knob overlooking the small valley below as well as the small creek that ran along its south side, and then started taking turns watching the movement below. With a slight breeze from the north, they decided it would be safe to build a small fire and cook some coffee. Todd drew the short straw, led the horses back a quarter mile from their overlook, set up their temporary camp, and then started a small fire. It wasn't long before the coffee was ready, so he helped himself to a cup.

Waiting what he thought was about two hours, he made his way back toward where Zack was set up, but Zack came running toward him before he was halfway there. "They're on the move! We got to go!"

Todd did a quick one-eighty and joined Zack on his headlong flight toward their animals. It only took a few minutes before they had extinguished the fire and mounted up, and several more minutes before Zack caught his breath and filled Todd in on what he had observed.

"I figure they got spooked findin' out we was somewhere over this direction an' decided to make a quick sale o' them cows. The reason I think that is 'cause Carter an' Morton showed up with Stockton an' three other gents. Them two snakes an' Stockton lit out after just a few minutes, headed north, an' the rest o' that bunch started movin' the cattle west."

"West? That just don't make any sense, at least not ta me. Why not just take them north instead o drivin' 'em up the Tonto an' then ta here?"

"Yeah, 'less they were tryin' ta avoid Green Valley for some reason, like maybe the over brands were still too fresh. From what I've seen, they're carryin' half a dozen different brands, an' they all look doctored. But I reckon they got some reason that makes sense ta them, 'r ta Stockton. I'm wonderin' if one of us ought ta track Stockton an' them two rangers, 'r just stick with the cows."

"I'm in favor o' stickin' with the herd, as I figure they'll all end up in the same place sooner 'r later. The only place I can figure they could take 'em north toward Winslow is way back ta the west, up either Pine 'r Strawberry Canyon, so bringin' 'em this way only puts more hard miles on 'em. 'Less they needed ta let 'em graze up some after bringin' 'em up from down below. 'Less they ain't takin' 'em north, an' if that's the case we'll need ta know where that herd ends up."

"That's prob'ly right, brother. The herd it is then."

For the rest of the day, the Creed brothers followed the herd at a safe distance, or at least what they thought was a safe distance. The five men working the herd pushed them hard all afternoon and nearly to twilight before bunching them up in the Star Valley. The only place with any real cover for the boys to camp and still watch the herd, and the men with it, was to the northeast of the valley, along the east side of Schoolhouse Canyon. But to get there, they'd have to cross a wide open area and chance being seen by one of the three men posted around the herd, unless they rode two to three miles back from where they currently sat their horses.

If they waited any longer, they could use darkness as their cover, but if they did they'd also be riding rough terrain in the dark. Opting to go while they still had some light, they took the chance that they could stay behind some of the low knobs and swells and not be seen. But halfway across the bottom of the shallow basin a half mile from the east end of the valley, they realized there was someone tracking them.

Even though it was all but dark by the time they had made it to the north side of the shallow depression, their animals continued alerting them to the fact their pursuer was staying close behind. Zack motioned to Todd to take the reins of his horse, double-checked the lead rope of his pack animal to ensure it wouldn't come untied, slipped his rifle from the boot and slid out of the saddle to hide behind a tree.

Todd continued on for a quarter mile before sliding out of his saddle, tying the horses off to some brush, and grabbing his rifle. Working back toward Zack, he only made if part of the way when he heard a horse coming toward him. Ducking behind an Alligator Juniper, he hunched down and waited. It was only a few minutes before a riderless horse came into view, walking toward their horses.

Clucking a call to the horse to calm it, he managed to walk up to it, grab the reins and lead it back to where he had stashed their horses. Then, heading back toward where he had dropped Zack off, he was almost to the previous spot when he could hear two men walking. Assuming one of them was Zack, he leaned up against a tree and waited.

"'Bout time you showed up. Who's our guest?"

"Why, it's none other than Seth Morton, Special Ranger, an' part o' the gang rustlin' the very same cows they was hired ta find. Now, he'd prob'ly like ta argue that he was just trackin' 'em an' tryin' ta catch up with us, but we both know that'd be a flat out lie. 'Sides, I stuck a rag in his piehole, an' his hands are tied behind him so's he can't take it out, so he ain't gonna be arguin' 'bout nothin'. Once we get ta the horses, I figure we ought ta move back up the canyon near a mile, so when we drop the gag they won't be able ta hear him yell an' force me ta knock him out. Though in a way I hope he tries it."

"Yup, sounds like a plan. Fast as they been movin' that herd, won't be any trouble at all ta find 'em again."

Chapter Eight

It was nearly two hours later when they found a good spot to camp and stopped for the night. Their travel had been severely impeded by the lack of any moonlight on a very cloudy night, as well as the rough terrain and having to lead yet another horse. Todd hauled Morton down from his saddle and tied him to a tree standing up with his face toward the trunk. Zack, in the meantime, built a small fire and put coffee on to cook while he dug around in the packs and found oats for the animals. After the critters were fed, he sliced two potatoes into a skillet of hot grease, peels and all, and then tossed in a couple of chunks of fatback.

Their meal finished, Zack grabbed one last cup of coffee, stood up and strolled to where Morton was tied while Todd cleaned all the utensils and put on another pot of brew. "Now, then, Mr. Seth Morton, if that's even your name, if I was ta pull that gag outa your mug, would ya stay nice an' quiet?"

Morton nodded that he would, but before Zack loosened the gag he made one more clarifying comment. "Ya know that if ya even make a peep louder than a squeak, I'll thump ya across the top o' your skull sa hard ya won't wake up for a week, if ever, right?"

Morton vigorously nodded acceptance of Zack's admonition, so Zack removed the gag and then started asking questions. "Who the hell is the big boss in this rustlin' scheme, an' where they takin' them cows?"

"Zack, you two got me fair an' square. Untie me an' let me have a drink o' water an' a cup o' coffee, an' I'll tell ya all I know."

"Todd, whattaya think? Ya wanna keep him covered while I take him off this tree?" While he waited for Todd to get into position, he turned back to Morton. "So Seth, ol' boy, ya know I'm gonna tie your hands in front o' ya, an' hobble ya so's ya can't run off, right?"

As Zack freed Morton from the tree, Morton complied with every command, and was soon sitting on a fallen log drinking coffee, seemingly content to have his hands and feet tied. But he wasn't exactly forthcoming with "all he knew" about the operation, prompting Zack to encourage him.

"Todd, 'member how that Apache showed us how ta get a body talkin'?"

"Man, do I! I thought that fella he was workin' on was gonna bleed ta death 'fore he finally started gabbin', an' then we couldn't shut him up. Lordy, he told us ever'thing from the day he was born ta the moment that Apache started workin' on him."

"Reckon it'll work on ol' Seth here?"

"Shoot, I imagine all ya have ta do is describe what you'll do if he don't start talkin, an' he'll be jabberin' like a jay."

"Yeah, most likely that's right. Seth, ya ever seen the Apache bleed a man? It's kind o' like what Maw taught me the Chinese did an' called 'the death o' a thousand cuts.' Ya see, we'll yank your boots off, an' start by makin' little slicin' cuts across the bottoms o' your feet. Ya don't tell us what we want ta know, we'll make a few more slices, slightly deeper, an' when you feet is all cut up we'll start up your legs…"

"Yeah, alright, I get the picture. I said I'd tell ya all I know, an' I will. No need ta be cuttin' on me. Look, me an' Jack came into this deal 'bout six months ago, when we was hired on by a couple o' ranchers from the Arizona Cattlemen's Association. We thought it was all legal an' above board, but it didn't take long 'til we was in it up ta our necks an' couldn't get out. The secretary o' the association had us framed ta the point we was gonna hang if we talked, an' all o' them was gonna ride away free. So yeah, I'm not real happy with 'em, an' I wanna see 'em swing if I'm goin' to."

"Well, get ta explainin', an' don't leave nothin' out."

"Jack told me there was some small time ranchers stealin' from the big ranches that were members of the association, an' they wanted us ta put a stop to it by infiltratin' the groups an' findin' out who the ringleader was. Time we got inta the group meetin's, it didn't take long ta figure out there wasn't a small rancher in that bunch. They all work for Sampson, just like the secretary does. And we ended up under his thumb as well."

"Sampson? Ya sure his name ain't Stockton? Ike Stockton?"

"We was told his name was Sampson, but Ike is right. There somethin' I'm missin?"

"Appears ta be. Ike Stockton is a rustler, an' has a gang that he always rides with, but they usually work the Northern New Mexico Territory and hang out in Southern Colorado from what I know of 'em. Up there, he mostly sells stolen cattle an' horses ta the Army. That the plan here?"

"Nope. The plan here is ta sell 'em ta the Commissary for the Indian Agent overseeing the Navajo an' Hopi, but them people will never see a single piece o' that beef. 'Tween Sampson, 'r Stockton,' the commissary an' the secretary, they figured out a way ta trick the government. The commissary buys old, spoilin' beef an' hauls it out ta the reservation while they send these cows ta Chicago, an' he shows the government the bill o' sale for 'em ta justify the price. Stockton handles the shipping ta Chicago, and the secretary handles everything else. They deduct all the costs an' split the profits equal."

"An' just how many cattle are they takin', an' from who? Say, isn't the secretary a member rancher, too? An' what's his name?"

"No more'n a dozen head from any one ranch at a time. An'

only the biggest ranches so they can blame it on the small ranchers an' homesteaders. They hold 'em just above where the Tonto dumps inta the Salt, gatherin' 'em up 'til they got 'tween two an' three hundred head, then they drift 'em up the basin tryin' to graze 'em as much as possible. You two threw a wrench inta their plans, though, when ya went askin' questions at the association office. Now they're talkin' 'bout shuttin' it down an' clearin' out.

"The secretary ain't a member, just a hired hand ta keep the minutes an' handle day ta day business at the office. His name is Campbell, Arch Campbell. Now, as ta where they're takin' 'em this time. I ain't got a clue. Usually they don't take 'em up the Tonto. They take 'em right through Green Valley an' up Pine Canyon an' straight ta Winslow from there. That's where the commissary inspects 'em, which only amounts ta gettin' a count. This time, I got no clue what they'll do with 'em 'cause they don't want ta take any chances on exposin' any of 'em ta gettin' caught. Jack's the one ya really need ta talk to, if he'll even talk now. Seems Stockton has told him he'll take Jack along an' make him a rich man. In fact, an' I ain't lyin', Jack is the one that talked me into joinin' up with him to do this deal."

"Well, that's sure a lot more'n we knew for certain, but we had an idea that's what was goin' on. But we don't aim ta let Stockton 'r the rest o' 'em get away if we can help it. Only problem we have now is catchin' 'em with rebranded cattle, but with your testimony I think we can still nab 'em an' try 'em all," Todd said.

"Be a sight better if we can catch 'em ourselves an' use Seth's testimony for backup. Sure would like ta take Stockton off the board, even if we do have ta split the bounty with the county. I know there's no bounty on Earl an' Micah, but there might be some extra on the rest of 'em. Seth, I got one more question for ya. What's your real name?" Zack prodded.

"Seth is my name, Seth Morton, but Jack is really Jack

Carrollton, not Jack Carter. I take it you already know Earl an' Micah, but the other three are Billy Taylor, Jason Colquitt an' Joe Haldiman. I don't think there's any money on any of 'em, part o' why Campbell hired us. Ya know, I could sure use some more o' that coffee, an' maybe a biscuit if ya got one."

"Yeah, why not? That's the last o' the pot, an' here's your biscuit," Todd said as he filled Seth's cup and handed him one of the hardtack biscuits. "Finish that, an' we'll have ta tie ya back up ta the tree again, Seth. You been right helpful, but I still ain't gonna allow you a chance ta escape."

"I ain't goin' no where, boys. I'm done for now, an' there ain't any place for me ta go. There's one more thing you need ta be thinkin' about. Well, two really. One, ya need ta keep me alive ta testify, an' two, when I don't show up tomorrow they're gonna send somebody out lookin' for me. There ain't no law 'round here right now 'cept you two, 'r jails ta put me in while ya chase the rest o' 'em. That puts ya in a real sticky spot, 'less ya start trustin' that I'm on your side in this now."

"Whattaya think, Zack? He does have a good point."

"Yeah, he does. But we can't do nothin' about it tonight. Let's get a good night's rest an' see what shakes out in the mornin'. Like Paw always said, 'Ya never know what the morrow will bring.' Seems ta me we always figure out a way ta handle whatever comes up, don't we?"

"That we do, brother. That we do. But for tonight, I reckon we can toss a blanket over Seth an' let him sleep against that log 'til mornin', an' then decide what ta do with him," Todd said as he banked the fire. Grabbing a spare blanket, he tossed it over Seth, and then grabbed his bedroll and laid it out on the opposite side of the fire pit from the captured outlaw. Zack followed suit with his sougan, and before long there were three men gently snoring.

***

Zack was the first to rise, adding sticks to the coals until a nice blaze was lifting its hungry flames up toward the coffee pot. After adding a few more of the bigger sticks they had gathered in the dark the night before, he kicked Todd's foot to make sure he was awake, and then set about graining the horses again. Seth was already awake and watching Zack's every move, but saying nothing.

Todd rolled out while Zack was busy with the animals, sliced up three potatoes and tossed some chunks of fatback into the skillet with the spuds, and then pulled the coffee pot back to keep the coffee from burning before yanking the blanket off Seth. The light was making itself known in the east, and broke over the horizon as they finished breakfast and doused the fire.

"You fellas decide what you're gonna do with me?" Seth inquired.

"Not yet, Seth, but we will shortly," Zack said, motioning Todd to follow him as he walked away from the camp. Fifty feet away, the brothers talked about the problems capturing Seth brought to the table, and made a decision about how to handle him going forward.

Back at the camp, they filled him in. "Seth, we're gonna cut you loose an' let you ride, but without any weapons. At least for now. You'll ride right in front of us, an' we'll tell you when an' where ta go. You make one bad move, try ta get away 'r signal somebody an' you're dead. I'm pretty sure ya know we're both crack shots an' quick with a gun, so ya know I mean what I say. As ta the noise shootin' ya will make, we'll take care o' anybody what comes our way. I don't figure they can get enough shooters close 'nough ta us ta do any damage 'fore we gun 'em down. But we'll leave that up ta you, 'cause the other way ta handle ya is ta gag ya an' tie ya to your saddle an' drag ya behind us, which will make ya a real fine target for any backshooter."

"What if shootin' starts? Do I get my pistol back then?"

"Depends on the circumstances, I reckon. Don't you, Todd?"

"Yup, it does. So what's your call, Seth, out front r' in the back?"

"Hah! Silly question, Todd. I'll take my chances out front."

Cherokee Parks

Chapter Nine

Ben took a few seconds looking at the young female before approaching. Several things were apparent: she was definitely a woman, albeit a young one, maybe in her early twenties; she had not been eating all that well, considering how her bones stood out; whoever or whatever she had battled had gotten as much or more than they gave, and they had given plenty. What wasn't obvious was whether she had survived.

As the Texan leaned over to check for signs of life and take a look at the wounds, she took a shallow breath and issued a venomous curse, but not one Ben expected. It was half spoken in English, but that wasn't his biggest surprise. The rest of what she said was spoken in Paiute, and the target of her venom was apparently her man, a white man. *What in the world is a Paiute gal doin' in Arizona Territory? An' why would her man cut her up like that 'less he figured ta leave her for dead?*

Creed reached out to touch her, just to let her know someone was there, and it nearly cost him as she lashed out with her knife, still clenched firmly in her hand. Jumping back, Ben called out to her. "Ma'am, I can help you if ya'll let me. I'm camped down below."

Her eyes fluttered open for just a second as she tried to see who was talking, but she slid into the unconscious world before she could respond. Ben checked her most obvious wounds, and then made sure he knew if there were any broken bones prior to trying to carry her back to camp. Finding nothing broken after a quick inspection, he stood up, looked around the scene, and then walked out following the direction of the blood trail until it headed downhill toward the creek. Satisfied no one else was around, and whoever left the blood trail wasn't coming back, he walked back to where he had found the woman. She was still out, so he looked around until he found her possibles bag, reloaded it with some of the things that had spilled out, swung it over his shoulder, kneeled down beside her and snatched her up in his arms.

Stopping only to retrieve his rifle from the tree where he had leaned it, Ben worked his way back to his hidden camp. He expected her to be a lot heavier than she was, even though she was only skin and bone, but she was like a feather.

Captain and Clem were standing alertly, most likely getting a whiff of the woman's blood, but as they got closer the animals started a nervous pacing. That is until Ben called out to them to calm down. The sound of his voice seemed to allay their fear, so they stopped pacing, stood nearby as he passed them, and then followed him into camp.

Carefully laying the woman on his bunk, he hung one of his metal buckets half filled with water over the fire, and then dug out some material for cleaning her up and bandaging her. Grabbing one of his pans, he poured some of the water in after it was warm enough and began cleaning her up as best he could. Finished with that, Ben set about finding something she could wear once she came around.

After twenty minutes of meandering around camp once he found what he had determined to be suitable clothing, he began to feel eyes on him, following his every move. Neither of the animals were acting suspicious or apprehensive, so Ben assumed it was his guest. From where he was, he could see her eyes were closed every time he looked in her direction. He drifted under the lean-to without looking at her, and when he was directly across from her he spun on his heels and stared directly at her. Catching her with her eyes wide open, he started laughing, and was pleased that she was laughing with him.

"How long you been awake?"

"Since you were washing me. Who are you, and why have you

saved me?"

"Name's Ben Creed. An' why wouldn't I try ta save ya? Mind tellin' me what happened that ya got inta such a fix? An' how a Paiute girl ended up down here?"

"Well, Mr. Ben Creed, I'll certainly try to tell you what brought me here, and caused me to be so badly injured. I am Chenoa of the Northern Paiute, the tribe you white eyes call Snake. I am in the land of the Southern Paiute because I was traded by the man I loved and thought was my friend. Turns out, I was just a piece of property to him, and the man he traded me to treated me like a slave. Two days ago, he tried to beat me, so I used my knife on him to protect myself. We fought all that day and into the night before he crawled off like the dog he is, and if I see him again I will kill him."

"'Nough said, Chenoa. I'll do what I can ta get ya healed up an' on your way, but I got work ta do so don't expect me ta wait on ya hand an' foot."

"I am in your bed, Ben Creed, but I will make my own later today so that you may rest correctly. And I will do all I can to make your life and work easier as I heal. The more I heal, the more I will do for you until the day comes when you ask me to leave or I find a new path to follow."

"Fair 'nough, Chenoa. I got some o' my old clothes here ya can wear 'til we can get somethin' better for ya ta wear. Ain't nothin' fancy about 'em, but they'll keep your hide covered."

"Ben, they will be fine. Please go on about your work and let me rest. When I can, I will get up and move. Oh, and thank you for taking care of me, for saving me. I have no way to repay you except to offer my friendship, which is yours," Chenoa said as she laid her head back and closed her eyes.

Ben could only shake his head as he walked away. Not only

was she obviously very intelligent, her English was better than most of the people he had met in the area, and she seemed to be a person who could be a loyal and dedicated friend. As he stepped into the cave, he looked back to ensure she really was sleeping. Grabbing a new pick and shovel, he stepped back out into the sun, and then covered the mouth of the cave again.

Picking up two canteens, Ben refilled them at the creek and then made his way back into camp. He dropped one canteen beside Chenoa, retrieved the pick and shovel, and made his way toward the claim on the south side of Tuscambia Mountain to clean out some of the loose material left behind when he had traveled to Prescott, and to gather as much of the exposed gold as he could. Not intending to do much about going deeper on this trip, his intent was to prepare for the work he had planned for the rest of the week as well as put away the easily converted gold for his next trip to town.

Keeping a close eye to both the trail for any sign of tracks indicating that others had crossed his little path as well as his back trail, Ben made it to the south claim quickly, and immediately went to work. Finding several large nuggets in the loose drift material, he was encouraged that this gold claim would be substantial. Using some of his canteen water to pan the sandy dirt, he was able to gather nearly an ounce of dust, which he poured into another leather bag separate from the bag holding the nuggets.

By midday, he had managed to remove as much of the loose material as possible and began chipping away at the quartz that covered what he thought was the main vein. Then just as suddenly as the small vein had appeared, it was gone. Sitting with his back to a large boulder, he looked over the area and tried to decide his best way forward. Stabbing at the ground beneath him, he thought he saw some glitter, so he scooped up a pan full and worked it.

It only took a few minutes to realize he had been sitting on better ground than he had been working, and grabbed his pick and shovel to work more of the material out from under the boulder. Three hours later, he had managed to pull out a large pile of material to be worked and started panning it out. Then he ran out of water, failing to save enough to quench his thirst. *Damn! I know better than that! Tomorrow, I'll have to bring more water so I don't run the risk of this again. One way or the other, it's gonna take me longer ta work this than what I'd figured, an' I still need ta find the real source o' this color...*

Loading up his gear, Ben headed back to camp, wondering how his new companion had fared throughout the day. Trusting that she had rested and consumed as much water as she needed, he began to go over his supplies in his mind with an eye toward what he could cook that would be good for her healing. Obviously some stewed vegetables and meat was the best thing he could prepare, even if it meant using up his dried meat supply forcing him to take a day or two away from his main purpose to hunt for meat.

As he approached camp, the smell of a campfire and coffee wafted up to him through the pines and juniper. Wondering if his mind was playing tricks on him, Ben picked up his pace. Walking into camp a few minutes later, he was stunned to see Chenoa not only had the fire going, but indeed had coffee cooking as well as a couple of pots over the fire. Whatever she was cooking smelled good, but she was nowhere in sight.

Calling out her name, there was no immediate response. But after the third attempt to locate her, her voice drifted up from the creek below. "I'm coming. You could lend me a hand with these canteens, though."

Having already shed the gear, Ben hustled in the direction of her voice, to find Chenoa resting on a fallen tree. Not only did she have all the canteens completely full of water, but a couple of gut bags as well. Without saying anything, Ben hoisted what he considered to be the heaviest of the containers over his shoulders, the gut bags, and then held out his hand to help Chenoa stand.

Once she was on her feet and standing steady, he decided that he needed to find out what she thought she was doing pushing herself so hard with so many injuries. "So, Chenoa, what the hell are you thinkin'? You tryin' ta finish the job o' gettin' killed? You need ta be layin' down, restin', not haulin' this much weight inta camp, 'r bein' up an about cookin' an' such."

"A very wise man once told me that people die in bed, Ben Creed. And I am not ready to die just yet. You saved me, and the least I can do is to try to help you until it is time for me to leave your camp."

"Chenoa, I'd think you'd want ta get healed up some 'fore ya try takin' care o' me an' my camp. Maw always told us that if we didn't take care o' ourselves first, we sure wasn't gonna be able ta take care o' nobody else."

"Very well, Ben Creed. I will take it easy for the next few days, but I will still do what I can to help. Even if it is nothing more than making coffee and cooking for you."

"That suits me just fine, as long as ya stick to it an' don't try ta haul a week's worth o' water inta camp again."

"I promise I will be more careful, and only do what is easy and simple for me until I am stronger. I have not yet started making an area where I can sleep, as I could not find a tarp for a cover to keep the rain out. Maybe you could assist me after we eat, as I know you must be very hungry after working all day."

"I don't see why you can't bed down under the same lean-to I use. There's plenty o' room, an' I just need ta move a few things out o' the way."

"Maybe into the cave, where they will be safe and dry instead of outside?"

Silver, Gold and Blood In Arizona
"You already figured that out, eh? Sure didn't take you long."

"Yes, though it is well hidden from the casual observer one who has lived in the wilderness can see it has been used recently, even after you have taken such good care to keep it hidden."

Chapter Ten

Ben was surprised at the flavor of the meal Chenoa had prepared, even though he had made the same meal several times over the last few months. He wondered which seasonings she had added, but was too busy at the moment devouring the food to ask. It wasn't until nearly an hour later that he had consumed enough that he felt completely sated for the first time in months. Not even the delicious meals in Prescott could compare to the savory and filling stew and vegetables he had just eaten. His only problem now was being able to stay awake to talk to his camp companion. Not even four cups of stout coffee could keep his eyes open, and before he knew it, it was morning.

The sizzle of fatback and potatoes frying as well as the smell of coffee mixing with the smell of fatback rattled his senses to full awake, though for a moment he could have sworn he was still sleeping. Sitting up and looking around him, Ben was somewhat startled that he had been covered against the evening chill, and that Chenoa was softly singing a Paiute morning song as she quietly went about her work.

"Dang, girl, what'd ya put in that stew last night that knocked me plumb out? 'R was it somethin' in the vegetables?"

Chenoa chuckled as she relied with a big, toothy grin. "Nothing, Ben, but you ate like a bear getting ready for winter. And I'm sure you needed the rest, or you would have not fallen asleep so quickly and easily."

"Well, it was a fine meal, I'll give ya that. But ya keep cookin' like you're doin' an' we'll be out o' grub 'fore ya know it. Keep in mind, I only stocked in enough for me, not for the both of us."

"Do not worry, Ben. There is plenty of food I can gather from the forest around us, and I'll be able to hunt in another week or so. Even if it is only rabbit or squirrel, it will replace the dried beef you brought, and there are many nuts and berries as well as greens I can gather."

"The way you make it sound, I won't have ta head for town for supplies any time soon. Even though I usually go in once a month ta either Prescott 'r Wickenburg."

"If I might suggest something for you to think about, do not make another trip to Wickenburg. Among the Apache, they say there are bad men there who would steal your claims from you if they only knew where they were."

"I've filed claims on the gold diggings in Prescott, an' got the paperwork all filled out on the silver claims just waitin' ta file 'em in Wickenburg. Once that happens, there ain't a soul won't know where my digs are at."

"And that is the problem. You must file your silver claims in Prescott as well, or risk death if you file in Wickenburg."

"An' just how do the Apache know all this?"

"They listen, and watch, and they know where your claims are located. They will not bother you, as you have been a friend to Apache and Yavapai alike, and to all Indians. Especially to me."

"That still doesn't tell me why I shouldn't file in Wickenburg. I go there about every other time I need supplies so's nobody can track me like if I was goin' ta just one place instead o' two."

"Each time you have left Wickenburg, you are followed. And each time they get closer to where you are digging. Just as you would have been followed the last time you left Prescott had you and your brothers not caught the man who followed you."

"An' s'pose ya tell me how ya know that?"

"It was told throughout the mountains before you left Prescott,

77

and you were also guarded closely as you left town. The Apache will not let anything happen to you, nor will they stop you from mining the gold and silver all white men desire. Now, it is time for you to eat and rest another day before you go back to your digging."

"I agree with the eatin', but not the restin'. I got plenty' o' that last night, Chenoa."

"Ben, you must learn to listen to me. Today, there will come a heavy rain just before noontime, and you might be trapped in your digs. The rain will wash away what hides your source of gold, and you will then know the secret to where your wealth will lie."

"Have I been talkin' in my sleep? How do you know what I been lookin' at up there?"

"It is as I say, as the mountains speak secrets to those of us who listen. Remember, your secrets are not just yours, but those of the old ones who came first. Those secrets are told on the breeze, and in the gargle and babble of the creek, and on the sounds of the owl and hawk and the coyote and cougar and bear. None of us are ever alone here, my friend, not in our presence or in our thoughts."

"Alright, woman, now you're startin' ta make me worry some. How close are these Apache watchin' me, anyway?"

"They are not close, only close enough to help you if you need it, and to protect you from enemies. Now eat, before it gets cold," Chenoa said as she placed a plateful of food in front of Ben along with a brimming cup of Arbuckle's.

Ben couldn't stop thinking about her warning about the weather, and decided another day in camp wouldn't hurt even though the sky was a clear, cloudless blue. Her caution about traveling to Wickenburg also rang home with him, even though he only planned one more trip south, and that just to file the proper paperwork on his silver claim. Besides, the more he learned about this Paiute woman, the more he wanted to know, and the only way he could see to do that was spend another day in camp with her asking every question he could come up with. Especially now that Chenoa had revealed that not only she, but the Indians who made their homes in the Bradshaw Mountains and surrounding area, knew a lot more about him than he knew about them.

After chow, Ben entered the small cavern to retrieve the feedbags and drop a scoop of oats into each one followed by drifting down to the meadow to check on his animals. While he only gave them a small ration every few days while in camp, he made sure they were grained up for the first few days before any trip as well as during the trip.

As he went about this chore, he ran a lot of things through his mind, wondering how he would open the conversation with Chenoa about how much she knew and how, as well as what other advice she might have for him regarding his claims and those watching him. Both friend and foe.

Back at the campsite, Chenoa was already putting things under the lean-to and dropping the overhead flaps in anticipation of the rain she had predicted. Ben decided that the best time to open the ball with her would be if the rain came and they were stuck under the lean-to for several hours, if that long. But she changed that plan as she worked.

"Ben, there are four men who would take all you have. Two in Wickenburg and one in Prescott who works with them. The fourth man lives in Phoenix. They are Mr. Simpson and Mr. Pendleton in Wickenburg, and Mr. Barriston in Prescott. A Mr. Meador of Phoenix owns all of them along with many more across the state."

"Barriston? The mining attorney?"

"Yes, he is the one."

"Well, I s'pose if there's somebody who could doctor claims

79

an' get away with it, it'd be him alright. So why do ya think I should file the final claim paperwork in Prescott with him there?"

"Because the assay office in Prescott is honest, while the one in Wickenburg is owned by Mr. Meador. And you can always file your claims with the county as well as the state, and there is another mining attorney there, a young man by the name of Whitaker, who is also honest. Mr. Whitaker is half Yavapai, but few know that, and he needs some new clients to start his business. He will guard your property with his life."

"I see. Seems you're pretty well connected, not ta mention in the know on all the goin's on 'round here."

"It was for other reasons I learned all of this, as I had no idea I would be living in your camp or owing you my life. I must also tell you that the man who felt he owned me as a slave also works for Meador and Barriston. If he survived the wounds I gave him, his name is Luke Weitz. You are why we were so close to your camp, even though he had no idea we were and I wasn't about to tell him. He expected me to lead him to you so that he could kill you, and when I refused he started to beat me. I wasn't going to let him do it again, even if it killed me."

"I see. Well, I'm glad I found ya an' was able ta keep ya alive, Chenoa, but I wouldn't say ya owed me your life. Seems ta me ya decided ta own your life 'fore I come along, an' all I did was ta give ya a chance ta do it. Now, how many others ya figure Barriston has under his thumb?"

"At least another two dozen men, but few are anything but townspeople. Several are miners, or have worked in mines, but most are drunks and gun hands. I would be far more concerned about Meador, but for the moment those in Wickenburg present a bigger danger to you. Might I suggest that before you go back to finish filing your claims in Prescott that you make extra improvements to them that would prove they are yours in the white man's courts?"

"I reckon that's a fine idea, though I don't really have all the necessary equipment an' lumber to build any structures on 'em."

"Ah, but you do have plenty of stones and rocks, and you have a willing helper to work on markers."

"Now, I never said I was gonna show you where the claims are, at least not 'til I make the final filings."

"Ben, do you think I do not know where they are? Why do you think I said it would be safer for you to stay in camp instead of being on the claims? I know that in a heavy rain the water flows heavy through both, and is why you were able to find all the nuggets and flakes of gold at your south claim. The silver is covered by heavy deposits of rock at your northern claim, much of which will be washed away today, and the source of your gold will also be uncovered by the rain flowing through the shallow wash."

Just then a clap of thunder broke their conversation, rolling and rattling through the air with a deafening roar in the high mountain air. A blindingly bright flash of lightening and another roaring, pounding roll of thunder, followed the first clap almost immediately. And then came the first cold drops of rain digging up dust as they smacked the ground. Within the next ten minutes, it was so dark Ben had to light the lantern so they could see inside the lean-to, even though the frequent lightning lit up everything as though it was the brightest of days.

Talking became impossible as the thunder kept rolling and clattering across both sky and landscape, not to mention the heavy rain hitting the top and sides of the lean-to. They had to settle for venison jerky and water for their midday meal, as the storm carried on for hours before finally letting up in the late afternoon. When it stopped, it was like turning off a faucet, changing from heavy downpour to nothing but sunlight filtering out in between the now scattering clouds.

Ben and Chenoa pulled the sides of the lean-to back up and tied them off again, thankful that they held and were properly placed to keep the rainstorm at bay. Chenoa promptly pulled out the dry firewood she had stashed in the lean-to and started a cook fire while Ben set about checking for damage to the campsite. It had weathered well, mainly because Ben had carefully selected it to start with, ensuring the creek wouldn't flood it out, and had made certain he put everything he could in the cavern. Further, it sustained little to no damage due to Chenoa's efforts at organization during her short stay. All in all, both campers were very pleased with how they had fared.

"Chenoa, first, thanks for makin' sure the camp was secured better, an' for predictin' that rainstorm. Any more comin'?"

"No, Ben, not for another two or three months when the summer rains come. I'll have your meal ready in the next hour if you want to go check the animals and drain the catch pots into the gut bags."

"Yes, ma'am. Will do," Ben said with a big smile, thinking how much Chenoa sounded like his mother when there were things to be done. Still, he did as he was told, just as he had always done at home. *Home. Dang, I sure miss the folks. Well, I ain't goin' no place 'til I get this minin' thing settled, an' I don't reckon the boys will be headin' home anytime soon, either.*

By the time Ben made it back to camp, Chenoa was dishing out leftover stew from the night before as well as some fresh fried potatoes and onions. It was just as delicious as the meal before, and once again Ben made a pig of himself.

"Chenoa, if I keep eatin' like this I won't be able to get onta the back o' my horse ta ride ta town."

The Paiute girl only smiled at first, and then commented, "I am pleased you like my cooking, Ben Creed, but I believe you will work it off when the time comes, probably starting tomorrow.

Make certain you carry an extra canteen for drinking and a gut pouch for washing the gold out. By this time tomorrow, you will know where to find all the gold, and the day after you must go to the silver claim. Within the next week, we must work together to make sure no one can ever mistake your claim by improving it beyond any doubt. And the week after that, we must travel to Prescott to see the attorney Whitaker."

"You keep sayin' 'we'. I been wonderin' 'bout that, if'n I shouldn' leave you here ta guard the camp. Might be a tad too dangerous for you ta show up in Prescott, 'specially if that Weitz feller made it, an' it's likely ta be a bit hairy as it is since Meador an' his cronies is expectin' me ta show up in Wickenburg."

"And my only concern was if I could ride the burro that far, or if I would have to walk it. The camp will be safe. The Apache will see to that. Our trip to Prescott will also be protected, and it will be once we are in town the trouble might occur. I do NOT fear Luke. Next time I will finish what I started with him, if he lives. And I will also help you with the association with the lawyer Whitaker. I feel I owe you, whether you want me to or not, and I will do all I can for you until it is time for me to leave your camp for another."

"That's the second time you've said that, Chenoa. Shoot, maybe I won't want you ta leave my camp, ever."

"Ah, but the choice is not yours, Ben Creed. It is mine. When I feel I have repaid you for your care and kindness, I will go. But I will always owe you my life, and will come to your aid if you ever call. However, I do not believe you to be the kind of man who would ever seek the help of another, though you are always quick to offer yourself. And because of that, I can never stay beyond what I decide is my time to leave."

"Well, sounds ta me like ya done decided it all, an' ya ain't leavin' much o' the choosin' ta me, includin' my own minin' interests. An' I reckon I'll go along with it 'til I can't. The day might come when we bump heads on somethin', an' bump 'em hard, girl, but for now seems like we're on the same path together. An' I reckon that's just fine by me. Say, what is it ya add ta the stew ta make it taste sa good?"

"My secret, Ben, given to me by my mother. And like your claims, I will not be sharing it anytime soon," Chenoa smiled.

Silver, Gold and Blood In Arizona

Chapter Eleven

Opting to follow the tracks left by the herd rather than get too close, the trio worked their way back down toward Star Valley. Somewhat surprised that the herd was still there, Zack motioned Seth to ride back to the east in an attempt to keep from being seen by any of those guarding the cattle.

Successful in making the move without being seen, they holed up in some heavy brush and posted a watch. Todd took first watch, but it didn't take long before Jack showed up and with the others started moving the herd north up Mayfield Canyon. Slipping back up through Schoolhouse Canyon, Todd and Zack were able to keep the tail end of the herd in sight until the herd was turned back to the northwest across the face of Diamond Rim.

Cover was sparse, but it wasn't long before Seth talked them into topping Diamond Rim at Gilliland Spring, and skirting the herd as they moved along. The drovers took a hard chance pushing the herd up the Verde River north through its narrow canyon. But only a mile and a half up the canyon they pushed them out due west toward Weber Creek. The going was tough for the trackers, but rougher for the cattle as the drovers pushed them hard over the rocky, up and down terrain.

The herd was pushed up Weber Creek until they hit Shannon Gulch, and then up the gulch until it turned north toward the Mogollon Rim. Just before dark set in, they bunched the cattle up in the flats below the rim and close to the new Mormon settlement of Pine.

The trio of trackers was left with little choice of camping sites that would remain hidden, and ended up over two miles back and up under the lip of the rim at Pine Spring in hopes they could have a small cook fire without getting sniffed out. Trusting that the drovers were as tired from their ride as their pursuers were, Zack took no time in getting a fire started and a pot of coffee on. Todd took over from there, chopping a couple of wild onions he'd found into the skillet with the last of their potatoes and the last of their fatback. An hour later, they had finished eating, cleaned up and set up their overnight camp, banking the fire and making sure Seth was securely tied to a log.

***

Morning came quickly, as the brothers wanted to make certain they were on the trail and ready long before the cattle drovers were, so as to make certain they didn't fall too far behind the herd just in case Ike Stockton showed up with new orders. He had a reputation for being unpredictable, which is what had kept him out of prison so far as well as making him a successful crook.

"My guess is they'll push the herd up onta the point above us, usin' a little cut in the rim due northeast o' where they bedded the cattle down. From there, once they top the point, it's near due north ta Angell, where they can load the cattle on railcars an' move 'em anywhere they want ta go. It's a hard three ta four day drive, not much water an' little forage, but the way I got it figured Winslow is gonna be way too hot for 'em right now an' they'll want ta be shed o' that herd quick like," Zack said.

"So, Seth, how do ya propose we get up on top without bein' seen? 'R bein' able ta follow 'em when there is little ta no cover once we get over the rim?" Todd asked.

"We take the hard route, up Weber Crick Canyon 'til we top the rim, then hightail it ahead o' 'em ta Baker Butte. There's still decent cover goin' north, 'nough we can stay outa sight an' still keep track o' the herd at least as far as Kinnikinick Lake. From there, we'll have ta use draws an' gully's an' pray it don't rain an' drown us. If they stay on that route, we can get ta Angell ahead o' 'em an' put a stop ta the whole shebang there. An' if they start elsewheres, we'll know that, too, an' we can change plans as we go dependin' on them."

"Todd, sounds ta me like Seth mighta made a good lawman if he'd just kept his nose clean. What do ya think o' his plan?"

"Sounds good ta me. An' I'll go one more, brother. Seems ta me ol' Seth here got hisself caught up in a real bad situation, so I been thinkin'. How's about we say he was workin' undercover once he found out what was goin' on with the secretary, an' his partner Jack an' the rest o' 'em owl hoots, 'til he caught up with us an' had somebody in the law ta tell it to, an' then he tied in with us an' helped bring 'em down. Sound reasonable ta you?"

"Yeah, it does. What say you, Seth? Ya ready ta honor that Special Ranger badge you're carryin'?" Zack asked.

"Damned straight I am! If it'll keep me from gettin' hung, I'd side with the devil! That mean I get my guns back? An' no more bein' tied up?"

"That's just what it means, Seth. But mark my words, one false move 'r slip on your part an' you can figure you're a dead man an' the story we tell will be the straight of it. But if you do this thing right, we'll even see if we can get you a job as a deputy with our sheriff," Todd clarified.

"Damn, men, I don't know what ta say, other'n thanks."

"Good, now help up load up the gear an then you can lead out an show us how you figure ta get us up on top an' ahead o' the herd," Zack said with a smile.

Three hours later, the trio rode out onto the flats above the Mogollon Rim after leading their mounts up the rough and steep Weber Creek Canyon. From there, they trusted that the herd would be behind them by at least an hour, if not more, and made a beeline toward the northeast side of Baker Butte. Once there, they set up a watch at two hour intervals to make sure they could see or hear the herd as it approached.

They didn't have to make the first shift change before the herd was pushed hard along the west side of the butte, just as Seth had predicted. The trio was able to stay well hidden in the trees and brush, following the herd by sound alone until late that day when the herd was bedded down alongside Willow Valley where Antelope Draw fed into it. Camping two miles northeast of the cattle, they made short work of setting up camp and getting plenty of coffee and chewing on a generous amount of jerky for their skimpy supper.

"Zack, we need ta stock up somewhere now that we got an extra mouth to feed. Grub is near gone already, an' you know how I get when I don't get my Arbuckle's."

"Well, there's a Mormon dairy ta the west o' Kinnikinick Lake that I reckon a feller could get some supplies at. Last I heard, they were runnin' a little tradin' post ta go with their milk sales. It's a hard day's ride there, but I reckon a man could get there, buy supplies an' meet the other two of us north o' Kinnikinick an' still be ahead o' the herd."

"Todd, it's your turn to load up supplies. Me an' Seth'll keep tabs on the cattle, an' if we ain't where we're s'posed ta be then find the trail an' hunt for us."

"Sounds good. I'll head out 'fore sunup. Now, how far north o' Kinnikinick ya figure ta be?" Todd asked.

"Three miles, at least. There's a little lake called Yeager Lake that usually has plenty o' good water 'bout three miles due north of Kinnikinick, and due east o' the dairy 'bout seven miles. By the way, there's a lake there at the dairy, most years anyway, an' plenty o' good, sweet water if it's full. Now then, if they push real hard an' camp at Yeager Lake, the best place for us'll be up Anderson Canyon at the springs there. It's all pretty easy ta find, sa ya should be able ta locate us."

"Yeah, by the sound o' our hungry belly's most likely," Zack said with a smirk. After a good chuckle all around, the trio fell into a quiet, almost worrisome silence, as though something bad was about to happen, but no one wanted to talk about it.

Morning came as quiet as the night before, Todd shaking hands before mounting up and riding silently out toward the Mormon dairy. Leading both pack animals, he pushed as hard as he could, and arrived at the trading post two hours before sundown. He gathered the needed supplies, loaded them and tied them down, paid the tab, mounted and rode out due east in hopes of finding Zack and Seth at Kinnikinick Lake.

As the day progressed in Todd's absence, Zack and Seth mimicked the flow of the cattle strictly by their sound. At midday, Seth pulled up to say, "At the rate they're pushin' the cattle, they'll be well past Kinnikinick, even past Yeager Lake by dark. There's several little lakes north o' there, but it's chancy if there's any water in 'em. I think our best bet ta make sure we connect with Todd is ta ride on up ta the springs in Anderson Draw. We'll be behind the herd, but at this rate I don't really think that matters as much as gettin' some grub in our bellies. Do you?"

"I reckon that's right, Seth. Ya reckon we're on the right side o' the herd ta find this Anderson Draw?"

"Yessir, we sure are. An' if we plan ta nail 'em at Angell, we'll need ta ride hard tomorrow, as we'll only be an easy day's ride out."

"How far out?"

"Maybe fifteen miles, tops," Seth answered.

"Then let's push on ahead an' get us a good camp set up. If I know Todd, he'll be Johnny on the spot by dark if not before."

Zack was correct in that by the time they made it to the springs at the top of Anderson Draw, Todd was only minutes behind them, having had to wait until twilight to skirt the south side of the herd as it moved on north. Seth had just finished gathering wood when Todd rode into camp shaking his head.

"What the hell got inta that bunch? They tryin' ta kill 'em cattle 'fore they get 'em ta Angell?"

"Yeah, we kind o' discussed that ourselves, Todd. But let's get that grub cookin', an' we can talk about it as we eat. I'm near starved!" Zack complained.

Todd had managed to pick up some fresh steaks from the dairyman, along with fresh dug potatoes, carrots and onions left in the ground from the year before, and was pleased as punch that the store also carried Arbuckle's. The trio ate like they hadn't eaten in a month, talking about how tired and hungry the drovers had to be by now.

"Whattaya think made 'em push on sa hard? Reckon Stockton 'r whoever he is gave 'em a deadline?" Todd queried.

"I figure that's the size of it, fellers. What with you upsettin' his apple cart, I reckon he wants ta be shed o' 'em cattle an' on his way outa this territory 'fore he gets nabbed. The more I think about it, the more I reckon Jack is also pushin' ta get gone, 'specially now since thay ain't seen hide nor hair o' me for some time now. He's got ta figure that either I'm dead 'r in jail, an' maybe singin' like a songbird if it's the latter. We never was really all that close, an' he knows I value my life over anybody else's so he'd figure me ta squawk like a jaybird if I got nabbed."

"Well, I got ta agree with ya on that, Seth. But there's just one thing. If it comes down to it, I'd like ta know we can count on ya ta back us up just like we'll do you if ya get inta a fix. I don't need ta think you'd turn tail an' run if it gets hot. 'Cause if that's the case, I'll plug you sure."

"I'll stand, Zack. I owe the two o' ya too much right now ta do ya dirty. 'Sides, I wanna see the look on Jack's face when we take 'em down."

"Alright, but you'd best know I'm holdin' ya to it. If this feller leadin' this bunch is Ike Stockton, he's pretty fair with a gun an' he won't hesitate ta kill whoever gets in his way, even his own men. 'Specially this bunch, that he's got no allegiance with other than havin' 'em do his dirty work. An' that includes your buddy Jack, no matter what he was told."

"Yeah, I done figured that one out. But I am wonderin' 'bout one thing. There's six men ridin' with the herd, Ike an' whoever he has lined up in Angell, an' just three of us. The odds aren't what I'd call in our favor, would you?" Seth asked.

"No, but that's the way it's always been with us Creed's. You can put the whole family tagether an' somehow the bad guys always end up with more guns than us, even if we add in our sisters. An' believe me, you'd much rather go up against any o' us brothers as ta go up against our sisters," Todd said with a smile.

"Even Ben? I've heard about his skill, an' the word is that you two are near as fast as he is. Trust me, I wouldn't want ta go up against any o' ya, for that matter. But still, I ain't that quick, sa it's likely I'm the one gonna get plugged 'fore ya can take the rest o' 'em out."

"How are ya with that rifle o' yours, Seth?" Zack asked.

"One helluva lot better'n I am with a Colt. Let's just say if I'm out huntin' with a rifle, I won't go hungry, an' I won't tear up much meat."

"That settles it then. We'll use you as a lookout man, overlookin' our play. The way I see it, even if they continue ta drive the herd as hard as they have been, we can still be in Angell an' get the layout long 'fore they ride in. How do the loading ramps an' corrals lay along the tracks, an' how big is Angell?" Todd asked.

"Maybe a dozen 'r so folks live there, mostly railroad folks like the agent an' his wife, a conductor an' his family, a storekeeper an' his brood an' a couple o' others, mostly just old folks. The corrals are ta the east o' town, an' the station is 'tween them an' the edge of town. The loading ramps are also on the east o' the corrals, an' the whole shebang sets on the north side o' the tracks. Even the houses an' the store. They all lay just a bit further north an' west o' the tracks than the station an' corrals, 'bout a tenth of a mile 'r so," Seth informed the brothers.

"Alright, then, sounds like we can keep it all out o' town if we do it right. No livery? An' what's the ground like? Flat? Any mounds 'r gullies we can use?" Todd continued with his questioning.

"No livery, just a big shed out by the corrals where riders put their horses an' tack up if they are stayin' a day 'r longer. An' no sleeping quarters anywhere either, 'less they leave an extra caboose 'r sleepin' car on the spur there. An' then it's just for railroad workers 'r big shots. The town sets on the edge o' Young's Canyon, an' west o' town there's two little rain fed draws that dump inta Young's Canyon, an' then it all runs north from there. Not much for cover."

"Enough, r' so it seems ta me. Whattaya think, Zack?"

"Yup, just fine. The only thing is, we'll need a place ta stash Seth where he can pick off any outliers with that Winchester," Todd responded.

"They'll be ridin' in from the south an' have ta cross the tracks ta get ta the corrals, sa chances are there'll be some cars settin' there ready ta load once they get the corrals filled," Seth said.

"Then I'm thinkin' we put you on top o' the car closest ta where they come in an' across the tracks from, an' me an' Todd'll set up inside the corral gates. That should put them smack in between us, an' be near like shootin' fish in a barrel. Now then, we got ta figure that Ike an' one 'r two men will be hangin' round the train r' the horse shed, an' most likely the Indian Agent will be there as well. Most o' 'em agents are cowardly little pencil pushers, but we still have ta account for him. From how you described the layout, we should be able ta stash our horses in the draw ta the west, and slip down the tracks real careful like ta get where we each need ta be. Seth, since you're goin' high, make sure ya go ta the far end o' the first car an' be real careful gettin' on top. Now let's sack out an' ride early."

Chapter Twelve

By the time the sun started peaking over the horizon, the trio had already covered well over half the distance to Angell, even though they were swinging as far west and into the trees as they felt safe doing. An hour and a half later, they were riding down the shallow draw that led directly into town, stopping to check and recheck both in front and behind them. Two miles from town they ran out of trees and had to depend solely on the sparse brush that lined the draw and provided their cover.

With just under a half-mile to go, they found a nice, well-hidden grassy patch with a good puddle of water and lots of brush to stake out the horses, and tied them off tight. Gathering all the guns and ammo they could carry they carefully shouldered and stuck their loads wherever they could find a place to hold a weapon or ammo and started working on down the draw. Slowly, as quietly as possible, they finally made their way to the short bridge crossing the draw. Todd and Zack used the little bridge as cover to slip up on the north side of the tracks while Seth made his way down the south side of the tracks toward the stock cars.

The sun was directly overhead when the brothers slipped under the corral rails and slithered themselves into place near the gates. They could hear Ike and the others talking, making plans to make themselves scarce as soon as these cattle were loaded. All but the Indian Agent, who was bemoaning the loss of his nice extra income, "nearly three times what the government pays me."

Zack worked into a new position, one where he could see the top of the closest stock car. Seth was in place, but too easily seen if anyone happened to look his direction. Zack motioned to him to move back further from the edge, and to remove his high-crowned hat. It took a couple of attempts, but Seth finally understood and repositioned himself, removing his hat and rolling it up to use as a cushion for his 1873 Winchester.

Moving back to his original spot, Zack motioned to Todd that both he and Seth were ready. As Todd motioned back, they could hear the sounds of the herd approaching, though they were still at least an hour or two from being close enough to the corrals to start the free-for-all. Both brothers used the corral rails as shade against the often brutal Arizona Territory sun, even though today wasn't bad with occasional puffy clouds drifting by overhead.

Seth wasn't so lucky, with nothing for shade on top of the stock car, and needed the extra canteen he had decided to lug along. He slurped down the last sip as quietly as he could, and hunkered down tight against the top of the car as the first of the cattle and lead riders approached the corrals. He could see the four men stride out from under the horse shed and toward the gates, and wondered how close they would get before trouble started.

His answer came, but not how he expected it to happen. One of the four men, obviously a railroader from the way he was dressed, grabbed the closest gate and swung it wide open, then casually walked back toward the group, making certain he was well out of the way of the cattle.

Todd wiggled even tighter against the rails, still unseen by anyone, mounted or otherwise. Then came the second gate, again opened by the railroad man, and again the Creed brother went unseen. An hour later, the cattle were all in the corrals and the gates closed in preparation for pushing them up the ramps into the stock cars.

Seth heard the sound of steam being added and felt the sudden jolt of the engine as the cars started moving toward the loading ramps. It startled him so bad that he nearly rolled off the top of the car. *When are those brothers gonna kick this off? It won't be long an' the crooks will have their business taken care of an' the men paid an' ridin' away.* His answer came just as his thoughts cleared his mind.

"That's about all there is, gents. You're all under arrest for cattle rustlin'. Drop any hardware you're carryin', an' walk slowly toward the depot buildin'. You're covered three ways from hell, an' there ain't no gettin' away now. That is unless ya decide ta try your luck, an' then you'll get a free ride ta Boot Hill." Zack's voice carried an air of authority Seth hadn't noticed before, but no one moved.

"If I were you fellers, I don't think I'd push him real far. He's in a real bad mood right now," Todd added to their confusion. "You'd best do what he says."

As though frozen in time, none of the outlaws moved, not even those mounted, until Seth caught the glimpse of movement from one of the furthest riders. Jack. *Don't do it, Jack. Just climb down an' start walkin' toward the depot like Zack told ya.* But Jack didn't. He tried to slip his pistol out of the holster, and had a look of both surprise and disbelief as the .44-40 slug ripped through his chest and blood seeped out onto his shirt.

As Jack fell and hit the ground with a thud, Zack called out again. "I'm startin' ta lose my patience, gents. Now get ta movin'." He had no more than finished speaking when another of the cowboys decided to test the fates, and died from Seth's rifle fire just as quickly as Jack had. The four men on the ground still hadn't moved a muscle, until finally the railroad man threw his hands in the air and started running toward the depot building, yelling at the top of his lungs. "Don't shoot! Don't shoot! I ain't in this deal! I'm just here to open the gates an' help load the cattle!"

Stockton used that movement as his means of trying to escape, grabbing his partner and the Indian Agent, throwing them down in front of him as he ran toward the horse shed. He kept moving, using the cattle and corrals as a shield until he ho longer could use either to keep any of the three men from shooting him. Just as Seth pulled a bead, Stockton jumped onto a horse behind one of the cowboys, using him as a cover as he pushed the animal toward the shed, where he shot the cowboy and dropped to the ground behind the only solid wall on the structure.

Even though he anticipated the move, Seth missed, hitting the solid pole that stood as the corner piece of the building sending splinters in all directions. Three other rounds also hit the side of the barn, all missing their intended mark. Another cowboy decided to make a run for it, but Todd dropped him not ten feet from where he started. The last two mounted men weren't mounted much longer, shucking their hardware, dropping it on the ground and hitting the ground running toward the depot. One of them, Micah Slate, was loudly yelling at the other. "Earl Carson, I ain't never gonna listen ta you again, if I don't swing for this! I knowed this thing was gonna go south, an' by gawd it did!"

"Zack, that feller standin' there with the Indian Agent is the Association Secretary. He's the one what hired me an' Jack," Seth called out as the two men were getting back to their feet. "Make sure he don't get away, an' I'll keep the shed covered in case Ike tries ta make another move."

"Zack, I got the boys covered, including the secretary an' the agent! G'won an' go get Stockton! Seth, keep us both covered!" Todd's clear voice rang out across the now quiet landscape.

With a reloaded and cocked Colt in hand, Zack quickly began tracing Ike Stockton's attempted path to freedom, cautiously working his way toward the shed. At the now splintered corner, he paused for a moment, peering around the corner into the all but empty structure. Three horses were loose in the far pen, but were still saddled. The bay he had seen Ike riding when he first saw him below the Mogollon Rim was there along with a copper sorrel mare sporting flaxen mane and tail and three white socks as well as a young gray gelding still hooked up to a buggy.

Counting legs, Zack deduced that Ike wasn't trying to hide among the animals and slowly worked his way further into the building. Checking every possible nook and cranny, he worked his way through the entire shed, with no sign of Stockton to be found. Not even his footprints.

Zack turned from the far end of the shed and then strode back to the splintered corner, stopping long enough to holler at Seth. "Seth, you didn't see anything movin'? Anywhere?"

"Nope, not so much as a tick. He ain't in there?"

"Nope, nowhere. Todd, you didn't see nothin'?"

"Nothin', but I been a tad busy tyin' these four fellers together. The railroad man fetched the station agent, who was hidin' in a corner o' the depot. He's got a real tale ta tell when ya get time."

"Fine, but I want Stockton. I'm goin' back through the shed again, an' give it an even closer look. Seth, ya might as well come on down an' give me a hand."

Zack stood at the corner as Seth scrambled down off the now stationary stock car and hurried to join him in his search. Together, they were just past halfway through the building when the engine steamed up and started down the spur headed for the open rails.

"Dammit! The train! We didn't check the engine!" Zack yelled as he ran toward one of the cowboy's horses, jumped into the saddle and started off after the engine. It only took a hundred yards for him to realize that the horse was too tired from the push to even begin to make up any ground on the engine. Reining up with a cacophony of profanities, Zack turned the exhausted animal back toward the corrals.

As Zack passed Seth, he said, "Follow me ta the depot. We need ta get some wires sent pronto, an' I'll want you an' Todd ta have 'em hombres gather up the dead. Looks ta me like the railroad might have some problems o' their own if the westbound has already cleared the last spur 'tween here an' Winslow."

Seth obeyed obediently, not wanting to cross Zack or the temper he was in over losing Stockton, and once at the depot he and Todd set about making certain they collected the dead cowboys, laying them in a row on the platform of the depot and covering them with a canvas they found. And although the prisoners grumbled, Todd informed them that it wouldn't take much prodding for them to join their dead comrades, which seemed to quiet any complaints. Half an hour later, Seth and Todd moved the survivors back to the side of the depot building, tying them securely to the hitching rails.

Inside the depot, Zack had put pressure on the railroad man left behind when the engine and tender pulled out, finding out he was the brakeman and as innocent as a lamb. Together, they calmed the station agent down and made sure he was capable of sending coherent telegrams both ways up and down the line. The first was to all the stations along the eastern line to check on the progress of the westbound passenger train, only to find it was still in Winslow waiting on some dignitaries coming down from the Navajo and Hopi Reservations.

Ordered to remain in Winslow until the rogue engine was either past, or had pulled off the rails somewhere along the way, Zack also made certain they knew the passenger train would be commandeered at Angell to carry deputies and prisoners to Flagstaff. The second was to the town marshal's in Winslow and Holbrook, informing them that if they had the opportunity to stop the rogue engine they should be careful in attempting to capture Ike Stockton, now wanted for rustling and murder in Arizona Territory. After considering adding more of a warning to the message, Zack decided that there wasn't a lawman worth his salt that didn't know about Stockton and how dangerous he was.

Next came a wire to the brand inspector's office in Flagstaff, alerting them that an inspector was needed in Angell as fast as one could get there to inspect over two hundred head of stolen cattle in an attempt to determine their owners, and to notify either he or Todd Creed at the Yavapai County Sheriff's Office regarding the original brand owners. He already knew that some of the ranchers were in on the rustling fix, or at least according to Seth they were, and he wanted to make certain they were made to pay for their deceit.

The next to last wire was to the Sheriff's Annex in Flagstaff to let them know he and Todd were coming in with four prisoners to be jailed overnight, along with four dead outlaws, and that they'd need the jail wagon to transport the living to Prescott the next day. The last wire was to the Sheriff's Office in Prescott apprising the sheriff of the basic facts.

"But what about all those cattle? What are we supposed to do with them?" the agent begged to know.

"Albert, was it?"

"Yes, sir. Albert Munson."

"Albert, make sure they get fed and watered, an' hold 'em here 'til the brand inspector inspects an' clears 'em, then let me know an' I'll tell ya where ta send 'em an' when."

"How long do you think that is going to take? I don't have the kind of budget to be feeding cattle, even for a day."

"Then I'd suggest you get on that telegraph o' yours an' let somebody above ya know what ya need, an' do it pronto. An' I don't want them stock cars moved either, at least not 'til the cattle are ready ta roll out. The cattle are evidence in a cattle rustlin' an' the stock cars are prima facie evidence of the fact the cattle were intended ta be shipped to other than the Indian Reservations." Zack was very proud of the fact that he had learned that tidbit of Latin from listening to lawyers try cases, and even more proud of the fact that the two railroad employees were satisfactorily impressed by his use of legal terminology.

He left it there, turning and striding through the door without another word spoken. Outside, he walked around the building to where Todd and Seth were holding the prisoners. Todd knew better than to interrupt Zack's mood, or his thoughts. He was the same way, as were all of the Creed men. Not that his sisters were any better, but they at least hid it better.

"Ahhh, Deputy?" the station agent asked fifteen minutes later, knowing he was walking on thin ice in approaching Zack, but it was critical he pass along what he had just learned over the wire.

"Yeah, what is it?" Zack snapped.

"The Omaha office has ordering a new engine to be sent here from Flagstaff, complete with two additional stock cars, a passenger car and a freight car. I've been instructed to load all of the cattle here into these cars, and make certain they get to the yard in Flagstaff where the brand inspector can look them over and report to both you and the office. The westbound is being held at the Winslow station until I signal that your train has left for Flagstaff."

"Fine. Thanks for tellin' us. Reckon that all makes sense. Any word on the engine that was here?"

"Yessir, I was coming to that. It was run onto the spur at Dennison and left. The engineer and fireman were killed, and the killer rode off in the station agent's buggy after wounding him. Oh, and there are two railroad detectives coming on board your train, ordered to assist you in any way you ask, and to stay, as Omaha put it, 'the hell out of your way.'"

Zack's mood lightened a bit at that, and Todd could see the anger over missing Stockton escaping on the engine was beginning to diminishi. "Again, thanks, Albert."

"A couple more things, Deputy. The brand inspectors will also be waiting in Flag for your train to arrive, and will arrange to guard the cattle until they are ready for release. The jail annex also sent word that the jail wagon will be held for you, but you'll also be taking three of their prisoners along with you to Prescott."

"Well, Albert, is that it?"

"Yessir."

"Good. Seems that things are workin' themselves out, don't it? Like Maw always says, 'Water seeks its own level, be it floodin' 'r dry as a bone.' Reckon that plays out more ways than one. Say, you got any coffee in that shack o' yours?"

"Nossir, but I can sure put some on," the agent replied, seeing another opportunity to get on Zack's good side.

"I don't reckon it's Arbuckle's, is it?"

"Nossir. I can't afford that, and the railroad would never pay for it either."

"Tell ya what. Wait a bit, an' I'll have some Arbuckle's here so's we can have some good coffee." Turning to Seth, Zack continued. "Seth, go fetch our critters, an' be snappy about it. Albert here is gonna brew us some Arbuckle's as long as we're providin' it. An' son, trust me, I need some good coffee right now, so get a leg on it!"

Seth could only smile as he started his trot back to where they had left their own horses. They were a bit further out than he gauged, forcing him to walk the last half of the trip with sore feet from running in boots. He was pretty glad to be able to ride back in, as he had developed a pair of blisters the size of pecans from all the walking of late.

His return to the depot was a glad one as well. Zack, Todd, Albert and Connor, the brakeman, were all wanting to have some of the best coffee known to the West. And by the time the second pot was finished, everyone was in a good mood and becoming friends with each other.

They were surprised to see their train arrive so soon after getting word it was coming, and within fifteen minutes the extra cars were dropped on the main track, and the engine was moved to connect to the stock cars allowing them to finish loading the cattle.

An hour later, the rest of the car was connected and not only were all the cattle loaded, but so were the horses and gear, while the bodies were placed in the freight car. A few minutes later they were all seated in the passenger car ready for the ride to Flagstaff. The brakeman decided to ride along with them, having lost his engine and tender, but still feeling responsible for the cars and cattle.

Chapter Thirteen

Anxious to see how much more gold had been washed out by the rain, Ben decided to continue working on the gold claim instead of moving to the silver claim as previously planned. As he climbed the last and steepest part of the trail approaching the big boulder he had been digging under, he couldn't believe what he was seeing.

The narrow gap a hundred yards down the draw, which he used as a means of hiding his trail, was blocked by big boulder. Or at least when he saw it he thought it to be a different boulder than the one he had been digging under. As he climbed up and over the ridge where the gap had been and looked down at his panning site, he was astonished to see that the boulder was the very same one. The area where he had been digging was now nearly full of runoff water.

What was most surprising was the glitter of gold dust, flakes and nuggets sparkling in the morning sun along the edge of the small pond created by the boulder blocking the draw. Climbing down to the water's edge, Ben started snatching up all the nuggets he could see. An hour later, he had filled seven leather pouches and stacked them under a small bush not ten feet from the boulder, and then pulled out his pan to work the flakes and dust. After another hour he had filled five more pouches with gold, and decided that he was actually wasting his time even though he had collected a large amount.

Following the concept he had originally considered, along with Chenoa's words, Ben worked his way up the draw, amazed at the amount of gold he was seeing as he worked his way up higher and higher up the draw along the side of the mountain. Roughly three hundred feet further up the slope, he came to what he had really been looking for all along. A wide vein of gold shimmering in a huge vein of rose quartz, the obvious origin of all the gold seen and found below. He chipped away a large chunk to have assayed along with some of the pouches.

Looking up at the sun, he decided he still had time to work his way around to where his silver claim was, just to see if Chenoa's prophesy regarding the silver being better exposed was true. An hour and a half later, he had made his way around and dropped down into the small draw holding his silver claim, only to find it was also acted as somewhat of a catch for the runoff.

Skirting the water marks where it had run down the draw, Ben turned to look at the rock face where he had been working. A large section of the face had broken off falling left and right, exposing a ten foot wide vein of silver in the new face of the slope. Scrambling into the open area, Ben grabbed up several rocks laced with the precious metal, and then several more that were all but composed of pure silver.

Patting himself on the back for leaving the pouches of gold hidden to avoid carrying that much weight, he slipped off his rucksack and stuffed several of the richest looking rocks into the bag, and then swung it back over his shoulder and turned to make his way out. Stopping for a moment, he glanced around in all directions to make sure he was alone, or at least that he couldn't see anyone watching him.

Satisfied he was undetected, Ben worked his way back to what was once his random set of trails into the find, picked one he hadn't used in a while, and then set out for camp. Even as careful and quiet as he was taking his circuitous route, he covered the distance in record time and was back near camp in less than half an hour. On the way back, he considered not telling Chenoa about the finds, and then decided she'd figure it out anyway and was fully prepared to tell everything over their evening meal.

But the smell of fresh venison cooking over an open flame

stopped him in his tracks. Quickly ducking off the trail Ben made his way around the campsite, getting a good look at everything as he did so. Nothing seemed amiss, and Chenoa acted as though nothing were wrong, so he decided it was just his nerves, and that there was probably a perfectly good explanation as to why there was a deer hanging in a tree on the edge of camp.

"Ben, why are you so worried that you feel you have to sneak into your own camp?" Chenoa called out as Ben sat there looking at her back.

He could only chuckle as he stood and strolled the rest of the way into the site. "Well, I smelled venison cookin', an' I know I didn't kill any deer an' I didn't figure you had, so I was a tad nervous."

"Ah, our visitor has been gone for several hours how, and had you been in camp he most likely wouldn't have been so generous. Oh, and before you get worried at seeing an extra animal with the others, he also brought me a pony to ride on our way back into Prescott on your next trip."

"An' just who the hell is this visitor? 'Specially one that knows about this camp, an' my stock?"

"Long Lance, an Apache warrior who has taken a liking to me and has decided to court me now that Luke is gone, or at least out of the picture."

"Long Lance? Never heard o' him. So how'd he know you was here an' didn't belong ta me?"

"We do not share any emotions, and do not sleep together. Such things are obvious to anyone who might stop to visit. That is among those few who know where we are camped."

"Yeah, all right, so he's one o' 'em what's been watchin' over me, eh? An' him an' his tribe all know how I carried ya inta camp an' all that, right?"

"Yes, and yes. I told him he is on a fool's errand, hoping to court me, as I am not at all interested in becoming the wife of another man, even an Apache named Long Lance or a miner named Ben Creed. I am more than capable of taking care of myself, and I will choose the man I wish to pledge myself to when I am ready, and not before."

Ben leaned back with a hearty laugh, and then sat back forward to ask, "How'd he take that? Not real happy ta hear it I'll wager."

Chenoa smiled back, and then turned back to her cooking for a few minutes before responding. "No, he was disappointed, but not surprised. He had brought the buck for me to eat to build my strength, but left not long after I stated my position. He left, and then an hour later brought me the pony, telling me that he had many ponies, and a large and empty wickiup for me to live in when I was ready to take him. When I gave him what must have been a half angry, half puzzled look, he explained that he would wait until I was ready. That no other man would come near me except you, and that one day I would know he was to be my man. I must say, he made his point quite clear, though he did so in an unappealing way. Are you ready to eat?"

"Yes, ma'am. I been hungry since I first smelled that deer cookin'. An' I reckon I got some news ta tell you over the chow. But let me get a cup o' that Arbuckle's for starters," Ben said as he stood, walked to the fire and poured himself a cup of coffee. Taking a sip, he couldn't help but smile again at how Chenoa had described the way she handled an Apache warrior. Taking the plateful of food handed him by his campmate, he walked to his usual stump, sat down and devoured a great meal, all but forgetting to fill Chenoa in on what he had seen and found that day.

The Paiute woman sat quietly enjoying her meal, smiling on occasion as Ben started to detail his day in bits and pieces between bites. And when he was finished, she merely smiled and said, "It is as I saw it in my dreams then. Ben Creed, one day in the not so distant future, you and your brothers will be very rich. But you will not stay here in the Bradshaw Mountains, or anywhere in Arizona. You will all be called home to assist your parents. Then you will move to another place where you will become even richer, but this time you will not be alone. That is all I have seen, Ben Creed, so I cannot tell you more."

"Lordy Lordy, I reckon that's plenty for one night! Just as long as I know I'm gonna live long enough ta spend some o' this money I'm gonna make, that'll tickle me plumb pink! Well, that an' knowin' I get ta eat this fine cookin' for a time longer 'fore Long Lance gets fat on it!"

Ben ducked Chenoa's empty cup as it flew past his ear, yelping as it went by. "Damn, I was just teasin', Chenoa. But ya know how much I like your cookin', an' how hard I been workin' these claims, not ta mention how hard I've worked ta keep anybody from findin' out where they are."

"Oh, don't worry. The cup was empty, and if I had wanted to hit you I would have. And yes, I know how much you have wanted these claims to work out after so many that have not. I also know that you wish to share any good fortune with your family, which is part of what makes you such a good man. Now, it is your turn to clean the dishes while I put away the meat. Then we must both rest, as tomorrow will be a very busy day."

Ben went about his share of camp duties, humming an old familiar tune that he had long forgotten the name of while he worked. Finished, he poured another cup of Arbuckle's and sat down on his stump to muse over Chenoa's ability to see into the future. He also wondered if that's what it really was, or just an inane ability to read minds, or maybe just feed off of what she saw in someone's expressions.

"It is what comes to me in my dreams, Ben Creed. Nothing

more. It only happens when I am very close to someone, those I have spent much time with or those who have done as you, and saved my life. Do not worry. If they offend you I will keep them to myself in the future."

"Now how did you know what I was thinkin'? I didn't say a word."

"No, but it was in the way you were watching me, and in your face as you did. There were many questions there, and I only guessed at what they might be based on our conversation after our meal."

"Well, ya don't have ta stop tellin' me what your dreams are, as long as the bad comes with the good an' you ain't holdin' anything back."

"I promise to tell you everything I dream about you, both good and bad. But now we must sleep, for tomorrow will be a very long day for both of us as I will be going with you to assist in marking out your claims. We must return with the gold you have hidden, as well as plenty of samples of the silver ore. We must also begin planning for the trip to Prescott, even though it has only been three weeks since you were there last. Going in early will throw off the timing of any who would desire to harm you, not to mention it is time to ensure your claims are properly filed with the assistance of James Whitaker. You will like him, and I am sure you will become lifelong friends."

"Settin' my schedule now, too, eh? Well, ta tell you the truth I was thinkin' on that on the way back in this afternoon. Considerin' what I saw after that rain, an' how much gold there was just layin' on the ground an' all the color in the silver claim, waitin' any longer would be fool's play. Let's get the monuments built tomorrow, an' start closin' up camp the day after that. And the next day, we'll load up an' head ta town. That work for you?"

"Yes."

"Are you sure you're healed up enough ta handle the hike an' all the work we got ta do?"

"Yes. I am much stronger now, almost completely healed. Walking and lifting rocks will help to heal me even more, as well as rebuild my strength. It is what I need. In the morning, I will pack some food to take with us so that we keep our strength up all through the day. But for now, I really must rest. I advise you do the same," Chenoa sounded very firm as she stood to walk to her bed, leaving Ben no chance to argue or agree, one way or the other.

As he rolled into his sougan, Ben tried to close his eyes and go to sleep, but no matter how hard he tried, sleep just wouldn't come. He could hear Chenoa's soft breathing as she obviously was sound asleep. He envied her tonight, being able to sleep so soundly while he couldn't clear his mind or get comfortable. The fact that these two claims were far richer than he could have ever dreamed was startling, and a source of concern going forward. Making certain the monuments were substantial enough that no one could just move them, or claim them as their own, was another concern. As was making another trip into Prescott this soon and finally declaring the exact location of these claims. He hoped Chenoa was right about this Whitaker character, as his trust of lawyers didn't run very deep.

***

Ben awoke to the sound of a camp already moving, and could smell the fresh coffee boiling along with fatback and potatoes frying. He never ceased to be amazed at how quietly the Paiute woman could move around camp, though he guessed the reason this morning was the fact he had slept so little and could have used another hour or two of rest.

"C'mon, sleepyhead. Breakfast is almost ready, and the stock still needs fed. At this rate, it will be noon before we get on the trail."

"Yes, ma'am, I'm up an' at 'em. Just let me toss some water on my face an' head down ta feed the stock. It won't take me long, an' I should be done eatin' 'fore the sun breaks the mountain," Ben replied as he jumped out of bed and grabbed a canteen. Sloshing some water on his face, he wiped it off with his sleeve and then headed to the cavern to retrieve oats for the critters. Twenty minutes later, both he and the animals were fed, the canteens were all full to the brim, and he was polishing off the last of the Arbuckle's.

"Ben, we need to be on our way," Chenoa's soft voice reminded him of the job in front of them.

"Yes, ma'am, I'm ready. Just let me pour down this last slug o' coffee."

"Well, let me fill the gut bags for water here in camp while you do, and then I will be ready as well," the Indian woman said grabbing the empty bags and heading toward the small creek, still running nearly full of water from the storm. Ten minutes later, she was back and placed the bags in a safe place Finding Ben already loaded with knapsack and canteens as well as his rifle, and ready to start out, she leaned slightly and picked up her tote bag complete with food and natural medical supplies, slung it over her shoulder without missing a step, and fell in behind Ben as he started up the trail toward the gold claim.

By midday, the monuments were placed at the proper corners of the first claim, including handwritten notes of ownership hidden nicely at the bottom of the piles of rock. Ben had taken time to grab up the twelve pouches on his way to the shady spot Chenoa had selected as the place to serve their meal. Thirty minutes later, each carrying half the leather pouches, they were on their way to the silver claim, where they repeated the process of marking that claim as well as filling Ben's knapsack with the best samples of ore they could find.

With an hour of daylight left, they headed down the trail toward camp, Ben amazed at the strength and stamina of the young woman he had found just two weeks before lying in a pool of blood. *She could put many a grown man to shame*, he observed as they made their way along the rough terrain while carrying a good amount of the weight. *Tougher'n boot leather an' salty as cured fatback. Sure glad she's on my side in all this. Don't ever want ta get on her bad side, that's for sure!*

Once they were in camp, and without missing a beat, Chenoa made supper using more of the venison and potatoes, adding in a can of stewed tomatoes for good measure. On this night, Ben had no trouble finding sleep, and was busy snoring in no time at all.

Chapter Fourteen

Cleaning up the campsite and removing as much trace as possible that two people had been there, in an attempt to keep the location hidden, took most of the day, especially when it came to the entrance to the storage cave. By noon, both Ben and Chenoa were ready for a break, having worked off breakfast all ready. Then came a surprise visit, and a change in both plans and actions.

Ben was leaning over the fire pouring himself a fresh cup of coffee when a shadow suddenly loomed over him. Looking up somewhat startled, beside him stood an Apache. The man had walked up on him as silently as though he wasn't really there, but that wasn't the only surprise. As he looked up, and up, and up, he finally got to the man's face.

There was a mild countenance reflected on the man's face that was belied by his very size. At six feet nine inches with a very muscular build, many of Long Lance's enemies had shirked in his presence, including those in his own community group. Ben, though, felt no fear after looking into the Apache's eyes and seeing that he was actually a very kind man. There was no doubt in his mind that if angered, Long Lance would be the most formidable opponent, and he had no desire or thought to angering this man.

"Ya'ateh. You must be Long Lance."

The tall Apache only nodded and replied, "Ya'ateh," followed by something else Ben didn't understand.

"Long Lance doesn't speak any English, Ben. He said that you look very tired, and asked if you slept well last night. I told him you did, but that you have worked very hard this morning," Chenoa clarified.

"I reckon that's just how it is, an' you can tell him I still have a lot to do before we pull out in the morning."

116

After a brief exchange, Chenoa translated the next conversation. "He says that we need not worry about doing anything more to hide our presence, including taking down the lean-to. He has a family that will use our camp while we are away. They will guard this place and keep all possible intruders away, and they will not enter the cave or use any of our supplies."

"Well, I wish we'd known that last night. We could have saved ourselves a lot of work this mornin'."

Another exchange of words between Long Lance and Chenoa resulted in both of them laughing before the Paiute woman translated for Ben. "He says he did not know we were leaving until this morning, after one of his warriors reported back to him that he thought we were moving the camp. He also said to tell you he is an Apache warrior, not a witch, so he cannot read minds."

Ben had to laugh, though he also wondered if Long Lance knew of Chenoa's ability to see into the future and possibly be able read minds as well. All he knew for certain was that he wasn't about to bring it up. "Tell him I said thank you, an' ask what we can do to repay him, an' the family stayin' here."

A moment later, the answer came. "Bring more tobacco, much more tobacco than what you have been leaving in the trees. Also, some candy. The hard, red kind. I think he means red rock candy."

"Well, that red candy comes in cinnamon an' cherry flavors as I recall. Which one does he want, an' how much?"

Several minutes of discussion later, the answer was, "The one that bites the tongue, or bring both mixed together and let the surprises begin in the mouths of his people. And bring lots."

When Ben looked into Long Lance's face, he could see the big man's smile spread at the anticipation of having some of the Apache expect one taste and get quite another. He had to smile himself, as the thought brought back memories of his father pulling the same thing on he and his siblings.

"Tell him he can consider it done, but I'm not sure how long we'll be gone this trip 'r when I can deliver."

After hearing what Ben said via Chenoa, Long Lance nodded, and took a few moments more before replying. "He says that when you return, no matter how long we are gone, will be soon enough. They were doing without the tobacco long before you came, and even longer for the candy, so when they get it they will be even more thankful than before."

Long Lance spoke again, the translation coming slowly. "He suggests we use what the Yavapai have named the 'Ghost Trail' to return to Prescott. He and his warriors will watch over us to make certain none follow us or try to pick up our trail until we are near Prescott, or at least the valley east of town. The 'Ghost Trail' leads into Lonesome Valley, but should save us many hours of travel as well as hide our movement. I think we should follow his advice."

"Do you know this trail, 'cause I sure don't."

"Yes, most of it. Let me ask him something." Several minutes later, Chenoa spoke to Ben again. "He will leave markers for us to follow as we travel. These sign will only be left if we veer off the trail, and will be removed once we pass so that no other can use them to follow the trail except those who already know it."

"Tell him I said thank you, but ask him why he's so willing to help me, a white man, when it is very likely that what I have found will bring many more white men into the area to take out the gold and silver."

Long Lance sat down and looked at Ben as his words were translated. He continued looking at Ben as he replied, and as Chenoa converted his words. "Because you respect the land, and have always been kind to both the Apache and the Yavapai, and now to a Paiute woman. It shows that you will treat all Indians with respect. White men would have eventually found what you have discovered and came here, so it is better that one who respects the land and the people get the benefit. Also, he asks that if you pass the land on to other white men, that you draw a promise from them to take care of the land and not destroy it as so many have done in the rest of the area."

Ben sat quietly for several minutes, looking straight back at Long Lance as he contemplated what to say next. "Tell him I am humbled, and that I will do my best to ensure the land and people are always respected. On that I give my word."

After the translation, Long Lance nodded, stood and walked to Chenoa's side, leaning over to whisper something in her ear. She giggled and blushed, but never stopped what she was doing as it happened. And then he was gone, though this time Ben saw him leave even though he heard no sound as the giant of a man walked.

"Well, I reckon that saves us a lot o' work, lady. An' if this 'Ghost Trail' is what ya say it is, we should be in Prescott 'fore sundown day after tomorrow. 'Specially if we don't have ta be so careful about where an' how we camp tomorrow night."

"This is true, but we still have much to do today so we need to eat soon and get back to work." The finality of Chenoa's tone told Ben that he needed to make sure he kept up with her frantic pace or he'd never hear the end of it. By late that afternoon, Chenoa looked around and declared the camp was ready for the Apache family to use while she and Ben were away, and began preparing their evening meal.

Ben breathed a sigh of relief at her statement, and seriously looked forward to getting some rest in the saddle the next day. As he poured a cup of Arbuckle's and sat down on his stump to wait for a plateful of grub, he marveled at how nice the campsite actually looked. It was far cleaner and more natural looking than he ever remembered, and he had always thought he did a good job

119

of removing most of the signs of his presence in the past.

***

An hour before the sun even thought about waking up, Ben and Chenoa were hoisting the packsaddles into place on the burro and loading the gold pouches and silver ore along with some of the essentials she determined were necessary for the trip. Working together, the packsaddles were loaded in half an hour, and Captain was caught up and saddled as well. Chenoa insisted on catching the Indian pony herself, as well as strapping on the Apache saddle. Ben garnered a new appreciation for the talents the Paiute woman displayed, and decided never to question her ability to do whatever she wanted at any given time.

As daylight began to brighten the horizon, they mounted up, Chenoa leading the way, and started toward Prescott. Ben was surprised that she started out due north instead of sliding northwest as he had always done, but by the time they reached the northern base of Tuscambia Mountain and picked up a faint trail he understood why. The trail was gentle, and they traveled quickly with little effort on part of the animals.

By the time the sun finally made its appearance for the day, they were already skirting Turkey Creek, following it until they were a half-mile from the Dandrea Ranch. There, she turned toward the west, starting a slow climb into the saddle between Moscow and Yankee Doodle Peaks, once again picking up a faint trail heading due north again.

By midday, Ben was surprised when Chenoa finally pulled to a stop longer than just to let the animals blow. "We will eat here and rest the animals for an hour. Do you know where we are?"

"Yeah, due east o' Mount Union, an' due south o' Mount Davis. We've covered a lot o' ground already, near ten, eleven miles by my best guess, an' for the most part it's been pretty easy ridin'. That puts us near halfway ta Prescott, an' we just hit noon o' the first day."

"Yes, but the next leg, between now and dark will take us much longer, as we need to avoid places like Potato Patch and all the mines dotted across the land. We will have to wind around some to accomplish that, and it will take a lot of time, Ben."

"Well, I reckon you know what you're doin', gettin' us ta this point so fast. You usin' any sign, 'r doin' this all on your own?"

"On my own so far, but going forward I will depend on the signs left for us to maneuver through the area. Still, we should be camping west of Groom Creek tonight, and will make it to Prescott by noon or shortly after tomorrow. Ben, I need to ask something of you before we reach Prescott. I only have the clothes I have on, your old clothing, not really suitable for the city. Do you think I could buy something to wear in town when we arrive?"

"Sure, whatever you want, Chenoa. I keep a room at the Congress Hotel, so I have my changes o' clothes there, an' I'll arrange for another room for ya near mine. That way ya can come an' go as ya please. Oh, an' I'll convert some o' this gold ta cash an' give ya however much ya want to spend on whatever ya want. I know one thing; I want a nice hot bath as soon as we get ta the hotel. Out there grubbin' in the dirt, a feller gets plumb covered with filth. And then I want a big ol' juicy steak with plenty o' fixin's."

"Oh, Ben, a bath sounds wonderful. It has been ages since I was able to take a real bath. One with soap and hot water, one that I can just lay in and relax until the water gets too cold. Could you also arrange that for me? They don't usually allow Indians to stay at the Congress, let alone receive any special treatment, so I'm not sure you can make all that happen. And if you can't, that's fine. I can always stay someplace else. I'm sure James can find a place for me."

"Nonsense. If the Congress wants ta keep my business, they'll do what I ask. Lord knows I pay 'em enough ta keep a room there, not ta mention how much money I spend when I'm in town anyway. They try ta keep you out, it will sure cost 'em plenty when I spread the word around town, that's for sure."

"Ben, I will not hold it against you if they decline, so don't do something like that. I really hate it when people use their power to get their way, and I certainly don't want you to do it on my behalf. Understood? Now, let's mount up and get moving agin, or all we have discussed will be in vain as we'll never get to Prescott if we start to argue over something so simple."

Without another word, Chenoa strode to the pony and vaulted herself onto his back. She only took long enough to look over her shoulder to make sure Ben was mounting Captain before she started out along the faint trail. Ben decided not to broach the subject again, seeing as how she seemed quite firm in her feelings about how some people used what they perceived as power over others to get what they wanted. He almost felt ashamed that he had even mentioned it, because he mostly felt the same way. But still, what good was it if he couldn't do something nice for her after all she had done for him?

As they zigzagged through the landscape, dodging the mines and keeping well away from Potato Patch, he worked out in his mind how he would make it happen without her knowing what he was doing. He all but ignored the trail, just following her lead, but remembering enough that he could make the same trip without any guidance if necessary.

By the time the sun was starting to dip low in the sky, they were at a quiet, hidden spot on Wolf Creek southwest of the community of Groom Creek cooling the animals down before allowing them to drink. Ben was amazed at how far they had traveled, and pleased as well. The thought of riding into Prescott from the east as opposed to his regular entrance from the south or southeast made him happy, and was sure to confound anyone looking to discover his claims.

It was a silent camp that night, with only a few words spoken between the pair of travelers. It wasn't until they had eaten and were beginning to settle in that Chenoa broke the silence. "Ben, I'm sorry if I sounded too harsh, it's just that..."

"No need ta explain, girl. I reckon in most situations I feel the same way. But you been a powerful help ta me, an' ya deserve ta be treated with the same accord an' respect any woman deserves. Hell, you can't help who your folks was, an' you bein' half Paiute don't matter a lick ta me. You're a young woman, a damn good-lookin' young woman at that, an' the Congress ought ta be happy as hell ta host a pretty girl instead o' 'em ol' fat wives o' rich men they specialize in."

As Ben looked over at her, for the first time since they had met he saw emotion spread across her face. She quickly turned her head, but he couldn't help but see the tears start to run down her face before she turned away. Apparently, he had hit a raw nerve, not at all what he intended.

"Chenoa, sorry if I said somethin' wrong. I didn't mean ta upset ya."

"No, Ben, you didn't. It's just that not everyone feels as you do, and it's been a very long time since someone told me how pretty I was. I didn't expect it, but I truly appreciate it. But again, don't try to force things at the hotel. I do not wish to create hard feelings in anyone."

"Shoot, all you got ta do is smile at 'em an' flash 'em big brown eyes an' they'll melt like butter in a hot skillet. Works ever' time for 'em sisters o' mine, an' I reckon women been usin' that trick for as long as time. You might as well use it, too."

Chenoa started laughing and shaking her head at Ben's remarks.

"Yes, even Indian women have been known to use the same tricks as white women to influence the minds of men, and sometimes other women. Even I have done so before, though I really hate to do it. Still, I will do so if it will get me a nice hot, soapy bath."

It was Ben's turn to laugh at the prospect of trying to keep Chenoa from her hot bath and a nice bed. He vowed to himself to do what he could to make it happen.

Chapter Fifteen

"I don't know who you think you are, young men, arresting me. I work for the United States government, and they will not stand for some local deputy to treat me they way you have. When those Washington lawyers get done with you, you'll be lucky to find a job as a dog catcher."

"Look, 'Mr. Indian Agent', you were involved in a cattle rustlin' scheme, buyin' stolen cattle an' who knows what else. I reckon when your bosses find out what you were up to they'll be happy to see you swing at the end of a rope with these other three."

"And what proof do you have that I knew these things you accuse me of? I was just here to take possession of cattle I bought for the Reservations."

"Todd, you got that Arkansas toothpick on ya?"

"Yup, I sure do."

"Is it sharp?"

"Yessir, as always."

"Reckon this critter will change his tune onct I start with that Apache truth cuttin'?"

"He'll sing like a canary bird, an' so will the others when they see it workin'."

"Seth, yank off that gub'mint man's fancy shoes an' socks, an' roll up his pants legs, will ya? Todd, lemme borrow that blade. Time we got ta the real truth 'fore we get ta Flag."

The two surviving cowboys looked at each other, and then to the Association Secretary, and finally at the Indian Agent. "Mister, I jus' believe I'd start talkin' an' not be plumb stupid. We seen what 'em 'Paches can do ta a man, an' it ain' purty."

126

"Now, Micah, don't spoil my fun. I'm lookin' forward ta takin' this lyin' piece o' cow dung down some. There are two kinds o' fellers I can't stand, liars an' thieves, an' he fills both boots."

"I know, Zack, but it jus' ain' human ta do what 'em 'Paches do to a man. 'Sides, I don' reckon the railroad is gonna like all that blood on the floor o' one o' 'ese fancy cars," Micah replied.

"You think I care what they think?"

"We do, deputy. We can't let you spill a man's blood. I don't know what you're planning to do, but apparently these two cowboys do. And we can't allow it," one of the railroad detectives spoke up.

"I thought your orders were not ta get in our way, mister. If I was you, I'd set back an' keep my mouth shut, got it?"

Seeing that Seth had carried out the request, Zack reached out to take the long, slender knife from his brother, "Thanks, Todd. Reckon ya can hold his legs for me?"

"I'll take one if Seth will grab the other."

A moment later, the Indian Agent's legs were being held securely by the two men, and Zack leaned over to the agent's left foot. He was ready to make the first cut when the Association Secretary stopped him, with a simple statement. "Deputy, I'll tell you everything you want to know, just don't make that cut. I know if that fool doesn't talk, you'll start on me. And the last thing I want is to watch him bleed to death before we reach Flagstaff, because I know it's a two day trip to Prescott and I'll be next. Tell me what you want to know, and let's not go any further down this road."

"All right, mister, but this story best be all of it, includin' this snake's part in it," Zack said harshly.

"It will be, including how Stockton talked us both into it.

Chances are you'll never catch him, but I'm pretty sure you'll have charges placed against him to add to those all ready out there. And Johnson, if I was you I'd cooperate as well. If you do, you might get to sit in a federal prison someplace for a decade or two instead of hanging here in Arizona. I'd settle for a chance to serve out my term, even as bad as Yuma prison is, and not hang in Prescott if I can convince some judge that I deserve leniency."

"Good thinkin', mister. Now, let's start with your real names an' take it from there. We all ready know Stockton was the ringleader, an' the charges we'll place on him, so you can skip right over him an' get to the two o' you an' your parts in it." Turning to the others watching, Zack said, "Todd, Seth, Connor, you fellers are gonna be the witnesses ta all this, so pay close attention ta what he has ta tell us." And then back to the man in front of him, he continued with, "All right, start talkin'."

Over the next hour, as they chugged their way to Flagstaff with a full trainload, the Association Secretary laid out the whole scheme, naming names and stating what part they each had in the theft enterprise. He even clarified that he was using the name Arch Campbell, but his real name was Layton Filmore, and he had been hired at the insistence of two prominent members of the association, Jack Parsons and Lawrence Murphy. The Indian Agent's name was Bill Johnson, as far as he knew, and Stockton was, indeed, the leader of the group. Stockton and Parsons had been childhood friends, and now Parsons' ownership of his sizeable herd began to come into question.

They had used Stockton's associates in Chicago to process the beef, as they were getting them at a seriously reduced price and were more than willing to make the extra profit while the government had paid full market value for them all ready, and the Indians ended up with outdated and rotting meat in the bargain. He closed by saying, "Deputy, I sincerely hope you relay to the judge and the district attorney my willingness to divulge all this information. I have no interest in hanging. Now, is there anything else you'd like to know?"

"Yeah, what part did the cowboys have in all this, and how much did they really know about what was going on?"

"Seth should have explained that to you all ready, as Jack Carter brought him in. Of course I recognize that Seth was a plant, and was not really working for us, which should add even more credibility to his statement and eventual testimony."

"Filmore, I need ta know about the two cowboys we have here, Micah an' Earl."

"They are as innocent as lambs in all this. They didn't even know until a few days ago that these cattle were stolen, and by then Stockton had them believing he would hunt them down and kill them if they even thought about pulling out. Why is it you think they are still alive? It is because, when the others decided to fight, they didn't. They were willing to take their chances in court after telling their side of things, while the rest knew they'd hang for sure."

"So what you're sayin' is they were coerced into workin' the cattle under threat o' death, is that right?" Todd asked.

"Yes, that's the size of it. I know Johnson and I are going to prison, and maybe the gallows, but these two men don't deserve that kind of ending to their lives. Yes, I understand that they have always skirted the law, and that Carson has been able to manipulate Slate into doing all sorts of things, so if either of the two of them should be charged with anything it would be Carson, but even he doesn't deserve to hang or spend years in prison."

Zack and Todd looked at the pair of cowboys, both hanging their heads looking at the floor of the railcar. "Todd, think we ought ta just let the judge hang 'em, 'r speak up for 'em?"

"Well, for all the trouble they gave us the last few years, might as well let 'em hang an' get 'em out o' our hair," Todd replied with a grin as wide as his face would allow.

"Now, daggone it, fellers. We was never that much…" Earl cut off what he was going to say when he looked up to see the brothers were both smiling. "How's 'bout we promise ta never cause no more trouble? 'R even leave Yavapai County for good?"

"Yeah, how's 'bout we leave the county?" Micah chimed in.

"Now, boys, I don't think you have ta go that far," Todd said. "Just behavin' an' stayin' out o' trouble will be good 'nough for us. Maybe if ya was ta get real jobs, an' stay with it instead o' gettin' run off 'r quittin' when the work gets tough, ya might even find out ya got real worth. How 'bout it?" Zack offered.

"Whatever ya say ya want us ta do, we'll do it, Zack. We ain't anxious ta hang, 'r set in no jail. Mama done tol' us that if'n we was ta get in trouble one more time she was gonna save the law the trouble o' dealin' with us. Me an' Micah is cousins, but my mama raised us both after his mama died, so when Mama says it, she means it."

"I reckon that settles that. Next time ya get in trouble, we'll just go tell your mother, providin' the judge don't throw the book at ya this time. An' yes, we'll speak for ya when it comes to the district attorney filin' charges. But one more time, boys, just one more time…" Todd was saying before getting cut short by Earl.

"There won' be no more, Todd, Zack. I know my word ain' much, but that's all I got ta give ya. An' if'n I break my word, ya can feel free ta shoot me on sight."

"Earl, I hope it never comes ta that, I really do. Truth be known, me an' Todd like you two, 'cept when ya get inta trouble like ya been doin'. I hope ya both learned a lesson here. That easy come money always has a string attached, where as money earned from hard, honest work spends easier an' slower, an' goes a whole lot further."

The two men nodded, then looked at each other again, and then hung their heads even lower than before, accepting the truth and praying that they could get out of this one with only a hard slap on the wrist, or a very short sentence in the local jail. But only time, and the grace of the judge, would tell.

As they pulled into the depot at Flagstaff, Indian Agent Bill Johnson started to cry like a child. "Oh, stop that blubbering, Johnson. You were all smiles when you were cheating the government and those Indians and pocketing all that money. Well, those were the wages of sin, you fool, and now they need to be repaid. You'd better just pray that you end up in Yuma and not on the gallows."

The slightly older man and soon to be former Indian agent suddenly sobered up and became quiet, even somewhat sullen. His face was ashen, and he was shaking like a leaf in a stiff breeze. As they removed the prisoners from the railcar, he tried to step off to the side but Seth yanked him back. Until he saw Jphnson's face, and then he helped him step aside to allow him to vomit. After several minutes, Johnson stood up and willingly stepped to the back of the line as they climbed into the jail wagon.

It was agreed that Seth and Zack would escort the prisoners to the Flagstaff office and jail while Todd would stay with Connor and the yard crew as well as the two railroad detectives until the cattle were all unloaded and the brand inspectors took possession. The horses were unloaded first, which Zack and Seth waited for so they could ride mounted instead of hitching a ride on the jail wagon.

As they were riding off, the brand inspectors showed up in a buggy, not quite what Todd had expected. "A buggy? For brand inspectors? Where's your mounts?"

"Stabled. Boss here don't want us ridin' 'round town 'cept in this confangled contraption. Damned if I don't feel all prissy an' such, like some city bred fool, havin' ta ride in this thing," one of the three men complained.

"Aw, you old hillbilly, it does my heart good to see you taken down some. One of these days, these things won't even need a horse to pull them around, and brands will be more complex and harder to read. Then cowboys won't be converted to brand inspectors, as it will require men of great intelligence and education to read them. Men like you will no longer be needed, or of any use to the cattle industry."

The old timer was seething, but Todd could tell the last one to speak was senior to the other two men with him, and that neither was ready to give up his job to rebut this smart-mouthed youngster, even though they were nearly the same age. But he decided that this wasn't the time or place to come to the rescue of the men older and more experienced than he.

"So which one o' ya is taking possession o' this herd? I need ta get ta the jail an' help the other deputies as well as get the rest o' these horses boarded someplace."

"That would be me," replied the young man. "I'm Jeffrey Townsend, manager of the Flagstaff office of the State Brand Inspector. We'll need to do a head count of the animals before you go anywhere, deputy, so be prepared to stay here until we've finished."

"Not likely, Townsend. I've been at it for more days than I care ta count, an' up since well before dawn today. I'm gonna go help my brother get the prisoners settled, board the horses, get me some grub an' a bath an' a good night's sleep. Any man that tries ta stand in my way isn't likely ta enjoy what comes next. Do I make myself clear?"

"Sonny boy, I reckon I'd pay attention ta what this feller says, 'specially if ya wanna stay on the right side o' the daisies. This here is one o' the Creed boys, the two deputies that cleaned up Flagstaff an' settled most o' the Injun troubles north o' here. They're the ones what brought in Manuel Mondragon, even though they had ta kill him ta get it done. So go right on ahead an' try your luck, but ya been warned."

"S-s-sorry, Deputy Creed. I wasn't aware of the circumstances that brought you here. Indeed, please go on about your business and we'll handle things here. Can I assume that you made a head count as they were loaded, something we can compare our numbers to?"

"Yeah, Townsend, we did. Two hundred eighteen head, most steer an' heifers with a couple o' young bulls. But if I was you, I'd head back to that office o' yours an' let these two men here do the rest. Every single brand has been doctored, an' I just don't believe you have enough experience ta be able ta figure out what the original brands were. Sure, you prob'ly have a system o' countin' cattle that'd make that job easy, but these two can sure 'nough get it done just as fast as you an' your system. Say, what is that system, count all their legs an' divide by four, 'r count their ears an' divide by two?"

The two older gentlemen nearly choked trying to hold back their laughter, and their young boss, though offended, simmered but held his tongue, deciding that he had it coming for being so pushy at the beginning of this encounter. "You're most likely right, Deputy Creed. I'll do just that. Fred, Joe, would you mind taking charge here, getting an accurate count and inspecting the brands? I'm sure you will do an exemplary job of it, and will bring me the list when you've completed the task at hand. I'll duplicate that list and send a copy to the Sheriff's Annex as soon as possible."

"As soon as possible will need ta be first thing in the mornin', Townsend, as we'll be pullin' out for Prescott with our prisoners shortly after daylight. An' if ya can't get it to us by then, somebody'll need ta ride ta Prescott with that list as soon as ya have it. Understood?" Todd had decided to really pour it on while he had the upper hand and Townsend was still reeling from finding out who he was.

"Yes, yes, of course. I know we'll need daylight to be able to check all the brands, but I'll send someone from my office to your Prescott office by late tomorrow. Is that all right?"

"Shoot, I'll even volunteer ta take it down myself. We got several brands that need sorted out down in Cordes Junction, an' I can do that on the way back from Prescott."

"Fine, Fred, there are several requests pending down in that direction, so I'll send Joe along with you. That way the two of you can split up the jobs and finish them faster than just sending one man to do it all. All right, I must be going, so let me know the results when you are finished," Townsend said as he popped the buggy whip over the horse's ears and bounced out of the rail yard at a trot.

"Thankee, Deputy Creed. He needed knocked down an' kicked in the teeth, an' ya shore done that. Joe, looks like we get a week 'r so away from his naggin' an' fussin, don' it?"

"Yessireebob, we surely do. Say, which one o' the Creed boys are you?"

"I'm Todd, an' you're both welcome. I don't really care for fellers like Townsend that toss their weight around like that. Served him right ta get his toes stepped on, but I might o' stepped a bit harder than I needed to."

"Naw, in fact ya coulda mashed down harder if'n ya wanted ta. Shore wouldn' o' hurt my feelin's none. Joe, what say we let this young feller get on his way an' get these cattle settled in for the night? An' thanks again, Deputy Creed. Wait 'til I tell the other fellers what ya done. Why, your reputation is gonna grow by double, an' it was all ready quite a purty damned big."

"Naw, don't do that, Fred. No sense kickin' a dead horse. He's taken all the hurt he's gonna need without tryin' ta gouge him any deeper."

"Well, if'n that's the way ya feel, we'll keep it ta ourselves, won' we Joe?"

"Yessir, mum's the word. Next time ya come this way, steaks are on me."

Chapter Sixteen

Just as Todd had predicted, they had their four prisoners loaded along with three that had been held at the Flagstaff office for transport to Prescott for prosecution. Two of the men from Flagstaff were well known to the brothers Creed, which prompted Zack to question one of them. "Sims, I see you haven't learned a lick since Todd an' me was workin' up here last year. Accordin' to the transport sign out sheet, you were arrested for the same ol' thing. Well, it looks like ya went a bit too far this time. Did ya really try ta stab Charlie when he went out ta pick ya up? An' with a broken bottle? I reckon ya must o' run out o' whiskey is the only reason ya had an empty bottle ta start with, right? But damn, son, why did ya beat that woman o' yours up sa bad? She's never done a thing against ya, even bailin' ya out a dozen more times that any sane person would o' done."

"Go ta hell, Creed. I thought I was done with the two o' you harrassin' me, but here ya are again. I get out this time, I'm comin' after ya, both o' ya, an' that fool Charlie Grimes. I'll see ya all dead an' buried 'fore I'm done."

"Well, well. Todd, did you hear him threaten us, an' Charlie? We might's well add them charges ta the list. Oh, an' Sims, just so ya know, we ain't afraid o' you 'r them threats o' yours. You try either one o' us an' they'll plant ya in that family cemetery o' yours. The judge ought ta just send ya ta Yuma an' get it over with. Might save your worthless life, 'specially if ya try us. An' I'll bet Charlie feels the same way. Now lay back an' shut up, an' sober up while you're at it. The only time you think you're the cock o' the walk is when you're still drunk."

Sims jerked against the chains in an attempt to reach Zack, but the man he was chained with yanked him back and slapped him around once he hit the floor of the jail wagon. "Sims, I done told ya ta behave 'fore I beat the crap out o' ya. 'Em Creed boys, either one, could take you with one hand tied behind their back, an' do it faster than I just parked you on the deck. Believe me, I know. I tried Zack there just over a year ago, an' I'm still hurtin' where he hit me. Damned near broke my jaw, he did. First man ever whupped me, an' he did a righteous job of it. You open that mug o' yours one more time an' they'll be sendin' me ta Yuma for doin' you in."

"Barker, I'm gonna pretend I didn't hear any o' that, just in case Sims don't make it ta Prescott alive. Let's see, says here you are charged with stealin' eggs from Mrs. Miller's coop. She finally caught ya, huh?"

"Yeah, me an' Peterson here. Never figured her ta be able ta use that double barrel shotgun that well. Loaded it with birdshot an' salt, she did. My fanny is still burnin' from that salt, but she sure stopped us both in our tracks with that one shot. She said the other barrel was loaded with double ought buck, an' neither of us was willin' ta test her. An' 'fore ya say it, it was a dumb thing ta do, I know. But dammit, we was hungry."

"Well, I doubt you'll get too hungry for the next ninety days. County'll keep ya fed, twice a day anyway. I reckon the judge will make ya work for her when ya get back home, you know, ta pay for the eggs she'd a had ta sell, an' not just the ones ya stole. 'Cause ya know she's gonna claim the rest o' her chickens quit layin' on account o' you disturbin' em, right? Best be on your best behavior goin' forward, don't ya think?"

Barker just nodded, lowered his head and leaned back against the wall of the wagon. His accomplice, Peterson, joined him, until Sims tried to move. Peterson grabbed him by the collar and yanked him, slamming him back down on the built in bench, squarely between he and Barker. "Sims, if you move again 'fore we pull up come dark, Barker won't get a chance ta do ya in, 'cause I'll be the one doin' it. An' Creed, ya didn't hear that, did ya?"

"Hear what, Peterson? Todd, what say we get this trip started, Seth, ya ready with the mounts? Me an' Todd'll take first draw on the wagon seat, an' we'll trade off as the day wears on."

"Fine with me. Let's pull out. I'll ride out front, just ta make sure we don't run into any unexpected visitors," Seth replied as he started down the street headed toward the road south through the Ponderosa Pine of Northern Arizona Territory. At the edge of town, he stopped to look back, making sure the wagon was coming. Assured that it was, he led both Zack and Todd's horses along with their packhorses and the string of horses taken from the prisoners and cowboys back in Angell.

Seth was glad to have been forgiven for his part in the rustling, as he never wanted to be a part of it anyway. Jack had pressured him to come along without giving him too many details, until it was almost too late to get out of it. Fortunately the Creed boys had shown him some mercy, the first real break he'd ever had, and one he was determined not to let get away. *No matter what it takes, I'll walk the straight an' narrow from now on, an' with any luck I'll do it wearin' a star.*

Several times throughout the day, Seth tied off the string of horses to trees along the trail and rode off the either side to make sure they weren't being watched, or riding into an ambush. Seeing nothing on his forays, he would ride back, gather up the string and wait for the wagon to come into view before moving on south again.

As they worked south, Todd and Zack decided to let Seth take the string for the whole day while they kept an eye on the prisoners in the wagon. The first day out was usually when prisoners caused problems, and they didn't want to have Seth put in any jeopardy. Stopping to rest the team and water them, first at Willard Spring, and then again at Woods Spring, they were making good time.

As they pulled out of Woods Spring, Zack caught sight of Seth and motioned him to ride back to them. When he rode up after leaving the string tied several hundred yards away, Zack explained what he wanted. "Seth, find us a nice flat spot near water and with plenty o' wood for a fire on south o' here a piece. 'Bout eight, ten miles south o' here, just north o' Red Hill, there should be a spot as I recall. Get them horses set up in a rope corral an' start makin' camp. We should be there just 'fore dark if all goes well. See ya in a bit. Oh, an' I hope you're a better cook than either one o' us. See ya."

"See ya," Seth said as he turned his mount, riding out to retrieve the string, and then on further south to make camp. Just as Zack had said, he found a nice grassy place north of Red Hill. Two small creeks fed into the area, dammed up by a family of beaver creating a nice pool of water for the animals, and for the men. Thanks to the beaver, there was an abundance of wood suitable for a good fire, and to sustain it for the night.

Seth first watered all the animals, and then created a large rope corral followed by stripping the packsaddles near where he thought the best place for the center of camp. Next, he stripped the saddles and rubbed all the horses down with some of the dried grass he found along the edges of the grassy area. Finally, he started the fire, and when it was hot enough he put on a pot of Arbuckle's and began peeling the few potatoes Todd had insisted on bringing along.

By the time he heard the wagon rattling down the trail, supper was all but ready to dish out, including enough for the seven prisoners. Ten minutes later, the wagon was sitting on the edge of camp and the team was being unhooked and led to water. In the early twilight, the team and wagon had been secured, and plates were being filled and passed around.

Earl and Micah volunteered to wash the utensils and plates, and were given permission to do so. All was going well until Sims stuck his foot out and tripped Micah as he walked past. Micah slowly stood up, turned to Earl and said, "Earl, since we's shackled tagether, hold up a bit. I got a little somethin' I need ta take care o' 'fore we clean stuff up."

Turning back to Sims, he reached out his bear like hand and grabbed the bigger man by the throat. Lifting him off the ground as high as he could, Micah said very calmly, "Sims, ya been lookin' for somebody ta work ya over, an' I'm just the one ta do it. Now you're a bigger feller, but I'm twict as strong an' just as mean an' o'nery." Zack, Todd and Seth had all started to intercede, but Micah called them off, "Stay back now, 'r I'll break his damned neck. Mr. Barker, if ya don' mind, give me a little slack on that chain so's I can do this skunk right."

Barker shook all the slack he could into the chain, and when he was finished Micah went to work on Sims. Ten minutes later, Sims was out cold, lying on the dirt of the camp, blood pouring out of his nose, mouth and both ears. Turning to the deputies and Seth, Micah said, "Sorry, fellers. But he had it comin', an' a lot more. If'n he gets out o' line again, I'll finish the job I started on him. Mr. Barker, Mr. Peterson, I ain' tryin' ta take none o' the fun out o' this for you fellers, but I've had all o' that sumbitch I can take."

When no one said a word, and all were just looking at each other wondering what to say, Micah turned back to Earl and continued. "Earl, we still got chores ta do. We'd best get to it, doncha think?"

Todd, Seth and Zack looked at each other and laughed deep and long. They were still laughing when Sims started coming around. He looked out of the slits that served as eyes, wiped his nose and shook his head. "What the hell ya laughin' at? Wait 'til I let your boss know that ya let another prisoner beat hell out o' me for nothin'. I'll make sure you lose 'em shiny badges!"

140

"Sims, do yourself a favor an' sit back an' shut up 'r we'll let Micah finish what he started 'fore ya passed out. As far as Sheriff Walker, you'll be lucky he don't do the same thing once we tell him what ya done ta start it. That is after he gets done laughin' at ya. Now if I was you, I don't think I'd upset any more o' these men if ya want ta live long 'nough to get ta Prescott. All right, men, time ta sack out. We got another long, hard ride tomorrow, an' another one just like it the day after. Seth, Todd, toss them blankets to 'em, an' let's hit our bedrolls. Seth, you're on the wagon tomorrow all day, an' I'll switch out with Todd at midday," Zack proclaimed as he walked to his sougan, dropped down and laid out flat with his head against his saddle.

***

The next day went like clockwork, no problems came up and once they got past Rattlesnake Canyon the trail smoothed out and they made good time. By midafternoon, they had reached Camp Verde, and decided to take advantage of Sally's good cooking at the Montezuma Café before pushing on toward Prescott. They reached the café before the Army patrons came in at the end of their day, and made sure that the prisoners turned in all their utensils after they ate. From there, they moved back up to the same spot Todd and Zack had always used, alongside Grassy Mountain.

Giving the horses the extra few hours of rest would be rewarded the next day as they pushed them even harder to cover the distance between where they camped in Copper Canyon and their final destination. As always, knowing that they would be jailed to await their trials, the prisoners started to become somewhat restless. All but Sims, Earl and Micah. Earl and Micah only hoped they would get a light sentence, but Sims was quiet for another reason. He wasn't taking any chances on upsetting anyone else riding in the back of the wagon for fear of his life.

Indian Agent Johnson started his sobbing again, but held it in as much as he could, while Filmore was moody and cross. Barker and Peterson also knew they would receive light sentences, or at least they hoped so, as their crimes were minor compared to the others. Still, Barker was fitful, and Peterson wasn't much better. As a result, Zack decided it best to keep a night guard, and took the first watch.

He woke Seth to take the second watch, after checking the prisoners to make sure they were all sleeping. Seth did the same several hours before daylight, but before he could wake Toss, he found Sims wide awake and trying to crawl to where Micah slept. He quietly walked up behind the man, grabbed the chain connected to the shackle on his legs and yanked hard enough to land Sims face down in the dirt. "Sims, when are you gonna learn? You need another ass whippin'? I'm sure we can arrange it here an' now if you'd like."

"What's goin' on?" Todd said from behind Seth. "Sims causin' more trouble?"

"He was tryin'. Ya know, I just believe it would save the county a lot of time an' energy if we was ta let Barker 'r Micah finish him off."

"That may be, Seth, but we still have ta haul him in an' make our best effort ta get him there alive. G'won an' get some sleep. I'll let ya know when the coffee is done. I reckon Zack plans on pullin' out long 'fore daylight shows, so I'll heat up the fire with plenty o' time."

"All right, Todd. I just hope I can get a couple hours o' sleep 'fore ya call me. Am I on the wagon again today?"

"Half a day is all, the last half. Zack wants ya to be ridin' the wagon when we get ta the office. That way he can explain ta the sheriff what went on, an' how ya come ta be helpin' us while your partner is dead an' prob'ly buried by now. That work for you?"

"Yessir. See ya in a few hours," Seth replied as he strolled to his bedroll and plopped down to rest for a few hours. It was still dark, with only the light of a half moon lighting the landscape, when he heard Todd rattling the coffee pot. Without waiting to be called, he rolled out to find not only Todd, but Zack up and around as well.

Again, as Todd predicted, they were rolling up Copper Canyon long before daylight even began to hint at the horizon. And when the sun did finally start to glow in the east, they had just crossed over Johnson Wash. Zack led the string of horses well in front of the wagon, and it wasn't until they had nearly reached Cox Spring that they saw him watering the horses.

Zack waited until they rolled up and got down before saying anything. "Gents, we're makin' good time. We ought ta be at Agua Fria not long after midday. When we get there, Todd, I'll ride the wagon on in with Seth. I need ta talk a few things over with him 'fore we introduce him ta the sheriff an' see if we can get him hired on."

"Figured as much, Zack. Though I had kind o' thought ya'd have him tend the string instead o' ridin' the wagon this mornin'."

"Thought on it, but we're gettin' too close ta Prescott ta do that. Best do it this way, so's he gets a fair chance, an' a good shake. 'Sides, we need ta make sure he stays safe ta testify when this shebang all comes ta court. The only question I have is, can we get Connor here ta testify in time. We need ta make sure the DA knows ta let him an' the railroad know ta give him plenty o' time ta travel ta Prescott. Well, let's roll if we figure ta get ta town 'fore full on dark." Without another word, Zack turned and walked to his horse, mounted up and turned west.

Switching at Agua Fria, Zack climbed aboard the wagon and settled in beside Seth. Over the next few hours, they went over and over the details of what had happened and how Seth came to work with them to bring the ring of rustlers down. When he was finally satisfied that Seth would give all the right answers when asked, and all without having to lie about any of it, Zack leaned back and went to sleep.

Seth could only smile, glad that he had become friends with these two brothers. He vowed again to follow the law, and become a good lawman if given the opportunity. As the sun was starting to dip low in the west, they started up the hill overlooking the town of Prescott, and Seth knew he was going to find out his fate within the next few hours. Just then, the prisoners started yelling and cursing, forcing Seth to pull up the team and set the wagon brake.

Chapter Seventeen

As they rode out of the trees along Lynx Creek and onto the flat just east of Prescott, Chenoa motioned for Ben to take the lead. Then she turned and rode back to the edge of the trees and made a sign. Riding back up to ride behind the burro, she settled in for the final five miles into town.

Ben motioned for her to join him up front, but she resisted. When she stayed where she was after three attempts, he stopped and said, "We aren't ridin' inta town 'til you come up here an' talk ta me. So c'mon."

Chenoa slowly moved the Apache pony up alongside Ben, asking, "What is it you wish to talk about?"

"Who were you signalin', an' what did you tell them?"

"Long Lance and one of his warriors. I was thanking them for their guidance, and for watching over us."

"Good deal. I kind o' figured that's what it was, but I wanted ta make sure. Now then, when we ride in I want you ta ride beside me, not behind. No need for that nonsense."

"But, Ben Creed, it is the customary way for an Indian woman to stay behind the man she is with."

"I know that, but I'm callin' on the French side o' you ta ride beside me as my business partner, so nobody gets the idea that you're my woman 'r such foolishness. 'Sides that, it will lend ta the story I'm givin' the hotel so's you can stay there without any grief about you bein' an Indian woman."

"Isn't that being deceitful?"

"Not really. You're half French, an' as far as I'm concerned you deserve what I can give ya, half Paiute 'r not. Now, I'm gettin' real hungry for that steak, so let's get a move on."

He nudged Captain forward without waiting for an answer, with Chenoa riding right beside him. It was just before noon when they hit the main street of Prescott, and rode up to Saltpeter Murphy's livery stable across the street from the Congress Hotel.

"Ben, you're back kind o' early, ain't ya?"

"Yup, I am, Salty."

"How long ya gonna be in town?"

"No idea yet. Just grain 'em up real good, brush 'em down an' such. Hell, you know better'n I do what they need. An' I'm gonna need ta rent that buggy o' yours while we're here. This young lady can walk the legs off the best man I know, but while we're in town she's gonna get a break an' ride in comfort for a change."

"It'll take me a bit ta get it wiped down an' rigged up for ya, Ben. Say half an hour 'r so? I didn't want ta say nothin' 'bout the gal, but since ya brought it up..."

"I found her all tore up out near my claim, an' she's been doin' the cookin' an' such for me since she got strong 'nough ta handle the chores. For what she done for me, I owe her more'n I can ever repay, but for now it'll have ta be new clothes, good meals, a good hot bath, an' ridin' in a buggy wherever she wants ta go."

"Suits me, but how ya gonna put an Indian gal up at the hotel?"

"She's French as far as I'm concerned, Salty. I'd appreciate it if that's what you'd tell anybody that asks."

"Sure thing, Ben. Ol' François oughta be real happy ta have somebody else ta speak French to, providin' she can speak that language. But I don't reckon Mitzi is gonna be real happy 'bout ya bringin' in your own woman."

"First off, an' let's get this straight. She ain't my woman, she's more of a business partner than anything, so make sure that's how ya answer those that'll ask. Second, you'll have ta ask her if she speaks French, I never bothered ta ask."

"Well, missy, do ya speak French?"

"Oui, Monsieur. Je parle français avec plusieurs autres langues."

"Damned if I know what she said, but it sure sounded like French ta me. Say, missy, what's your name anyway?"

"Chenoa. And I am pleased to make your acquaintance, Mr. Murphy. I said I speak French along with several other languages. Are there any other questions you'd like me to answer?"

"No, ma'am, that'll do it for me. An' just call me Salty, if ya would. That's what all my friends call me, an' I'd sure like ta include ya among my friends if ya don't mind. Ben, whattaya want me ta do with them packsaddles?"

"We'll be taking them with us, Salty, along with the saddlebags an' our personal gear. I'm headin' across the street ta get our rooms settled an' order up hot baths for 'bout two hours from now. 'R should I wait on orderin' them baths, Chenoa?"

"I think it would be best to wait, Ben, as I will need new clothes first, and some food as well."

"Fine an' dandy, Chenoa. Salty, can ya help Chenoa load the buggy while I'm over there?"

"Well, Ben, if 'em bags is as heavy as they look, that buggy won't handle 'em. You'd be better served ta use that buckboard o' mine, at least 'til ya get that load where it's goin'. Then ya can switch back ta the buggy if'n ya want to. That work?"

"Yessir, Salty. That'll work out just fine."

"Good, I can hook up the team pronto, as the buckboard is already clean an' ready ta go. Even greased the wheels the last time it was used, an' that'll give me a afternoon ta get the buggy all ready for ya. Well, Miss Chenoa, shall we get to it? You just show me what ta load in the buckboard, an' me an' Clete, we'll get it done." Then, turning to the back of the building, he called out, "Clete! Get on up here! We got work ta do, pronto!" Then back to facing Ben, he said, "Give us 'bout fifteen minutes an' we'll have it ready for ya."

Ben nodded, turned to Chenoa and said, "I'll be right back, soon as I let 'em know ta give ya a room next ta mine if they got one, 'r 'cross the hall. But at least on the same floor."

"Fine, Ben, if you're sure it won't cause any problems. I'll see you in a few minutes, but I'd better help Salty and Clete for now."

Ben strode quickly across to the hotel, bracing himself for any grief his sudden and early return might cause, not to mention his bringing a guest. Inside the hotel, Claude was at the desk waiting for Ben to enter. "Mr. Creed! You're back early! I saw you ride up to Salty's a few minutes ago, and have sent Beatrice and Maude up to prepare your room. I also saw that you had someone with you. Will she be staying here as well?"

"Yup, as close ta my room as possible, Claude. An' we'll be needing baths later, but right now we need ta get the young lady some new clothes, an' get some grub in our bellies. An' no, we won't be eatin' here this time, figured we'd go see Jason an' Margarite at Renner's Café. Might make a couple more stops along the way 'fore we get back here, but that'll give ya time to get the room ready for the young lady as well. Keep in mind that she is my guest, an' all charges will be billed ta me. Got it?"

"Yessir, Mr. Creed." Then, leaning forward, Claude whispered, "Is she an Indian girl, Mr. Creed? Will I have to face any criticism over her staying here?"

"Nothin' ta worry about, Claude. She's French, an' just been out in the wild for a bit. That'll change the way any woman looks 'r dresses, don't ya think?"

149

Leaning back with a look of relief on his face, Claude responded, "Very well, sir! We'll see to it that she is treated with the utmost care and respect during her stay. It will indeed be a pleasure to have such a lovely woman here with us. And, Mr. Creed, you'll be pleased to know that the rooms on either side of yours are empty. The one on the left is adjoining, while the one on the right is not. Would you like the one on the left?" Claude said with a wink.

"Not at all. The one on the right will be perfect. Claude, she is more like a business partner, an' not a romantic interest, so quick access in not necessary, while privacy is. Understood?"

"I'm sorry, Mr. Creed, I didn't mean to imply anything to the contrary, and I apologize if it sounded that way."

Ben had to keep from laughing out loud at Claude's sloppy attempt to cover his faux pas, but only because Claude had assumed, like most people would, that if Ben had a beautiful woman in his company that there was more going on than business. "No problem, Claude. We should be back in a couple o' hours, an' if Chenoa is like most women we'll need help carryin' in all the packages o' clothes she'll buy. Other than that, we're travelin' light, like I always do."

"We'll be ready and waiting, sir. You are definitely one of our most valuable and respected guests, Mr. Creed, and we will do all to make this current stay as comfortable as we can for you both."

Ben was all ready halfway through the lobby heading for the front door as Claude finished trying to butter him up. It wasn't working, but the Congress was still the best hotel in town, and it wouldn't do any good to tell Claude he was as full of it as a Christmas goose, or that he would stay at the Congress until a better hotel came along. As long as they didn't cross him when it came to Chenoa or anyone else he brought in.

Back at Salty's, the buckboard was all ready loaded, and Clete was finishing hooking up and readying the team. Chenoa was standing beside the buckboard smiling while she and Salty carried on a conversation. They turned to Ben as he approached.

"Ben, daggone if this ain't just not only the purtiest gal in Prescott, maybe all o' Yavapai County, but I'll be danged if she ain't 'bout the smartest one, too. An' quick as a whip. Sure glad I got ta meet her, an' call her friend."

"Now, Salty. I wouldn't go that far. I'm just an average woman at best, but I appreciate the accolades you've heaped upon me."

"Yessir, Salty, now ya know why I brought her ta town with me, an' why she's what I consider a partner good 'nough ta ride the river with. But you're too old for somebody as young as her, an' she's got a fistful of admirers already, not one I'd like ta go up against when it comes ta her."

Chenoa was blushing listening to the two gush over her, and finally said, "Ben, that's enough. We'd best be getting aboard and making our stops before the two of you continue making such a fuss over me."

"Make that three fellers, ma'am. An' anything ya need, ya just let me know. An' if anybody gives ya any trouble while you're in town, let me know, will ya? I'm too homely ta even think 'bout standin' next ta a woman as handsome as you, even though I ain't too old, like Salty here. But I'll sure 'nough knock the dickens out o' any fool that gets out o' hand 'round ya, ma'am."

"Thank you, Clete, I do appreciate that. And you are not 'too homely', not at all. You are a fine specimen of a man, and any woman worth her salt would be proud to stand with you. Ben, really, we must be going. I am famished, and you promised me a nice, big steak. Not to mention that I need to purchase some new clothes, and that will take some time."

"Yes, ma'am. Fellers, thanks for takin' such good care of

Chenoa while I was across the street. Salty, I'll drop the wagon an' team off tonight when we're all done."

"We'll keep an eye out for ya, an' you just wave at us an' we'll trot across the street and gather it all up for ya when you're done. See ya later."

By the time Salty had finished talking, Ben and Chenoa were seated on the buckboard, ready to pull out. Ben flicked the reins and turned the team toward Renner's and a good meal. It only took ten minutes to pull up in front of Jason and Margarite's small café, and during that short trip Ben couldn't help but notice the looks they got as they rode along.

Stepping inside, Jason looked up from his customary table at the back, and called out, "Ben! Get on back here. The two o' ya can sit at my table. I'll bet ya want a nice, big juicy steak, medium rare as I recall, an' lots o' spuds an' whatever other vegetable the ol' woman has back there. An' how 'bout you, young lady?"

As Chenoa sat down, she smiled and replied. "I'll have the same as Ben, only not quite as much, and coffee, plenty of coffee, if you don't mind, sir."

"Jason, this is Chenoa. Chenoa, one o' my oldest friends here in Prescott, Jason Renner. His wife is the cook, an' man can she cook. The two o' you could go head ta head in a cook off, an' the judges would have ta take a month o' Sunday's ta figure out the winner."

"Now, Ben, stop making it sound like I'm something I'm not. I'm sure Mrs. Renner is a far better cook that I."

"Why, thank you, sweetie. Ben, what brings you back so soon? This pretty young gal get ya in here early? Oh, an' I all ready got the steaks, fresh corn an' spuds on. Got Sophie watchin' 'em for me. Now, ya gonna introduce me 'r not?"

"Sorry, Margarite. This here is Chenoa, an' Chenoa, I'm sure ya

152

figured out that this is Margarite, Jason's wife and the main cook here. Naw, got business here in town, Margarite, an' we made this our second stop, well third for me. Stabled the horses at Salty's, an' made a quick visit ta the hotel. Then here for a pile o' the best grub in town, just like I promised Chenoa 'fore we even left camp."

"Goin' ta the assay office again? An' stoppin' ta see Barriston, an' from there ta the county clerk's office?"

"Partly right, Jason. First, we'll go see James Whitaker, an' then whatever he tells me that's what I'll do from there."

"Whitaker? I keep hearin' he's a damned fine lawyer, but I don't know of a soul what's hired him. You know somethin' the rest of us don't?"

"Maybe, but he comes at Chenoa's recommendation, an' that's good 'nough for me."

"I take it ya hit the mother lode, Ben, 'r close 'enough ta make sure your claim is good an' tight. Not a word will leak out from me, you can count on that," Jason said in a whisper.

Ben only nodded, and then leaned back as Margarite brought out a fresh pot of coffee and two cups. "Give me about ten more minutes, an' I'll be bringin' out your food, Ben. Say, where'd you find this pretty young gal anyway?"

"She was hurt real bad when I found her close ta camp. I carried her in an' patched her up best I could, an' within a few days she was takin' on chores for me 'round camp. Been a real pleasure havin' her there, that I'll tell ya for sure. An' Margarite, 'fore ya get the wrong idea, she's more of a business partner than anything else, an' there ain't nothin' goin' on 'tween us, all right?"

"Don't be silly, Ben, We woman can tell such things, an' I seen that right off by the way the two o' ya looks at each other. There ain't no hearts an' stars in either o' ya's eyes, only respect an'

153

friendship. At least for the time bein', but don't neither o' ya rule out somethin' more in the future, hear me?"

Just then, a harsh voice rang out from the front of the room. "Hey, Renner. When did ya start feedin' squaws in here? Damned if I know if I wanna continue givin' ya my business."

Chapter Eighteen

Ben started to stand up, anger chiseled across his face, until Chenoa grabbed his arm and said, "I'll take care of this one, Ben. It is time I stood on my own here in Prescott, as you will not always be at my side when these things happen."

Without waiting for Ben to respond, Chenoa jumped out of her seat and quickly walked directly at the offending individual. Once she stood directly in front of the man, she started in on him. "Sir, and I use the term loosely, do you assume I an Indian from the way I look? Or the color of my skin? Or just the way you perceive me? I am FRENCH, understand? Where were you when I needed rescued? Probably sitting in some bar guzzling bottles of courage, none of which ever worked. You are a coward of the first degree, and you can thank your lucky stars that I just saved you from a severe beating, possibly saving your life. My escort is the man who saved my life, and my dear friend Ben Creed. I assume from the look in your eyes that you know who Ben Creed is, and what he is capable of. Now, you can apologize to me, or I can walk back to our table still offended and turn Mr. Creed loose on you, your choice."

"S-s-sor-r-ry, ma'am. I didn't really mean anything by it, honest. I was just teasin' Renner. I apologize, my sincerest apology, ma'am. Please forgive me."

"This time, but if you or any of your dirty friends ever insult me again, Ben Creed will be the least of your worries. Now, all of you, go bathe, you stink." Chenoa calmly turned around and walked back to the table, sat down and smiled at Ben and the Renner's. "Margarite, is that steak done?"

"Honey, I'll go check, an' bring out your food as soon as it's ready. Jason, make sure them cups don't run dry now, an' get 'em

155

somethin' ta eat with 'sides their fingers. Chenoa, that was the bravest thing I ever saw, an' girl, you're welcome ta sit at my tables anytime ya want. Now I know you're just half French, an' half Indian, but I don't give a hoot in hell one way 'r tother. Jason an' me is proud ta have ya as a friend, if ya don't mind that."

"And I am just as proud to call you friends. I'm sorry if I caused a disturbance, but he needed taken down a few notches. And I'm quite sure he'll be back to eat here, but will think twice, maybe three or four times, before he opens that big yap of his again."

Margarite was still laughing as she stepped back into the kitchen. They could hear her reciting what had just transpired to her assistant, Sophie, and then both women laughing. A few minutes later, both Margarite and Sophie brought out their plates, filled to overflowing, along with a couple of extra platters of potatoes and vegetables. Once the plates were carefully placed on the table, both women gave Chenoa a big hug, and then returned to the kitchen to prepare the other orders that had come in.

Jason had remained quiet; with a big grin spread across his face, until he finally spoke. "I reckon I'd best get ya another pot o' coffee, but 'fore I do, Ben, I see why ya brought her ta town. She's a by gawd spitfire, for sure. If push ever come ta shove, I'd want her on my side, for damned sure. Chenoa, if I was still single an' twenty years younger, you'd have ta beat me off with a stick."

"Thank you, Jason," Chenoa replied between bites, and then dug back in to her plate of food. She was still eating when Ben declared he was about to burst, and continued eating until Margarite asked, "Girl, where do you put it? Skinny little thing like you must be plumb hollow. Ya's best save a spot 'r two for some o' my fresh apple pie, 'cause ya ain't gettin' out o' here without eatin' at least a slice of it."

"Oh, I'll have room. It's just that I haven't had such good food in a very long time, and I have to admit I was very hungry when we arrived here," Chenoa said, cleaning the last of the food off her plate and then pushing it aside. "There, now I'm ready for that pie, if you please."

Once again, Margarite was laughing as she stepped into the kitchen, returning with two plates, both with two slices of apple pie centered on them. "Now you just let me know if ya need some more. I got three pies left back there, but if ya want another slice ya'd best call for it quick like, as there are a bunch in here that'll be wantin' some as soon as they finish eatin', even ol' loudmouth over there. Oh, I'd so love ta tell that bunch I run out o' pie, but that'd only drop me ta their level."

Ten minutes later, their plates were once again empty, and they were sipping the last cup of coffee for this visit. "Chenoa, ya ready to go get some new clothes, 'r should we go see Whitaker first?"

"Yes, I am ready, if I can still walk. I'm absolutely stuffed, Ben. We'd better go see James first, and then find someplace that will sell me some fashionable clothing. Shall we?" she said as she rose from the table, followed immediately by Ben standing up.

"How much we owe ya, Jason?"

"Not a red cent. This one is one us. It was a real pleasure ta meet ya, Chenoa," Jason said standing up and reaching out to shake her hand.

"Oh, c'mon now, Jason. You can't stay in business puttin' on such a feed on the house."

"I said it was on us, an' that's the end of it, Ben. I figure you'll be back ta see us more'n once, an' we'll make plenty off ya then. 'Sides, once word gets 'round town 'bout Chenoa takin' ol' Muley down, well, that'll only send more folks here ta eat with us. Danged if the two o' ya won't be real good for business, real good."

157

"If you're sure, Jason. An' I can guarantee we'll be back several more times 'fore we leave town again. Well, Chenoa, let's get movin' while we still can," Ben finished as he shook Jason's hand and turned for the door, only to be met by Margarite.

"You ain' gettin' out o' here without givin' me a hug, ya rascal. An' you, too, Chenoa."

A minute later, they were outside at the buckboard, climbing aboard. "Oh, goodness. Ben, can you give me a hand. I think I ate too much."

"Shoot, I might need a hand myself!" Ben replied as he helped Chenoa climb up onto the seat. Walking around to the other side, he had to use the seat rail to pull himself up. Finally seated, he admitted, "I don't believe I've ever ate so much in all my life. Danged if I have. Well, we'd best get movin' if we're gonna get that hot bath 'fore dark."

Chenoa gave Ben directions to the office of James Whitaker. Fifteen minutes later, they were seated in his office, introductions made and their business stated. Whitaker leaned back in his chair, looking at Ben, and then at Chenoa, and then back at Ben.

"Mr. Creed, can I assume you have properly marked your claim, and that you feel it is substantial in value?"

"Yes on both accounts. Here is a sample o' the gold I panned an' picked up off the ground downhill from where the main deposit is," Ben said, handing two of the pouches to the lawyer. "And here is a sample of the silver I picked up at the main vein where it was exposed."

"Have you taken these samples to the assay office, and filed those claims there?"

"Not yet. Chenoa felt it was best ta bring 'em ta you 'fore we did anything else. Now then, I did file a claim last time in town, but it wasn't really for these claims. It was for an old claim o' mine. Not sure I trust anybody in this deal, which is why we're here. What do you recommend?"

Whitaker was still looking over the silver sample, and took several minutes before answering. "Ben, this is very heavy with silver, some of the richest I believe I've ever seen. And the gold speaks for itself. I'd say that if these claims pan out, you will become one of the richest men in Arizona Territory. In fact, you will be as wealthy as the wealthiest men in the entire west. Now then, here's what I'll offer, and we'll negotiate from there on my fees. We settle on that, and then I'll give you my recommendations. I want two percent of everything taken from both claims, since we don't know which will be the richest claim. How does that suit you?"

"How's half a percent suit ya? I figure ta cut two o' my brothers in with an equal share o' what's left after what I give you an' Chenoa, an' that's for them workin' the claim with me, if they will, an' I'd planned on givin' Chenoa five percent."

"No, if I'm going to be your attorney of record, meaning I will represent you in any matter that arises, whether it is related to the claims or not, I will need more than that. I'll settle for a full one percent, or you will have to pay my standard office fees for representation in all matters. Look at it this way; should you end up selling your claims in the future, our agreement ends there. All I want is a very small share of what you pull out, no matter how many other partners you eventually have. And I will also prepare any needed paperwork for those partnerships, and represent you should you decide to sell. Further, I will personally monitor the processing of any gold, silver, lead or any other mineral pulled from those claims. That's a mistake too many miners make, not getting paid for the other minerals pulled from their claims."

"Hold it right there, James. You just sold me. I'd o' never thought about the other minerals, an' I reckon that alone is worth another half percent. We got a deal."

"Very well then. I'll draw up the paperwork giving me one percent of the proceeds of the claims and any sale of those claims in the future. In the meantime, I want you to duplicate this paperwork, making a copy for my records. Once you've completed that, take your copy to the county clerk's office for filing. They will give you a detailed receipt for that paperwork, but you'll have to ask for it. Once you have that receipt, and not before, then take your samples to the assayer's office and make certain you receive receipt there as well, detailed by the type of material and weight. DO NOT, I repeat, DO NOT leave any copy of the claims there. I do not know that I completely trust the local assayer, but he is all we have, for now. You may tell him the approximate locations of these claims, but not their actual locations, or how they are marked. Understood?"

"Yessir, I got it. Now, how much I owe ya for this first visit?"

"Nothing. Let's get those assay reports first, and by then I should have our agreement ready for signatures. From there, we'll have a better idea what we're dealing with."

"Fair 'nough. Chenoa, how 'bout I drop you off ta get your new clothes, an' I'll head for the county offices an' the assayer's office. I can take care o' that while you shop, an' we should get done about the same time."

"Yes, that sounds perfect. James, thank you so much for helping Ben. I'll chat with him about what he intends for me, as I really don't care to make anything from his hard work. I suppose we'll see you again several times over the next few days, and again when the assayer finishes his report. Like you, I wish we had another assayer here, but I know of none outside of Tuscon or Phoenix, and even then I don't know that they aren't connected to Barriston."

"There is one in Flagstaff, but he is too well established to consider relocating here. There is, however, a young man just completing his studies that I might be able to convince to set up shop here. But he won't be ready for another six months or so. Unfortunately, he doesn't have any financial backing, so it will be hard for him to establish himself no matter where he goes, unless I or one of my clients decide to assist him," James said looking directly at Ben.

"We'll talk about him when the time comes, James. Of course I'll want ta meet this young feller 'fore I decide anything."

"Of course, Ben. Of course. When the time comes, I'll bring him around to meet you both. I should forewarn you, he is black, but I doubt that makes any difference to a man like you."

"You're right, I could care less about the color of a man's skin. It's what he made of that I look at. Chenoa, let's get out o' here 'fore James has all my money spent 'fore I make it," Ben replied with a laugh.

Ten minutes later they were downtown, a block off Whiskey Row, where Ben pulled up in front of Mrs. Devereaux's Millinery and Ladies Apparel. "Ben, this looks too expensive. Isn't there another shop you can take me to?"

"This one will do just fine. The Widow Devereaux is a nice old gal, an' word has it she treats every woman that enters her door the same way. That alone is worth a lot ta me, an' it ought ta work fine for you as well. C'mon, let me introduce you."

"And how is it you know this woman?"

"I helped her out a few years back, when I first came here. She was just north o' town with a loose buggy wheel. I set it back in place an' tightened up the nut good 'nough ta get her the rest o' the way ta town. Got her over ta Salty's place, an' him an' Clete fixed up that buggy proper like. After that, she came lookin' for me at the hotel, insistin' on buyin' my supper. We had a nice chat over our meal, but I still paid. I even thought her an' Salty might get together, but it never happened. Not for Salty not tryin' though. Anyway, I think you'll like her," Ben said as he opened the door to let Chenoa inside.

"Mercy me, if it isn't Ben Creed! Where have you been, young man? And why haven't you stopped to see me? And who do you have here?"

"Ma'am, this is Chenoa, a very good friend an' business partner o' mine. She needs a passel o' new clothes, all on me, so whatever she needs, I'm payin'. Chenoa, this is Madge Devereaux, an' this is her place. I'll gonna leave you in her capable hands while I take care o' the rest o' my business."

"Yes, yes, of course. Chenoa, it is my pleasure to meet you. Ben, we ladies will see you in, say, an hour or so. Chenoa, I have the most delightful new dress that I'm sure will fit you perfectly, and look absolutely gorgeous on you. Oh, and I have a hat and bag to go with it. You will be the talk of the town, trust me."

Madge was still talking as Ben slipped out of the door and made his way to the buckboard. At the corner, he was tempted to make it the block over and hit The Palace, but decided against it. Pulling up in front of the county offices instead, he made his first stop the Sheriff's Office, checking with Mrs. Bishop to see if either his brothers or Sheriff Walker were in. A few minutes later, he was invited back to the sheriff's private office.

"What brings ya back ta town sa soon, Ben?"

"Hired me an attorney, an' filin' on my claims. I was wonderin' if my brothers had made it back yet, 'r when they might be here. Any idea?"

"As a matter o' fact, Ben, I heard from 'em a couple o' days back. They're bringin' in a load o' prisoners from Flag. If they left day before yesterday, which I figure they did, they should be in here sometime late today. You need 'em for somethin'?"

"Well, sort o'. Kind o' depends on the assayer's report I reckon. Damned if I ain't gonna try ta hire 'em away from ya 'fore they get hurt."

"Ben, that actually works for me. I don't know how much longer I want ta hang on here. This might just be my last year. I'll tell ya this, them two are the finest deputies I've ever seen anywhere, but they've made more'n one enemy workin' this job, an' some o' 'em enemies is real bad people. I'd just as soon see 'em move on ta somethin' else an' get shed o' this county, 'r at least take a low profile."

"Glad ya won't be upset if I can get 'em ta quit ya, Sheriff. You an' me ain't always seen eye ta eye, but we always understood each other."

"Now that's a fact, Ben. An' call me Jeff, will ya? How long ya figure ta be in town this time?"

"I don't know for certain, Jeff. At least a week 'r so I reckon. Just tell the boys I'm in town an' stayin' at the Congress as always. I don't think they'll find me on Whiskey row this round, as I have a ton o' business ta handle. Well, that an' I brought along a guest this time."

"Really? That French gal the town is buzzin' about? The one some say is Indian, an' the rest are afraid ta say?"

"Yup, that's the one. Damn, word sure travels fast here, don't it? Hope I don't have any trouble on account o' her, but I won't let nobody put her down 'r talk bad about her. Jeff, she was in pretty bad shape when I found her. Man she was with sold her ta a varmi't named Luke Weitz. He worked her over, but she gave as good as she got. He slunk off somewhere, an' I don't know if he lived 'r died, not that I care either way. Anyway, I patched her up, an' as soon as she could she took over my camp, cookin' an' such, doin' more'n any woman I ever seen 'cept maybe my own mother. She's had a real hard time, but I'm tryin' ta fix that. She's half French an' half Paiute, an' all woman. A terror of a woman when pressed, but one helluva a woman by any measure."

"Where is she now?"

"Mrs. Devereaux's, gettin' outfitted with new clothes. I got two more stops, an' then I'll go back an' pick her up. She'll be stayin' at the Congress in a room next ta mine, an' I reckon she'll be ready for a good, hot bath as much as I am. Least that's what she said."

"I hear she nailed ol' Muley ta the floor over ta Renner's, but he's all mouth anyway. I'll see if I can get around an' meet this gal 'fore ya leave town, Ben. Oh, an' I heard tell Weitz showed up in real bad shape. He's still 'round town some'eres, an' talkin 'real mean 'bout some Indian gal. Says if he ever finds her, he'll kill her. Best keep an eye out for him, just in case. An' I'll let the boys know ya want ta see 'em as soon as they can. For now, try ta keep from shootin' up the town, will ya?"

"I'll do my best, Jeff, but trouble always seems ta hunt me down an' jump in my face. Well, thanks for the warnin', but I need ta get movin' if I'm gonna finish up my business an' get back ta that gal 'fore she spends ever' dime I got."

Ben left the Sheriff's Office and walked down the hall to the County Clerk's Office, stepping inside to see the same woman at the counter as was always there. "Hello, Martha. How you doin' today?"

"Just fine, Ben. You bring in more paperwork to be filed?"

"Indeed I did. Here ya go," Ben said, taking the paperwork for both claims out of his pocket and laying them on the counter in front of the lady. "Oh, an' my lawyer says I need to make sure an' get receipts for these, if ya don't mind."

"Sure thing, Ben. Just give me a minute to record these, and I'll get you a receipt. Can I also assume you'll be leaving these papers here to be filed with us?"

"Yes, ma'am, those are your copies."

"Fine, have a seat and I'll call you when they've been recorded," the middle-aged woman said as she disappeared into the back of the office.

A few minutes later, she returned and called Ben to the counter, handing him his receipts. "Good luck, Ben. I hope these two claims are the ones that make you rich. Oh, and that'll be a dollar."

Fishing a dollar out of his pocket, Ben placed it gently on the counter, picked up his receipts, winked at Martha, and then turned and walked out of the office, and the courthouse. Climbing into the buckboard, he started the team toward the assayer's office. The assayer was standing at the door with his closed sign in hand when Ben pulled up. "Hold up there, I need ta drop off some samples for testin'."

"What is it with you miners? Why is it you always come right at noon, or just as I'm closing the office for the day or trying to get away for a few minutes for personal business? Well, come on in. Bring your samples."

Ben reached into his saddlebag to lift out one pouch of nuggets and one of dust, along with the chunk he had chiseled out of the wall of rock, and then grabbed two sizeable chunks from the silver claim and started for the door. "Say, I never have asked your name, mister."

"Hutchison, Mike Hutchison."

"Mind if I call ya Mike?"

"Not at all, Mr. Creed."

"Well, why don't you call me Ben if we're gonna be on a first name basis."

"Fine, Ben. What have you got for me this time?"

"Samples from two claims, one silver an' the other gold. I hate ta ask, but my lawyer wants a receipt for both by weight and type of material. I assume that's not a problem."

"Not at all. Let me weigh them and write down a general description for you, and I'll make sure to register them as from your claim. Do you have the claim paperwork?"

"Nossir, but there's a copy at the lawyer's office, an' one at the county clerk's office. The lawyer said that's all you'd need, other than a basic description of where they're located."

"Yes, as long as I can verify the claims by checking either copy. I can have your reports done day after tomorrow, unless you want to pay for a rush service."

"Yeah, I'd like ta know pronto, Mike. A lot of things hinge on those reports, includin' my bringin' on more partners."

Over the next several minutes, Ben described the monuments they had used to mark the claims, and then shook out the gold flakes and dust into the scale pan and dropped three large nuggets on the assayer's desk along with the large chunk from the gold claim, followed by placing the two rocks with silver on the desk as well. Assayer Hutchison raised his eyebrows at the dust, and then hefted the three nuggets, followed by picking up the rock laced with gold and each of the two silver rocks.

"Ben, it looks like you've hit a good strike in each claim, if they remain consistent. All right," he paused to weigh the dust, "you've got 10 ounces of dust here, and if it assays out at ninety-five percent this small amount alone will bring you about two hundred dollars at today's prices."

Pouring the dust back into the pouch, he placed the three nuggets in the pan, and carefully weighed them. "Two and a half ounces here, and from the looks they should assay out at eighty-five percent, or another sixty to sixty-five dollars."

Placing the gold laced rock in the pan, he took a moment longer to weigh it, and them placed the two silver rocks in the pan and weighed them together before pronouncing his initial thoughts. "Impressive gold, Ben. Very impressive. The silver as well, weighing eight troy pounds and eleven ounces, and it should assay out at about sixty percent, or about eighty dollars. Of course those are just rough numbers, subject to my final assay findings. Now, I can have your results by late tomorrow afternoon, but it will cost you twenty dollars."

"No problem," Ben said digging into his pocket, and then flipping a double eagle before laying it on the counter. "Make sure ta include the findings on any other minerals, like lead 'r copper, in those reports, will ya? Now for the receipt."

A few minutes later, Ben had his second receipt and was on the way to the Bank of Prescott to exchange four gold pouches for cash. Finished there, he headed for Mrs. Devereaux's to retrieve Chenoa. He almost swallowed his tongue when Madge handed him the bill, a hundred eighty-three dollars forty-five cents. But he was certain it would be worth every penny.

Cherokee Parks

Chapter Nineteen

Zack jumped down from the seat and ran to the back of the jail wagon, opened the lock and slung the door open. "What the hell is goin' on back here?" It didn't take long to get his answer.

"Johnson's been whinin', sayin' he was gonna kill hisself, an' Sims cracked an' said he was gonna help him here an' now," came the answer from Earl. "We was just tryin' to keep 'em both away from each other, an' Sims kinda got hisself hurt. Real bad from the looks of it."

"All right, start climbing' out o' there, real slow like," Zack ordered.

Todd rode up from where he had been out front, handing the reins to Seth, who had joined Zack at the rear of the wagon. "Zack, why we unloadin' here? We're less than a half hour from the jail."

"We need ta check on Sims, maybe Johnson. Seems Sims went after Johnson an' got beat back for his trouble. I can't see either one o' 'em 'til we get the rest o' these numbskulls out. Just keep 'em guarded while I go inside. Seth, lend Todd a hand watchin' 'em once they hit the ground."

Finally, with the three prisoners, Micah and Earl, chained together, and Peterson on the ground, leaving only Barker, who was chained to Sims, and Filmore, who was chained to Johnson. Before climbing inside, Zack handed his Colt to Seth and then climbed into the back of the wagon. Barker said, "I ain' gonna give ya no trouble, Deputy, an' I'll watch your back just in case Filmore there, 'r Johnson, tries ta pull somethin'. I don't reckon Sims is gonna be up ta tryin' anything. Not sure he made it through that attack alive."

One look at Sims told Zack all he needed to know to verify Barker's comments. There was a big depression on the side of Sims' skull as he lay on the floor of the wagon. Johnson was still all but motionless, except for his shoulders shaking as he sobbed. Filmore had a smile on his face, anticipating what came next.

"Filmore, see if you can get Johnson outside so's we can clean him up a bit." Turning to tell Todd and Seth that two more were coming out, he continued by saying, "Johnson is gonna need cleaned up some. He's got a big cut alongside his cheek an' it looks like maybe his nose is busted. Sims is dead, an' I'm gonna take Barker off his chain an' send him out as well."

"All right, Filmore, get a move on. Johnson, ya ain't dead, so move it!" Once they had cleared the door and were on the ground, Zack turned to Barker. "So, Barker, who done the deed?"

"Damned if I know for sure. I reckon we all did, in a way, as we all had a part in yankin' him back an' stompin' him ta the floor. All but Johnson. That yellow sumbitch just sat there takin' a beatin'. Never lifted a hand ta fend off Sims, like he wanted the bastard ta kill him an' get it over with."

"All right. Well, I reckon we'll never know for sure then, but I'm bettin' either you 'r Filmore dealt the kick ta the head that done him in." Leaning over to unlock the chain holding Barker to Sims, Zack finished by saying, "Now drag him out o' here so's we can toss the body over my saddle an' get loaded back up again, but this time you're gonna be hooked up ta your buddy Peterson."

"Suits me fine, Deputy. At least it won't be ta that crazy Sims. He was crazier'n a pet coon, that one was."

As soon as Barker had drug Sims through the door, Zack also stepped back out of the wagon. "Todd, do me a favor an' hook Peterson an' Barker together. How's Johnson look?"

"Pretty bad, Zack. Looks like his cheekbone an' nose are both broke, an' that gash on his cheek is real deep. He'll hold 'til we get ta the jail, but he's gonna need the doc real quick like once we get there."

"All right. Micah, you an' Earl climb back in. Barker, you an' Peterson are next. Seth, reckon ya can load Sims across my saddle an' tie him tight so's he don't fall off?"

Seth nodded, and then turned to untie Zack's horse from the lead rope and lead him up beside the body. Waiting until the first two pair of prisoners were back in the wagon, he then hoisted Sims lifeless body onto the saddle. Taking a pigging string, he made a loop around Sims legs, and then walking to the other side of the horse, he reached under and grabbed the loose end of the thin rope and secured the hands of the corpse so that Sims wouldn't fall off on the short trip into town.

"Here, hold this rag against your face to help stop the bleedin'," Todd said to Johnson as he helped him to his feet. The sobbing had stopped, but there was no denying the look of desolation and desperation on the prisoner's face, or what could be seen of that face. "Filmore, do yourself a favor an' give him a hand, will ya? Don't make this any tougher'n on all of us than ya have to."

Filmore did as asked, but it was pretty obvious that he did so grudgingly. Once they were back inside and seated, Zack closed the wagon door and slammed the lock closed again. "All right, boys, let's get ta the office, an' hope nothin' else happens along the way. We ought ta be there in half an hour 'r so. I don't s'pose Doc is gonna be real happy 'bout gettin' called out after dark, but that undertaker ought ta be all grins an' giggles. Let's roll," he finished as he and Seth took their seats and Todd climbed back aboard his mount.

As they rolled up in front of the jail, they were surprised to see the sheriff walk out to meet them. "Boys, glad ta see ya made it. Who's the dead one?"

"Graf Sims."

"One o' you boys do it?"

"Nossir. It happened in the wagon just outside o' town. He tried ta do Johnson in, an' the rest o' the prisoners put a halt to it, killin' Sims in the process. Johnson's hurt pretty bad, an' is gonna need Doc ta come treat him."

"All right." Turning to the deputy at his side, Sheriff Walker said, "Shorty, go fetch Doc an' the coroner. Pronto."

The young man, whose nickname belied his height at six feet four inches, turned and trotted toward the county stable to get his horse, and was seen just a few minutes later headed toward the north end of town and Doc's office. In the meantime, the sheriff yelled back inside the building for the jailer on duty that night. "Morrison, get on out here! We got prisoners ta lock up!"

Turning back to the Creed brothers, he said, "I see ya got some help. Ain't that one o' the pair o' Stock Association's Rangers?"

"Yessir, it is. Seth here got trapped in a bad deal by his partner, the one we knew as Jack, but he got out by lendin' us a hand in catchin' the real culprits an' haulin' 'em in. He's a good man, Sheriff, an' I reckon ya might want ta put him on the payroll," Todd offered.

"You boys standin' behind him on this?"

"Yessir, we are. He's worth it, for sure. Damned good rifle shot, but a tad slow on the draw, at least compared ta us anyway."

"Well, all right then. What's your name, son? I don't remember."

"Seth Morton, sir."

"Seth Morton, eh? Well, Seth, come on by the office first thing in the mornin' an' we'll get ya sworn in an' give ya a badge. Now, who are the rest o' these prisoners?"

"Two o' 'em are regulars, but they got drug into the rustlin' thing when they was hired on as cowboys. They got tricked, an' was told if they tried ta take off they'd get hunted down an' killed for their trouble. Earl Carson an' Micah Slate. We've had 'em in here before for a number o' petty crimes, but I don't reckon this time they had a clue until it was too late. The one all banged up is Bill Johnson, the Indian Agent that was buyin' stolen cattle an' takin' part in sendin' 'em ta Chicago ta be butchered, all while deliverin' old an' rotten beef ta the Reservations. Then there's Layton Filmore, who was usin' the name o' Arch Campbell. He was the Arizona Cattlemen's Association Secretary, an' the third leg in the scheme. The last one o' that bunch is Ike Stockton, but that sumbitch managed ta get away on us," Zack filled the sheriff in.

"Stockton? I didn't know he operated anywhere but New Mexico Territory, an' hid out in Colorado. Ya sure it was him?"

"Yessir, an' Filmore will attest ta that as well. I don't think he's real happy about gettin' nabbed while Stockton got away slick. We'll need the DA ta issue an arrest warrant for rustlin' an' murder on Stockton as soon as he can get to it. Now then, we got Chuck Barker an' Hank Peterson, arrested up in Flag for stealin' eggs, of all things, 'cause they was hungry."

"Well, well, quite a crew, eh? An' Sims? What was he arrested for?"

"Seems he beat his woman near ta death, an' then tried ta stab Charlie Grimes with a broken bottle when Charlie went out ta haul him in. He even threatened me an' Todd, sayin' he was gonna get both o' us an' Charlie when he got out, that he'd see us dead 'fore he was done."

"Not too smart, was he? Well, since you boys didn't figure out who done him in, we'll just call it an unfortunate accident on the trip in an' call it good. Ya got the transport sheet there handy?"

173

"Yessir," Todd replied, handing the folded paper to Sheriff Walker.

"Where do ya want me to put the body, Sheriff?" Seth asked as he prepared to unload Sims.

"Just lay him on the ground here by the door for now, Seth. The undertaker ought ta be here 'fore long, an' he can take care o' the body from there. Say, I'll bet you fellers are gettin' hungry 'bout now. Seth, ya got a place ta stay here in town?"

"No sir, I don't."

"An' I'll wager you're short o' cash as well, right?"

"Well, yessir, I am."

"Tell ya what, why don't you just bunk here in the jail tonight? We got a cot set up in the room next ta the jailer's office. You can sleep in there. Zack, I'll have Shorty take care o' the wagon an' team, an' Seth's horse as well. Yours, too, if ya want me to."

"Naw, we'll take care o' our own animals, Sheriff. We board 'em at Cooper's, right across the street from Mose Brody's boardin' house, where we keep a room."

"You sure? Yeah, I know ya are. Well, I'll see ya when ya come in ta file your reports in the mornin'. Seth, once I get ya sworn in, I'll need a report from you as well. C'mon in an' let's get ya settled in," the sheriff said as he grabbed Seth by the arm and turned to go inside the jail. Then, stopping short, he called out, "Say, 'fore I forget it, Ben was by lookin' for ya earlier today. Said he'd be at the Congress, but not ta look for him on the Row this trip. Got a young Frenchwoman travelin' with him this time, just so ya know."

The brothers looked at each other in surprise, and then Todd shrugged his shoulders and said, "Not much really surprises me 'bout brother Ben, but travelin' with a Frenchwoman? Now that's a new one, even for Ben. Let's go get the horses boarded, get cleaned up an' see if we can find somethin' ta eat 'fore my belly thinks my throats been cut."

"Hell, my belly's all ready there! Let's ride, brother," Zack replied as he strode to his horse and swung into the saddle, picking up the lead rope for both packhorses. Ten minutes later, they were dismounting in front of Cooper's Livery, where they were met at the door by Mack Cooper.

"Kind o' late, ain't ya, boys?"

"Yeah, we are, Mack. Sorry. Ya mind strippin' 'em for us, an' brushin' 'em out an' grainin' 'em real good for us? Been a real long day."

"Not at all, boys. I hear Ben's in town with a real pretty young woman. Ya seen him yet?"

"Not yet. We just rode in about an hour ago, an' had ta take care of a few things at the Sheriff's Office. I reckon we'll find him in the mornin' an' see what this is all about. We'll let ya know whatever we find out, Mack, so there ain't no rumors goin' around that don't need ta be."

"Now, ya don't think I'm a gossipin' old woman, do ya?" Cooper asked with a laugh.

"Naw, but you can help by tellin' the real truth when ya hear somebody speculatin," Zack said with a smile. "Say, what's still open where we can get some grub?"

"Danged if I know. Renner's is closed, an' I doubt ya wanna pay the price at the Congress. But I'll wager Maybelline'd be glad ta whip somethin' up for ya. All ya got ta do is ask."

"Well, that works. We need ta go clean up some anyway. Zack, she favors you, so you can ask her when we get over there."

"Yeah, well the way I see it, she favors you, so you can ask."

175

The brothers were still trying to decide who would ask their hostess as they opened the gate to Brody's yard. "Nevah ya mind who' her favorite, boys. She loves ya both," Mose said with a hearty laugh.

"Mose, what're you doin' settin' out here in the dark?"

"Just enjoyin' the evenin', boys. G'won an' warsh up, I'll have the ol' woman start gettin' ya somethin' ta eat, an' I reckon youse gonna want plenty o' coffee ta warsh it down with," the whiskered, elderly black man said as he slowly stood up, reaching out to shake the boys' hands as they approached the door. "Say, I heared tell brother Ben come ta town agin, sportin' him a fancy lookin' gal."

"Yeah, Mose, we been hearin' the same thing. Can't tell ya any more'n that, though. But we'll let you an' Maybelline know what we find out when we catch up with him," Todd said. "Seems he's the talk o' the town these days, eh?"

"Not sa much him as her, the way it come ta me. Hear she's a real fine lookin' French lady, but some is sayin' she's Injun. I reckon the truth lies in between, that she's half o' each. Leas' ways that how I gots if figuahed. G'won now, an' lemme tell Maybelline ya'll is back an' hongry."

It wasn't long and the brothers were seated at Maybelline's table, with coffee all ready poured for them and food being prepared as they sipped. Conversation took a back seat once their plates were filled, and refilled, and filled again. Maybelline was smiling a huge smile as she watched the boys devour her cooking.

Finally, she just had to say something, even if they couldn't answer with their mouths full. "Sho' glad ya boys likes mah cookin'. Shoot, ya can eats heah anytime ya's hongry. Ya's like mah own chillin, ya know that don' ya? Aw, don' try ta answah me, ah's jus' tellin' ya how much ah loves ya, boys. Sho' don' know what me an' Mose is gonna do if'n ya'll was ta leave us. But the way it's bein' told 'roun' town et days a comin'," she finished,

176

wiping a tear from her eye.

"Now, Maybelline, I don't believe we're plannin' on goin' no where any time soon. An' we love you an' Mose as well, not ta mention that you're the best cook in the county an' keep the cleanest an' most comfortable boardin' house in two hundred miles, maybe further. Me an' Todd love stayin' here. You know that, don't ya?" Zack managed to say between bites.

"Woman, quit yer blubberin' now an' let the boys eat. Boys, we's damned proud ta have ya, no matter how much longah it is."

Cherokee Parks

Chapter Twenty

As was their custom, the boys were up with the sun, washed up as good as one could do without a tub full of hot water, and dressed in clean clothes. Maybelline had coffee on for them, and was busy frying eggs, ham and potatoes. Just as the food was ready to pull off the stove, she reached inside the oven and pulled out a pan full of biscuits, sliding them into a basket and setting them on the table. A minute later, the rest of the food was served on platters meant to be emptied. "Git ta eatin', boys, 'fo Mose gits heah an' beats yuns to it."

And eat they did, but making sure to leave plenty for their host, who joined them as they were finishing their meal. "Mose, where ya been? We near cleaned up the grub an' left ya hungry."

"I wuz ovah ta Mack's. He needed a bit o' he'p hookin' up the buggy 'fore ya. I know, ya didn' order no buggy, but it looks ta me an' him et ya got a lot o' travelin' 'roun' town ta do taday, too fer ta walk an' all that climbin' up an' down from 'em hosses'd be too much. Mack said it'd be on him, no charge. Reckon he feels like me an' the ol' woman. Yuns is right valuable customers, an' need ta get some special like treatments from time ta time."

"Well, I can tell you we really appreciate the way you an' Maybelline treat us, an' how Mack tends ta our horses an' gear. But it's us that ought ta be doin' somethin' special for the lot o' ya."

"Ah, ain' no setch thang, Todd. Now g'won an git ta takin' care o' yuns business. I'll warsh up all 'em dirty clothes an' get 'em hung ta dry for ya whilst yuns is gone. I don' reckon yuns'll be back ta eat lunch, 'r supper tonight, but ah'll sho' have breakfas' ready again in the mornin'."

"Thanks, Maybelline. Todd, she's right, we'd best get ta movin'. We got a lot ta handle today, for sure. Mose, Maybelline, we'll see ya in the mornin'."

Across the street, Todd saw Mack pitching hay into the feed bunks for the regular boarded horses, and called out to him. "Mack, Mose spoiled the surprise! What did we do ta deserve such a treat?"

"Aw, the buggy needs used now an' again ta keep it limbered up. I just greased it an' cleaned it up again yesterday, an' figured maybe you fellers'd enjoy sittin' on a soft seat for a change. I'll bring it right out for ya, just gimme a minute."

Shortly Mack drove the buggy out from the back of the barn, pulled it up to a stop and jumped down. "There ya go, boys. Who's drivin'?"

"I reckon we'll take turns as we go, but for now I'm drivin' this rig. Let's see if I can remember how…" Zack said with a big smile aimed at Mack. "Thanks, Mack. Seriously, you don't have any idea how much this means to us. We'll bring it back 'fore it gets too late, if Ben don't hold us up from gettin' here."

"Yeah, well, I got me a helper that'll be here after seven. Tonight, I'm gonna get me a good night's rest, one way 'r tother. Reckon I'll see ya in the mornin', though. Oh, an' the buggy is yours ta use 'til ya get ready ta leave town again. I'll see ya later," Mack said turning back to the barn and resuming his chores.

Twenty minutes later, they tied off the buggy horse in front of the courthouse and climbed the steps, heading to the Sheriff's Office. As they entered the office, Seth came out of the sheriff's personal office with a big smile on his face, followed by the sheriff with an equally big smile.

"Hey, boys. Good mornin'," the sheriff said, echoed by Seth. "Welcome my new deputy, will ya? I reckon you boys are right. He'll make a right handy deputy. Now, I'll need all three o' 'em reports 'fore the DA comes around this mornin'. Oh, an' stick around town in case he needs ta talk to ya. I got ta go take care of a couple o' things, so ya can leave 'em reports with Mrs. Bishop. See ya later, fellers, an' try not ta tree the town while you're here."

The three deputies walked back to a large room with several desks set at regular spaces, each with a chair, a stack of papers, and an inkwell and pen. "Grab a seat, Seth. This is where all the deputies fill out reports, an' 'em that's usually close ta town come ta do their daily business. Sheriff say what he's gonna have ya doin'?" Zack asked.

"Yeah. I'll be workin' around the jail for a month 'r so, 'til I get a few dollars saved up an' learn more about the law. Just the few things we talked about this mornin' made my head hurt. Shoot, I didn't know there was so much to know ta keep the peace."

"Yeah, an' just when ya think ya got it all figured out, they up an change one law 'r three 'r four. But after a while, ya just focus on all the main ones an' let the sheriff worry over the rest. He'll send ya where he needs ya, an' usually give ya an idea which law has been broke an' who needs arrested," Todd replied. "Let's get those reports filed, Zack, an' see if we can find big brother."

"You fellers mind if I tag along today? I don't need ta be back here 'til about four. I take my shift startin' at six tonight 'til six in the mornin'. I just need a short nap for I get started tonight, as I slept better last night than I have in quite a spell."

"No problem here, Seth, as long as your report is finished when ours are."

For the next half hour, all that could be heard in the room was the dipping of pens into the inkwells and scratching sounds as ink was applied to paper. Finally, Todd said, "That should do it for me. How 'bout you two?"

Both Zack and Seth stood up, Seth replying, "Just waitin' on you two."

Without another word, they headed for Mrs. Bishop, stopping just long enough to introduce Seth to the official gatekeeper for the sheriff. Reports handed over, the trio headed outside, where Seth was surprised to see they were using a buggy.

"Yeah, Mack Cooper, the feller where we board our horses, told us to use it while we're in town. Todd, your turn ta drive. Let's head for the Congress an' see if we can find Ben."

Loaded up, ten minutes later they were tied off in front of the hotel and walking inside. Ben and Chenoa were just heading into the dining room, and every eye in the place was fixed on the French and Indian woman, including the trio. She was a vision of beauty, dressed to kill in her new clothes.

"Boys, there ya are. Come on, join us for breakfast."

"Well, we'll join ya for coffee, but Maybelline fed us all ready," Todd responded.

"Speak for yourself, Todd. All I got at the jail was coffee, if that's what ya wanna call it, an' nothin' last night as we got there after the prisoners were fed," Seth interjected.

"Ben, this here is Seth Morton, one o' the new deputies. He helped us bring down that rustlin' ring we was sent out ta get, an' did a fine job."

"Seth, you're sure welcome ta join us. Boys, this is Chenoa. Chenoa, my brother Zack, brother Todd, an' you heard that this is Seth."

"A pleasure to meet all three of you. Zack, Todd, I've heard a great deal about you, all good I assure you," Chenoa said with a chuckle. "Ben, I'm starving."

"Yes, ma'am, Shall we?"

Stepping into the dining room, they were stopped short by François. "Excuse me, but you do NOT have a reservation. Mr.

Creed, even if you are a guest of the hotel you will require a reservation. And I'm afraid we do NOT allow Indians in our dining room."

"Are you referring to me, sir?" Chenoa said, stepping up to stand directly in front of the maître d'. "I am French, sir, and do NOT appreciate the rude treatment inflicted on both I and my friends. I insist on an apology, NOW!"

François seems somewhat taken aback, but soon recovered, saying something in French. Whatever it was, it only angered Chenoa even more. "What kind of a French accent is that? It certainly sounds like a phony to me. I challenge that you are even French. Maybe Belgian, but NOT French." From there, she lit into him in French, throwing out one sentence after another until he finally succumbed to the pressure.

"My apologies, Mademoiselle. Of course you are welcome here, and will always be welcome here, escorted or not and with or without a reservation. Please, follow me to your table, and I will summon your waiter immediately. I assume you'll all want coffee?"

"That is correct, sir, and thank you for your apology. I am sorry if I also offended you, but I'm certain we will become good friends, just as Ben Creed is my best friend, and these other gentlemen are fast becoming my best friends."

François graciously led the group of five to a large table off to the edge of the dining room, but not far from the entrance to the kitchen. As promised, he summoned a waiter, giving him explicit instructions on taking care of these guests, including bringing them two fresh pots of coffee, not any that had been sitting in the back unused.

Turning to the group, but looking directly at Chenoa, he paused for a moment, and then said, "Please, if you need anything during your stay here at the Congress Hotel, let me know. No matter what it is, I am at your service." Then he turned and disappeared.

"Chenoa, just what the hell did you say to him?"

"Oh, I'm afraid I couldn't possibly repeat it all, but I think he is now a believer in my French heritage, and will enjoy letting others know if they should question it."

"Well, it suits me just fine. That's two men I've seen you dispatch with just your tongue, an' I'd hate ta see what you'd do with a knife."

"On, Ben, I believe you know what could happen, but let's not get into that here. I'm sure you'll inform your brothers and Seth here about the conditions of our first meeting, and why we are still together. Boys, let me tell you myself so there is no question later. Ben is a great friend, and if he has his way I'll also be a business partner. But that's were it ends, as there is no romantic involvement on either side."

"So, I reckon that means there's a chance for us, doncha think, Todd?"

"Hah! Not likely! If she's all ready turned Ben away, I doubt we'll be able ta get an inch closer'n he did," Todd said.

"Now, Todd, don't sell yourselves short. It's just that Ben and I have a different kind of relationship, one that cannot possibly become romantic, but one that will last longer than most marriages. Seth, if you are a friend of the Creed's, you can also count yourself as eligible, though I must warn you I do have a history, and there are several suitors already pitching themselves as the best choice."

The waiter slowly approached the table with a questioning look, but Chenoa calmed him by motioning him closer. He respectfully took their orders, and then hustled off to the kitchen, bringing yet another fresh pot of coffee to replace the already empty one on the table.

Twenty minutes later, after some idle chitchat, breakfast was served, and talking almost ceased entirely, leaving Todd and Zack to wait quietly. Finally, after the platters were emptied, Zack asked, "So, Ben, Sheriff Walker said you were lookin' for us. What's goin' on?"

"Thanks ta Chenoa, I reckon I've hit it, an' good. 'Specially the gold claim, but the silver claim might be just as good." Looking around the now almost empty dining room, Ben leaned in toward the center of the table and continued speaking, his voice even lower than before. "I should have the assay reports this afternoon, an' the claims have been filed at the county clerk's office. An' I've hired an attorney. Now, here's what I'm thinkin'. If these assay reports are what I think they'll be, I'd like ta have you boys file right next ta me on both claims, an' then I'll cut ya in for an equal split o' what I ain't all ready promised, with me keepin' fifty-one percent."

"Ya reckon it'll pay that big, Ben?"

"Yup, I do. 'Nough that we can take good care o' the rest o' the family, an' only work at what we wanna do for the rest o' our lives. But first we'll have ta work it, an' work it hard ta make sure it pays right, an' then we can sell it off for a bunch an' let somebody else work it. We'll have ours an' can walk away rich."

"Ya say the assay repots will be in today?"

"Yup, had ta pay extra for it, but I'll go by about four an' pick 'em up. Seth, sorry, but this is a family deal, an' I already got plenty o' partners," Ben explained.

"Not a problem, as long as somebody else is payin' for this chow. What your brothers have done for me is all I need. An' I don't know if I'll ever be able ta pay 'em back."

"Well, if we go ta workin' the claims, we'll need a few extra pairs o' hands, an' I'll pay real good," Ben added.

"Nope, I'll pass. I'm a real lawman now, an' I reckon I'll just stay that way 'til I get planted, 'r get too old ta wear a star."

"Suit yourself, but the offer stands in case ya change your mind. Oh, an' breakfast is on me, Seth, so don't worry about that. Now then, what are you boys' plans for today?"

"Rest an' relax as much as possible, an' stay handy in case the DA needs ta talk to us. I need ta swing by the gunsmith, get my Colt worked over some. I'm thinkin' maybe he can file off the trigger throw some, so it takes less ta squeeze it. That an' I'm thinkin' on maybe a new Colt. I reckon this one's had too many rounds through it all ready," Zack stated.

"Yeah, I was thinkin' along the same lines as Zack. Even if we partner up with you minin', Ben, I reckon there'll still be a need for a good gun, an' ya never know when 'r where."

"Well, do what ya need ta do, an' let's meet back here for supper about five. I should have all the details by then, includin' the reports. Chenoa, reckon we might invite James ta join us?"

"Yes, that's a splendid idea. If those reports are honest, you will need to start laying in supplies for digging, depending on how many men you have to hire besides these two partners of yours. And James can be a wonderful source of information as well as mining knowledge when it comes time to start. Ben, I need to tell you that James is also interested in me, but I will not allow him to pursue that interest until this is all settled. And I mean settled as in your claims sold."

"Very well, that's good to know. I suppose we should go by ta see him yet this mornin', 'fore he makes other plans. Gents, we got a few things ta take care of this mornin' 'sides invitin' the lawyer ta join us, sa let's split up an' meet back here at five. I'll let François know we'll be in, an' ta save us another big table, now that I know he won't give me any guff."

186

As Ben walked to where François was standing, the boys and Seth escorted Chenoa to the lobby, where they all waited for Ben. After a few minutes, he joined them and they all strolled out the front door toward their respective conveyances.

"Creed, you mangy cur. Get your hands off'n my woman. In case that breed didn't tell ya, I own her, lock stock an' barrel."

"You must be Luke Weitz. The way I hear it, ya left her ta die, an' that's tells me ya give up any claim to her, not that anybody could claim her less'n she allowed it. An' she ain't allowin you."

"We'll see about that."

"Mister, that man there is Ben Creed, an' the three o' us are Yavapai County Deputies. Two of us are brothers o' his, so there ain't much chance o' you gettin' out o' this fix you've put yourself in," Zack did his best to help Ben diffuse the situation.

"Oh, just like I figured. Cowards, an' ya need ta be four ta one ta stand agin' me."

"Boys, walk off a bit, an' stay out o' this one. Take Chenoa with ya, an' don't let nothin' happen to her. I see five more like him standin' in several places, tryin' ta hide. Locate 'em, an' keep 'em covered, will ya?" Turning his full attention back to Weitz, Ben said, "Cowards? You were the one who tried ta cut up a woman, an' that tells me you're the real coward here. Too bad she didn't finish the job, but I hear tell she near got it done. An' the way I see it, the odds are six ta four in your favor. Ought ta be a real heyday for the undertaker, plantin' the six o' ya. 'Cept I'm tellin' your pals standin' back there that if they want ta live ta see the sun set today, they'd best stand clear an' not reach for them guns o' theirs."

Glancing quickly off to the side to make sure Chenoa and the boys were clear, and the three deputies were ready, Ben again put his full focus on Weitz. "Now then, you yellow belly woman beater, care ta try a man? Guns, knives, fists, your call. A fight ta the death, if ya please, coward.''

"Guns is fine with me, Creed, I hear you fancy yourself real fast. Well, we'll just see how fast ya really are." While Weitz was talking, he drew, even clearing leather before the first slug ripped through his heart, and a second shot entering in nearly the same spot. The only shot he got off drove into the street at his feet.

A second later, more shots rang out, as Zack and Todd each fired at Weitz' support, and another second later another shots as Seth took out a third man. The remaining two men who had stood with Weitz threw their hands in the air, wanting no part of the death raining down on the streets of Prescott at the hands of the Creed brothers, plus one.

Looking around, Ben first checked to ensure his brothers and Seth were still standing, and had not been hit, even though the only shots he had heard were his, the single shot fired by Weitz, and the shots Zack, Todd and Seth had fired. Next, he looked to Chenoa, making sure she was safe as well. She was, and was on the move toward Weitz' prone frame. He tried to reach her before she reached the corpse, but she was moving too fast.

As she got to Weitz, she started kicking his dead body, cursing in Paiute first, then French, and then a mixture of the two along with a few words Ben recognized as German. Once Ben finally reached her, wrapping his arms around her to hold her in place, she was reduced to sobs.

"Oh, Ben, I am so sorry it came to this. I hated that man so much, and was afraid he lived to torment me again. Now that's over, but I'm sorry you were forced to do it. And Seth and your brothers, all of you were in danger because of me. I feel so bad. Please, take me back to my room. I need to be alone for awhile."

"Yes, yes, of course. But it wasn't your fault, so no need for you ta feel bad. None at all. We're all safe an' sound, an' Weitz will never mistreat another woman, an' that's somethin' we can all be happy about. As to 'em others, I have no idea who they were, but I'm sure the city marshal will find out an' let us know. You didn't know any o' 'em, did ya?" Ben asked as he escorted Chenoa back into the hotel. He couldn't help but see the look of fear on François's face as they walked past.

"No, I don't think so. Then again, I didn't get a good look at any of them. I was too busy watching Weitz. I wanted to try to warn you that he tries to get the jump on his opponents, and that's how he started thinking he was fast with a gun. He met more than his match, but it was coming to him sooner or later. Please, take me upstairs."

Cherokee Parks

Chapter Twenty-One

"Ben, this is getting to be too frequent, even though I know this wasn't your choice. Still, this time I have four bodies, as opposed to just one the last time you were in town. The saving grace is that three Yavapai County deputies were involved as well, even though two of them are your brothers. I believe two of the dead men were wanted, maybe all four, as I can't be sure about Weitz and the other man. The two that didn't draw are suspects in a minor crime that happened here in town last month, but I can't put anything on them as yet. There will be some reward money coming on the others, and I'll let you know about them when I find out exactly whom they all are. The young lady, Chenoa, I believe her name is, is she all right?" City Marshal Jim Dodson inquired.

"I think she'll be fine, Jim. She's up in her room recomposin' herself. Weitz cut her up real bad an' left her ta die, but she did her best ta make sure he near died as well. Like I've said before, she gave as good 'r better'n what she got. Anyway, I found her near where I was camped out by my claims, hauled her in and doctored her as best I could. She got real strong real fast, an' 'fore I knew it she was takin' care o' my camp, cookin' an' all manner o' things. She's now a good friend an' business partner."

"Yes, I got most of that from Zack and Todd. Scuttlebutt has it that you have hit the big one, or two with two claims. Any truth to that?"

"Don't know just yet. I'll get the assay reports back this afternoon, an' I'll know then if the claims are really any good."

"Just so you know, Barriston is asking a lot of questions about your claims, and has sent one of his thugs to the County Clerk's Office for a copy of your filings. You'd better keep a close eye all around you no matter where you go from now on. I don't trust that snake Barriston any further than I could possibly throw that three hundred pound body of his. The claim jumping is all out in Sheriff Walker's domain, but I still hear things. Like you have been trailed, but lost your trackers somewhere out in the Bradshaw's."

"Yessir, I have. But now I got some Apache warriors helpin' ta keep 'em off my trail, though I don't suppose that'll last much longer if these claims are good. We'll end up doin' a lot o' work around 'em, an' haulin' ore in for processin'. Hard ta hide that kind o' movement, but by then it'll be near impossible ta jump my claims."

"Indeed. Ben, let's go over what happened one more time, just to be on the safe side, and then I'll let you go on about your business."

For the next several minutes, Ben recited the chain of events as they had happened once they stepped out onto the boardwalk in front of the hotel right up until Weitz and the others were lying dead in the street. Marshal Dodson stopped him several times to clarify something he said, and then allowed him to continue. Finally, Dodson said, "That's all I need for now, Ben. I assume you'll be around town for several more days, just in case I need to ask you something, or the city attorney has any questions. Say, is that Chenoa?"

Turning around, Ben saw Chenoa striding up to them, a sweet smile across her face, wearing a different dress with a matching hat, acting as though nothing had happened. "Jim, this is Chenoa. Chenoa, this is City Marshal Jim Dodson. We're just finishin' up here, if ya can give me a couple more minutes."

"Pleased to meet you, Chenoa. Ben, I've finished, so go on a about your affairs, and take good care of this lovely young lady. I must say, I now understand the buzz around town, especially among the women. Ah yes, jealousy is in full bloom in Prescott this year. Now then, I really must be going," Dodson finished, reaching out to shake Ben's hand before swiftly walking away to catch the coroner before he could get away.

"I see the boys an' Seth left all ready, sa we can go, 'r we can stay here at the hotel a bit longer if you want."

"No, I'm fine now. I guess I was just upset at seeing that worthless piece of humanity again, and as you said, he won't be beating or cutting up any more women where he's going. We really should get to James' office and invite him for tonight, and then could we have coffee, and maybe some pie at Renner's? I'd really like that."

"Sure, I wanted ta go see Jason today anyway. The lawyer it is, an' then coffee an' pie at Renner's, if Margarite has any. Ya know, she don't bake ever' day."

"Yes, I know that. But she told me she'd bake another apple pie this morning, just for us. Well, just for me is what she really said, but I'll be happy to share with you," Chenoa said teasingly.

"An' if my brothers show up, you won't have any choice but ta share with them, too."

"Oh, silly, you know I would. Now let's get a move on. Just talking about that pie is making me hungry, and it wasn't all that long ago we ate breakfast," Chenoa said as they reached the front of Murphy's Livery to find Clete waiting with a shiny black buggy with a single leather seat and a canvas cover, pulled by a beautiful sorrel mare with flaxen mane and tail, and three white socks, brushed out and glistening shiny in the sun.

"Oh, Salty, that is the most beautiful buggy I've ever seen. I will be honored to ride around Prescott in it with Ben," Chenoa gushed as Salty came walking out of the barn.

"Ma'am, that buggy is my pride an' joy, but it's gonna play second fiddle ta you ridin' in it. You don't know how many fellers have come by here wantin' ta know who ya are, where ya come from, an' if Ben's got a claim on ya. I swear, you can sure have your pick o' the litter 'round here. But I reckon that's how it'd be no matter where ya go," Salty said, beaming with pride.

"That ain' ta mention how many folks is startin' ta board here now. Barn's near full up, an' we added another dozen horses ta the corral. Hear tell Mack's business has picked up as well," Clete added.

"Well, that's real good, Salty. You an' Mack both run good stables, an' it's high time ya got ta see some return," Ben said as he and Chenoa climbed into the buggy. "We'll take good care o' this rig, an' bring it back every night we use it, so it gets stored inside. But for now, we need ta get movin'. Lots ta take care of yet 'fore we meet back here at the Congress at five. We'll likely drop it back off 'tween four an' four thirty, if not before. That all right?"

"Well, that was nice of him," Chenoa said as they climbed into the buggy and started for Whitaker's office.

Leaving Chenoa in the buggy, Ben squeezed in a few minutes with James, who gladly accepted the dinner invitation, and further cautioned Ben about getting into any more trouble. "Keep in mind, we haven't signed that agreement as yet, and if you need me to defend you on some charge or another it will cost you an excessive amount as your attorney of record," Whitaker said with a grin.

James, too, had heard that Barriston was inquiring about Ben's assay reports and had gotten copies of the claim filings, but he assured Ben that he had taken steps to guarantee no one could jump his claims, no matter their worth. Ben was beginning to see why Chenoa had recommended this young man, and was learning to trust him unlike any other attorney he had ever met or dealt with in the past.

"Not ta worry, James, not this time anyway. It was a case o' self-defense supported by three lawmen who were also involved. I can also tell ya that Chenoa is no longer in danger as a result o' Luke Weitz, 'r any from her past. That's part o' the reason I want her ta receive that five percent of the take, so she can buy her way ta wherever she wants ta be, an' be beholdin' to no man again."

"I want the same thing for her, Ben. She certainly deserves it, even though she has to deny part of her heritage for the time being. The problem with her is that she is so strong willed, and insists that she wants no part of any fortune you may create. In time, though, I think she will see the advantages independent wealth can give her, and accept it. Even if it is begrudgingly. Well, I have a lot of work to do, not only on your behalf but also for several other new clients, who, by the way, have come to me as a result of your becoming my client. Among those new clients is your friend Jason Renner and his wife."

"Really? Well, I hope your business continues ta grow, James, an' I know you will represent all fairly and honestly. We'll see you at five then, at the Congress, an' I should have the official reports in hand when we meet," Ben said, reaching out to shake the attorney's hand before turning to the door and excusing himself.

Climbing back into the buggy with Chenoa, he said, "Girl, I'm glad we got the buggy this mornin'. Lord knows it would o' looked strange ta have such a fine looking woman dressed so well riding in an old buckboard. An' I'll guarantee this buggy has much softer seats than that wooden one."

Chenoa only smiled and nodded in agreement, tied her flowery hat down tight and said, "Quickly then, driver, to Renner's and some of Margarite's world famous apple pie."

Ben laughed as he popped the reins to push the horse into a trot. A few minutes later, Ben pulled the buggy up in the half empty lot next to Renner's, as the entire front of the building was all ready full of horses tied to the rail and a pair of wagons sitting at angles. The lot where he parked was also filling up with wagons and buggies, and he had to wonder where they were going to sit if the café was that busy.

Inside, it was packed wall to wall, but Margarite spotted the couple as men and women alike stepped aside to allow them to walk toward the back. "Ben, Chenoa! Come on back ta your table. Wondered what took ya so long ta get here, then we heard ya had a spot o' trouble. You all right, Chenoa?"

"Yes, I'm fine, Margarite. Absolutely fine."

"Oh, ya ain't gonna ask about me?" Ben teased.

"Oh, I know you. No matter what gets throwed at ya, ya come out smellin' like a rose. I take it 'em brothers o' yours is fine as well."

"Yeah. S'prised they ain't been by here. They're haulin' Seth with 'em as well today, so they got three badges 'tween 'em now. Say, while I'm thinkin' about it, make sure they get whatever they want on me, just let me know how much I owe ya whenever I come in an' I'll settle up for 'em."

"You got it, Ben, "Jason replied. "Now, coffee an' some grub? Margarite's got a bunch o' pot roast cookin' back there. Been at it since long 'fore daylight. 'R she can toss on steaks for ya if that suits your fancy."

"That pot roast sounds wonderful to me. I assume you have lots of vegetables to go with it? And that you saved us some apple pie for dessert?"

"I sure did, Chenoa. Ben, same for you?"

"Yup, Margarite. Pot roast will sure do the trick, but let's get that coffee goin' first. Jason, ain't that your job?" Ben finished with a laugh.

"Yes, Jason Renner, do you expect me ta do it all 'round here?" Margarite joined Ben and the others in laughing. "Ben, it don't look like it time most folks get here ta eat, but if it weren't for that ol' man o' mine, I don't know what I'd do with this place. Now then, let me get your meals dished up an' brought out for ya," the half owner of the café said as she disappeared into the kitchen.

Jason poured their coffee, and then sat down with Ben and Chenoa. "Chenoa, like I told Ben, I'd heard a lot about that new lawyer in town, an' that he was a good one, but nobody was tryin' him out. But me an Margarite got some legal stuff that needed handled, an' I wasn't about ta hire Barriston, so we paid him a visit. We wasn't there ten minutes 'fore I hired him ta handle all our legal stuff. I figured he all ready saved me ten times over what he charged us."

"Yes, James is a very bright man, and with a brilliant legal mind. So many people turned away from him because he is half Yavapai, but he was in the top three in his class at the University of Richmond Law School, and was hired by Eagleston and Morriarity of Denver upon graduation. He worked there for only a year, and left when they refused to take on an Indian client, even though the case was eventually an easy win, and his first case and win. That's when he decided to come back home, here to Yavapai County where he was born."

"Well, my my. Quite a story, an' I'll wager there's a whole passel more ta that boy'n what we've all ready learned. All I know is, he's my lawyer from here on out. An' if anybody is ta ask, I'll tell 'em he's as good as they'll find anywhere." Margarite sat the plates down on the table in front of her guests, and Jason stood up at the same time. "I'll get ya some fresh coffee, then I got ta get around the room an' talk ta folks. Enjoy, an' hopefully I'll get ta chat with ya a bit more for ya leave," Jason finished as he moved out into the room, talking to first one table, and then the next.

A few minutes later, Margarite sat down with them, saying, "I need ta get off my feet for a bit. Hope ya don' mind. Aw, I know

197

ya don't. Say, Jason tell ya we hired that friend o' yours as our lawyer? Yeah, I know he did. Well, here's why. Business has been growin' steady, an' we need ta add on an figure out some new buggy an' wagon parkin'. That, an' we've decided to stay open two hours later, which means we got ta hire more help. This whole thing, buyin' that lot next door, dealin' with the town officials, an' everything else is more'n either one o' us wanted ta deal with on our own, let alone spend the time it takes ta do it."

"I reckon that's where a good lawyer really earns his pay, ain't it? An' like the two o' you, without us even havin' a formal agreement signed, I figure he's all ready saved me a bunch, an' helped me earn a bunch more."

"Ma'am, excuse me. I wanted ta stop by your table an' apologize again for my rudeness yesterday. Mama raised me better'n that, an' she had ta rolled over in her grave at the way I was actin'." It was the man who had insulted her in the café the day before, and had gotten taken down several pegs for the trouble. But this time he was clean and properly dressed instead of looking like a ragamuffin. "My name is Rufus Muldowney, but my friends call me Muley. Ma'am, if ya ever need anything, I don't care what it is, if I can take care o' it I'll do it, 'r do my level best. Sorry for intrudin', but I needed ta get said what I did."

"Why, thank you, Rufus. May I call you Muley? I really appreciate your coming to apologize to me without it looking forced. That means a great deal to me. And you can consider me a friend as a result of your politeness and honesty."

"Thankee, ma'am. Thankee," Rufus said as he carefully backed away, facing Chenoa but keeping a wary eye on Ben as he departed.

Before he had gotten four steps away, Ben called him back. "Muley, you workin'?"

"Not right now, Mr. Creed."

"How many o' your friends are good hands an' needin' work?"

Rubbing his freshly shaven chin, Rufus pondered for several seconds before answering. "I reckon there's maybe five, maybe six. Several o' 'em fellers got little ones, an' they is havin' a bad time."

Ben stood, reached into his pocket and pulled out six double eagles, and then extended his hand to Rufus. "Here, take these. Keep one for yourself, an' give the other five to 'em you're sure need the help. No promises, but if all works out well, we'll be needing a handful o' good, hard workin' men. But I will promise you this, if I hire you an' you cross me, well, let's just say you don't wanna do that. All right? Now, I should know something in the next three 'r four days, so come find me then, an' bring these friends with ya."

"Yessir, Mr. Creed! An' I guarantee ya won't be sorry! Not one little bit! Nosirree," Rufus said, nearly tripping as he backed up and bowed simultaneously, finally turning and striding outside and out of sight.

"That was very nice of you, Ben. And I do believe you just made another friend for life," Chenoa quipped.

"I believe you may be right. An' you have another guardian who would die 'fore they'd see any harm come to ya."

Chenoa blushed, dropped her head low for a moment, and then looked directly into Ben's eyes. "You mean like how I would die before I saw any harm come to you? And I'm sure all your friends and family feel the same way about you."

"No, I mean like the way I'd die 'fore I saw anything bad happen ta you, partner. You ready for some o' that pie?" Ben changed the subject before either of them said anything they'd regret.

Cherokee Parks

Chapter Twenty-Two

After a few stops to let Chenoa pick up a few more items of clothing and some personal things, as well as Ben buying a new hat and stopping to order several new packsaddles, anticipating the need for them to haul ore, they swung past the assay office to pick up the reports. When Chenoa started to climb down, Ben insisted she not. "I've got ta have a few words with the assayer, an' I won't be able ta say the things I need ta say if you're there."

Chenoa nodded her understanding, and settled back on the seat to wait as Ben climbed down. Inside, it took a couple of minutes before Mike came back to the front to greet Ben.

"Ben, you're just a tad early, but I should have the reports finished in the next couple of minutes."

"Mike, I appreciate you gettin' 'em done so fast, an' I appreciate ya not lettin' folks like Barriston know what they say 'fore I do. There's no doubt where the claims are, 'r at least the general vicinity, since they're public record now. I figure Barriston has all ready sent off some men ta check the filings for the exact location, but I reckon they'll meet up with a big surprise if they get too close. I also figure 'tween Barriston an' Meador an' those he owns in the minin' business are all ready tryin' ta figure a way ta shanghai me an' steal my claims. I want ta make sure ya ain't connected to 'em, 'r feedin 'em information."

"Ben, I want nothing to do with those scoundrels, or how they do business."

"Fine, I'll take your word for it, for now, Mike. Now then, my reports, if you please."

"All right, just give me a minute or two to bring them up," Mike said as he turned and then walked behind the curtain serving as a door to the back room. A moment later, he returned, handing the reports to Ben.

"Well, well, well. Looks like I was right. The dust comes out at one ninety-nine percent pure, an' the nuggets at ninety-seven percent pure. That ought to make the veins at least sixty percent 'r close to it. Add in the nine present copper an' five percent lead, an' it ought ta pay real well. I see ya did two reports on the silver. Why?"

"I broke the two rocks up separately and assayed them that way. As you can see, they are very close to being the same."

"Yup, one's seventy-two percent silver an' the other is seventy percent, an' both contained roughly eight percent copper an' six percent lead, two percent gold, an' whatever these other mineral are. So the veins I took 'em from ought ta run close, if we can get the ore out fairly clean. Let me fill ya in on a few more things, Mike. If Barriston sent any more critters out ta try ta find me, they'll likely end up like Weitz. He got paid ta track me, but he lost me 'cause he was countin' on Chenoa ta lead him to me an' she was havin' none of it. He tried ta kill her, an' she like ta done him in while he was at her. I don't even have ta be there ta know my claims are nice an' safe, an' most anybody that gets too close will be stayin' there. Ya see, the Apache are guardin' my camp an' claims, an' they'll make sure anybody who gets close will disappear."

"Sounds like you're pretty sure you'll get to work your claims without interference, Ben. I know that several of the really good claims I've assayed over the last two years have ended up belonging to Barriston, or Meador behind the scenes. But I have no proof of any wrongdoings."

"Mike, do you make a good livin' here?"

"I have been since I came here."

"Look, we're all meetin' at the Congress at five ta have dinner.

Me, Chenoa, my brothers an' Whitaker, my attorney. I'd like for ya ta join us."

"I'd love to join you, Ben, I surely would. I'll close down a bit early and be there by five or shortly after."

"Good. There's a few more tings I want ya to know, an' I want ta help ya grow this little business o' yours, 'cause there's a few people that don't fully trust ya. Some think ya pass off information ta Barriston, an' I want ta make sure they know ya don't. There's even talk o' bringin' in another assayer as soon as he finishes his schoolin', but I ain't sure there's enough business ta support two o' ya. Well, I'll see ya at five," Ben said shaking Mike's hand, and then turning for the door.

"Ben, before you go, let me tell you what I know of Barriston. Yes, he has sent his thugs by here threatening me several times, including this morning asking about your claims, but I have always resisted, trying to ignore his threats as much as possible. I lost my wife just over three years ago, and came here to get away from Meador in Phoenix, where he was putting pressure on me to do the same thing Barriston wants me to do here, divulge assay information. Ben, my children are still in Phoenix, living with my sister-in-law. Normally, they come up here every summer, but this year they're going to summer school to try to get a leg up on their schooling. You see they attend a private school, the one where my wife's sister teaches. That's the only way I could possibly afford for them to attend, but Meador and Barriston both know where they live and attend classes, and have sent me veiled threats regarding their safety, so anything I can do to take them down will suit me just fine," Mike gave his lengthy explanation.

"Good, glad ta see you got an idea where I'm headin' by invitin' ya ta dinner. I won't give up anything that's rightfully mine without a fight, an' I always come out on top," Ben declared.

"Ben, there's plenty of work, and likely to be a lot more for a good assayer's office. In fact, if it continues to improve, I'd be glad to hire a good man to assist me."

"Make sure ya let Whitaker an' Chenoa hear ya say that tonight over dinner, all right? Now, I got ta get movin'," Ben said as he walked to the door and stepped through it.

Outside, he crawled into the buggy, picked up the whip and snapped it over the mare's ears urging her into motion. Not looking at Chenoa during the first block, she finally punched him in the side. "Well, how do the reports look, silly man?"

"Oh, they look just like assay reports, nice an' neat, tellin' how much o' this an' how much o' that."

"Ben Creed, you'd better stop playing around and tell me what they say!"

"Naw, I'm gonna wait 'til dinner, an' let everybody find out at the same time. Oh, an' I invited Mike ta come along. We're gonna use him ta turn the tables on Barriston an' his whole outfit."

"Can we trust him?"

"I think so. He don't like bein' threatened by Barriston or Meador either one. An' apparently they been layin' on the threats every chance they get."

"Are you sure you don't want to let me see those reports, or at least tell me what they say, before dinner? After all, I did help you, didn't I."

"Yeah, ya sure did, Chenoa. Let me just say they're real good reports, an' you'll all be real happy ta hear and see 'em. But I'm still gonna make ya wait," Ben said with a big grin.

Chenoa sat back with a huff, and then started laughing. "Oh, all right then. As long as I know the reports were good ones. Now then, if I might ask, where are you going to get the money to hire more help, besides your brothers if they do decide to throw in with

205

you? And all the supplies, like the packsaddles you just ordered, or the mules or burros to put them on?"

"Let's just say I'm a member in good standing with the Bank o' Prescott, an' since my brothers will work for a part o' the claims they'll get their take when we process the ore. Just like you, James an' I will get ours at the end. Oh, an' I'm gonna keep your room at the Congress so you'll have a place to stay anytime ya come ta town while we're workin' the claims. I figure we need ta work the gold first, since it seems ta be easier ta collect, an' then we can use those monies ta finance the diggin' o' the silver as well as the gold. In the meantime, I got plenty ta pay for all the supplies an' hire any men we might need, includin' our new friend Muley."

"Well, aren't you just full of surprises. I suppose your complete plans will be discussed tonight over dinner?"

"That's the plan, all right. But there's a lot more to it, includin' how ta trap Barriston an' Meador, but I ain't got that all worked out in my head yet I may have ta hold off on that for a day 'r so. Any more stops we need ta make 'fore we head ta Salty's?"

"Just one, Ben. I ordered some new shoes and another new dress from Madge. It will be perfect for tonight. I hope you don't mind, but remember you said whatever I wanted you'd pay for."

"Yes, of course," Ben said as he turned the buggy toward the downtown area and Mrs. Devereaux's. It took nearly twenty minutes for them to get away from Madge, who insisted on showing Chenoa some new goods, even though they repeatedly told her they were going to be later for dinner, and that Chenoa wouldn't have enough time to change if they didn't leave immediately.

It was nearly four-thirty when they pulled the buggy up in front of the hotel. Clete came trotting across the street to retrieve the buggy while the bellboy was quickly grabbing the boxes out of the small bed box behind the seat. Following Chenoa inside and up the stairs to her room, she left Ben behind to handle the rest. Ben just smiled, grabbed his few things and headed inside, stopping just long enough to let François know there would be six at their table instead of five.

"Monsieur Creed, I feel I should let you know that the only wait staff I could free up to take care of your table is Mitzi. I sincerely hope that isn't going to be a problem, seeing as how close you and Madam Chenoa are."

"I don't see any problem, François. First of all, Chenoa an' me are just very close friends an' business partners. There is nothin' romantic 'tween us." Ben hoped he didn't put François off with his gruff tone, but he was getting tired of explaining the relationship between he and Chenoa. "'Sides, my younger brothers will be here, an' Mitzi can flirt with 'em all she wants. But if you would be so kind, please let Mitzi know this is gonna be a very serious business meetin', an' ta stay away from the table 'cept when she comes to bring the food 'r fresh coffee less'n we motion for her. I don't really care ta have any big ears nearby as we talk about certain things, an' not just hers, if ya know what I mean."

"Oui, I understand completely, Monsieur. I still have time to move your table back away from the others even more, and even to relocate a few of the other tables and chairs to the storage room. It doesn't appear we will require them this evening, as I do not anticipate it being busy. Do not worry, Monsieur Creed, I will make your meeting as discreet and secure as possible for a hotel dining room. Please excuse me while I make the preparations..." François said as he scurried away.

Ben couldn't help but smile at the difference in the way the maître d' treated him now that Chenoa had trimmed his ears. Though keeping his room at the hotel during his absences as well as his spreading money around had to begin to have some effect as well. Realizing that he was about out of time, Ben took the stairs two at a time, turned down the hall and trotted to his room. Inside, he quickly changed, doffing his new hat and then checking himself in the mirror. *Yup, this new hat sure looks better on me than that Derby I been wearin' in town.*

Satisfied with his look, Ben stepped into the hallway just in time to see Chenoa also leaving her room. Offering his arm, she gladly took it, as the new heels she was wearing left her just a bit off balance while she adjusted her walk to fit the shoes. At the bottom of the stairs, everyone in the lobby turned to stare at the couple, the women jealous of the way Chenoa looked, and the men jealous of Ben having such a beautiful woman on his arm.

At the entry to the dining room, François met them with a more than gracious smile and deep bow. "Monsieur, Mademoiselle, welcome to the dining area of the Congress Hotel. Your table is ready and waiting for you. Will your guests be arriving soon?"

"They should be arriving at any moment, François. And thank you for your graciousness. It is a pleasure to dine with you again."

"Ben, there ya are," called out Zack.

As Ben turned to look, he couldn't believe how his brothers were dressed. Both were wearing suits similar to his, and wearing new hats also similar to his. "Boys, glad ya could make it. We're expectin' two more ta join us, but we might as well take a seat an' get started with some coffee."

"Are we late, Ben?" James Whitaker asked as he entered the hotel lobby from the street accompanied by Mike Hutchison. "I ran into Mike outside, and we introduced ourselves."

"No, you're right on time. Shall we?" Ben nodded to François, who led them to their table.

"Will this arrangement be suitable, Monsieur Creed?"

"Perfect, François. Just right. Thank you," Ben said slipping

François a gold double eagle and winking at him.

The Frenchman's face nearly split in two from the huge smile. "Monsieur Creed, please alert me to anything that you might need. I am at your service," François said with a bow nearly to the floor, before he made his way back to his stand at the dining room door.

Introductions were finished before they all sat down, but once they were all seated Mitzi arrived with two fresh pots of coffee. Ben half expected her to pout, or at least try to sneak a wink or two, but she maintained a professional appearance and attitude. Carefully pouring each a cup of coffee, she asked, "Will there be anything else at the moment?"

"No, thank you, young lady. And may I compliment you on your service. Too many are careless when pouring coffee, but you did so with perfection," Chenoa said with a disarming smile.

Mitzi curtsied and nodded, and then left the table without saying a word, though Ben could see a look of confusion on her face. Apparently she didn't think she would like Chenoa, but she had been totally disarmed with just a kind word.

"Gents, what say we order before we start talkin' over the reason why we're all here? Maybe we ought ta finish eatin' 'fore we light up the conversation…"

"Ben, let's order first, and then look over the reports. As I understand it, only Mike, you and Chenoa have seen them," James offered.

"James, he wouldn't even let me see them, so I'll be as surprised or disappointed as the rest of you."

James laughed, but knew better than to say anything. To save him, Ben asked, "You all know what you want ta order, 'r do ya need more time ta look at the menus?"

Laying their menus aside, the general consensus was that they were all ready, so Ben motioned for Mitzi to approach. Quietly, she not only took their orders, but made some recommendations for a few meal add-ons. Once she had the final order, Ben's, she asked, "Would anyone like more coffee before I turn your orders in?"

Making it around the table, she refilled every cup perfectly once again, placed the pot down, curtsied again, and then headed for the kitchen.

Chapter Twenty-Three

Ben cautioned his tablemates not to show any unnecessary reaction to the reports, as he didn't want anyone to know just how valuable his claims were outside of those seated with him. As the four reports were passed around, it was obvious that the others had to work to contain their excitement. Especially his brothers, and Chenoa, who almost choked on her coffee when she looked at the gold reports. Whitaker, being a lawyer, had practiced a look of non-expression all during his schooling and while practicing in Denver, and now had it down perfectly.

"Ben, I must say, these are even more impressive than what I expected, even after your glowing words yesterday. That said, we'll need to meet first thing in the morning to finalize our agreement, as well as lay out the shares for your partners.

"Damn, Ben. Am I seein' this right?"

"Yes, Todd, there ain't a thing wrong with your eyes. My question is, are ya ready ta turn in your badges an' start minin'?"

The two younger Creed brothers looked at each other, and then Zack gave Ben his answer. "You're damned straight we are. We just need ta give Sheriff Walker notice. Can't just up an' quit him."

"Oh, I don't think Jeff will object any, an' likely let ya go pronto."

"Well, we got this case with the rustlers we'll have ta testify on, but after that we should be good ta go." Todd said.

"Fellers, ya can always come back ta town ta testify. I plan on pullin' out in a week, an' I want ya ta ride out with me. I seriously don't think Jeff will object at all."

"There somethin' ya ain't tellin us? Like ya already talked to

211

him?" Zack asked.

"Yeah, I did, an' all ya got ta do is let him know you're all done with bein' deputies. In fact, he said he's thinkin' about hangin' it up himself, but don't let him know I told ya that."

"Well, then I guess you'll have our good comp'ny, as long as Chenoa is doin' the cookin'. We've both ate enough o' our own cookin, an' plenty o' yours as well, so if she ain't doin' the cookin' ya'd best be for bringin' along a camp cook. An' I mean somebody that really knows how ta cook," Todd said with a chuckle.

"I reckon ya'd best be for askin' her, 'cause it's all up ta her."

"Oh, of course I'll do the cooking, as long as you three clean up afterwards. Is that a deal?"

"Deal!" the Creed brothers all agreed simultaneously, followed by a laugh.

Mitzi hesitated to approach the table, balancing several heavy plates on her arms, until Chenoa saw her predicament and motioned for her to bring their meals. Nearly all conversation stopped until after all the plates were served and a fresh pot of coffee was placed on the table. Accordingly, Mitzi once again made herself scarce after making sure each person at the table had what they needed.

It was several minutes before any sign of conversation started again, the diners thoroughly enjoying their food. Finally, Mike started it rolling again by saying how happy he was to be working with such fine people, and stating that by the end of the summer he was going to need to hire an assistant. Turning to James, he said, "I understand you might know of someone who might be interested in coming to Prescott to work, is that correct?"

"Why, yes, that's correct. He is a young black man, and a very hard worker just as honest as the day is long. Are you certain that you will have an adequate amount of work to be able to support an assistant?"

"Yes, I'm nearly there now, and I'm certain that once more miners find out they can get a fair and honest report here, something they never get in Wickenburg, my business should pick up even more."

"Very well then, let me know when you're ready, and I'll let you know when Samuel has finished his schooling and testing. Let me also tell you that I had my own misgivings about you until I saw these reports and see that Ben invited you to this dinner. But now, I can wholeheartedly give you my support, and feel safe in sending you any of my new clients. Chenoa, don't you agree?"

"Yes, I do. I hear truth in his words and see it in his eyes. He will always do his best to take care of any who cross his path. We must help him make certain his family is also safe, James, Ben."

"Yes, ma'am. I'm workin' on a plan ta do just that. After we meet with James in the mornin' I should have it all worked out. 'R at least by noon anyway, after I talk ta the sheriff an' City Marshal Dodson. Got ta keep it all real legal like, right James?"

"Indeed. Just let me know how I can be of assistance."

"Good. Mike, I want ya to know you'll be handsomely rewarded for your help in takin' down that pond scum, one way 'r tother, an' if I have ta guard your kids myself then that's what I'll do. Now then, so far here's how the split goes down, if I've done my math right. Chenoa, you get five percent of all the profit and proceeds from the claims, James you're gettin' one percent, Todd, Zack, ya each get twenty-one an' a half percent, includin' from the sale. Now, that ain't all. I want the boys ta file claims on each side o' my two claims. James, ya handle that for 'em, make sure they do it all right. Now, I can't speak for Chenoa 'r James either one, an' I can't say there'll be any valuable ore there, but if there is I'm gonna want twenty-one an' a half percent o' whatever ya strike there. An' when I sell out, an' ya got ta know I will, I want all the claims ta sell as one unit on the gold an' one on the silver. If they do, then I'll want forty-nine percent o' the sellin' price. Once the claims are sold, all other partnership agreements cease ta exist. Agreed?"

"Fine by me, big brother," Zack replied.

"Same here," Todd chimed in.

"And for me as well, considering I didn't really want any part of it in the first place," Chenoa added.

"I am in agreement as well, as I fully intend to try representing the buyer after the sale is consummated, unless they already have legal representation, as most large mining firms do."

"Good, now that's settled, the next thing we need ta talk about is where ta get the ore smelted an' processed. James, that's on your shoulders. I just want to make certain we get a fair shake, an' not a penny of it goes ta Meador or Barriston. Which pretty much rules out Wickenburg, right?"

"Absolutely, although choices are thin from your claim location. I believe Meador has his fingers in the Crown King smelter, but even if he doesn't the chances of getting them to take on yet another mine might be difficult at best. They are running twenty-four hours a day now. I wouldn't rule them out since they're roughly five mines away, but still… Now then, the next closest would have to be Mayer, which does a really good job for such a small smelter, especially for silver, primarily because of the large stamp mill they have installed. They're about a dozen miles away, and currently only have three small operations they process for, so they'd be a good bet. The rest are getting too far out to be wise choices, from twenty to some forty miles out," James explained.

"Well, sounds ta me like you're gonna be makin' a trip ta Mayer real soon, an' if it all works out you'll be down there real regular like, an' ya might even be haulin' Mike along on occasion," Ben laughed.

"All right, brother, so ya got it figured out how ta haul the ore? There ain't hardly no water up where I think you've got the claims, an' damned few trails an' fewer roads. An' what about timbers?"

"Good questions, Todd. I figure ta buy a dozen mules an' packsaddles for 'em. That ought a handle the haulin' initially, dependin' on if we can get an agreement with the smelter at Mayer. We don't really need any water since, for the most part, there's a little pond that was created by a heavy rain, the one that exposed the source of the alluvial spread downhill. For starters, we can pan a lot of gold, an' there's nuggets scattered all down that slope. That'll keep us plenty busy for a couple o' weeks for sure. Then we can start chipping away at the vein an' go in a ways without havin' ta use any timbers. We need to do some work on the silver claim ta show improvements on it so we don't lose that claim ta some technicality, but for now we'll concentrate on the gold. It'll bring in a lot more money an' help ta finance the rest."

"Well, that sounds good for now, but what about when we do need timbers?" Zack commented.

"I figure ta hire a dozen lumberjacks, 'r more, that ain't afraid ta use saws and adz ta hew out timbers, an' only pick out the best trees, not just clear off trees for the sake o clearin' trees. When it comes ta movin' the timbers, we can use the mules there as well. An' once we have the timbers we need, we can use the lumberjacks that want ta stay on as miners, an' replace them that decide ta leave."

"How long ya figure ta be out on the first trip?"

"Three ta four weeks, 'til we have enough ore ta pack out on a dozen mules, dependin' on where we have ta go. We can leave camp an' the claims for a week at a time if need be, an' if we take care o' the Yavapai an' Apaches they'll keep anybody from tryin' to jump in and steal 'em in our absence. Chenoa, tell the boys what that cost is, 'cause they won't believe me."

After laughing for a moment, she took a sip of coffee, and then looked around the table before answering. "Several pounds of red rock candy, half cherry and half cinnamon, and several pounds of tobacco. I priced them today, and the total cost will be, if we can afford it, is around twenty dollars."

"That's it? That's all? Ben, what else did ya promise? There's got ta be more'n that," Zack said shaking his head. "Ya sure ya didn't offer Chenoa up as a squaw ta one o' the chiefs?"

"I'll have you know that I will choose my next man, and no one else will do any picking for me. NEVER again will that happen to me!"

"Sorry, Chenoa. I didn't mean ta offend ya," Zack apologized, realizing he had just jeopardized any possibility of a close relationship of any kind with the Paiute woman.

"Oh, I know, Zack. I know you were just teasing, and I'm sorry for blowing up like that. You couldn't possibly know what I've been through. Tell you what, one of these days I'll sit with you and Todd and fill you in. How's that?"

"Yes, ma'am. That'd be good," Zack replied, breathing a sigh of relief at escaping this beautiful woman's wrath.

"Well, I figured on buyin' about twenty pounds worth of each, candy an' tobacco. Give 'em a real treat. Think that'll work?" Ben laughed, joined quickly by Chenoa, who added, "That and give them lots of tummy aches, and maybe a few toothaches. They might not be thanking you after a few weeks!"

"Well, I guess we'll just have ta deal with that when it happens," Ben stated, suddenly kind of saddened by the prospect of creating rotting teeth. That was one of the things his mother had always kept after her children about, keeping their teeth clean and not eating too many sweets. To his knowledge, it had worked on all of them, as, even though they all loved pastries, they rarely overdid it with anything else sweet. "James, let's get back ta business for a bit, shall we? What do ya think the smelter will charge to smelt all out ore?"

"Well, that's hard to say. Often, smelters will give a better price if the loads are considerable in size, as they can process a larger amount without having to reset or spend time cleaning out the melting vats between different mines. That's why the mining corporations try to buy up as many mines in close proximity as they can, to reduce both mining and smelting costs, and if they can develop enough ore they simply buy out the local smelter or build their own. Also, the processes are far different for gold and silver, and many times the cost is on a sliding scale depending on just how rich the ore is. Some try to gouge clients by charging extra if there is a large amount of copper or lead mixed in the ore, and even try to lower the grade of gold or silver by calling it dirty ore. So, what is my answer? Well, Mike and I will have to take the assay reports along with as many samples as you can provide us along on our trip to Mayer, and let them gauge the costs from there. And you can trust us to negotiate the best possible price we can get, but to do so we'll need to get an estimate on the amount of ore you'll be taking in, and how often you deliver it. One thing you might also want to consider is stockpiling your ore with the smelter until you have enough to make it worth their while to run your product."

"Can we trust 'em ta keep our ore separate, an' not slip some away for their own use from time ta time?"

"The quick answer is, no, but a way around that is to post a guard on their site to keep a close eye on your ore. Yes, that would be an additional cost, but unless you can deliver at least forty tons a month of ore that cost would be saved by processing the larger amounts of tonnage. Keep in mind that the smelters use the troy

217

ounce and pound to weigh ore, so a ton avoirdupois is actually closer to two thousand four hundred thirty troy pounds, and forty ton Troy is really closer to thirty-three ton avoirdupois."

"Avera... what?"

"Avoirdupois. What we use as the standard rate of weight measurement, Ben," Chenoa said quietly.

"Oh, well I knew there was a difference, I just never heard it called out by name, I guess. Sounds like ta me we'll need ta hire a guard then, since the three of us can't pull that much ore in a month o' Sunday's. I figured if we could load twelve mules with a eight hundred pound load each, that'd be near ta five ton in four weeks. How many Troy pounds would that be, you mathematic whizzes?"

"Close to twelve thousand one hundred fifty, give or take a pound," James answered. "That sound right, Mike?"

"Right on the button, James. Say, where'd you learn all that? I thought only assayers and other people in the mining trade knew those things."

"Besides law, I studied mining, as I considered taking a job for a coal mining company back east. That was before I received the offer from the firm in Denver, and decided I needed to live in the West, not the East."

"Will wonders never cease," Ben said. "Chenoa, this lawyer friend o' yours just continues ta impress me. James, sure glad you're on our side in this deal. Ain't you, boys?"

"Well, now if he can also use a Colt 'r a Winchester with any accuracy, 'r set a good horse, I'd say he's a real bargain an' a man we can count on."

"Zack, keep in mind that I am half Yavapai, so setting a good horse is second nature to me. My father also taught me how to shoot, not necessarily as fast as your reputations indicate, but quite accurately, and with any number of weapons. Add in knife work, and I believe I can ride with the best."

"Confident, too, ain't ya? Yessir, Ben, I reckon he'll do ta ride the river with," Zack said, reaching out to shake James' hand. "That makes us a pretty formidable crew, I'd say. We just need ta make sure anybody else we bring on will stand hard an' loyal. We won't have room for 'em that'll cut an' run at the first sign o' trouble."

"I got some men in mind already, Zack, but if ya happen ta know of any, have a chat with 'em 'fore we leave town."

Cherokee Parks

Chapter Twenty-Four

Over the next half hour, and dessert, the conversation drifted from one topic to another, but nothing of great importance was discussed. Finally, Ben called the meeting concluded, and suggested they all get a good night's rest as there would be much to do the next several days.

"Yes, and Ben, let's start by you, Chenoa and I meeting at eight o'clock in my office. I'll go in early and complete our agreement, and have it ready for you to look over and sign. The document detailing how the shares are to be split, I can do over the next couple of days and make copies for all those involved. Mike, I'll have my buggy readied and swing by your office after I finish with Ben and Chenoa. With any luck, we can be in Mayer shortly after lunch, meet with the smelter ownership, work out a deal and be back not long after dark."

"James, I'm going to call you on your abilities with a horse. I think we can make better time in the saddle than we can in a buggy."

"Yes, I agree, however it is far more professional looking, especially with all the paperwork I'll be carrying, for us to appear in a buggy. But trust me, I have a good, stout buggy and a fine buggy horse. Not to mention that the ride will be far softer and simpler than in a saddle, Mike. Some another time, I'll accept your horseback challenge, except I won't need a saddle to outride you," James Whitaker finished with a hearty laugh.

"Well, all right then, James. I'll see you in the morning. Who knows, maybe I can even drum up some business while I'm there with you."

"As might I, good sire. Chenoa, gentlemen, here's a last toast to good fortune and a successful enterprise, as well as to good friends. May all things work to our advantage, and may all our hopes and dreams be fulfilled," James closed, lifting his glass high.

With that, they all accepted the toast graciously, and began to file away for their separate accommodations. Ben stopped to pay the tab with François, after leaving an eagle and a double eagle on the table for Mitzi, who had been the most professional he had ever seen her as a waitress.

Walking to the maître d', he said, "François, that was very well done, an' I want ya ta know how much I appreciate all ya done ta make it so." Looking at the handwritten tab, Ben added another thirty dollars to it and gave that amount to the Frenchman, putting another big smile on the man's face.

"Why, thank you, Monsieur Creed. I must apologize for the way I've treated you in the past. I considered you to be a ruffian and a trouble maker, but you are, indeed, a true gentleman."

"Well, François, I wasn't always the kindest ta you, so let's just call it even an' leave it at that, shall we?" Ben said, reaching out to shake hands.

François replied, "Consider it done, my friend. Anytime you need anything while here at the hotel, please feel free to ask me. I will do all I can to accommodate you, and any of your guests."

"I'll do it. Now, if you'll excuse me, I need ta get Chenoa upstairs, an' I need ta hit the sack. Got a lot ta handle in the next few days, an' tomorrow is all jammed up all ready." Smiling at the maître d', Ben turned to extend his arm to Chenoa, who quickly latched on and allowed herself to be led through the lobby and up the stairs, and then down the hallway to her room.

"Ben, thank you for getting everyone together. I felt there was more that could have been discussed, but there was still so much that we talked about. What didn't get discussed wasn't all that important, and can be covered individually over the next few days before we leave town. One thing, when it comes time for a guard, are you considering Muley?"

"Yes, ma'am, I am. An' I might use Muley an' his pals as lumberjacks, an' I reckon that's somethin' they can handle as well as work in the mines later on. Hungry men treated right will work hard, do whatever they're asked ta do, includin' fight for the boss if need be. An' they just may need ta fight for us if things don't go the way I hope when it comes ta Meador an' Barriston. Now then, I'm whupped, an' need some sleep. We can talk more on this stuff tomorrow. G'night, Chenoa. Sleep well."

Inside his own room, Ben quickly undressed and flopped down on the bed, expecting to be sound asleep in minutes, but sleep just didn't come right away. Instead, he went over the entire meeting in his mind, wondering what it was that Chenoa wished they had talked about. He fell asleep finally, still working things over in his mind.

***

As the sun slipped in through the window, it found Ben all ready up and dressed, still fussing over what it was Chenoa thought they should have covered. Then, after several more minutes of contemplation, he finally gave up and decided to just let her speak her mind when she felt like it, and he'd go with the flow of it.

Quietly slipping out of his room, he started down the hallway on his way to the restaurant for coffee. "Ben, give me time to put on my hat and I'll join you for coffee. I'm still full from last night, believe it or not, and coffee is all I need this morning."

As Chenoa closed her door, Ben stood in the hall smiling at the resilience of this young woman. She managed to not only stay with him throughout everything, but had even outlasted him more than he'd ever admit to anyone else. As he stood looking at the walls, he failed to hear her close her door or approach him, and was startled when she took his arm. "Shall we, Ben?"

Thirty minutes later, they were standing on the boardwalk in front of the hotel, waiting on Clete to bring the buggy across after waving at him from the doorway as the stepped outside. "Mornin' Ms. Chenoa, Mister Ben."

"Good morning, and please just call me Chenoa. The Ms. is just too formal for an exchange between good friends, don't you think?"

"Yes, ma'am," Clete replied with a big grin. "Have a fine day now, hear?" he said as he turned and trotted across the street and back to the livery stable.

"We got some time 'fore we need ta be at James' office. Any ideas?"

"Yes, who are you planning on purchasing the mules from?"

"Salty. Why?"

"Maybe it might be a good idea to have him start looking now, today, instead of waiting any longer."

"Well I had planned on talkin' to him after we meet with James. Startin' ta deal with Salty always seems ta take longer than I ever plan, so I wanted ta make sure I did it with some time ta spare."

"I think I can handle that for you. What say we take the buggy over, and stay seated while we deal with him?"

Ben nodded, helped Chenoa climb into the buggy seat, and then hoisted himself up to sit beside her. Swinging the buggy around, he waited for a wagon to go by, and then swung to a stop in from of Salty's double barn door.

"Somethin' wrong, Ben?" Salty said as he stepped outside.

"Not a thing, so far, Salty."

"Salty, we have a small problem that only you can help us with. Have you got a moment?"

"Sure, Chenoa. What can I do for ya?"

"We are going to need a dozen big, healthy, strong, well trained mules, each as close to the same size and conformation as the others. And we're going to need to look them over before we buy them, at a fair price by the way. Oh, and the real problem is, we'll need them in five or six days at the very latest. Can you help us out?"

Salty pushed his hat back on his head, revealing a healthy head of red hair. "Pretty tall order, Chenoa. Pretty tall. But I think there's a feller out in Chino Valley with a bunch o' mules he might sell, but I ain't sure they won't be a pile o' money. I'll see what I can do for ya. Can ya check back with me day after tomorrow an' see how I'm doin?"

"Yes, of course. And I hope you don't let me down, or I just don't know what we'll do. Ben, we'd better move it or we're going to be late for our meeting. Salty, thank you. I know you'll get it done for us," Chenoa closed the conversation, turning to face forward in the buggy indicating for Ben to get moving.

Down the street and around the corner, Ben pulled up to a stop. "That was as slick as I've seen of late, young lady. Aren't you near ashamed o' yourself, the way ya done Salty after he's been sa good to us?"

"Oh, nonsense. He knows what it's like to deal with a woman with a strong mind, and he also knows he'll make money on the deal. Maybe not as much as he would in dealing with you, but still a goodly sum. It that why you stopped here? To admonish me for starting a business deal?"

"Yeah, I reckon that was a big mistake. Lord a mercy, lady, remind me ta never get in your way on anything ever again," Ben said with a chuckle. "Why, it just ain't healthy."

"Oh, Ben, you're making fun of me again. Aren't you?"

225

"Well, yes an' no. Let's just say I think I'll let you do all the bargainin' from now on. You're one tough cookie, that's for sure, an' I reckon you're right. You'll get a better deal from Salty than I ever could, an' all 'cause you're a woman, an' one he knows he can't take advantage of, not that he would take advantage of any woman in the first place."

"Fine, I don't mind at all. Now, we'd better get a move on if we are going to be at James' office on time. Have you got your plan all worked out on how to do Meador and Barriston in?"

"Not yet. I need ta talk ta a couple more folks 'fore I can do that. Figured we'd pay each o' them a visit after we seen James," Ben said as he clucked the buggy horse forward. Several minutes later, they were in front of James Whitaker's office, ready for their quick meeting with him.

Twenty minutes later, Ben had reviewed and signed the agreement with James, starting the lawyer's official handling of all things legal for Ben and his brothers as well as Chenoa. From there, they stopped to see Jim Dodson, who had just arrived in his office at city hall.

"Good morning, beautiful lady. Who's this galoot you're stuck with?"

"Good morning, Marshal Dodson. This man? He came with the horse and buggy. Not much else I could do, is there?"

"All right, you two. Jim, ya got a few minutes?"

"Sure, Ben, what can I do for you?"

"In private, if ya don't mind, Jim." Sitting in Dodson's office, Ben told him what was on his mind. "Jim, I've just gotten my assay reports, an' it looks like we got us a really good find. I've hired James Whitaker ta handle all the legal on it, an' I'll wager Barriston has all ready sent men out ta try to jump the claims while I'm still here in town. Barriston is an arm o' Meador out o'

Phoenix, an' word has it they've stolen several of the better claims of late."

"Yes, I've heard most of that all ready, but what can I do to help you take them down?"

"Keep an eye on Mike Hutchison an' his office, as well as James Whitaker an' his office, just in case. Meador, through Barriston, has made threats ta Mike, even threatening harm ta his family, an' I see 'em steppin' that up as well as addin' James ta their mix. There may be more I'll need, but for starters that'll help. Last thing I want is for anything ta happen ta them two fellers."

"You got it, Ben. Just let me know whenever ya need something, and I'll do my best to help out."

"One more thing. My brothers are turnin' in their badges an' comin' with me as partners. There's a feller named Seth Morton that's been hired by Jeff Walker. I think he's gonna be one helluva lawman, so lend him a hand if the opportunity arises, will ya?"

"I'll do it. Anything else?"

"Not for now. Well, we got a lot o' things ta cover today, so we'd best get movin'. Appreciate the help, Jim. I truly do."

Fifteen minutes later, they pulled up in front of the county courthouse just in time to see Zack and Todd come out, accompanied by Seth. "Hey, boys. I see ya all ready took care o' meetin' with Jeff. How'd it go?"

"A lot better'n I figured, Ben. We're still on the payroll for a couple more days while we finish puttin' together our travelin' expenses for reimbursement an' some other paperwork. But when that's all finished up, we'll turn in our badges an' be ready ta help ya out with whatever ya need ta help get this show on the road," Todd filled Ben and Chenoa in. "Oh, an' he said he was half expectin' ya ta show up this mornin', so he wasn't surprised when I told him ya might be by."

"Good deal. Well, get your business handled, because over the next few days there's a lot ta be handled 'fore we move out. Seth, whattaya think o' all this?"

"Sure surprised me that these brothers o' yours helped me out the way they did, but not that they're goin' with family ta do somethin'. That's the way it should be."

"Chenoa, guess we'd best go see Jeff. He's been wantin' ta meet ya anyway. Oh, an' the grub's on me at Jason's if ya get by that way, includin' you as well Seth. See you boys later."

Ben took Chenoa's arm and led her up the steps and into the building without stopping to look back, knowing without looking that all eyes were on Chenoa. Inside, Mrs. Bishop said abruptly, "Go on in, Ben. The Sheriff is waiting. I'll bring in coffee as soon as it's done."

"No need, Mrs. Bishop. We'll only be a moment, an' we got a lot o' other places ta go yet today, 'specially this mornin'. But thanks anyway. Oh, and this is Chenoa. Chenoa, the real brains o' this place, Mrs. Bishop."

Mrs. Bishop immediately had a flustered look on her face, but quickly recovered, as Chenoa said, "Isn't that the way of it, Mrs. Bishop? Women run the world and let the men think they do, but only occasionally do they give us any credit. Well, I suppose that's the curse we must live with, at least for now. It is a pleasure to meet you."

"They pleasure is all mine. Say, after the Sheriff gets to meet you, why don't you join me here and let the boys have their chat?"

"You know, I'll just do that. Shall we, Ben?"

"Yessir, Ben, she's prettier than everybody's been sayin', for sure," Jeff Walker said after being introduced to Chenoa.

"Thank you, Sheriff. Now, please excuse me, as Mrs. Bishop

228

and I have a few things to discuss while you men talk," Chenoa said excusing herself.

"Ben, what can I do for ya?"

Ben explained the same things he had laid out for Marshal Dodson, and asked for the same protections for Mike and James that he had of the Marshal, to which the Sheriff agreed.

Cherokee Parks

Chapter Twenty-Five

While Ben and Jeff talked, Mrs. Bishop poured Chenoa a cup of fresh coffee, and then sat down with a serious look on her face. "Chenoa, I know this town has been sort of rough on you, but you have beaten them all at their own game with charm, beauty and brains. Now then, I know the sheriff is considering making this his last year in office. The times have changed too much, and so has the county as well as Prescott itself. I almost hate it that the Creed brothers are leaving, but I certainly understand why. In fact, I guess I'm sort of jealous about their ability to leave. But that's not why I wanted to talk to you. I have a pretty good idea what Ben is asking of the sheriff, and I want you to know I'll do anything I can to help."

"Why, thank you, Mrs. Benson. That's awfully kind of you, considering the amount of work you must have all ready."

"Now, young lady, if you going to be friends you're going to have to call me Ruth. Understand?" Without waiting for an answer, she went on. "My nephew and his friend hit a nice vein of gold in the Wickenburg Mountains, but they lost the claim to claim jumpers, and Barriston ended up in control of it. Well, he and Meador. They are evil men and all their cronies need to be jailed, and for a very long time. You just let me know what you need me to do, and I'll do it. We need to make certain everything done is all legal and above board, as I would hate to see some big city shyster get them off on a technicality, wouldn't you?"

"Yes, indeed! And we'll just keep this between us, Ruth, but I may be by to see you more and more often as time goes by. We'll be leaving for camp in just under a week, so for now there really isn't much we can do, but whatever I can think of in the meantime, I'll certainly let you know. I hear Ben and the sheriff wrapping things up, so I'd better finish this delightful coffee and be ready."

"Be ready for what, Chenoa?"

"Oh, Ben, I was just saying that you should be about finished and I should be ready to leave as soon as you are. Thank you again for the coffee, Ruth. I really appreciate your hospitality."

"Oh certainly, dearie. Any time, Chenoa. Ben, this is a delightful young lady you've associated yourself with, for a change. I hope some of her rubs off on you, but I suppose that's asking too much."

"Yes, ma'am. I'm pretty set in my ways all ready, but she sure is a delight. On that I'll agree. Mrs. Bishop, Jeff, see ya next time we come ta town."

Outside, after loading back up in the buggy and starting toward their next stop, Ben said, "Ruth? I've known her for a couple o' years now, an' never been asked ta call her by her given name. so how do you rate?"

"Oh, it's a woman thing again, Ben. Don't try to understand it, just accept it."

"Yeah, all right. Look, I'm headed ta the mercantile warehouse. We're gonna need a lot more supplies. I took down what I thought was a three month supply last trip, but you an' me went through a lot of it. I know the boys can eat a lot, well, like I do, so we're gonna need ta lay in quite a lot o' grub. I'm gonna order two boxes o' dynamite so we can open up the mouths o' the veins once we get the lose stuff cleaned up, an' several hammers and drill bits to use ta set the dynamite as well as plenty o' fuse. I'm orderin' picks an' shovels as well as anything else I think we might need. Includin' more canteens an' a couple of barrels so we don't have ta haul water ever'day. But I'm leavin' the food orderin' ta you, so make sure ya lay in enough to hold all four of us for at least two months, if not three. Might as well load up them mules good goin' out the first time, don't ya think?"

232

"Good. I was afraid I would have to fight you on what to bring along, even though what you stored wasn't all that bad. Do you get the grain from Salty?"

"No, that's our next stop, the granary. I figure we'll be taking six, maybe as many as eight horses along with the twelve mules, sa we'll need quite a bit o' grain."

"Why so many horses?"

"Zack an' Todd each have two, an' I reckon they'll want ta bring 'em, both. I got Captain, an' I been tryin' ta deal Salty out o' a real nice blue roan geld he's got there. That's six, an' your pony is seven. Now, if ya want a horse, pick one out an' ya can give Long Lance his back so he don't think ya owe him anything, an' I'll see about that geld, which'll make eight horses," Ben said, doing the math for her.

"Yes, Ben, that's a good idea. I would like to talk to Salty about that blood bay filly he has. I saw him putting the saddle on her and working her around the corral some, but she needs finished before most people could handle her. However, I think I can settle her down in half a day if he'll sell her to me, and even have her trail ready before we leave."

"Yup, she's a fine lookin' horse, no doubt, but trail ready in less'n a week? I highly doubt it."

"You buy her for me and watch and learn, cowboy. We Indians have a way with horses, in case you didn't remember."

"Well, I hope ya prove me wrong, an' she handles everything all right. Ya gonna want a saddle as well?"

"Yes, that would be nice, and a good hackamore, as I don't like stuffing metal into a horses mouth. Actually, a bosal with a very long mecate so I can adjust the length of the reins to what is needed as she develops."

"An' you think you can control that horse with a hackamore?"

"Oh, yes, as you will see. And if she isn't ready when we are, I will pay you back for all the costs. It seems, thanks to you, I'm going to have some money of my own to spend."

"Pretty sure of yourself, ain't ya? Guess I'd best pipe down, since ya all ready showed me how capable ya are no matter what it comes to. Well, let's start gettin' this order laid out so they got plenty o' time ta make sure they get everything in that we'll need if they ain't all ready got it." Walking to the desk in the back of the building, Ben introduced Chenoa to the middle-aged, greying man sitting there. "Carlton, this here is Chenoa, an' she's gonna handle some o' the orderin' for this trip. It'll be a sizeable amount, since I'm gonna need some minin' tools as well."

"Ben, good to see you again so soon. Chenoa, so you're the young lady who has this town turned on its ear? I can certainly see why! Ben, how soon will you need your supplies?"

"Five, six days tops, Carlton. Ya should have most o' what we'll need, but just in case I wanted ta get by as soon as I knew when we were pullin' out so's ya'd have time just in case."

"Still, that's not much time if I'm out of stock on something. Just a second, let me get Marisol to help Chenoa with the foodstuffs. By the way, we have just added canned and dried meats to our supply lists, in case you'd like to try them out, Chenoa. Fresh meat is not always too easy to find in the summer months, and these are just the ticket to hold one over. I'll be right back. Let me find that woman o' mine."

A few minutes later, Carlton returned with his wife, who happily led Chenoa away, both women chattering away as they discussed what would be needed for four healthy adults for three months. In the meantime, Ben and Carlton started compiling the list of mining supplies, all of which Carlton had in stock, including the dynamite, caps and fuses. Chenoa and Ben finished up about the same time, meeting back at Carlton's desk.

"I hate to ask, Ben, but since this is such a sizeable order, and even though I know you've hit a good strike, or at least that's the word, I'm going to need some money down to secure these items."

"Sure, Carlton. Two, three hundred dollars hold ya?"

"Oh, goodness. I was thinking of more like a hundred. Three hundred will nearly pay for everything."

"Well, let's make that the way of it then," Ben said as he counted out three hundred dollars in double eagles. "I know ya need the money ta lay in more supplies, 'cause from the looks of it we're makin' a pretty big dent in what ya got in stock. Ya always treated me fair, Carlton, an' I want ta be as fair as I can with you. Chenoa, we'd best get a move on, doncha think?"

"Yes, indeed, Ben. My, where has the time gone? If we don't hurry we're going to be late again. Carlton, Marisol, it's been a pleasure, and I'm sure we'll see each other again, even after we take possession of this order."

Turning toward the door, Ben had to hurry to catch up with Chenoa. Outside and in the buggy, it was obvious Chenoa was irritated. "What's the matter?"

"Carlton is what's the matter. Marisol let it slip that he beats her, hitting her in places where it never shows. She also thinks he is keeping a mistress, which might be the real reason he wanted money up front from you for the order. Ben, please, not a word of this or he might really hurt her if someone else were to find out. But please, we need to find another supplier for our supplies before the next trip, if Carlton is still in charge."

"Yes, ma'am. We'll turn James loose on findin' us a good supply source, all right?"

Chenoa just smiled, and then asked, "Where to next, driver?"

"The saddle maker, but that comes after lunch at Renner's. I'm gettin' real hungry. How 'bout you?"

"Oh, good. If you had said anything besides we were going to eat you might be walking right now, because I'd have thrown you out of this buggy," Chenoa said with a hearty laugh.

"Chenoa, Ben, looks like ya just beat the noon rush. The boys are all ready here, an' just ordered. Ya want ta sit with 'em, I reckon, so get on back there ta your table. I'll get you some coffee an' take your order. Sophie's doin' a lot o' the cookin' today, an' I hired her sister Clarice ta help out. Gettin' ta be more'n two people can handle these days," Margarite said, as she all but led them to the back of the café.

"Thank you, Margarite. And as long as these women take your cue when it comes to cooking, it will be just fine. That is as long as you have some fresh apple pie for dessert today," Chenoa said.

"Oh, sweetie, I sure do. I have one pie set aside just for you an' Ben, an' his brothers an' Seth, too."

"Where's Jason?" Ben queried.

"Oh, he'll be out front shortly. I got him in the back washin' dishes from the breakfast run. Why? Ya need him for somethin'?"

"Well, no, not really. Just had a couple o' questions for him is all. But if ya got him workin', they'll wait."

Within a few minutes, Margarite had filled their cups, brought out a fresh pot of coffee to place on their table, and taken their order. The group started talking about their morning activities, including the fact that Ben and Chenoa had all ready started ordering supplies, and asked if there was anything the boys wanted to add that maybe they had missed.

They said no, but after a few minutes Zack asked, "Chenoa, any chance ya know how ta make corndodgers?"

"No, I do not. I've heard of them, but I've never had one, or even seen one that I know of. But I'd be happy to learn if there is someone who will teach me."

"We can ask Maybelline Brody if she'll show ya. She's our landlady, an' she makes some o' the best corndodgers we've ever had," Todd said. "I'm sure she'll do it, an' be real happy to."

"Dang, corndodgers? Like Maw makes?" Ben asked.

"Yessir, just like Maw makes. She whips up a batch for us ever' now an' then if she knows we're gonna be doin' some hard ridin'," Zack answered.

"Man, a batch o' corndodgers would sure be good ta chew on out workin' the claims. Chenoa, I insist ya learn how ta make 'em 'fore we leave town. I got a half day o' doin' things that ya don't need ta tag along on, an' that ought ta be plenty o' time ta learn," Ben said firmly. "But we might need ta order more canned corn an' flour, 'r whatever it takes ta make 'em…"

"Not to worry, Ben. I'll learn how, and take care of adding the ingredients to the supply list. As long as you leave me the buggy while you're doing your other chores."

"Reckon that settles that, then. Boys, find out if Maybelline'll teach her, an' when she wants ta do it, an' I'll make sure Chenoa is there. Even if I have ta walk all over town while the buggy just sets around gatherin' dust."

"Oh, Ben, you have such a flair for the dramatic. I don't know why you didn't become an actor on Broadway. I'm beginning to think you're worse than most high society ladies with all their airs."

"Whoa, Ben. I think she just called you a woman. Didn't it sound like that ta you, Todd?"

"Well, sort of. But she's right, Ben. You're startin' ta whine a lot in your old age," Todd heaped even more on their older brother.

"All right, you two. That's plenty, less'n you're ready ta step outside an' try me on for size. An' Chenoa, if you don't quit tryin' ta stir the pot, I'll turn you over my knee an' give ya what for," Ben said with a big grin.

The gentle teasing continued as they ate, until Jason joined their table, pouring himself a cup of coffee from the fresh pot he brought with him. "So, Ben, Margarite says ya got somethin' ya need ta talk ta me about. What can I do for ya, my friend?"

"Jason, I almost hate ta even ask ya for a couple o' things, but then again I don't, considerin' what I might need ya ta do. First, there's Mike Hutchison and James Whitaker. Try best ya can ta keep an eye on 'em, make sure nothin' happens to 'em. In the long run, I'm gonna try ta take down Barriston an' Meador, an' the two o' them is all part o' the deal. Mike's all ready been threatened, as well as threats ta his family, an' if push comes ta shove they may need ta be hid out for their safety."

"No problem there, Ben. I got several other friends I can count on ta help out if it comes ta that. What else?"

"I'm gonna need ta switch suppliers. I been usin' Carlton Stockdale, but I think there's a problem there, an' I need ta know where else I can get all the things we'll need once we get started. For now, I got near everything we'll need ta set up ordered from him, but by the time we need more I'd like ta get the supplies elsewhere."

"That's not a problem either. I been hearin' things 'bout Carlton I don't like as well, but he's always been about the cheapest an' with the best selection o' goods. There's a new place openin' up, but they're still organizin' an' loadin' in merchandise, if ya don't mind dealin' with Mormons."

"I got no problem with them 'r what they believe in, as long as the supplies are good an' priced right an' they got big enough numbers ta keep us goin'. After this first trip out, I figure ta add in another half dozen men, so the supply needs will be increasin' from then on."

"First chance I get, I'll go have a chat with 'em, make sure they'll sell ta ya first off, as sometimes Mormons will only sell ta each other, an' second that they'll be stockin' what a minin' outfit needs as well as plenty o' grub supplies. Anything else?"

"Nope, that's it for now, but a few more things might pop up goin' forward. Like even more men. Oh, an' tell Muley I need ta see him in the next few days. I might have some things him an' his friends can do while we're still out on this first run."

"He comes in ever' day for coffee, an' a meal if he's got any money. Sometimes a couple o' his friends come along, but they sure ain't regulars. Still, I'll let him know next time he shows up here. Well, if that's it, I see I'd best get ta movin' 'round some, make sure ever' table gets a howdy an' has coffee."

"That's it, Jason. An' thanks, I knew I could count on ya," Ben said, reaching out to shake Jason Renner's hand.

"All right, folks, here's some o' that apple pie Chenoa was askin' about. Anything else I can get ya ta top off your meal?" Margarite said, placing the entire pie on the table with clean plates and forks.

Cherokee Parks

Chapter Twenty-Six

"Oh, Ben, that's the very hackamore I want, right there. Built on a good rawhide bosal, and with a long mecate braided from mane hair instead of tail hair," Chenoa said, stopping to look in the window of the saddlery before they stepped inside.

"I'll have ta admit, that's a real nice one. Well, let's see how much Ralph wants for it," Ben said opening the door. They were immediately hit with the smell of leather and oil, a smell Ben had always liked. He stopped to take a deep breath before continuing into the depths of the shop.

"Ben, you're back all ready? I told ya it'd take me a few days ta make up them packsaddles the way ya want 'em."

"I know, Ralph, but that's not why I'm here. I need ta add ta that order, like eight more packsaddles an' a dozen headstalls ta be used on mules for trailin'. Bad part is, I'll need 'em all in the next five 'r six days. Say, how much ya want for that hackamore hangin' in the window?" Ben changed the subject slightly to avoid listening to the saddle maker complain that he'd need more time.

"Now that one was made by a Mexican down along the Rio Grande. Cost me plenty, I'll tell ya that. But it's been hangin' there for near a year now, 'cause nobody wants ta pay my price. Here's what I'll do for ya, Ben, since you're bringin' me sa much business. I'll let ya have it for ten dollars over what I paid for it."

"That still doesn't tell me the price, Ralph."

The saddle maker scratched his chin for a minute before answering, as though he were doing some addition to see what he was going to sell it for. "Fifty dollars, Ben."

"Naw, I'll give ya forty, 'cause if I know you ya only paid thirty-five for it."

"Forty-five, an' that's just what I paid for it."

"No, Ben, he still wants too much. It's been hanging there so long that it will need a lot of cleaning and some work to put it back into a usable order. Forty is the top price one should pay."

"You heard the lady, Ralph, an' trust me, she knows what she's talkin' about."

"Ya takin' your marchin' orders from a woman these days, Ben?"

"Careful, Ralph. There's nothin' that's keepin' me from takin' a fast trip ta Phoenix an' gettin' what I need there. But I'm tryin' ta save time, an' ta throw ya some business here local."

Ralph puffed up like an old bullfrog, but soon settled down. "Sorry, Ben. Business has been pretty good, an' I been workin' my tail off tryin' ta keep up. Then ya come in an' place the biggest single order I've had in some time an' I talk down to ya. Ma'am, sorry."

"Ralph, this here is Chenoa, one o' my partners. She's sharp as a tack, an' bright an' quick as well. She knows what she's talkin' about 'r she don't talk. She wants that hackamore, an' we need ta order her a saddle if ya don't all ready have one that'll suit her."

"All right. Pleasure ta meet ya, ma'am. I sure see why all the young fellers has got their tails in a knot an' get all tongue-tied when anybody mentions ya. Let's see if I still ain't got that sidesaddle in the back, an' then we'll talk more on that hackamore."

"I'm not at all interested in any sidesaddle, sir. We're going to be riding in some pretty rough country up in the Bradshaw's, and I'll need something far more substantial. Keep in mind that for the last several years I've been forced to ride an Indian saddle, mostly an Apache saddle, so I certainly wish to ride something built properly and well-built for starters."

"Yes, ma'am. I've got a saddle with a small seat I built for a young man last year, but he got killed in a ranch accident, an' his paw declined ta pay for the saddle afterwards. Let's see, where did I put that saddle. Oh, I remember! It's in the back. Let me bring it out an' clean it off for ya." Ralph quickly disappeared into the back room, and then came out carrying a dusty saddle badly needing soaped and cleaned.

"Sorry it's so rough lookin, ma'am, but I've neglected it figurin' I'd never get it sold 'cause most cowboys want a bigger seat than this one has," Ralph said as he wiped it down.

"Here, let me do that while you and Ben talk. I know there are several other things he's going to want, or at least I think there are," Chenoa said taking the slightly oily rag.

As they walked away, Ben made sure he stood where he could keep an eye on Chenoa as she inspected the saddle. She was thorough, flipping the saddle over to check the tree as well as under the skirts, looking over the stitching to make sure it was done correctly. Flipping it back over again, she made sure the cantle was solid, and stood high enough for her frame. She seemed satisfied with the size of the seat, though he wondered if it shouldn't be slightly larger to accommodate her derrière. But he guessed that she knew better than anyone what would be comfortable for her.

Next, she inspected the fenders, as well as all the support stitching, followed by checking the swell, horn and gullet. She went over every inch of that saddle, all appearing to just wipe it down, but Ben knew how she operated. She was inspecting every seam, cut and stitch, leading him to believe that she knew more about saddles than many working cowboys. Finally, she nodded that it would work for her.

"Ralph, we all ready know ya collected some money on that saddle when ya took on the job o' buildin' it, an' ya said ya didn't ever think ya'd sell it, so now comes the questions. How bad ya wanna sell it, an' how much do ya want for it?"

"Ben, I need a hundred fifty, bottom dollar, for that saddle."

As Chenoa approached, she said, "No, too much. But I know you need to make some money just to keep the doors open through the thin months, when the cowboys can't work and have no money for repairs of new equipment. Make it a hundred fifty for the saddle and the hackamore, and you'll almost have a deal. I'll need a new horsehair cinch, and a good saddle blanket in that hundred fifty, then you'll have yourself a deal."

"Now how the hell, pardon the language, ma'am, but how am I s'posed ta stay in business at that rate?"

"Ralph, you have already made several critical mistakes in dealing with me. You assumed that since I was a woman, you could take advantage of me. Second, you also assumed that Ben was going to be easy to convince of the pricing, as he has always been when you dealt with him. I can't do a thing about what he has agreed to pay your for the packsaddles, and I have no problem regarding you making a small profit on the headstalls and other accessories he's ordered. But when it comes to buying equipment for me, I will NOT allow him to spend more than what things are worth.

"Third, you yourself admitted that you had no one even remotely interested in either the saddle OR the hackamore, even keeping the saddle in the back room where no one would ever see it. In other words, you considered them to be dead inventory, and you long ago spent what money you did collect on the saddle up front, probably for the supplies it took to build it in the first place, but with nothing, not a penny for the labor involved. With me, you have a chance to reclaim some lost expenditures and lost time, but you aren't going to take advantage of anyone here today. Is that clear?"

"Yes, ma'am. Crystal clear. But I still need more'n a hundred fifty for all you want. But you make it a hundred seventy-five an' we got us a deal."

Chenoa just shook her head, turned to Ben and said, "I'll make due with what I have now. I guess Ralph has decided to keep his items until they completely fall apart and he has nothing but dust and memories of what they once were."

"Oh, all right, lady. One sixty, but that's as low as I can go."

"And you guarantee the stitching for at least a year?"

"Yes, ma'am."

"Then we have a deal," Chenoa said reaching out to take Ralph's hand.

"Good. Ben, do me a favor an' leave her ta home next time ya come in. Lord knows she'd have me givin' her the shop if I'd let her," Ralph said with a laugh. "Seriously, she's tough ta deal with, but fair, an' she knows what things are really worth, no doubt about that."

"Yessir. I keep tryin' ta tell folks that, but, like you, it seems they all got ta learn on their own. Now then, you gonna have everything ready for me in five days, right?"

"Yeah. I'll have ta bring in that Jacobs boy ta help, but it'll be worth it, since your brothers have brought me in some work ta be done on their saddles as well as them buyin' a few new things like saddle blankets. Seems this is gonna be a big trip, an' from the sounds of it real regular like as well. Just let me know whatever ya need, an' I'll handle it for ya. An' if ya need to, ya can send Chenoa in on her own anytime an' never worry 'bout her."

"Thanks, Ralph. Good ta know. Chenoa, we need ta get movin'. We all ready been here longer I figured we would, an' we still got more places ta stop if we're gonna be ready to roll out in five 'r six days."

"Yes, indeed. And Ralph, if all goes according to plan, I'll be in sometime in the next couple of days to pick up my saddle and such. I'll need them to finish a mare I'm looking at buying, so I can have her trail ready in time."

"That blood bay filly Salty's workin' on? Oh, she's a fine one, but trail ready in six days? Ma'am, ya might be dreamin' on that one."

"Careful, Ralph, you're startin' ta question her again. If she says she can do it, I'm bankin' she can."

"Yeah, I reckon that's right. Well, I got ta get busy if ya want your order ta be done. I'll see ya when I see ya," Ralph said as he turned toward the back, and the stockpile of work in front of him.

Outside, Chenoa said, "Why are so many men so hard to convince that a woman is more than capable of taking care of things, or that we aren't stupid?"

"Maybe it's 'cause sa many women play dumb so men will take care of 'em. Just like a feller ain't real interested in keepin' a rattlesnake for a pet, but he'll keep a bull snake anytime."

Chenoa was so busy laughing that she nearly missed the little step on the side of the buggy, and all but fell in face first instead of climbing in. Once seated, she responded, "Ben, I suppose that's the perfect analogy. And I agree, too many women act dumb on purpose, but you should hear them talk about it when there are no men around. You can be glad I'm not one of those women, or you'd be in a world of trouble about now."

"Now that's a fact, an' don't I know it."

"I need to have you take care of a few more items for me, but I also should let you know that I ordered some new cooking pots and utensils for camp, as well as some tin cups and plates, enough to feed a dozen people if need be. Also, I ordered two new coffee pots, as yours are all but burned up."

"That's fine, as you're in charge o' the camp an' ya need what ya need. Now, what else do ya need?"

"First, I also ordered new blankets and a pair of large tarps, as we'll need to expand our sleeping areas and create more shelter in case of bad weather. I knew you'd approve, but I didn't want you to be surprised when it comes to loading everything to haul out to the camp."

"All right, now what do ya need that ya don't want ta ask me for?"

"Men's clothing suitable for the trail and camp, including a good pair of boots. I have spent so much time looking like a ragamuffin, dressed in Indian clothing that is now in bad need of repair, as well as your old clothing, that I want to wear something that in new, and all mine. I also am going to need a pistol and a rifle, as I am going to be in camp alone much of the time. And I'd also like for you to see that I am quite proficient with both, something we can do before you decide to buy them for me. That means we must find someplace where we can shoot without interruption. I know we still have many things to do, but I feel this is very important, as important, or more, than my learning to make corndodgers for you and your brothers."

"Agreed. The clothes are the easy part. We can head ta Morgenstern's right now an' get ya outfitted with all the clothes ya think you'll need, an' from there we'll head ta the hotel an' I'll fetch my Henry. After that, we'll decide whether 'r not you get the weapons. Ya sure ya don't want a huntin' knife like the one I wear, 'r maybe a good skinnin' knife? Usin' the camp knives for such things is cumbersome, but ya still managed ta skin an' cut up that buck Long Lance brought in."

"Yes, some good knives of my own would be much appreciated, indeed."

"Well, as long as ya promise not ta shoot me 'r cut me up, I

247

don't see why not," Ben said with a smile as they turned the corner headed downtown and to the stores that were there.

An hour later, Chenoa had what she considered the best clothing for the trail and for camp, most of it from the boy's selection at Morgenstern's, including a good, sturdy pair of boots. Back at the hotel, Ben had the bellboy carry her packages up to her room while he stepped into his room to retrieve his rifle and a box of .44-40 cartridges. He was surprised when he stepped out into the hallway and she wasn't waiting there. Tapping on her door, she called out, "Just a few more minutes, Ben."

Five minutes later, she came out looking like a young man, with her long, black hair tucked up underneath the hat she had picked up. Ben almost didn't recognize the young woman standing in front of him, and thought back to something his mother had said often, "Clothes make the person, or at least make them acceptable in good company." He nodded in appreciation of how she was dressed, and agreed that she definitely looked ready for both trail and camp.

Outside of town several miles, they found an open area with a good view all the way to the hill off to the side. Ben took a chunk of wood he found about a hundred yards from the buggy, and set it up on an old stump, making sure it could be easily seen from where the buggy was, and then trotted back to where Chenoa was already holding the Henry.

Chenoa walked off about thirty yards from the buggy, perpendicular and behind the buggy far enough away from the horse so as not to spook him, and with Ben standing beside and behind her lifted the Henry, took quick aim and squeezed off the first shot. The chunk of wood flew off the stump in half a dozen pieces. She levered in another round, and picked out the largest of the pieces, blowing it to smithereens, following suit with the next largest piece, and continuing until there were no pieces large enough to hit at that distance.

"All right, ya made your point with a rifle. You want a new Henry, 'r would ya rather have a new Winchester?"

"Oh, I like the way this Henry feels and shoots. A Henry will be perfect. Now then, if you'll hand me your Colt and pick out some targets for me, let's see how I do with it."

Slipping the Colt out of its holster, Ben flipped it around butt first and handed it to Chenoa. Looking over a tree at about thirty feet, he said, "How about that little branch about four feet off the ground on the left hand side. Reckon ya can hit it?"

Without responding, Chenoa fired from the hip, clipping the branch off clean. "Now, for that smaller one down a touch on the right hand side," she tucked the Colt into her pants and turned her back to the target. In a spinning move, she drew and fired, again from the hip, snipping the twig off right at the trunk of the tree. Looking at Ben with a sheepish smile, she said, "I can draw better, and faster, using a good holster with a tie down. Now you know why the men I've known have never let me have a pistol or a rifle."

"Damn, girl, where'd ya learn ta shoot like that?"

"As I told Zack, my father taught me how to shoot, but that was for hunting. After my father left, another man came to live with our tribe for a time. He was on the mend from getting shot, and was most likely what you would call a gunslinger or shootist. Anyway, as he began to heal, he would practice shooting. He saw my interest, and let me shoot with him until I was as fast as he was, though he always said I was even faster then he. Fortunately, I have never had to face a man to find out how fast I might or might not be. I truly hope that time never comes, but I do want to be prepared."

"Sold. Tomorrow we go buy you a new Henry rifle, a new Colt, both chambered like mine, in .44-40 so ya can use the same cartridges, an' if we can find one that fits ya we'll get you a new gun rig with a tie down holster. No need ta demonstrate with knives, 'cept that we'll see if there's a real knife maker in town an' you can get your pick o' knives an' sheaths for 'em. Now, let's get back ta town an' find some grub 'fore it gets too late."

It was a quiet trip back, as Ben contemplated over the many things he was learning about the Paiute woman on the seat next to him.

Chapter Twenty-Seven

Once again, morning came early for the Creed boys. Zack and Todd sat drinking coffee with Mose and Maybelline, talking about their upcoming venture with Ben and Chenoa, when Maybelline asked if they were still going to keep their rooms or move on.

"Maybelline, not only are we gonna keep our rooms, but we'd like ta pay two months in advance, though we plan on bein' back in a month 'r so. But we got a favor ta ask ya."

"Shoot, Todd, ya jus' tell me what ya needs, hon, an' ol' Maybelline'll do her bes' ta get it done."

"Well, we'd like for you ta teach Chenoa how ta make corndodgers. We're gonna have some long days, an' bein' able ta snack on 'em treats, well, that'd make any man's day."

"Why, sho' 'nough, ah'd be happy ta teach her. You jus' bring her on 'roun' any time."

"This afternoon be all right, if she ain't all ready got plans?"

"Like ah said, any time, chil'. Ah been a dyin' ta meet this gal since ah fuss ah heared about her."

***

Across town, Ben and Chenoa were sipping coffee in the dining room of the Congress Hotel, discussing their plans for the day. First would be to have a chat with Salty about the filly and the blue roan, and see if he would sell then, followed by a stop to pick up some weapons for Chenoa, and then to look for a knife maker in town, if there were one. Short of that, she would have to settle for factory made clothing available at any of the stores in the business district.

"And Ben, don't forget that I need to learn how to make those corndodgers, and order what I'll need for them once I figure out what that is. If Salty lets us have that filly, I'll need to spend a few hours every day getting her ready, depending on how far along she all ready is."

"Yes, ma'am, I haven't forgot about them corndodgers. My mouth's been waterin' just thinkin' about 'em. Well, I'm about coffee'd out for now. You ready to light out?"

"Yes, let's get started. I'm really starting to get excited how, but I have to tell you I wasn't all that thrilled at the prospect of spending months and months in a mining camp after spending so much time in the wilderness in the past. But now, Ben, I am truly excited about this."

Dressed far more casually than in days past, Ben waved off Clete as he started to bring the buggy across for them. Walking across the street, Salty saw them coming and met them at the doors. "What can I do for the two o' you this mornin'?"

"Salty, I really like the looks of that little filly you've been working with. Any chance you'd sell her? To me?"

"Well, yeah, I reckon, but she's a month 'r so from bein' ready."

"I'd like to take her as she is right now and finish her myself. How much do you want for her?"

Salty gave Chenoa a long, hard look before turning to look at Ben, and then back to Chenoa. "I was thinkin' two hundred dollars finished, an' I got ta tell ya I ain't all that comfortable lettin' her go 'til she is finished. Ya think ya can handle her?"

"Yes, I do. And I'd like to take her with us when we ride out next week. So what do you say?"

"Well, let me tell ya a few things 'bout her what ya don't know. She was feelin' her oats yesterday mornin', so I took her out ta the track an' let her go. That little gal can fly, I want ya to know. She's as fast as any horse around here, maybe faster. Her mama an' daddy both had good speed an' a ton o' bottom, so I reckon she will as well. She's light an' quick footed, an' shows a considerable amount o' brain. I reckon she's 'bout the finest little filly I've had the pleasure o' workin' in a real long time."

"All right, Salty, we know what ya think of her, but how much ya want?" Ben asked.

"I reckon unfinished like she is, a hundred fifty should be about right."

"No, too much, Salty. How about a hundred, and a promise that you get to board her any time we're in town, along with all the other horses and mules except those belonging to Todd and Zack."

"Ben's all ready gonna board 'em with me anyway, so what am I gainin' there?"

"Well, you spent so much time selling the filly to us when I all ready wanted to buy her that I thought it only right I do the same to you. Now then, a hundred dollars?"

Salty stood silently, looking first at Chenoa, and then to Ben, and back again, then turning to stare off into the barn before finally turning to give his answer. "A hundred twenty-five an' she's yours. An' not a penny less. Hell, you're gettin' a horse gonna be worth a helluva lot more in a year 'r two when she starts throwin' babies."

"All right, Salty. Danged if I'm gonna stand here a half day an' listen ta the two o' you haggle. You'll be down ta pennies o' difference if I let this go one. Consider her sold at a hundred twenty-five. I'll bring ya some money later on today, since I need ta square up with ya anyway. Any word on them mules?"

"I should hear somethin' back yet this mornin', Ben, maybe by the time ya come back around."

"Now, what about that blue roan geld? Ya wanna sell him?" Ben asked.

"Well, I was gettin' him ready ta sell, but I reckon he's finished enough to let him go."

"How much?"

"After that deal for Chenoa, I'm near scared ta say. Whattaya think he's worth to ya?"

"I'll give ya seventy-five, Salty. That work?"

"Naw, I need a hundred."

"That's too much, Ben. He's really only worth about eighty," Chenoa chimed in.

"Dangit, I should o' knowed she's have somethin' ta say on it. All right, eighty dollars then."

"Good deal. Chenoa, we need ta get movin'. Still a lot ta do this mornin'."

Ten minutes later, they were standing in front of a shop with large, bold lettering on the window stating *LOSHKAREV FINE WEAPONS*, and below it in smaller lettering, *Viktoravich Loshkarev, Proprietor*. There were several very fancy rifles in the window along with a small assortment of mostly Colt and Remington pistols. To both their surprise, there were also a nice assortment of knives for various purposes.

Stepping inside, the smell of gun oil and gunpowder permeated the air. Looking around, Chenoa was stunned at the number of new weapons on display, as well as the number of used and reconditioned ones, and the wall completely filled with boxes of cartridges of all sizes and calibers.

"Ben, it is so good to see you again," came a small, youngish voice from the bowels of the building. "I'll be right with you."

A moment later, a young man in his late teens appeared, "What can I do for you this morning, Ben?"

"Nick, where's your paw?"

"He and mother are on their way to New York, if not there all ready. Mother's sister and her family are coming in on a steamer from Russia, and my folks are there to welcome them and bring them home to Prescott. Now, what can I assist you with?"

"I need ta have my Colt tuned up again, maybe take a touch of trigger pressure off, but not too much. An' I most likely need ta have the barrel on my Henry cleaned up some."

The door to the shop had just opened, and another voice said, "I reckon we'll both need the same thing, Nicky. Ben, fancy meetin' you an' Chenoa here," came Zack's all too familiar voice.

"Mornin' Zack, Todd. What brings the two o' you here sa early?"

"Most likely the same as you, with both pistols an' rifles, though we both been thinkin' on new Colt's, dependin' on how tough ol' Nick there is ta deal with."

"Now, you men know we always have the best prices in town, and that we always treat you right. So, Ben, let me have my uncle Sergei look your Colt over. He speaks no English yet, or at least very little, but he is as good a gunsmith as my father. You can drop your Henry off next time you go by and we'll get it cleaned up really nice. And my mother's brother, Boris, has also joined us in the business as a knife maker. Take a look at what we have on display, and if there is something that interests you just let me know. Zack, Todd, might as well hand me your pistols as well, let Sergei look them all over at the same time. And you can drop off your Winchesters anytime as well."

Once the Colt's had all been handed over, Nick disappeared into the back of the building while the group began wandering around looking at the items on display. Chenoa immediately headed for the knife selection, and picked out five knives she wanted, one for use as a hunting knife, one as a skinning knife, and three for camp knives. Nick stepped out, and walked straight to her to pull the five knives out for her to examine further, then carrying them to the front counter as she accepted them.

Ben was looking at the Colt's, and chatting with Todd and Zack about what they might want in the way of new pistols, and how they would have to be modified for their personal use. Nick joined them next, asking, "Are these the new ones you're interested in?"

"Yes, how many ya got in stock, Nick?"

"I guess that depends on how many you're buying, Ben," he replied with a laugh.

"I'm thinkin' five, Nick, all in .44-40, an' a rig with a tie down for Chenoa. One each for me an' my brothers, an' two for the lady. We'll want them all set up exactly the same, light trigger pulls an' such. Just like mine is set up now, but with even lighter trigger pulls."

"Fine, that will leave me one for display until the next shipment comes in. Papa is bringing that shipment back with him, so it should be here in the next two weeks. How soon do you need them?"

"Three, four days from now. And' I'll want another Henry with the sights adjusted like mine, and sighted in ta take the whiskers of a fly at a hundred yards. That an' I reckon we'll need five hundred rounds o' .44-40 cartridges ta go along with the rifle an' pistols."

"Very well, I can have Sergei get started yet today, and have the Colt's and a Henry ready with time to spare. Now, as to that gun rig, I have one that should be perfect for the lady. Ma'am, if you'd like to try this on for size," he said reaching under the counter and pulling out a holster and belt and handing them to Chenoa.

The French and Paiute woman strapped the rig on, and then tied the holster down. Reaching for one of the new Colt's now lying on the counter, she slipped it in and out of the holster several times, making certain is slid properly. After several times, she suddenly drew and aimed at an imaginary target. Repeating the motion several times, she turned back to face the Creed brothers, all looking rather startled at the speed she displayed.

"Yes, Nick, this will be perfect. I'll take it."

"Ben, you knew about this? Damned if she ain't near as fast on the draw as our sisters," Todd commented.

"Yessir, I did, though it was just yesterday afternoon when I found out."

A tall, thin man stepped out from behind the curtain separating the front and back of the shop and said something to Nick. Nick responded, laying the three pistols on the counter. "Sergei says they are all very clean, and that he appreciates it when people take good care of their weapons. He has adjusted the trigger pulls on each as far as he feels safe in doing by installing new shorter springs, and suggests you step to the back and try them by firing them into the sand bags. Now, if you'll follow me, please."

Not waiting for a response, Nick Loshkarev turned to the back, stopping only to hold the curtain open for his guests. Ben grabbed the new rig for Chenoa as they walked by picking up their Colt's and following Nick into the back. At the very back of the building a wall of sandbags were stacked up, and from looking it seemed to Ben that they were double stacked, maybe triple stacked.

Stepping to the front, Todd drew and fired two rounds into the bags, and then turned to Sergei and Nick to say, "Perfect. Just right."

Zack followed suit, nodding his acceptance, followed by Ben, who also agreed the trigger setting was exactly what he wanted. He then handed the Colt to Chenoa, who repeated the same motion as the men, except that she seemed intent on showing them just how fast she could draw and fire. Turning back to the others, she said, "That is exactly how I'd like to have my Colt set up, Ben. And before you ask, Zack, yes, I'm as accurate as I am quick. You can ask Ben about my prowess with a rifle as well. Gentlemen, shall we go back to the front and see how much Nick intends to charge for all this?"

Following Nick back to the front, Ben couldn't help but smile at the friendly eye exchange between Sergei and Chenoa. *I s'pose language don't matter much when mutual interest is concerned.* Standing at the counter, Chenoa asked, "Are there sheaths available for those knives, Nick?"

"Yes, and they are included with the price, ma'am."

"And the price for everything, rifle, knives, pistols, holster and belt, gunsmith work and cartridges?"

"Ben, do you want two hundred grain cartridges, or two hundred twenty-five?"

"Two twenty-five, Nick, if you got five hundred rounds of 'em."

"Oh, I do, and then some," Nick laughed as he set about totaling the figures, and finally came to a total price, prepared to dicker with this strong minded woman, as the word had all ready spread throughout the town that she was a tough negotiator. "That comes to four hundred dollars."

"No, not unless you are triple charging for the gunsmithing services, young man, as well as too much for the gun rig and knives. Now, I don't begrudge you for the skill and talent in creating those beautiful knives and sheaths, nor do I begrudge anyone trying to make a living at any trade, and I know there are set costs of the Henry rifle and Colt pistols. I also know you'd love to tell your father how much you made the shop on a big sale such as this. But the real point is, this is a large sale and discounts can be allowed for our doing business with you. Now, sharpen that pencil and let's hear a more reasonable number if you wish to consummate this deal today."

Nick couldn't help but smile, as everything he had heard about this gorgeous woman was correct. Sergei leaned over and said something to him in what Ben decided had to be Russian, and the two of them walked to the curtain to call Boris in. No one had seen the third member of the current shop staff, and all were surprised when a giant of a man stepped into the room with them. At roughly the same height and build as Long Lance, Ben couldn't help but wonder how a battle between the two of them would turn out.

After a few exchanges between them, Boris spoke. "I haf tol' Nikolai to sell knives lower. I go now," he finished stepping through the curtain and disappearing.

The chat continued between Nick and Sergei for several more minutes, seemingly heated at times, until Nick took a deep breath and started running numbers again. Finally, after starting over several times, he said, "Three hundred seventy dollars, today only."

Chenoa laughed, saying, "Today only? Why, are you going to sell all this before tomorrow? Highly unlikely, Nick. Tell you what, three hundred sixty, and you get to make a decent profit on everything. Deal?" she said, putting her hand out to shake.

Ben thought her hand would drop, she held it out so long, but finally Nick took it, saying, "Ben, this is a good woman. You need to keep her with you when you buy anything. Soon, though, businesses will begin closing their doors when they see her coming," he closed with a big laugh.

"Don't I know it, Nick. Don't I know it! " As Ben started counting out the money, he commented, she has sure been worth her weight in salt on this deal, an' I'm sure glad ta have her as a partner."

Chapter Twenty-Eight

"Chenoa, Maybelline said she'd teach ya how ta make corndodgers any time ya was ready. Ya got time this afternoon?"

"Why, yes. I believe so. Ben, is there anything you need me for this afternoon? You're not buying anything else today, are you?"

"No, I don't plan on it anyway. I do need ta pay a visit ta the bank, an' see what Salty found out about them mules. We still need ta go see James an' see what he found out yesterday in Mayer, make sure we got a deal with the smelter there, but that shouldn't take too long."

"Don't forget, now that we bought that filly I'll need to pick up my saddle, blanket and hackamore so I can start working with her tomorrow."

"I reckon I can take care o' that this afternoon if we don't get to it yet this mornin'. But I'm gonna need the buggy, so I'll have ta drop ya off an' come back an' pick ya up later."

"Yes, of course, Ben."

"Tell ya what, Ben, meet us at Renner's for lunch an' we'll deliver her ta Brody's from there. Me an' Todd are all but done with what we need ta get settled up on, now that you took care o' the new Colt's an' fixin' the old ones."

"Not ta mention all that ammunition ya bought. Ya plannin' on startin' a war, 'r finishin' one?" Todd asked.

"Neither one, boys. Just figured we ought ta make sure we got plenty just in case. Never know, somebody might try ta pin us in somewheres, an' we'll need all the grub an' ammo we need ta outlast 'em. Remember, there's a couple o' fellers what don't want us ta keep what we got, an' they'll go ta extremes ta take it away if we don't take 'em down first. But I have ta say, with four guns with the kind o' skill we got, they'll be real hard pressed ta pull it off."

"Oh, we ain't forgot, but it's been real quiet around town, big brother. Nobody is talkin' much about where the claims are located, 'r showin' any interest in movin' in. An' that's mainly 'cause o' the Creed reputation, even if they don't know we got one more just like us when it comes ta shootin'. 'Sides, if we'd a known how tough she was ta deal with, we might o' saved us a few dollars all ready just by lettin' her handle it," Zack observed.

"Yessir, she's tougher'n Maw is when it comes ta dealin' with merchants. Chenoa, what say we go find James an' get the word on the smelter, an' then go by the bank. That won't take too long, an' by the time I finish there it'll be time ta meet the boys for lunch. Boys, see ya at Jason's," Ben said as he lightly popped the buggy whip to coax the horse forward.

"We'll follow ya ta see James, an' split up again afterward!" Todd called out as they urged their own buggy onward.

Fifteen minutes later, they were all standing outside Whitaker's office, wondering where he was, as he was normally open by nine, and it was all ready ten thirty. As they prepared to leave and start checking around town for him, the young lawyer came walking down the boardwalk, one arm in a sling and with a bandage wrapped around his head.

"Good morning, gentlemen, Chenoa. I was hoping you'd be by."

"James, what happened to you?"

"Oh, it's nothing, really. At least Mike didn't get hurt, and my injuries are really nothing serious. Just a knot on my head and a sprained shoulder."

"Dammit, man, what happened?" Ben insisted.

"Mike and I were on our way back from Mayer, still about a

263

dozen miles out, when we were attacked by half a dozen riders. There are a few slugs in my buggy, but none of them hit Mike, my horse or myself. We had each taken both pistols and rifles, sort of expecting some trouble, so we were pretty much ready, and while I kicked the mare loose Mike started firing back at them. I believe he hit one or two before they pulled back, though. I was trying to pull the buggy to a stop and reaching for my rifle at the same time, a big mistake as it turned out, when we hit a hole in the road and the buggy almost bounced me out. I smacked my head on the roof support and caught my arm in the cross section piece, twisting my shoulder something fierce. Mike had to drive me in and take me to Dr. Martinique's office after dark."

"Any idea who they were?"

"No, I didn't really get a look at any of them, but Mike said he thought he knew a couple of them. He should be here soon with my buggy. He was taking it over to Murphy's to see if they could repair it first thing, and coming by here when they were finished. Well, I'm sure you're very interested in what we found out in Mayer, so let's step inside and take care of that, shall we?"

Once James was seated at his desk and had his document case open and the necessary papers pulled out and placed on his desk, he looked up at the others, who had quietly waited for him to speak. "You will be thrilled to know that the Mayer stamp mill will take all of the silver ore you can deliver, no minimum tonnage required. Same for the smelter. As to the gold, they were a bit more selective, until I told them there would little stamp work required initially, as most of the gold was in flake, dust and nugget form, and showed them the samples we took along, though the latter forms of gold will undoubtedly change. They then agreed to stamp and smelt gold under the same conditions as the silver, but in the final agreement they stated they had changed their mind on the minimum tonnage, and would require a minimum of two ton of gold ore.

"Now then, the next thing is the copper and lead smelted out and separated is also included, since they are a small smelter and can easily separate the 'dirty' ore from the rest in the finished product. Now, for the pricing. For silver, they wanted sixty cents per Troy ounce for refined silver, but we settled at forty cents after discussing the possible drop in the market value of ninety-nine percent silver from the current dollar and a quarter to a dollar, though I really don't see that happening for another year or two as Congress debates it over and over. Gold is much more expensive, so they are asking three dollars per Troy ounce if the gold standard holds at the government established twenty dollars sixty-seven cents an ounce for ninety-nine percent pure product. Again, these prices will not fluctuate with the tonnage, as long as they have at least two tons of either gold ore to process on any delivery made to them. I trust this is acceptable to you."

"Yessir, it sure is. Good prices, no doubt. I hope you locked 'em prices in 'fore ya left down there," Ben stated the obvious.

"Yes, I did, and I have the signatures of both Charles Tucker and Emmitt Browner on paper guaranteeing them."

"Good deal. Next question. Why in hell haven't ya notified the sheriff?"

"Oh, Mike took care of that last night. In fact, I expected Sheriff Walker to have been here all ready. But maybe he came before I arrived, and will come by again later."

"James, you're acting rather nonchalant about this trouble. Why? Do you think we'll think any less of you if you were frightened?"

"No, Chenoa. Remember where I was raised, and what we faced back then. I felt no fear, especially with Mike along. Turns out he is a very good shot, quite capable with a rifle. But what I did feel was anger at myself for being so clumsy. Ah, here comes Sheriff Walker now."

"James, as soon as we say howdy ta Jeff, we'll take off an' let ya get your report filed. Maybe Mike'll show up an' he can tell the sheriff who he thinks they were. Oh, an' tell Mike we'll be a Renner's for lunch, an' he's welcome ta come by an chat. You can come, too, if ya want ta."

"Thank you, Ben, but I'm behind in my work after being gone all day yesterday and coming in so late this morning. But I'll sure let Mike know."

Greetings were passed around once Walker joined them, but Chenoa and the Creed's left to take care of their business while James filed his report. Splitting up, Ben and Chenoa headed directly downtown to the bank, while Zack and Todd headed to places unknown.

Zipping along, Ben nearly missed seeing a little boy run out into the street, but managed to swing the buggy just wide enough to miss the child. They were nearly to the bank, so Ben didn't stop until they pulled up to the front of the building, and then said, "Chenoa, take care o' the buggy while I go check on that boy."

Chenoa stood on the boardwalk watching as Ben hoisted the boy high into the air, making him laugh, and then sat him carefully on the boardwalk giving him a sound talking to. When he was finished, the boy's mother shook Ben's hand, and Ben started walking back in her direction. The glint of steel caught her eye, making her look up to find where it was emanating from. Ben saw her looking and also started looking, first along the tops of the buildings. He saw what she was looking at almost too late, jumping into a doorway just as the rifle fired. The bullet ricocheted off the iron doorframe and slammed into the boardwalk.

Removing his hat and peeking around the edge of the doorframe, he could see that the bushwhacker was still there, rifle pointing in his direction. Not seeing any way he could get out of the doorway without the risk of getting shot, he contemplated his next move. *If only Chenoa had somethin' ta shoot with...* Just then a shot rang out from her direction, and then another. Peeking out again, the bushwhacker was slowly sliding forward on the roof of the facade, and then fell to the ground with a thud.

Stepping out and then running to see who it was that had taken the shot at him, he could see Chenoa standing beside the buggy with a rifle in hand. Behind her stood the bank president and one of the tellers looking at each other in disbelief. A small crowd had all ready started to gather around the body, and wild speculations were all ready starting.

"Somebody go fetch the marshal 'r one o' his deputies, an' be quick about it." Turning the body over, Ben didn't recognize the man, but thought he had seen him with some of Barriston's thugs. He hoped Dodson would know him, and if this backshooter was who he thought he was, Barriston was really beginning to turn up the heat. *I wonder if he did send out a crew ta try ta poach our claims, 'r if he's just figurin' on makin' sure we never get back to 'em.*

Standing back up, Ben looked across the street toward the bank. Chenoa was still standing there, rifle in hand with both the teller an' the banker standing with her. "Somebody tell Dodson 'r one o' his deputies, whoever shows up, that I'm at the bank," Ben said to no one in particular but everyone standing there in general.

He walked across the street, fully intent on completing the business he came here for in the first place, but wondering how anyone other than James or his brothers knew he'd be visiting the bank this morning. Deciding that someone figured out that he was spending a lot of money around town, and would eventually have to head for the bank to get more cash, they had posted a man across the street to lay for him. Then again, they might have several more men placed around town just waiting to take a potshot at him, or his brothers or Chenoa.

"Raymond, I take it that's your rifle Chenoa used?" Ben said taking the rifle from Chenoa and handing it back to the banker.

"Yes, Ben, it was. Damn, she's a helluva shot. I couldn't have made it, I'll tell you that. Any idea who he was?"

"Nope, not yet anyway. Maybe Marshal Dodson will know when he shows up. Mind if we step inside? No sense in havin' all them folks starin' this direction if we can avoid it. Chenoa, you all right?"

"I think a better question is, are you all right?"

"Yes ma'am, I'm fine. I'm thinkin' we need ta head back over ta Loshkarev's an' see if he's got your rifle set up, 'r maybe one o' 'em Colt's. No sense in all of us not packin' from here on out."

Grabbing his saddlebags from the buggy and stepping inside the bank, Ben asked the banker if they could talk in private instead of in the lobby, and have someone stay with Chenoa while they talked. Assured that she would be well guarded, they stepped back into the bank president's office.

"What can I do for you, Ben?"

"I need to pull out five thousand, Raymond, to pay for all the things we need ta set up the operation. An' I reckon there'll be a few more costs I haven't encountered as yet. Seems there always are."

"How soon do you need it?"

"Right now, Raymond, if ya don't mind. I need ta pay some things off this afternoon an' first things in the mornin' as well as make sure Chenoa's got some money on her for anything she wants ta buy."

"You certain these claims are going to pay off enough for you to get your money back?"

"Yes, more than certain. That an' a whole lot more. Now, I

need ta get movin', so if you'll kindly get the money for me, I'd appreciate it."

"Yes, of course, Ben. Just a minute, please." Stepping to the door, the banker called out to one of the tellers, and then spoke softly to him when he came to the door. "Give Miller about ten minutes to gather it up for you, and bring it in to be counted. And I insist you count it before you leave my office, Ben, just to make certain we're all in agreement on the exact amount."

"Never had to do that before, Raymond. What's goin' on?"

"Well, we've had a minor run, and most of our deposits have been placed in a bank in Phoenix so we're a bit short on cash until the Wells Fargo shipment arrives day after tomorrow. Any more withdrawals like yours, and I'll have to temporarily close the doors. That's the last thing I want to do, Ben, as it is a sign of a bank's weakness to do such a thing."

"Whattaya think brought on this run?"

"What I believe and what I can prove are two different things, but I believe Randolph Barriston and Manuel Meador are behind it. They tried to buy me out last month, but I turned them down flat. They gave me sixty days to reconsider, telling me that they would make sure I suffered and went broke if I didn't play along. Barriston laughed, saying when they were done with me, they'd be able to buy the building off the auction block at a sheriff's sale and then open their own bank where this one stands. I think this run is the start of that pressure."

"Tell ya what, any money I don't need ta spend, I'll bring back in, an' we'll deposit all our money here as it comes in, if ya can guarantee that much silver an' gold will be safe here. Sure save me havin' ta send it ta one o' the big banks down south."

"You got it, Ben. In fact, I'll put on two or three more guards to protect the place during business hours, as well as at least one at night, even though I don't believe anything short of a half a case of dynamite could crack open our new vault, if even then."

"Then we got us a deal, an' I'll be sure ta let my brothers an' Chenoa know about it."

A light tap came to the door, and the teller stepped into the office, heavily weighed down with gold coinage. It was soon counted out, signed for, and Ben loaded it into his saddlebags and was on his way around town again, though he did remember to take out two hundred dollars and give it to Chenoa..

Chapter Twenty-Nine

"Ben, when did you say you're leaving town?" Jim Dodson asked.

"Middle o' next week, Jim. Still got quite a lot ta handle 'fore we pull out. Why?"

"Just wondering what the body count will be by the time I get you out of town. I understand we can attribute this one to Chenoa, correct?"

"Yessir, she saved my hide by takin' this one off the roof 'fore he got me."

"Yes, that's what all the witnesses are saying, which leaves the two of you in the clear, as always in your case."

"Know who he is, 'r who he works for?"

"Yes, he's one of Barriston's thugs, one Frank Tolleson. I've been waiting for him to show his face around town, as I had paper on him all ready. I suppose Raymond told you what Barriston told him, right?"

"Yeah, he did. Seems ta me him an' Meador are tryin' ta take over a lot of things, like they know somethin' the rest of us don't."

"I agree, Ben. I think maybe they are trying to corner what could be a valuable mineral rush. Yours is not the only good strike in the Bradshaw's this year, not to mention those on the Wickenburg side or down along the Agua Fria and Big Bug, or up at Jerome. Copper is going higher and higher, though silver and gold have been price regulated by the Federal government. Still, with enough ore being stamped and smelted it could amount to a great deal of money, and power."

"I reckon you're prob'ly right, but if all works out they'll be lookin' out from Yuma's walls instead o' ruinin' good folks that have worked hard ta get what they got. We done here? Chenoa an' me got ta meet the boys at Renner's for lunch, an' I need ta warn 'em ta be on the lookout for backshooters. Chenoa is gonna be at Brody's most o' the afternoon, but I'll be movin' around town quite a bit. Thinkin' 'bout parkin' the buggy at Brody's an' takin' Captain, 'cept that kind o' make me a better target out in the open. Well, Jim, let me know if ya need anything, like me ta talk ta the city attorney or DA. See ya 'round."

Foregoing a stop to see Salty, or to pick up Chenoa's saddle or a weapon, Ben chose instead to go directly to Renner's after stashing his saddlebags under the seat of the buggy. Pulling up there, he saw Muley and two of his friends walking toward the door.

"Muley, got a minute? An' bring your friends along, will ya? Chenoa, go on inside an' order me a steak an' taters. Margarite will know what I want, an' if the boys are in there tell 'em I'll be right in, please."

Without questioning Ben, Chenoa did as she was told even though it ran against her nature to take orders from any man. Muley tipped his hat, followed in suit by his companions, as they walked past her, causing her to speak kindly to each of them. She hoped Ben would fill her in the next time they had a moment alone.

"Muley, I got a job for ya, after ya introduce me ta these two."

"Yessir, Mr. Creed. This one is Bart Baker, but we call him Bear Claw 'cause he can eat more bear claws 'n any three men. An' that one is Jed Smith."

"Pleased ta meet you boys. Now, let me ask ya if ya got more men like these that can be trusted, Muley."

"Well, yeah, just like ya asked me about tother day. They's Carl Sawyer, an' Big Mike Murphy, Rooster Case an' Stumpy Jackson.

273

All good men whut I'd trust wit' my life."

"Good, 'cause that's likely what it'll come ta. Now let me ask ya somethin' else. Ya happen ta know who all works for Barriston?"

"I do, 'em bunch o' reprobates," Jed Smith answered. "An' I can point 'em all out ta anybody whut wants ta know."

"Good. You can tick one o' that list, a Frank Tolleson. Chenoa took him out this mornin' after he tried ta bushwhack me. But here's what I need from ya. Get all your men together, only them what can be trusted not ta switch sides, an' start slippin' 'round town findin' where they're at. I figure they got a few more posted around that are intent on killin' me 'r one of my brothers, maybe even Chenoa. An' if it looks like they're set up ta bushwhack one of us, find one o' us, 'r Marshal Dodson, an' let us know. Other'n that, try ta keep an eye on Mike Hutchison an' James Whitaker. They tried ta hit them yesterday east o' town an' failed."

"Mr. Creed, if ya need more men, I can get my cousins. They're all good mountain folks, an' tough'n boot leather," Smith said.

"How many o' 'em are there?"

"Four, an' thar's another three 'r four more fellers I know of whut I can trust if ya needs 'em."

"Here's the deal, men. We're pullin' out the middle o' next week ta work my claims. An' them claims are good ones, real good ones. Barriston an' Meador got their eyes on stealin' 'em, but I want ta turn the tables on 'em an' take 'em down. Sa let's add Raymond Alvarez, the president o' the Bank o' Prescott, ta that list ta watch over since they threatened him as well."

Digging into his pocket, Ben counted out twenty double eagles, handing them to Muley. "Hire twenty good men ta handle all this, an' give 'em each a coin. Once we get the claims set up ta mine proper, along with a good camp, I'm gonna need some men that can handle big timber. There ain't no sawmill, 'r a big water source ta power one anywhere near, so it'll mean cuttin' mine timbers by hand, enough for two mines, an' I'll need some men experienced with minin' ta help work the ore. On top o' that, I'll need several men ta stand guard over our ore while it's at the smelter in Mayer, make sure none of it disappears. That job'll start in about a month, while it will likely be six weeks 'fore I start addin' the others. An' I'll be payin' proper wages ta ever man what comes ta work for us. Keep it under your hats, but start sortin' out the ones I'll need. Now, if ya want ta come on in, I'm buyin' lunch today, gents," Ben said as he slapped Muley on the back and started for the front door of Renner's.

Joining Chenoa, Margarite, Jason and the boys at their table, Ben let Margarite know that Muley and his companions were eating on him this time, and to let them have whatever they wanted. As she scurried off to take care of another table, Ben filled those remaining at the table of the events at the bank, and his hiring Muley and friends to help shadow those he felt might be in danger as well as to monitor the movement of Barriston and his thugs.

"Ben, we can handle whatever comes up, so no need ta give us any help, is there?" Zack asked.

"Well, considerin' the one what came after me was a backshooter, yeah. You don't know where they might be hidin' any better than I do, 'r how many there might be, if any. I'd sooner have a handle on it, at least as best we can 'til we leave Prescott."

"I s'pose that's right, Zack. You an' me can cover each other, but not if we don't see 'em 'til after they fire off a round. An' if they don't miss, well, I'd sooner have somebody figure out where they're hidin' first, like Ben says," Todd lamented.

"You boys still up for takin' Chenoa ta Brody's for me? I need ta move around town an' take care of a few things while she's there, an' still get back ta pick her up in time ta get some grub tonight."

"Ben, we have all ready talked about it, while you were talking with Muley, and they are, indeed, delivering me to Maybelline for my cooking lesson. Pick me up when you can, and be safe as you move about. In fact, I am finished eating, so as soon as you men finish we can get started."

Ben and the boys hurriedly took the last few bites of their food, Ben tossing down what he thought would be enough to cover all the meals plus some, and hurried outside. A few minutes later, the boys were introducing Maybelline and Chenoa, who hit it right off, and then excused themselves and headed for the downtown area. They wanted to try to keep tabs on Ben, but he was nowhere to be found. Heading toward the Congress, they spotted him at Salty's just as Ben and Salty stepped inside.

They joined the pair just in time to catch up with the conversation. "Yessir, Ben, they're some fine mules, damned fine if I have ta say so. Ol' Allred has 'em well fed an' well trained, but he ain't gonna let 'em go cheap. We'll need ta ride out so you can see 'em yourself, an' you can strike a deal with him yourself."

"When can ya get away, Salty?"

"Right now, if ya wanna. Clete can handle anything that comes along."

"Ben, ya sure ya don't wanna wait 'til mornin' an' take Chenoa along? That gal can sure work a deal better'n any o' us."

"Zack, Todd, good ta see ya. Naw, Allred is a hardcore Mormon, an' he don't cotton ta women havin' too much ta do 'cept cook an' clean an' get pregnant. Best just me an' Ben go out, though I got ta agree with ya on her dealin'. Damned if she didn't even beat me down an' got the best o' me like no one has ever done. But I ain't Allred."

"Understood, Salty. I was just askin'," Zack said.

"Boys, make sure ta stick close to her, even while she's at Brody's. I don't want ta take no chances on her gettin' hurt. She's done too much for us all ready, an' deserves ta have a good, safe life from here on out."

"We'll take care of it, Ben. You an' Salty keep a close eye on the way out an' back ta where ever you're goin.'"

"Chino Valley, Todd. We're ridin' out ta Chino Valley. Ya ready, Salty? All I got ta do is saddle Captain an' I'll be ready ta ride. Well, after I fetch my Henry from my room."

"Go get it, an' I'll have Clete saddle him up for ya."

Ben was back in under five minutes, to find the boys had departed, Captain saddled, and Salty mounted on his black geld ready to ride. Grabbing his saddlebags from the buggy, he tossed them behind the saddle, tied them on and swung into the saddle. An hour and a half later, they dismounted at the Allred place in front of the corral containing the mules. Ben noted that Salty was right about several things. These mules looked sound, and were tall, very tall. As he stepped into the corral, the mules lined up to look directly at him, and allowed him to inspect their feet and legs without question or difficulty.

"Like what ya see there, mister?" a tall, well-built man dressed in black said from where he now stood beside Salty.

"Yes, I do," Ben said as he checked out the last mule, and then walked over to climb back out of the corral. "Ben Creed is the name, sir."

"Allred, Joshua Allred, Mr. Creed. How soon you looking to buy these mules?"

"Now, if the price is right. Providin' ya can deliver 'em ta Salty's by tomorrow."

"I suppose I could have my boys deliver them by noon tomorrow, if that's one of your conditions, though we don't normally deliver any animals. You have to understand that if anything happens to them on the way into town, they are still your responsibility, right?"

"Yessir, not a problem as long as I have your word they'll be handled with care."

"You have that."

"I guess all that's left is hearin' the price, Mr. Allred."

"Very well, then. I need two thousand dollars for the lot of twelve. Cash money, and no paper money either."

"Pretty steep price, ain't it? I'd think fifteen hundred would be more like it."

"You would, huh? For the best mules this side of Missouri? Mules that can carry an eight hundred pound loaded pack, or carry a man thirty miles a day in the saddle, day after day. These mules are too well trained to let them go cheap. No sir, you've got to do much better than that."

"So, they'll take a saddle as well, eh? An' carry an' eight hundred pound pack? How far?"

"As far as you need them to go, and as often. These mules are all three and four year olds, and have at least a dozen good years of work in them, provided they're well cared for."

"All right, would you consider seventeen fifty for 'em?"

Allred stroked his chin for several minutes before answering. "No, I think not, not if I have to send my boys to town with them. You pick them up here, and maybe."

"All right then, eighteen hundred delivered ta Salty's in Prescott by noon tomorrow. An' I'll pay in gold coin as soon as they land in Salty's corral. Last offer I'll make ya."

Allred turned to face Ben, studying his face for several minutes before answering. "You've got a deal, Mr. Creed. And you're getting the best crop of mules I have ever raised. At least next to those I'm keeping to farm around here, but those are simply not for sale, not for another two or three years anyway. If you need more in the future, I'll have another six young mules like these ready by next spring. You are a shrewd man, Mr. Creed, as I swore I wasn't going to let them go for less that two thousand. Seems you have bested me, young man. But you are welcome back anytime."

"Appreciate that, Mr. Allred, I truly do. An' if there's ever anything I can do for ya, just let Salty know an' he'll pass the word on ta me."

They shook hands, Ben nearly wincing at the firm handshake the stout Mormon man gave him, and hoped he hadn't let on. Salty was all ready mounted by the time Ben got to Captain and swung into the saddle. They turned and headed back to town at a swift trot, slowing to a walk a mile from Allred's place.

"How's your hand, Ben?"

"Just gettin' the feelin' back in it. Why the hell didn't ya warn me about that handshake?"

"That would o' took the fun outa watchin' your face an' knowin' ya was gettin' the same thing everybody else gets when they make a deal with Allred. Sure surprised me that ya never showed a thing, Ben. I figured ya's at least flinch, but ya didn't."

"Well, it took all I had not ta! I'll tell ya that!"

The two men laughed, and the picked up the pace to a trot again, covering the ground to Prescott at a good rate. They had just slowed to a walk again about two miles north of Prescott when the shots rang out. Both men ducked down, and then two more shots rang out off to their left in a clump of trees.

"Stay here, Salty, an' let me see what the hell is goin' on," Ben said as he spurred Captain in the direction of the shots, his Colt drawn and ready. But Salty didn't stay behind; he was riding a step behind Ben and Captain, his black glistening in the sun and his Colt drawn as well.

Chapter Thirty

Just as they reached the trees, Ben could see the figures of four or five men standing in the center of the cluster, mostly hidden by the leaves and branches. Sliding Captain to a halt, he landed on the ground running before his horse had even stopped, heading directly at the men.

"Hold up 'ere, Ben. It's me an' my cousins. The ones whut I tol' ya 'bout outside o' Renner's," Jed Smith called out. "We trailed 'ese two out, a pair o' snakes Barriston uses ta work folks over 'r ta get rid o' 'em. Don' guess 'ey'll be doin' nobody else in any time soon."

Ben, followed by Salty, who had joined him, walked into the trees to where the men all stood in a circle. "They dead, Jed?"

"Naw, we just winged 'em is all. 'Ey oughts ta come too sho'tly. Buford, toss a dab mo' water on 'em, will ya?" After nearly emptying a canteen over the faces of the two men, they finally came up gagging and spitting, cursing at those standing around them.

"Now look here, you two, that's enough 'r I'll let these fellers have their way with ya. I hear they can skin a squirrel in his sleep, so I don't think I'd push me 'r them too far. Mind tellin' me what you two were doin' hid out in these trees, an' who you're workin' for?"

When neither man responded, Ben turned to Smith and asked, "Jed, ya know their names?"

"Yessir. 'At biggun, he's Charlie Alcott, an' the tother one is Curtis Mitchell. I hear tell 'ey's both wanted up in Oklahomer, runnin' whiskey ta the Injuns an' stealin' horses. An' 'ey's both on Barriston's payroll."

"Thanks, Jed." Turning back to the two men now seated on

their fannies on a fallen tree, Ben said to the bigger of the two men, "So, Charlie Alcott, ya work for Randolph Barriston, eh? How many more men he got out tryin' ta kill me 'r my brothers, 'r anybody close to us that they can figure out?"

Charlie's reply was to try to spit in Ben's face, but he didn't get the chance as Ben slipped his Bowie out of the sheath and laid it against his neck. "Now, Charlie, that wasn't a bit hospitable, an' if you're gonna be like that, well, I might have ta try ta get my answers another way."

"Ta hell with you, Creed, an' this bunch of damned hillbillies ya hired." For that one, he got a swift kick to the ribs from one of the men from Kentucky.

"Still haven't learned a thing, have ya, Charlie?" Turning to the men, Ben said, "Whichever one o' ya has the fastest horse, go get the sheriff 'o one o' the deputies as fast as ya can. Try ta make it back 'fore ol' Charlie here bleeds ta death, will ya?"

As one of Jed's cousins left, headed for his horse, Ben said, "All right, Jed, you an' somebody else yank his boots an' socks off, if he's wearin' any, an' roll his pants legs up as far as ya can." When Charlie tried to put up a fight, those remaining at the site pinned him down and removed his boots and socks, leaving a few more bruises up and down his body.

"Now, keep holdin' him down, 'specially his feet. You boys ever hear of 'r see an Apache interrogatin' a man? They got this thing I learned from 'em similar ta the Chinese 'death of a thousand cuts'. The trick is, ya start at their feet, slicin' across the bottoms of 'em, an' then ya move up ta their legs, an' keep workin' on up 'til they either talk 'r die. An' chances are that if it gets that far they're gonna die even after they do talk, 'cause the Apache won't do nothin' ta stop the bleedin' like we whites do."

Stepping to Charlie's feet, Ben leaned over and made a quick stroke across both of Charlie's feet, and then stood up and laughed.

"Gee, I reckon my Bowie is so sharp Charlie never even felt the cuts. But he will shortly, when they start ta bleed even more."

"You're a lyin' sumbitch, Creed. That Apache bluff ain' gonna work on me."

"Really? Take a look at that grass where your feet are, an' tell me that ain't blood," Ben said, stooping over to make yet another quick slice. "Now who is it you work for, an' what were ya doin' out here in these trees?"

Charlie Alcott looked down at the grass, and began to feel the gravity of his situation. "If ya sent for the sheriff, ya ain't about ta bleed me out, Creed."

"Really? We still got ol' Curtis here, an' we can all say he was the only one that got caught. Why, it'd take nothin' ta make you just disappear, would it fellers?"

"No sir, Ben, it sho' wouldn'. If'n he don' take too long ta bleed, we can have 'im buried in less'n an hour, an' ya know the sheriff ain' gonna be here by then," Jed Smith replied.

Ben squatted at Alcott's feet, flipping his knife and catching it by the handle. "Charlie, I'm still waitin'." When Alcott still didn't say anything, Ben swiped across his feet again, making Alcott yank them back this time.

"That hurt, dammit. Now cut it out, Creed."

"Not 'til you either talk, 'r die, Alcott. An' if ya talk, whatever ya tell us ya'd best be ready ta tell the sheriff as well, got it?"

"I'd be signin' my death warrant."

"Well, from the looks of it you've all ready done that right here an' now. Man, you sure can bleed. Jed, I think we might ought ta start on Curtis, 'cause it don't look like Charlie is gonna last too much longer."

"No, don't you cut on me! I'll tell ya whatever ya want ta

know! Just don't cut me!"

"Alcott, you just lost all value ta me. Boys, drag him off an' start diggin' his grave."

"Wait a minute, dammit! I'll talk, too, but only if ya help me stop the bleedin, an' not 'til the sheriff gets here other than ta tell ya Barriston hired us an' another dozen 'r so men ta make life hard for ya, even kill ya if we don't think we'll get caught. An' he sent another dozen men ta raid your claims. He done sent for more men from Phoenix that should be here by the first o' next week."

"You the same ones that tried ta stop Mike Hutchison an' James Whitaker east o' town?"

"Yeah, that was us. Didn't figure a pair o' city dudes ta be carryin' rifles, or know how ta use 'em. Now how 'bout some bandages ta wrap around me feet an' stop the bleedin'?"

"Boys, toss him his socks an' boots back. He ain't gonna bleed ta death from those thin little cuts. Now, if they hadn't started talkin' the cuts would have gotten deeper an' deeper the further up his legs I went, an' time I'd have got to his upper legs he'd have been losin' consciousness from the blood loss."

"Yessir, ain' much diff'rence 'tween whut 'em 'Paches does an' whut 'em Cherokee does wit' a knife. Seed whut was left of a feller when they got done skinnin' 'im onct. Sho' warn' purty, fo sho'."

"What say we get these two loaded on their horses an' start for town. We can turn 'em over ta the sheriff if we cross him on the way." Turning to face Charlie and Curtis, he continued. "An' if ya think ya can change your minds an' not talk, the sheriff'll prob'ly let ya go an' we'll find ya an' finish what I started. Do I make myself clear?"

Both men nodded, and slowly went along with Smith an' his cousins toward the horses, while Ben and Salty went to retrieve their mounts. Meeting back on the road, they started to ride toward town, running into Seth and Sheriff Walker with the Smith rider about a mile out.

"Whatcha got here, Ben?"

"A couple o' Barriston's men that was sent out to cause us some worry. They were in on that attack on Mike and James as well, an' they said they're ready ta talk. Best lock 'em inside the jail away from the windows 'r Barriston is likely ta have 'em shot where they lay."

"All right. I trust you'll be by with a couple o' these men ta fill out reports an' file charges against em yet today, right?"

"You got it, Jeff. But for now I need ta check on the boys an' Chenoa, make sure Barriston's men haven't gotten close to 'em yet. Me an' Salty got a couple other things ta handle, but I'll be by shortly. These fellers can go with ya now an' tell ya what they saw an' did. Jed, you an' your cousins follow the sheriff in, will ya?"

Smith nodded, as Ben and Salty put their mounts into a slow, ground-eating trot. They dropped back to a walk at the city limits, Ben riding directly toward Salty's barn. "Ben, ya said we had some things ta take care of. Whattaya got in mind?"

"You still got that safe in your office?"

"Yessir."

"Would ya mind stashin' somethin' in it for me for a few days?"

"Ya all ready know the answer ta that. But what are ya wantin' to put in it?"

"My saddlebags, after I take a few things out first."

"Ben, that don't tell me a thing."

"All right, Salty. I'm carryin' five thousand in double eagles in 'em, an' after I pull some money out I'll need a safe place ta hide the rest. What with pullin' out the eighteen hundred for Allred tomorrow noon, an' havin' ta slip around town ta pay for supplies, new weapons an' some other bills, I'll be dippin' into it several times 'fore we leave town."

"Whew! That's a chunk o' change, Ben. But I'll sure 'nough let ya keep it in my safe, but why not leave it in the bank?"

"Hours. Like most banks, they open too late an' close too early for me. At least it seems like they're always closed when I need ta get some money out."

"Well, ya know either me 'r Clete is always there, so whenever ya need ta get some out, just come a callin'."

Ben just smiled, knowing that his money would be well hidden and safe. It wasn't long before they rode up to the front of Salty's barn, but Ben dismounted at the door instead of the hitching rail and led Captain inside and to the back. Clete was no where to be seen, until Ben stepped inside Salty's office carrying his saddlebags, and there Clete sat on the floor in a mess of papers with a pretty young woman holding a towel against the back of his head.

"Clete, what happened?"

"Aw, two fellers come in here throwin' their weight aroun', wantin' ta look over the buggy. I told 'em no, an' one o' 'em smacked me on the back o' the head. I can't tell ya much after that, 'cept when I come to there was two other fellers standin' over me 'long with Marshal Dodson, an' Mary Ellen here holdin' this towel ta the back o' my head. That second pair o' fellers is out back, waitin' on you an' Salty ta get back."

Just then Salty stepped in, asking pretty much the same thing, cursing that all his papers had been yanked out of his desk, ending with, "Mary Ellen, what the heck are you doin' here?"

"I came by to pick up my horse for a ride, and found Clete needing aid. It was rather scary at first, with all those men and the Marshal, until I found out what had happened."

"Ben, glad ta see ya made it back. Me an' Stumpy here, we was follerin' a pair o' Barriston's men when they come 'roun' heah," Bear Claw began explaining. "Well, we was standin' 'roun' the corner o' the barn when we heared the trouble start, but when we didn' heah no yells for help we jus' waited. Didn' know they'd knocked ol' Clete thar plumb out. Anyways, we finally decided we'd bes' come in an' check on him, an' found 'em two fellers a tearin' into the office heah. So we thumped 'em real good an' drug 'em ta the back stall an' tied 'em up. Time we got 'et done, the Marshal showed up, an' 'en Miss Mary Ellen heah come walkin' in. Clete had come 'roun' by 'en, an' tolt the Marshal whut happened, an' him an' one o' his deputies hauled 'em rascals off ta jail. Tol' us 'et us an' Clete needed ta come by his office an' sign some papers, an' reckoned Salty'd bes' come in as well."

"Thanks, Bear Claw, Stumpy. Why don't you go on an' head ta the Marshal's Office an' take care o' that. I s'pose Salty an' Clete will go in as soon as Clete is ready ta go, right Salty?"

"Yeah, if I can find somebody ta watch the place for half an' hour 'r so."

"Shoot, I'll do that for ya, Salty. Clete, you feelin' up ta movin' around some?" Ben asked.

"Yeah, I reckon so. Mary Ellen, I sure wanna thank ya for tendin' ta me like ya done. Reckon I owe ya, 'cept I don't know how I'll ever repay ya."

"Oh, Clete, you silly man. I know exactly how you can repay me. Take me to dinner, or on a picnic. Just take me anywhere you want."

Clete blushed a deeper red than Ben thought he had seen in a very long time, but it was pretty obvious Mary Ellen was quite serious, and quite interested in this sort of homely stable hand. Clete struggled to his feet, a bit wobbly at first, but steadied as he started to walk. "Boss, ya ready?"

"Yup, but we'll be takin' the buggy for this trip, Clete, since the buggy horse is all ready hooked up. Ben, we'll be back as soon as we can so's ya can use it ta get the rest o' your business done today." Then leaning in close, he softly said, "The safe's open, so ya can stash 'em saddlebags after we all leave. When we get back, I'll even give ya the combination so's ya can get into it whenever ya need."

As soon as the barn was empty, Ben threw the saddlebags into the safe, after removing two thousand dollars and stuffing the coins in his pockets, and closed the door, making certain it locked. He then stepped out into the breezeway, looking around for something to do. Leading Captain to the stall where he was normally kept, Ben stripped him down and put him away. Then climbing into the mow he started forking hay down to the animals below, finishing by tossing hay out into the area between the corrals.

Climbing back down, he then forked hay into the feed bunks in the corrals, making sure there was enough for all the animals there. Back inside the barn, he gave Captain a ration of oats, but stopped there, not knowing which animals got oats and which didn't, or how much Salty and Clete gave them. He was still contemplating what to do next when Salty pulled the buggy up to the door and helped Clete down.

"I see ya done most o' Clete's chores all ready. Appreciate that, Ben. I don't reckon them two ruffians are gonna see much daylight for several months ta come, time we finished pressin' charges on 'em. Bear Claw an' Stumpy get back here? They said they was comin' back ta keep an eye on ya."

"Haven't seen 'em, Salty. How long ago was that?"

Stepping out of the shadows at the back of the barn, Bear Claw spoke up. "Good, 'et means we was hid out real good, boss. Me an' Stumpy been here near half an hour all ready, makin' sho' warn' nobody come sneakin' 'roun' heah."

"Thanks, men. I'm good, though. G'won home now, will ya?"

Cherokee Parks

Chapter Thirty-One

"Salty, I put the package away all ready, but I don't need ta know the other thing we talked about. Now, I need ta get movin' as I told Chenoa I'd go by an' pick up her saddle an' tack, an' see if her weapons are ready. If I don't hurry, the shops will be closed 'fore I get there an' I'll be terrible late ta pick her up. I'll drop the buggy off once I get her picked up and delivered back here to the hotel."

"No hurry, Ben. We'll be here for a long time tonight, sortin' through and refilin' all this paperwork, so take whatever time ya need."

Ben walked to the buggy, crawled in and was sitting in front of the saddle shop as fast as he could get there. Stepping inside, he was met at the counter by Ralph. "Ben, didn't expect ta see ya quite so soon. What can I do for ya?"

"I need ta pick up Chenoa's saddle, blanket, cinch an' hackamore, an' ta ask if ya have a good scabbard that'll fit that saddle."

"An' I s'pose ya want me ta toss that in as well."

"Naw, I'll pay ya for it, as well as give ya however much ya need right now."

"Well, add twenty dollars for the scabbard an' latigo strings ta hang it on the saddle. I could use a couple hundred dollars now, if ya can give it ta me. I've had ta hire a pair of men ta help me get your order ready, an' they'll need ta be paid shortly."

"No problem there, Ralph," Ben said as he counted out two hundred dollars in double eagles and lay them on the counter. "Mind helpin' me carry this stuff out?"

"Not at all, Ben," Ralph said as he scooped up the blanket, cinch and hackamore after retrieving the scabbard and placing it on

291

the counter. If you'll grab the saddle an' scabbard, we're good."

Ben placed the saddle and scabbard on top of the rest of the tack once Ralph had placed them in the box behind the seat. They shook hands, and without a word Ben jumped back into the buggy and turned toward Loshkarev's.

As he pulled up out front, he could see Nick inside turning down the lights, so he knew he'd have to hurry before the door was locked. Rushing inside, he called out, Nick! Don't close up just yet!"

"Ben, we were just going out to eat an early dinner, and then come back and continue working on your guns. What do you need in such a hurry?"

"I wondered if Chenoa's new Henry is ready, an' ta see if at least one o' the new Colt's are ready."

"Yes, we treated the Henry sights to match yours, and we have two of the Colt's ready to go."

"That's perfect. I need the rifle, an' just one Colt. Oh, an' that gun rig for her as well. An' I'll give ya some money if ya need it."

"Well, I could use a hundred or so, if you have it on you. You don't need any of the cartridges now?"

"Naw, just the Henry an' the Colt an' the riggin'. I still got a good amount o' cartridges," Ben said as he counted out ten double eagles onto the counter.

"Ben, that's more than I need right now. "

"Yeah, but it also cuts down what I'll have ta pay ya later, Nick," Ben said as he picked up the rig and stuffed the Colt into the holster, taking a second to hook the leather loop over the hammer, and then grabbed up the Henry and headed for the door. "Thanks, Nick. See ya in a couple o' days," he said as he stepped out onto the boardwalk and toward the buggy.

Out of the corner of his eye, he saw movement, and swung around with his Colt drawn and pointing in the direction of the movement. "Easy now, boss. It's just me an' Tom," Jed Smith said as he stepped out of the shadows.

"What are you doin' here, Jed?"

"Just keepin' an eye out for ya. Got a couple o' the boys watchin' Zack an' Todd, an' a couple more over ta Brody's, makin' sure Ms. Chenoa is safe an' sound."

"Thanks, Jed. Reckon I'm gettin' more'n I paid for with all you fellers watchin' out for us so close."

"Naw, we owe ya all the watchin' we can give ya, boss. Ya know, ya kind o' hurt Bear Claw an' Stumpy's feelin's, tellin 'em ta go home. They didn't, though. They's watchin' over Mr. Hutchison right now, an' two more is watchin' that lawyer feller, Whitaker, an' two more is keepin' an eye on the bank an' Alvarez. We don't figure ta have none o' Barriston's men get even close again, let alone thump somebody like they done Clete. Oh, an' just so ya know, there'll be men watchin' outside Brody's an' the Congress all night just ta make sure nobody comes sneakin' 'round with larceny in their hearts."

"Damn, Jed, do ya think all that's necessary? I mean, me an' the boys can pretty much take care o' ourselves, an' Chenoa ain't no slouch even by a man's standards."

"Yessir, we do. Ya hired us ta keep Barriston's men at bay, an' by jingo that's just whut we'll do. Ya see, ever one o' us has a bone ta pick with Barriston an' them snakes he keeps aroun'. We even got men watchin' him ta make sure he don't go slinkin' off when things start gettin' too hot for him."

"Well, I reckon that makes sense, an' it's good ta know ever'body has some skin in the game, Jed. Includin' all you men. I s'pose all I can say ta that is, try ta get as much rest as ya can, an' thanks for makin' sure we do. Now, I need ta get ta Brody's 'fore Chenoa thinks I forgot all about her."

Jed stepped back into the shadows and disappeared as Ben popped the whip and set the buggy into motion. It was still daylight as he pulled up to a stop in front of Brody's and walked up to the porch to find Mose sitting there with a double-barreled ten gauge lying on his lap. Mose, been a while. How ya doin'?"

"Ben, yessir, been a long spell, ain' it? Ms. Chenoa is inside, an' I reckon her an Maybelline is 'bout done with the last batch o' corndodgers. Say, she's a real pistol, ain' she? Sharp as a tack an' quick as anything I ever seed. Her an' Maybelline is the bes' o' friends now."

"Yeah, she has that effect on ever'body she meets. Say, Mose, I hate ta ask, but why the shotgun?"

"Oh, I seen a couple o' fellers a sneakin' 'roun' heah a while back, an' figured 'ey was a tryin' ta get clost ta Chenoa."

"I hired some fellers this afternoon ta keep an eye on her an' my brothers. Might o' been some o' 'em as I know they been around."

"Naw, they showed up sho'tly after the firs' pair, an' all but run that firs' pair off. I knows some o' 'em fellers. Good men all, an' treats me like a equal, even though mos' o' 'em fought for the South durin' the war. An' ya can count me in if'n it comes ta a fight with Barriston an' his bunch. That dirty sumbitch done stole all he's a evah gonna steal from me, an' 'at's a natural fact'."

"Yeah, don't seem ta me like he's got too many friends, at least around Prescott. An' he's sure in my crosshairs, right along with the feller he works for, that Manuel Meador out o' Phoenix. I may not get Meador, but takin' Barriston out will sure hurt his operation."

"Like I said, count me in. Now what say you an' me sees if'n we can get 'em womenfolk ta let us sample 'em corndodgers?"

"You bet!"

Stepping inside the front door of Brody's home and rooming house, Ben and Mose walked directly back to the kitchen. After both men taking seats at the table along with Maybelline, Chenoa poured them each a cup of coffee, and then refilled Maybelline's. "I suppose you two want to see if my corndodgers will pass the test. What do you think, Maybelline? Shall we allow them to sample my cooking?"

"Yeah, honey chil', let 'em at 'em corndodgers. Lawd knows what we gonna do with sa many if'n we don' let's the men get started eatin' 'em."

Both Mose and Ben grabbed one each from the platter sitting in the middle of the table, and started eating. "Oh, my, Chenoa. These are just like my Maw makes, maybe better. Maybelline, is this your recipe?"

"Well, it was, 'til Chenoa added a twist to 'em. Danged if'n ah ain' gonna use her recipe from now on. An' ah done et sa many ah cain' take anothah bite, ah sweah."

"Yes, I agree. We have been sampling all afternoon, since the very first batch, and I am so full I may even have to skip breakfast tomorrow. But I certainly see why you men love them so much out on the trail. They are absolutely delicious."

Mose was already on his third one when Zack and Todd walked in, each taking a seat at the table and being served coffee by Chenoa, followed by each grabbing a corndodger and joining in the praise of them.

"Maybelline, how many ya figure you gals made today?"

"I quit ta countin' at fo'teen dozen, Ben. Why?"

"You got a big flour sack I can have?"

Maybelline answered by stepping into her pantry and then

handing a flour sack to Ben. "If you don't mind, ladies, would ya mind fillin' this sack up with corndodgers, an' then we can eat the rest," he finished with a laugh.

"And just what are you going to do with these, Ben?"

"Oh, not me. Todd an' Zack. Boys, there's a bunch o' men out an' around town that's been watchin' over us today, includin' a couple keepin' an eye on things here. Would ya mind takin' this sack out an' havin' 'em spread these around ta the rest? Lord knows there's still plenty for us, but we might need a fresh batch ta take with us the day we pull out o' town."

"You sure there's gonna be any left time we get back in here, Ben, Mose?"

"Oh, we'll leaves ya a couple, boys, won' we, Ben?"

"Oh, yeah, maybe three 'r four, if you don't take too long."

Each grabbing two as they stood and grabbed the bag, Todd said, "Well, Zack, sounds like we'd best find 'em fellers right quick like, eh?"

"Yep, let's get to it!"

Once the boys were out the door, Ben said, "Chenoa, let's take a few more o' these an' head for the hotel. See if I can eat four or five more 'fore we get there. But we need ta get movin' 'fore it gets full on dark. Maybelline, I appreciate ya teachin' Chenoa how ta make these corndodgers, an' I'm glad ya got on so good."

"Ben, boy, when are ya gonna larn? Long as a body does me right, like you Creed boys has done, ah can gets on wit anybody. Now Chenoa, tha's a whole new thang. Why, she's like a sistah, an' if'n somethin' was ta happen to ya, she can come live wit' us'n if'n she wuz of a min' ta. 'Cep' ah reckons she's got a plenty o' places ta puts her boots, but she still welcome heah any o' time."

"Thank you so much, Maybelline. And you, too, Mose. From

the moment I arrived I felt like I was right at home, just like these Creed boys have made me feel just like a sister to them. You have all been so wonderful to me," Chenoa said, dabbing at a tear.

Ben was surprised to see such an open sign of emotion and hear the care in the Paiute woman's voice, having become accustomed to her being stoic and hiding any feeling she might have about anything from everyone. That was a small part of what made her a top-notch negotiator in his mind; her ability to deal based on strictly price and value, with no apparent emotion involved.

After hugs all around, and handshakes between Mose and Ben, the younger couple hustled out to the buggy and climbed aboard. As Ben swung the buggy around, headed toward the hotel, a figure suddenly stepped out of the shadows to stop him. "Thankee, boss, fer sendin' out 'em corndodgers. Ain' had nothin' like 'et fer a passel o' time. We done passed 'em on ta the nex' bunch o' fellers."

"An' who are you, if ya don't mind me askin'?" Ben queried.

"Ah'm George Smith, one o' Jed's cousins. An' ovah yondah is my brothah Billy. We's gonna be keepin' an eye on 'em brothahs o' yorn tanight."

"Thanks, George. Much appreciated."

They were down the street and around the corner before Chenoa spoke. "Ben, just how many men did you hire to watch over us? So far, I've counted nine, and I actually think I may have seen three or more but I couldn't be certain."

"Well, I thought I was gettin' eight 'r ten tops, but I gave Muley twenty double eagles an' told him ta hire twenty good men, but I sure didn't figure he'd find that many, 'r that quick. Seems in spite o' the growth an' all goin' on around Prescott, there's still plenty o' good men needin' work. Good ta know, 'cause we're gonna need guards at the smelter, as well as at the bank later, an' both lumberjacks an' miners. These twenty an' a few more ought ta be plenty, an' gettin' started now, testin' their loyalties an' resolve, is a good thing to do."

"Yes, Ben, it seems to be a good plan, especially if they keep our business associates safe as well as us, and can be counted on later as trusted employees at the claims. I just worry that they may be left flat if things change with you selling out after you have your nest egg."

"Men like that go from hard time to hard time, Chenoa, an' only a few ever get a good break that lifts them up. An' a few o' 'em will make their own breaks an' rise up, but that's not too many of 'em. Oh, I'll do what I can to make certain they are well rewarded for what they do for us while we're at it, an' hope they spend any money they get wisely."

"I knew that about you all ready, Ben, and your brothers are just like you. I can only assume your entire family is that way, and were taught those values by your mother and father."

"That about sums it up. Maw an' Paw always seemed ta be hard knuckled an' tough on us, but now that I'm growed I sure see the value o' what they taught us."

As they pulled up in front of the Congress Hotel, Clete came walking slowly across the street to meet them, his bandage still firmly in place. "Clete, what happened to you?"

"Well, Ms. Chenoa, I just got my head in the wrong place," he replied, winking at Ben.

"You're all right then?"

"Yes, ma'am, just got a bit of a headache is all, but even that's goin' away."

"Well, take good care of yourself, and by all means be more careful."

"Yes, ma'am. I sure will," Clete said as he took their place on the buggy seat and started to turn it across the street to the stable.

"Say, Clete, we'll leave the saddle, blanket, hackamore, scabbard an' cinch in the buggy if you'll put 'em up in the tack room for me."

Clete only nodded as Ben and Chenoa lifted the rifle and gun rigging out of the back of the buggy.

Cherokee Parks

Chapter Thirty-Two

"Can ya handle this stuff goin' upstairs, Chenoa?"

"Certainly. By the way, could I get some cartridges from you? I'd like to fill the rifle and Colt, as well as the belt if you have enough."

"Sure, just give me a few minutes ta take care o' some business at the front desk," Ben said just before stuffing the last of his corndodgers in his mouth. "Then maybe we can come have some coffee 'fore we turn in."

The bellboy appeared, offering to take everything upstairs for Chenoa, but she shook him off, thanking him for the offer. As she climbed the staircase, Ben stepped up to the counter to find Claude's brother, Leslie, handling the night desk chores. "Leslie, I'd like ta pay up front for the next couple o' months, both rooms," Ben said counting out fifteen double eagles on the counter. "That ought ta do it for the next three months, right, Leslie?"

"Yessir, Mr. Creed. You know you have all ready paid for at least a month in advance, don't you? And that's enough, actually for both rooms, two months if it was just your room, sir."

"Naw, didn't know I'd paid that far in advance, but that's fine. That'll handle anything we need for a bit. All I ask is that our rooms be kept fresh and secure durin' our absences."

"Oh, yessir. Claude and I see to that without asking, and now even François has taken an interest in seeing to it that your rooms are at the top of the list for being kept clean as well as making certain only the maids are allowed in."

"Good deal. I don't see François tonight. Where's he hidin' out?"

"Believe it or not, Mr. Creed, François has taken the night off. Is there something else I can take care of for you?"

"Well, Chenoa an' I will be down for coffee shortly, but that's it."

"Very well, sir. I'll see to it you have a nice, quiet table," Leslie said motioning to the dining room to get someone's attention.

As Ben walked across the lobby and started up the stairs, he could see out of the corner of his eye that Leslie was giving Mitzi specific instructions, which brought a big smile to his face. Stepping inside his room and delving into the closet for cartridge boxes, he pulled out two while taking stock of the remaining boxes. After taking two, he was down to his last box, making the order for five hundred rounds timely for their trip into the Bradshaw's. He even considered asking for another five hundred rounds when he stopped to drop off his Henry in the next day or so.

Stepping back into the hallway, then double-checking to make sure his door was locked, he stepped down to Chenoa's room and tapped on her door. As she opened the door, he could see she had taken time to freshen up, though she still wore the same clothes as earlier. The only sign of her having spent the afternoon cooking was a small spot of flour on her pants leg.

"Ya might take a moment ta brush that flour off after ya put these someplace safe," Ben said as he handed her the two boxes of .44-40 cartridges. "Ya know, I never thought ta ask if you wanted two hundred grain slugs, 'r if the two twenty-fives were all right."

"Oh, the two twenty-fives are perfect. I rarely need to fire at great distances to bring down deer for food, so the weight of the two twenty-five is good as it has a bit more stopping power at closer ranges. Also, wind does not affect the two twenty-five as much as the smaller slug, though elevation does and one must be careful to give enough lift on longer shots," Chenoa demonstrated her knowledge of ammunition as she brushed off the flour, and the placed the cartridges under the edge of her bed before returning to the door. "Shall we?" she finished by stepping into the hallway to join Ben.

Descending the stairway at a casual pace, Ben glanced out through the lobby doors in the direction of Salty's to see two men, who he assumed were among those he had hired, leaning against the barn. They waved, and he nodded in return.

"Yes, Ben, I saw them as well. I think they were eating my corndodgers. Gee, I hope they enjoy them."

"Anybody that don't like 'em corndodgers has lost their sense o' taste. Mitzi's got us that table right over there, an' it looks like she just brought out a fresh pot o' coffee," Ben said as he saw Mitzi slightly motion them in her direction.

As they sat down, Mitzi asked, "Will there be anything else besides coffee?"

"Not for us, Mitzi, but if you could take a pot of fresh coffee and a pair of cups to those two men leaning against Mr. Murphy's barn, I would really appreciate it. And just tell them to bring the pot and cups back when they've finished, and I know they will do so gladly," Chenoa asked the waitress.

Mitzi curtsied, and disappeared into the kitchen, coming back out a few minutes later with a pair of tin cups and a large battalion style pot. She smiled as she carried the pot and cups past Ben and Chenoa, outside and across the street, speaking to the two men while serving them, and then hurrying back into the hotel dining room. Stopping at their table, she said, "They said to tell you thanks, ma'am." And then Mitzi was gone from sight again.

"My, my, she certainly doesn't act like several others have told me she acts in front of you. Why is that, Ben?"

"Oh, I think she's most likely scared ta death o' ya. 'R she thinks there's more goin' on 'tween us than what there is, an' she done lost out. Whatever, I don't know, 'r care, as long as she stops pesterin' me."

"Now, Ben, you know you enjoyed the attention, especially from such a pretty young girl. In fact, I think I should tell her that you're still available and to have at it."

"Don't you dare, Chenoa! I like things just the way they are right now. Now finish that coffee an' let's go get some shuteye," Ben said, only half kidding.

Ten minutes later, they were saying good night in the hallway and going into their respective rooms.

***

Ben was up, sitting on the edge of the bed in the pre-dawn light contemplating how to dress for this particular day. He still needed to go by the sheriff's office, and he needed to remember to take his Henry in to Loshkarev's so they had all the time they needed to clean out the barrel. Noon would see the mules come in, and he would want to look them over before laying down one thousand eight hundred dollars in gold coin. He decided that wearing his best wasn't a good idea, though he did really like his new hat and would wear it instead of the Derby.

It had cost him a pretty penny, but was the most comfortable hat he had ever owned or worn. *Whoever this Stetson feller is, he sure come up with a good hat. An' if it lasts like that feller said ta me tryin' ta get me ta believe all he bragged about, I won't need another hat for at least ten years. Just somethin' funny 'bout buyin' a hat at The Palace instead o' in a shop 'r store.*

Picking out a clean pair of tan, woolen trousers and a light blue linsey-woolsey shirt, Ben fastened the shirt and then sat down to attach the suspenders to the trousers, pulling on a fresh pair of socks before pulling on the trousers. Stomping into his boots, and then strapping on his gun rig, Ben finished by plopping the hat on his head. Picking up his Henry so he wouldn't have to make a trip back up the stairs, Ben started for the door.

Before he could reach the door, there came a light tap. Carefully opening the door, half expecting Chenoa, there stood another hulk of a man dressed in frontier leather and carrying a Sharps rifle. "Mr. Creed, jus' figured we'd bes' let ya know we done took two more fellers ta task fer sneakin 'roun' the hotel. 'Ey was a tryin' ta get inta Ms. Chenoa's room in the night, but me an' Hank done stopped that. 'Ey's over ta the city jail now, as the marshal done picked 'em up 'bout a hour ago."

"Thanks, an' what's your name?"

"I'm Ferd, one o' Jed's cousins, an' 'et feller yonder is my brothah Hank. Thanks fer 'et coffee las' night."

"You can thank Chenoa. She was the one who sent it."

"Reckon we'll do jus' 'et, when we sees her. But ah reckon ya paid fer it, sa thanks. Well, we'll be goin' ta get some sleep. 'Ere's another pair o' fellers outside watchin' all ready."

The big man just turned and ambled away. Ben stood there with his door open, just looking into the hall, when he heard Chenoa open and close her door. Stepping out to join her, she said, "Ben, I need a substantial breakfast this morning. I think a visit to Renner's is in order, that is unless you have other plans."

"Nope, that suits me just fine. Them corndodgers quit on me about halfway through the night, an' my belly is plumb empty. Shall we?" Ben asked, noticing that Chenoa had strapped on her rig as well. He almost didn't notice it, as it seems to be a natural looking part of her.

Stepping out onto the boardwalk, they didn't see Clete or Salty ready to deliver the buggy, so they started across the street. Out of the corner of his eye, he could see two more strange men watching over them, and trusted that they had been hired by Muley. Just as they reached the barn, the double door swung open wide. And

305

there stood both Clete and Salty.

"Sorry, Ben, we're gettin' kind of a late start this mornin'. We both had a long hard night, wakin' ta ever' noise. Only reason we got any sleep at all was knowin' 'em fellers ya hired was awake an' makin' sure ever'thing was quiet. Buggy is ready; we just hadn't brought it up yet. That was next, after we opened the doors. Chenoa, I seen that saddle an' hackamore. Real fine lookin', an' ought ta do the trick. That is if ya can get that filly ta take it," Salty said with a big smile.

"I'll be by around noon or shortly after, Salty, and we'll just see what she's got. But Ben, you'd better get me some coffee and feed me if I'm going to live that long," Chenoa said with a smile as she climbed into the buggy Clete had just brought to the front.

"Don't forget that delivery for ya at noon, Ben."

"I won't, not for a minute, Salty. Say, I need ta make a withdrawal this mornin, 'fore we get too far."

Taking quite a lot of the remaining double eagles from his saddlebag, but making sure to leave two thousand, Ben said, "Now, I'm in the same shape as that gal there, weak from hunger, so we'll see ya at noon, pard," Ben replied as he climbed aboard the buggy and popped the whip launching them down the street.

As they made their way to Renner's, it seemed that at every corner there was someone watching them, three men when they pulled up in front of the small café. Climbing down, Ben said, "Todd an' Zack must be here all ready. That sure looks like Zack's horse Blue, an' Todd's horse Morgan is tied up right beside him."

Inside, Ben was proven correct, as his brothers were all ready seated and drinking coffee. "Ben, you're near late to buy. Thought I was gonna have ta arm wrestle Zack again to get him ta buy."

"Who said I was buyin' anyway?"

"Aw, now Ben, you're the rich one in the family, least ways next ta Nellie anyway."

"Now, don't go ta comparin' me that that tightwad girl. She's still got the first penny she ever earned, doncha know."

"Ben, Chenoa, just heard ya. I'll get ya some cups. Big hungry 'r little one?" Jason asked.

"Big ones, both of us, Jason."

"Steak, eggs and taters comin' right up, same as the boys ordered," the co-owner of the café said as he ducked back into the kitchen.

"Boys, glad I caught ya this mornin' first thing. I'm changin' plans. We done told everybody we'd pull out the middle o' next week, an' that's what Barriston an' his cronies are thinkin'. So, instead, we're pullin' out day after tomorrow. Chenoa, sorry ta cut your time short on gettin' your filly ready, but we need the element o' surprise. I'll go around an' order a few more things as well as tell the merchants I want ta have everything ready first thing in the mornin' day after tomorrow. I figure if we can hit the trail by mid-mornin', we can make a good distance 'fore we have ta camp, an' be in a place where we have good cover an' plenty o' water. Then we can be in camp by late the next day, an' have ever'thing unpacked an' put up by noon the day after that. We'll rest that afternoon, an' you two can get the layout down 'fore we head up ta the gold claim. Any questions?"

When none came after several minutes, Chenoa spoke up. "Don't worry about that filly, she'll be ready by tonight. But what about the packsaddles, will they be ready? And the Colt's, will Nick have them finished?"

"Yeah, 'cause I'll light a fire under both of 'em ta make sure. I'm droppin' off my Henry ta be cleaned this mornin', boys, an' I suggest ya do the same with your Winchesters so we can pick 'em up yet this afternoon. Now then, I see ya got your best horses out. Any special reason for it?"

The boys looked at each other and laughed before Zack answered. "Ben, our whole lives you always plan ta leave a certain day 'r time, an' ya get itchy footed an' pull out a day 'r so earlier. Most o' the time ya don't even tell nobody, ya just leave. But I reckon ya need us an' Chenoa ta go along this time 'r ya wouldn't have said a word. An' we decided we'd best limber our horses up some 'fore we ride out."

"Damn, am I that predictable?"

"Only ta those that know ya like family, Ben."

"Reckon I need ta make some changes ta how I do things. Hate bein' predictable. That's the kind o' thing that gets a feller killed."

The boys nodded, sticking this tidbit of information into the memory banks for a time when they might need it for their own safety. Chenoa also tucked it away, adding a new piece of information to her all ready vast knowledge of survival.

Chapter Thirty-Three

Agreeing to meet at Loshkarev's at ten, the four finished a hearty breakfast and went about their individual business. Ben and Chenoa drove directly to Porter's Saddlery, not needing to take Zack and Todd along as they were all ready riding their repaired saddles on new blankets. Ben was intent on making certain Ralph and his helper would be able to have the packsaddles and tack ready by the next afternoon or evening.

"Ralph, how's it goin' on my order?"

"I'll have it all finished up by Monday next week, two days ahead o' schedule, Ben."

"Not soon enough. We've been forced ta change plans, an' I'll want ta have it all ready ta pick up late tomorrow. Not a word ta anybody, an' I mean not a soul, 'bout the change o' plans."

"Yeah, I hear tell Barriston's men have been takin' potshots at ya, but I also hear ya hired a bunch o' tough ol' mountain men ta counter anything them skunks do. That true?"

"Yessir, an' so far they been makin' sure nobody gets close to us. Now, about my order. Can I pick it up tomorrow?"

"Ben, your brothers have picked up their saddles. I assumed you were paying for their repairs as well, so I'll need to add that onto your bill. Other than that, your order is all but done, but I wanted time to check over all the stitchin' since I ain't doin' all the work myself. I brought in Jimmy Jacobs, an' he's a real fine hand but kinda green yet, an' I hired Mando Armendariz as well. Now he's a real fine saddle maker from a long line o' saddle makers in South Texas, but I still wanna check over his work."

"As long as I can have everything by tomorrow night, I don't care what ya have ta do, Ralph," Ben said, sounding a bit irritated.

"Ralph, you'll have to forgive Ben here. It's been a real strain on him, having to lay out so much money to get this enterprise started, and what with that bastard Barriston trying to stall us and actually do us harm, well…" Chenoa let her words drift off.

"Aw, hell, I understand, Chenoa. I truly do. An' I ain't gonna hold it against him for bein' short with me. Shoot, I was short with both of ya the other day when ya come in. Ben, I'll make sure it's all done an' ready ta go, even if I have ta stay here all night. What's more, I'll even guarantee that if any o' the stitches come lose we'll fix 'em next time ya come in."

"Thanks, Ralph, but don't you do that anyway, you old rascal?" Ben asked.

The saddle maker had to laugh, "Yeah, I do, but I know you're gonna be workin' 'em packsaddles pretty hard. So, that said, I'll even give ya a year's guarantee that our work will stand the test. Fair 'nough?"

"Plenty fair, Ralph. An' 'fore I forget, throw in one o' them regular packsaddles ya stock for horses, as I picked up that blue roan geld Salty had, an' I'll need ta use him for packin' as well. Now, how much I owe ya, includin' for the boys saddle repairs?"

The price was stated, and Ben counted out enough double eagles to cover it, plus a pair extra. "Give Mando an' Jimmy each one, will ya? I appreciate ya takin' 'em on, an' a little bonus might help ta keep 'em workin' hard for ya, Ralph. Well, we need ta hightail it, but we'll be back with a wagon about four tomorrow afternoon."

"Best make it six, Ben, just ta make sure we got it all wrapped up."

"All right then. Chenoa, let's get ta movin'. See ya tomorrow, Ralph."

The next stop was at Carlton Stockdale's warehouse, to ensure all their supplies were ready, and to add a few more items as well as make the last payment on what they needed. Carlton's wife was at the desk when they walked in, but spoke without looking up.

"Marisol, what's wrong? Why won't you look at us? Stand up here and let me see your face," Chenoa said.

Slowly shaking her head no, Marisol stayed seated. Chenoa walked around the desk and placed a hand under the woman's chin, lifting her face upward, and then brushing her hair aside. There was a big bruise across her cheek combined with a black eye. Ben was instantly furious, but held his tongue as Chenoa tried to get Marisol to stand.

"I can't stand today, Chenoa. That is why Carlton has me at the desk, because my leg is hurt."

That was all Ben needed. "Carlton! Get your ass up here! NOW!"

From the back of the storeroom came the sound of someone walking heavily, until Carlton stepped out into the open behind the desk. "Yes? What is it? Oh, Ben, it's you. I was just assembling the last of your ord..."

He didn't get to finish his sentence as Ben's right uppercut dropped him where he stood. Grabbing a pitcher of water from the corner of the desk, Ben poured it on the prone man's face until he came up blubbering. "How's it feel, big man, gettin' knocked on your fanny by somebody your own size? So, you like beatin' your woman, do ya? Wait 'til I get the word spread all over town that ya beat your wife an' we'll see if you're still in business time we get back ta town."

"By gawd, Ben, it's none of your business what goes on between a man and his wife."

"It is when I'm doin' business with a wife-beater. I won't tolerate it!"

311

"But she…"

"I don't give two hoots in hell what she did 'r didn't do, understand? She's a woman, plain an' simple, an' needs ta be treated like one. Ya wanna punch on somethin', try me, ya road apple. An' it might do ya some good ta get the crap knocked outa ya. I'll bet ya don't lay a hand on that sweetheart ya got on the side, though."

"What are you talking about? I don't have a…"

"Yeah, ya do. The whole damned town knows it. You don't want your wife, give her the business an' leave town with your concubine, but if I ever hear that ya laid another hand on Marisol I'll beat you ta a pulp. Got it?"

"But, but, Ben, I love my wife. It's just that…"

"I don't give a damn what your excuses are. Treat her right 'r I'll take care of ya real good. Now, ya can start by apologizin' to her."

Still lying on the floor, Carlton managed to get up on one knee in front of his wife, and said, "Marisol, I'm sorry. I truly am. And I promise to stop seeing Amy, and I also promise to never lay another hand on you. Will you forgive me, please?"

"No, I won't. Not until you prove to me that what you are promising is true. Carlton, if you touch me again, or come home smelling of her perfume, I'll kill you in your sleep. I'll take no more!"

Carlton hung his head, whimpering, "Please, dear. I'm so sorry."

"Aw, get up, you fool. I need ta find out if my order will be ready ta pick up day after tomorrow, an' we need ta add a few things. I can't stand ta look at ya. Chenoa, you an' Marisol handle it, will ya? An' when you're done, let me know an' I'll come in an pay it all off. But, Carlton, the money goes ta Marisol, not you, an' if I was you I just believe I'd let her handle all the money from now on," Ben said firmly before turning and walking out onto the boardwalk.

Twenty minutes later, Chenoa called him back inside, where he counted out the necessary double eagles to pay for all of their supplies, handing Marisol two extra coins and telling her, "You hang on to these, just in case ya need 'em. An' don't ever hang your head again. Oh, an' make sure Carlton don't blab a word of us pickin' up our supplies day after tomorrow. We'll be loadin' early that mornin', so I'd appreciate it if ya was here an open early."

"I'll see to it that all of your supplies are ready to load, and I'll have someone here to help you load as well, Ben. And thank you. I guess I just needed someone to take my side for a change. Carlton will never hurt me again, I swear it," Marisol said with a strength in her voice Ben had never heard.

Back outside, Chenoa gave Ben a hug and said, "Ben that was the nicest thing I've ever seen you do. Well, next to saving me, that is. I appreciate it."

Ben didn't know what to say, as what he did was what he had seen his own father do to a wife beater back in Colorado City when he was a young man. To his way of thinking, it was the only thing a man could do to help a woman in trouble. Without a word, he helped Chenoa into the buggy, crawled in and headed for the granary.

Satisfied that they would have all the sacks of oats ready for him the next day, he paid the bill in advance and they started out for Loshkarev's to meet the boys, hoping that Nick and his uncles would have everything finished and ready to pick up, even though it was several days ahead of schedule.

"Nick, how's it coming? Everything ready? We'd like ta take it all now, if we can, provided we can get them rifles cleaned pronto," Ben said to the young man as they met at the counter.

"Yes, as a matter of fact, Ben, all the Colt's have been set up the way you want them, but the rifles will take at least an hour. Now, I have a question. Are you going to keep the Colt's in your saddlebags, or wear them?"

"Tell ya the truth, I figured on stashin' mine in my saddlebags. Why?"

"Well, Sergei and I were talking, and he said it would be a real shame to wrap them up and put them where you might have trouble getting to them when needed. He suggested that, quite possibly, you hadn't thought about hanging a cross draw holster on your rigging. There would still be plenty of room for your knives and sheaths, provided the extra holster was mounted correctly."

"Yeah, I've seen a few of those cross draw rigs, an' a lot more with a two hand draw setup. Never really cared much for either, but considerin' what we might be up against at any time, it might not be a bad idea ta have the second Colt in reach. Let's see what ya got, an' we'll decide from there."

Nick called out for Sergei, who stepped out of the back room, taking the three rifles from the Creed brothers, looking them over and then disappearing into the back room again. While Sergei had been handling the rifles, Nick had stepped into the back room and came out carrying four cross draw holsters, laying them out individually across the top of the counter. "These were made by a Mexican fellow my father knows, a Mando Armendariz from down around South Texas he said. The quality is top notch, and can have conchos mounted if one is so inclined. Would you like to try one?"

"Yeah, I believe I would. How 'bout the rest o' ya, wanna try one out?" Ben asked, thinking that Mando had done a lot to stay busy.

"Yes, I would, Ben. I've used one before, and found it somewhat cumbersome when doing other things. But as long as they can be removed when there is no danger, I'd like to see how this one feels."

"Lady makes sense, brother. Reckon I'm with her," Todd said, with Zack nodding in agreement.

Slipping the new holsters onto their gun belts, the foursome followed Nick into the back room, feeding cartridges into their new Colts as they walked. Facing the sandbags again, Chenoa was the first to draw, snapping her first Colt out and firing two quick shots, followed by flipping the first gun into her left hand, drawing the second Colt and firing two more rounds.

As she turned around, the men were all looking at her with a renewed admiration of her gun handling skills. Ben was next, performing the same routine as the Paiute woman, with the same result. Zack and Todd followed suit, but neither was as quick to pull the second pistol.

"Take some gettin' used to, but I just believe it might come in handy on the trail. Not so much around camp, 'r just movin' around, but damned handy if a fellow happened to be in a fight with more'n one shooter," Zack was the first to comment. "I believe I'll take one, dependin' on how much ol' Nicky here tries ta soak us."

"They are fifteen dollars each, and I'll even apply some oil to slick them up if you'll give me a few minutes."

"Todd, how 'bout you?"

Todd only nodded, followed by Ben saying, "All right, Nick. You got a deal. An' we'll wear the Colt's out today as well. We'll step outside ta wait while ya get the boy's Winchester's an' my Henry cleaned up."

"Very well, Ben," Nick said taking Ben's gun belt and starting to oil the new holster. "Would you like to take your cartridges along as well?"

"Yeah, I reckon we might as well."

"Very well. Now if you'll give me twenty minutes to finish oiling your new holsters and put the cartridges together... Oh, and I'll package the knives and sheaths for you, Ms. Chenoa, so you can take them along as well."

"Make sure Sergei does a good job o' cleanin' the lead out o' them barrels, Nick," Ben said as they stepped outside. "Oh, an' if anybody asks, you have no idea when we might be pullin' out o' town."

"That's pretty easy, Ben, as I really don't have any idea when you might be leaving. Not that I even care, as long as the bill is paid before you leave town," Nick responded with a laugh.

It was nearly a half hour later that Nick opened the door to let the group know the rifles were ready, the additional holsters were slicked up, and everything had been wiped down. Additionally, the cartridges were all packed into two wooden cases, and Chenoa's new knives were carefully tucked into their sheaths and wrapped in heavy oilcloth.

It took ten minutes to carry the crates of cartridges out and get them situated in the buggy, even with Boris and Sergei assisting. When they were finally finished, Ben said to the boys, "Chenoa an' me got ta be at Salty's at noon. The mules are due ta be delivered by Allred's boys, an' Chenoa is chompin' at the bit ta get stared on that filly o' hers. Might be somethin' ta see, if ya want ta swing by."

"See ya at Salty's here shortly then, Ben. Yeah, I don't know about Zack, but I want ta see what this gal can do ta settle a horse down, considerin' how tough she is on people," Todd said with a laugh.

"See ya there, then," Ben said as he held the door open for Chenoa as they stepped inside. "All right, Nick, what's the bottom line today."

"With the additional cartridges and the new holsters, four hundred twenty dollars, Ben, less the two hundred you've already paid leaves two hundred twenty."

Ben quickly counted out eleven coins onto the counter. "There ya go, Nick. We're good ta go 'til I need somethin' else. Oh, an' if Chenoa ever comes in when I ain't around, treat her right from the gitgo, an' put whatever she needs on my bill an' I'll pay ya next time I'm in after that."

"No problem, Ben. She is too tough to deal with for me to do anything but treat her right, and I know father and mother will agree after dealing with her just once. Have a safe journey, my friend, and return in one piece. Oh, and make certain you bring Chenoa around once in a while to see Sergei, will you?" Nick said with a huge smile.

Ben couldn't help but laugh, as he had seen Sergei peeking through the curtain separating the front and back rooms, and Chenoa sneaking smiling looks in Sergei's direction every time she got a chance. "By golly, I'll just do that, Nick. Chenoa, we'd better get a move on if we're gonna make it ta Salty's by noon. Shall we?" he said, giving her one more chance to smile in Sergei's direction before he turned her toward the door.

"I'm glad you and Nick had such a good laugh at my and Sergei's expense. I'll remember that, and believe me when I say you will get paid well for that, Ben Creed. Now, take me to my horse, quickly, driver." Seeing the look on Ben's face, Chenoa couldn't help but break into laughter. Unfortunately, her laughter didn't last long...

Cherokee Parks

Chapter Thirty-Four

As they rounded the corner to the street running between the Congress Hotel and Saltpeter Murphy's Livery, shots rang out. Ben and Chenoa both reached for their Colt's, not knowing exactly where the shots came from or where they were intended to go. Ben swung the buggy to the side of the street as near Salty's as he could get, and the pair jumped up taking cover behind the buggy.

Ben could see Zack and Todd's horses all ready tied to the rail on the far side of Salty's double barn doors, and guessed that they were spread out, one on each side of the opening. At the far corner of Salty's barn lay a man in the dirt, and he could see two more across the street lying at the corners of the Congress.

"All clear, Ben," came a familiar voice from the corner nearest he and Chenoa. "We got three o' em whut tried ta ambush 'em brothers o' yorn, but one got away. Bear Claw, Rooster an' Muley lit out ta hunt him down. 'Ey ought ta be back sho'tly," Jed Smith said stepping out from the near corner of the barn. "Stumpy got hisse'f nicked, an' ah reckon we ought ta send fer the doc. Carl an' me an' Big Mike is fine, an' ah reckon some o' my cousins'll be 'long sho'tly as well, boss. 'Fo' an fohgets ta tell ya, we done grabbed two more ovah ta Whitaker's a few minutes back, an' run off a pair up ta the assayer's office as well. Seems like ol' Barriston is gettin' right nervous."

"Indeed, it sure looks an' sounds like it, Jed. Chenoa, why don't you get inside with the boys, an' I'll take the buggy on up ta the door." Without waiting for Chenoa to respond, Ben was all ready in the buggy, moving it along the few feet to park it next to the door, thinking that it might be best to get all the cartridges unloaded inside the barn instead of driving a powder keg around town.

"Say, Ben, you're gettin' kind o' dangerous ta be around, ain't

319

ya, son?"

"Sure seems like it, Salty. You an' Clete all right?"

"Yeah, we was both back in the office when the boys showed up an' all hell busted loose."

"Good. Say, I've got five hundred rounds o' .44-40 cartridges I need ta store here 'til mornin' after next, if ya don't mind. I guess I don't need ta tell ya that's when we're leavin', an' ta ask ya ta keep that to yourself," Ben said facing the stableman.

"Yeah, I figured as much. Ya been too active this mornin', an' it looks like Barriston has figured out somethin's up as well. An' yeah, ya can set 'em cartridges over in the stall next ta the one we keep Captain in. That's where we been puttin' the tack that belongs to you an' Chenoa, an' there ain't nobody goes inta that stall 'cept me an' Clete. Might ought ta just pull the buggy in an. make it easier, not ta mention so's nobody will know what we're unloadin'. Fact, I'll have Clete do it 'fore 'em mules show up, which ought ta be real soon," Salty said pulling out his pocket watch and looking at it.

Taking a few steps back toward his office, he called out, "Clete! Come on up here!" When his assistant walked up, Salty quietly said, "Move the buggy up ta stall seven. We need ta unload some boxes inta the stall, pronto!"

Zack and Todd walked up to join Salty and Ben, followed by Chenoa, Jed and Big Mike. "We'll lend ya a han', boss. Done sent Carl ta fetch the doc, an' ah was wonderin', Mr. Murphy, if'n it'd be all right if'n we wus ta bring Stumpy inside 'til the doc gets heah."

"Hell, if the man's hurt, put him in my office. Clete, after ya move that buggy, help these men put Stumpy in my office, an' fetch a bucket o' fresh water an' some clean rags."

"Yessir, Salty! I'll do 'er!" Clete called back as he climbed into the buggy and picked up the reins.

Ben, Salty, Zack, Todd, Jed and Big Mike made short order of unloading the cartridges and storing them in the assigned stall, while Chenoa and Clete tended to Stumpy, even after the doctor and Carl arrived. They had no more than placed the last of the cartridges in the stall when Muley, Bear Claw and Rooster returned dragging a man by his heels, followed by a city deputy.

"Mr. Creed, will you tell these men to let go of that man so I can arrest him? I've got two more men coming along with the coroner to retrieve those bodies outside, and I'd like to send this one to jail while I conduct my investigation."

"It's all right, men, ya can let go o' him now."

"Ah don' reckon 'e's goin' nowhars, deputy, less'n ya carry 'im. Ol' Rooster thar thumped 'im right good when he tried ta fight us off. Rooster thumps 'em, 'ey stay thumped fer a bit," Bear Claw explained.

Ben had to turn away to keep the deputy from seeing him laugh, and even then he almost lost it. As he turned back to face the others, he could see little snickers escaping the others as well, even Chenoa. A few minutes later, Rooster retrieved a bucket of water and tossed the entire contents into the man's face. Even then, it took a few minutes before he regained full consciousness, just in time for the arrival of the two additional deputies, who immediately placed him in cuffs.

"Don't look like much has changed, Ben," Sheriff Walker said as he entered the barn. "Folks still gettin' shot up around you. But I hear you ain't the one doin' the shootin'."

"Not lately, Jeff. These men I hired are makin' sure Barriston's men stay off our backs, an' cuttin' em down if they try. All but the one Chenoa removed from polite society a couple o' days back."

"Yeah, I heard about that shot. Ray Alvarez is still talkin' about

321

it. But let me get ta why I'm here. Your friend Barriston has filed a complaint against you an' your men, sayin' you're injurin' 'em and havin' 'em arrested, even killed, for no reason. Heard he's filin' with the city as well."

"Well, there's been plenty o' witnesses ta prove him wrong, so I doubt anything will come of it. Dodson has taken the reports an' done the investigations on several o' these things, an' if I know Jim, Barriston will be lucky he don't get arrested."

"Yeah, pretty much the way I see it. One more incident in the county an' I'll be huntin' him myself. He come inta the office just a little while ago, just a huffin' an' a puffin'. Lawdy, as big as he's got, it's a wonder he made it up the steps ta the courthouse. Anyway, he wanted ta report that a body o' men he sent out ta inspect some properties got shot up by the Apaches an' wantin' me ta notify the Army ta have 'em arrested."

Ben couldn't contain himself, and both he and Chenoa were consumed by laughter for several minutes before Ben could say anything. "Jeff, I reckon that was Long Lance an' his warriors. They said they'd keep a close eye on my camp an' claims, an' make sure nobody got close to 'em. That 'body of men,' ta use what were prob'ly Barriston's words, was most likely snoopin' too close ta my camp 'r my claims, prob'ly figuring ta move my markers an' stake out my claims for Barriston 'r Meador. Serves 'em right. Any o' 'em get killed?"

"Yessir, in fact three of 'em. An' six got severely wounded, while three had minor wounds, accordin' ta Barriston anyway. Not bad, considering it was a 'body' o' twelve men ta start with. Sounds like 'em Apache got a nick in on ever' one o' 'em bastards. An' you're right, it serves 'em right for doin' Barriston's dirty work. I just smiled and said I'd check into it for him, but I all ready figured they was after your claims. I'd appreciate it if there was some way ya could let me know for sure."

"Jeff, let me talk to ya in private, if these folks will excuse us for a bit," Ben said, taking the sheriff by the elbow and leading him out the back of the barn. Under a tree at the back of the corrals, Ben stopped to fill the sheriff in. "Jeff, we're pullin' out day after tomorrow, first thing in the mornin', an' I don't plan on comin' back ta Prescott 'til I have to. I doubt any o' 'em Apache speak a word o' English, 'r if they'd talk ta about the white man's law even if they did. I can still find out, which I figure ta do anyway, but it may be some time 'fore I could get word to ya."

"I heard tell ya made a deal with the smelter down ta Mayer. That right?"

"Yessir, James made the deal for me as my lawyer. That's where him an' Mike was comin' back from when they got shot at."

"I also heard you were gonna have your own guards set up down there. That so as well?"

"Yessir."

"Good plan, an' ya can send word through any o' 'em men 'bout whether they was tresspassin' on your claims 'r in your camp, 'r even near 'em, an' I'll see to it the survivors get charged with tresspassin'."

"Jeff, I understand that Barriston has sent for more men, some out o' Phoenix, an' I figure that as soon as word gets out that we're leavin' town, he'll make a hard run at us. I'm gonna have these men I hired follow us out, even set some o' 'em out outside o' town where they can take positions ta fire from. Once we hit the timber, I reckon Long Lance an' his men will take over from there, an' no matter how many men Barriston sends it won't be enough. 'Tween the four o' us an' Long Lance, they'll pay one helluva price."

"I might just have ta drift out an' take a position myself, hombre, so I can report the real truth, not whatever Barriston an'

323

his men try ta claim. Might even bring Seth along, an' see if he's as good with a Winchester as the boys say he is."

"Hah! The more the merrier, Jeff. An' I reckon the men will be glad ta have the law settin' with 'em. They don't know what I got planned yet. So far, other than Chenoa an' the boys, only Jason Renner, Nick Loshkarev, Marisol Stockdale, Ralph Porter an' Salty, you're the only one that knows, so keep it ta yourself, all right?"

"Sure thing, Ben. Say, I also heard ya had a dozen Allred mules comin' in at noon. Wonder where they're at? It's well past twelve now."

"Yeah, I was beginnin' ta wonder myself, an' figured if the didn't show by one I'd ride out ta see," Ben said starting to walk back to the front.

Just then the noise of a large number of animals being led resounded through the barn. Ben could see Clete running out through the doors, presumably to open a corral gate to let them in. "Well, I guess that must be my mules. Let's go get a look at 'em."

The entire barn emptied out as the mules were led into a corral. Within minutes, the Allred boys had the halters off and the mules were lined up at the feed bunk munching on hay. Ben was impressed at how well behaved the mules seemed to be, and was pleased that they were just as promised by Allred himself, as well as apparently the same mules he had looked over before.

As he climbed through the fence to get a closer inspection, he was joined by his brothers along with Jed and Carl, who apparently knew their mules well. After twenty minutes of looking them over, Ben climbed back through the rails and headed for the barn.

"Boss, if ya don' mind me sayin' so, ya got yourself the best mules 'is side o' Missoura. Me an' Carl both checked 'em, an' 'ey's as strong an' healthy as any we evah seed," Jed said, joining

Ben outside the corral.

"That's what I came up with, Jed. An' thanks for you an' Carl checkin' 'em for me. Appreciate it. Now, I just got ta pay for 'em," Ben said as he continued into the barn. Seeing Muley standing at the door as he approached, he said, "Muley, I need ta see you as soon as I get these mules paid for. Got a little change o' plans I need ta tell ya about."

Salty had all ready opened the safe and pulled Ben's saddlebags out, handing them to him as he stepped into the office. "Ya gonna have anything left ta put back in here, 'r can I close it up?"

"Close it up, Salty. I got plenty, but I figured I'd take what I don't need back ta the bank later today 'r first thing in the mornin'."

Stepping back out into the breezeway, he walked back toward the front, where three young men dressed in black were standing. "All right, gents, which one o' you Allred boys is in charge?"

"That would be me, sir. My name is Joseph, and these are my brothers, Brigham and Malachi. Father told us to bring these mules here, and that you, assuming you are Mr. Creed, would give me one thousand eight hundred dollars. Is that your understanding, sir?"

"Yes, I'm Ben Creed, and that is the agreed upon price." Reaching into the saddlebags, Ben started pulling out coins, counting them out into Joseph Allred's hand. When he reached one thousand, he had to switch the saddlebag around, having emptied the first pouch. Pulling out more coins, Ben continued counting, reaching into the bag until he had reached the additional eight hundred. As he pulled out the last ten coins, he dropped them into his pocket, saying, "Well, that's it boys, ya done cleaned me out."

Ben shook hands with each of the Allred boys, and then watched as they walked to the hitch rail and mounted nearly identical black mules, turned and headed toward home, keeping perfectly abreast of each other as they rode.

As he turned to enter the barn, he was met by Chenoa. "You bought something without me? Ben? After you said you wouldn't? And I heard how much you paid for those animals. Disgraceful. Why, Ben Creed, they're worth a thousand more than that if they are as well trained as they seem to be," she said with a smile broadening across her face. "I see my bargaining skills are starting to rub off."

"Well, I did take a page out o' your book, Chenoa. An' Carl an' Jed have blessed the deal as well, so I guess I done all right, eh?"

Chenoa only nodded, but with her big smile still across her face.

"Good, now it's time to see if you are all talk when it comes ta workin' a horse, 'r if ya really know what you're doin'. But I got to meet with Muley first. I'll see you in a bit," Ben said as he started to seek Muley out.

Finding him standing with his friends, Ben motioned for Muley to follow him out the back of the barn deciding that the tree where he and Jeff had talked was as good as any place. "Muley, I need ta let ya know somethin' but I don't want ever'body in town ta know. We're loadin' up an' pullin' out mornin' after next, several days ahead o' schedule. It's gettin' too hot here in town, an' I'm afraid o' somethin' happenin ta Chenoa 'r my brothers. We can handle loadin' all the packsaddles an' lead ropes an' halters here at Salty's an' the only thing we'll need ta finish loadin' is the bags o' oats an' all our supplies at Carlton's place."

"Ya just tell us what time ta meet ya, an' we'll help ya load up the supplies, boss."

"Good, that's part o' what I had in mind, Muley, but there's a lot more to it. Figurin' that what I heard is right, Barriston is on a tear after his men gettin' all shot up by the Apache, not ta mention the job you men have done on 'em. The way I see it, he's gonna try ta hit us outside o' town, 'fore we turn inta the timber. I'm gonna want your best marksman ta set up in the trees 'r wherever they can ta get a good look at what's goin' on as we pass 'em. Anybody that tries, they can open fire on 'em an' take 'em down. The Sheriff even said he'll bring a man along an' set up with 'em."

"How many men ya want out there?"

"As many as you think will be a good number, but they all need ta be crack shots. Half o' the rest I'd like ta have ride out 'fore we do, an' the rest after us. Now, once we turn into the timber, the Apache will pick us up from there, an' I doubt anybody will get close enough ta cause us any harm after that."

"I'll take care of it, boss, I sho' will."

"Muley, I'm not done. 'Fore we head out, it might not be a bad idea if ya was to slip by Whitaker's office, an' Hutchison's office, too, an' let 'em know ta keep their heads down as we're pullin' out. An' swear 'em ta secrecy, will ya? Now then, I reckon it will be some three, maybe four weeks 'fore we have enough ore ta take ta the smelter in Mayer, an' I want ta have those crack shots settin' there ta guard our ore when we dump it there. An' I'll want 'em ta keep an eye on it 'til it's finished in the smelter an' ready ta haul out, but I ain't sure where that will be just yet 'r I'd tell ya ta have 'em stay with it. Now then, after that first load is run through the smelter, I'm gonna need the rest o' the men ta start cuttin' timbers for the mines, an' then start workin' the mines for us."

"Sho' sounds good ta me, boss, an' I know the rest o' 'em fellers'll be glad ta get back ta workin' agin."

"Muley, I can't ask the men ta just hang on with just you askin' 'em ta do it, so I'm gonna give ya some more money ta hold 'em over 'til we get goin' real good. Here's eight hundred dollars, forty a man, for ya ta pass out among 'em. Oh, an' 'fore I forget it, I didn't buy any saws 'r axes, 'r adz 'r any other timber workin' tools, so the men that'll be workin' timber will need ta bring their own tools. Now, I'll get ta somewhere I can buy anything else we need, 'specially when we start settin' timbers in the mines, but 'til then I'm countin' on the men ta help us out."

"That sho' ain' no problem, boss, 'cause we all got 'em kind o' tools an' setch. An' ya ain' got ta give us no money ta get us a goin'. We'll make due with what ya done give us."

"Nonsense. Most o' the men got families, an' if nothin' else it'll help out at home while they're out workin'. An' one more thing. My name is Ben, not boss. I want ever' man workin' for an' with me ta call me Ben, not boss. Now pass the word when ya pass out the money, an' ya can tell 'em that the next man that calls me Ben is fired," Ben said with a big smile, knowing that there would be several slips of the tongue before they all got into the habit of calling him Ben, and not boss.

"Yessir, bo... uh, Ben, I'll sho' let 'em know."

"Good. Now, Chenoa is gonna show us boys how ta finish a horse for the trail lickety-split, an' have tha little blood bay filly ready ta go when we pull out. Let's go see what she's got up her sleeve, shall we?"

"Ought ta be somethin' ta see, fo' sho'."

Chapter Thirty-Five

As they walked through the breezeway, not a man could be seen. Stepping outside, Ben could see a crowd lined up around the small corral off to the left of the barn where Salty worked any animal he was trying to train. It was deathly quiet as the men leaned against the rails, starring intently at what was happening inside that corral.

Joining the others, Ben was amazed at what he was seeing. Chenoa was walking around the corral in a twisting, winding circuit of steps, with no apparent reason to where she walked. And the filly followed right behind her. No bridle, no headstall, nothing. Just following. After several minutes of this, Chenoa stopped to face the filly, then reached up to place her hand on the horse's face. The filly never flinched, never moved a bit, even as the Paiute woman blew in his nose, and then walked around the animal, keeping her hand on the horse at all times.

Two trips around and Chenoa stopped on the left side of the horse, pushing down at the base of the horse's neck. After a minute, it was as though the horse began to understand what was wanted of her, and dropped to one knee with the other leg stretched out in front. Chenoa swung her leg over the back of the filly, and then pulled at the base of the mane encouraging the horse to rise to all fours again. Gently tapping her heels to the filly's flank she started to walk in a circle around the corral.

After two circles, the young woman again tapped the flanks, urging the horse to go faster, repeating the skill until the horse was at a slow gallop. Next she had the filly going in the opposite direction, switching leads as naturally as though she had done it all her life. Still not a man had uttered a word, but they all gasped when Chenoa brought the filly to a sliding halt with just the tap of her toes to the horse's front legs.

Slipping off the horse's back, the filly started following Chenoa again, this time to the edge of the corral where the woman swung the saddle blanket onto the filly's back, followed by lifting the saddle into place and pulling up the cinch nice and snug. The filly never moved a muscle; she just stood there as though frozen. Then came the hackamore, which the filly dropped her head to accept willingly. Rechecking the cinch to make certain it was still snug, Chenoa stepped into the stirrup and swung her full weight into the saddle.

Adjusting the reins slightly, Chenoa pulled ever so slightly against the reins, followed by the filly backing up until she backed into the rails on the opposite side of the corral. Without any apparent movement by the rider, the filly immediately stepped to the center of the corral and stopped, but just for a second. Suddenly she started spinning to the left, and just as suddenly stopped, and then reversed direction. Stopping once again, she remained stationary for a full count of ten, and then started walking forward.

"Would someone please open the gate for me?" Chenoa said quietly. Salty, standing by the latch, did as requested, and then stepped back to where he had been standing. The filly began to walk toward the gate, but stopped before going through the opening, until Chenoa urged her forward. With no other traffic on the street, she urged the filly to a full gallop, slowing just enough to negotiate a complete turn and a return at full speed down the street at the corner.

No one had noticed until Clete said, "She did all that without touchin' the reins. I never seen the like."

Twice up and down the street at a full gallop, and without Chenoa using her hands, the filly seemed to be on an invisible string, turning at each corner after slowing enough to ensure she could make the turn and not lose her passenger, and then running as fast as she could toward the other end of the block.

Then, after two complete trips up and down the street, the filly slowed to a walk about midway coming back up the street and turned back into the corral as though she knew exactly what to do and when. In the corral, Chenoa dismounted, loosened up the cinch and started to walk away from the filly. When the filly started to follow, Chenoa made a signal with her hands, and the filly not only stopped, but also turned to stand where Chenoa had climbed down.

After several minutes of standing at the opposite end of the corral, Chenoa took a swig from a canteen hanging on the fence, and then turned to walk back toward the filly. Removing the cinch, she slipped the saddle and blanket from the horse's back and tossed them onto the top rail of the corral. Clucking to the filly, the horse turned to walk toward her, gently placing her chin on Chenoa's shoulder. The French and Paiute woman reached up to scratch between the horse's ears, and then slipped the hackamore off and tossed it over the saddlehorn with a practiced ease.

Taking the filly's nose in her hands, Chenoa slowly and softly blew into the horse's nostrils again, and then scratched between her ears again. Walking the length of the animal, she slowly rubbed along the horse's spine, stopping to scratch at the base of its tail, and then walking very closely around the rear of the animal she repeated her actions in reverse. At the horse's head, she again blew into its nostrils, and then turned to walk away, making a slight motion with her hand as she opened the gate and stepped out.

"Salty, she is far more ready than you led us to believe. I would feel comfortable riding her in a hailstorm or into a gun battle, and could do so with complete confidence in her. She is a fine horse, and I declare her trail ready."

"Ma'am, if ya don't mind me sayin', you did things with that filly that I could never have done, not in a hundred years. Ya sure made a believer out o' me when it comes ta horses, 'r most anything else. If ya say ya can do it, I know without a doubt ya can. An' I'll bank on it ever' time," Salty declared.

"Why, thank you, Salty. That means more to me than you'll ever know," Chenoa said walking into the barn with her saddle, blanket and hackamore.

"All right, gents, shows over. Time ta get back ta business. Chenoa, Zack, Todd, I'm startin ta get hungry again. Renner's?" Ben asked.

"Sounds like a winner ta me, Ben. Meet ya there," Zack said, nodding to Todd as they turned to retrieve their horses.

"Ben, I swear, that woman can train anything ya put in front o' her. Why, I never seen anything like it. She had that critter followin' her around like a puppy after fifteen minutes o' walkin' around it an' talkin' to it, an' then walkin' off an' ignorin' her. An' the things she had that animal do, well, it was short of a miracle is all I can say," Clete said as he joined Ben and Chenoa, taking the saddle, blanket and hackamore off her hands and carrying them back to the stall next to Captain's as they walked back toward the buggy.

"Now, Clete, I hope you don't start rumors about me being some sort of a witch with animals, or say things that could make other people start to think that way. Lord knows there will be plenty of that when those mountain men start telling it."

"You act like that's happened before, Chenoa. Has it?"

"Yes, once, a long time ago back in Idaho. I was about twelve, I think, when it happened. It really hurt my mother, and I just don't want it to start again and hurt any of those I care about. But enough of that. Let's go eat, good sir. And after we eat I need to pick up some supplies for corndodgers and repay Maybelline, as well as spend half a day tomorrow making enough for our trip."

"Sounds like a deal straight out o' heaven, Chenoa. Let's go," Ben said enthusiastically as he flipped the reins to get the buggy horse to walk slowly out of the barn. Once into the street, he popped the whip, and within a few minutes they were sitting outside Renner's Café, lucky enough to find a spot right in front.

"Well, well, about time you showed up," Todd said as they sat down at the same table as always. "We been sittin' here waitin' on ya ta arrive, but we done ordered ours. I told Jason an' Margarite you were comin', so they left cups for ya," he continued as he filled the pair of cups sitting empty.

"And you didn't order for us as well, Todd? Shame on you," Chenoa chided him.

"Au contraire, mademoiselle. But we did order for you."

"Oh, so now you're going to start speaking French, young man?"

"Naw, just asked François how ta say a couple o' things, but that 'bout all I remember."

"Well, if you'd like to learn, we'll have plenty of time in camp for me to teach you."

"Hah! That's hard ta believe, I plan on keepin' these two so tired all they'll want ta do in camp is sleep an' eat," Ben said, putting a damper on things.

"Yeah, leave it to you ta hinder my education, Ben," Zack said, getting into the conversation.

"Trust me, boys, I'll make ya so rich you'll be able ta learn ten new languages once we get done at these digs."

"Shoot, Ben, sounds like maybe Margarite an' me need to close this place down an' join ya in this little adventure."

"Jason, I love ya like a brother, but I got all the partners I can handle for now. An' I don't pay that good, surely not as much as ya make here on a good day."

"Oh, Jason, you ol' fool. Why, your back would give out the first week an' then Ben would have ta run ya off. Now get these folks a fresh pot, will ya?" Margarite said as she started placing platters of food onto the table. "An' Jason, they don't even have their plates an' utensils yet. Ya best get ta crackin', old man, 'r I'll have to replace ya!" Margarite said with a chuckle. "Lord knows, I don't know what I'd ever do without that man. I could no more'n run him off than I could stop eatin'."

As the co-owner and waitress hustled back into the kitchen, the quartet sat sipping coffee, waiting for their dinnerware to appear. Jason was scrambling, having gotten carried away joking about mining with Ben when he should have been paying closer attention to their needs. But he recovered nicely, and the diners were able to eat their fill from the platters of food while it was still hot.

"Boys, I need to fill ya in on how I want this ta go day after tomorrow. But until we get started, we need ta keep all keep our heads down. No sense takin' any risks this close ta leavin' town. I've been around an' paid for everything all ready, so the only things left are ta go by Ralph's an' get all the tack, an' for Chenoa ta pick up supplies ta replace Maybelline's and enough more ta make us a big batch o' corndodgers ta take with us. So if you'll let her know that Chenoa will be by in the mornin', we'd appreciate it.

"Now then, I figure you're gonna want ta take both your horses, just in case, an' Chenoa will be leadin' that Apache pony. Add in Captain an' the blue roan geld I bought off Salty, an' the dozen mules that makes twenty animals ta tend to. The way I see it, if we each take three mules, we'll be leadin' four animals each. An' 'fore ya ask, I bought that blue roan geld off Salty, so I'll be leadin' four as well. The only stops we need ta make once we leave Salty's is the granary for the bags o' oats, 'cause we'll have all ready loaded the cartridges, and then Carlton's for all the rest o' the supplies. We'll need ta meet at the Congress dining room for breakfast an hour an' a half 'fore daybreak, an' be at Salty's an hour later ta get the mules all set up an' the cartridges loaded. From there ta the granary, but that stop shouldn't take too long, not for ten sacks o' oats.

"The real time killer is gonna be loadin' the supplies at Carlton's, but Muley an' some o' the men are gonna be there ta help with that. If all goes accordin' ta plan, we need ta be toppin' the hill east o' town by ten at the latest. I figure, leadin' that many animals, we'll be travelin' kind o' slow, but we should still be able ta turn into the timber along Lynx Crick by ten thirty. By chewin' on corndodgers an' sippin' water, the only stop we'll make that day, other than ta let the critters blow, is when we make night camp.

"We should get picked up by the Apache shortly after we ride inta the timber, which leaves us in trouble all the way from Salty's 'til we hit that timber. So, here's what I got set up. I'm havin' the best rifle shots among those workin' with Muley ta slip out early an' take up positions along the way, so they can guard our flanks in case Barrington gets real stupid an' tries somethin'. It might warm you boy's hearts ta know that the Sheriff Walker an' Seth will be out there among 'em, rifles in hand."

Looking over at his younger brothers, they were both smiling. "Well, that Seth sure can handle a Winchester; I'll give him that. An' he ain't one bit bothered by pullin' down on a man," Zack said.

"Good ta know. Now then, the rest o' the men will be split 'tween in front o' us an' in back o' us. I'll take the lead, Chenoa, you follow me, an' then you boys can pick your poison about which position ya wanna take. But once we hit the timber, Chenoa takes the lead, an' keeps it all the way ta camp. The rest o' us can switch up if we're of a mind to. Chenoa will call a halt at midday, but it will be a dry camp, just long 'nough ta stretch out your legs, 'r we won't make it ta our camp 'fore dark. Leadin' as many animals as we are, an' them loaded down heavy, we night be pushin' it ta make it anyway. 'Specially if there's any trouble along the way, 'r if we get hit 'fore we even leave town. I don't think I need ta press the reason why we need ta keep this quiet, do I?"

"No sir, ya don't. But ya missed one thing, Ben. We each have a packsaddle, an' can take on part o' the load on our spare horses. They won't like it at first, but they'll settle in after a few minutes. Shoot, they'll be fine 'fore we even get close ta the city limits. Might be a good idea to load them with the oats, an' put the cartridges on the mules, though," Todd mentioned.

"Well, that sure helps, an' yeah, as long as they don't toss 'em oats on the street that'll be fine. An' if we each take three bags o' oats on our spare critters, an' toss the last bag on one o' the mules, that shouldn' load 'em down too much. Just so ya know, I told Muley ta have his sharpshooters down ta Mayer in three weeks to guard our ore once we dump it there, but I let him know it might take as long as a month."

"Ya think we can get enough ore ta load twelve mules in less than a month, Ben? You figurin' both silver an' gold?"

"No, Zack, just gold. You'll see why I say that once we get there an' get started workin' the digs. If we figure eight hundred pounds a mule, we should have enough in dust, flakes an' nuggets alone to load three, maybe four mules. An' once we start clearin' out the vein, we should be able ta load the other eight with rough ore inside of a month."

"There's really that much in nuggets, dust an' flakes, Ben?"

"You won't believe it until you see it, boys. I've seen it, an' it's all I can do ta believe it."

"Ben is right, boys, there is a lot of dust. It is easy to pan out, and the flakes and nuggets are everywhere one looks, at least in the watershed below where the vein is located. The vein is thick and heavy with chunks of gold. It is, as Ben said, almost unbelievable even after one sees it for themselves."

"Ben, why do I think you're not only anxious ta get movin' on this, but usin' all this as a trap for Barrington."

"Well, in a way I s'pose I am, Todd. But we can lay up here in town an' have ever' thug he hires take potshots at us 'til they get us, 'r draw 'em out onta our ground. Barriston has made a personal trip up ta see the sheriff all ready, so it sure won't surprise me if he decides ta make a trip out ta supervise the attack on us. If it comes, that is. An' with Jeff out there along with a deputy, maybe more if I know that rascal, we'll have the law on our side, an' they can take him down for orchestratin' the whole thing."

"All right, just so we got an idea what might come our way. Chenoa, ya ready for all this?"

"Yes, I am. Barriston has caused all of us enough trouble that it's time to put him in his place, a dark jail cell or hanging from a rope. And this thing goes back even further for me than it does for you Creed's. Even further back than Ben knows or thinks he knows. Once Barriston is finished, I will tell you the rest of my story."

Cherokee Parks

338

Chapter Thirty-Six

The details settled, the four soon to be travelers quietly finished their breakfast and sat sipping coffee. Each had their own thoughts about what might happen, and how they would handle any trouble that surfaced. Finally, Ben spoke again, "Any thoughts anybody wants ta share?"

"Yeah, Ben. Them mules ought ta be runners as well as good pack animals, an' if they were trained ta ride they might do ta use as somethin' else 'sides for packin', not ta mention they might do us well in a runnin' battle."

"Yeah, I thought o' that as well, Zack. Dependin' where Barriston tried ta hit us, if he even does, we might want ta light out as fast as they can go an' try ta get inta the timber long 'fore we get anywhere near Lynx Crick. But it all depends on where an' how hard they come at us what we end up doin'. With me up front, just follow my lead, an' Chenoa once we hit the timber. They may try ta follow us inta the trees, an' it may be a bit 'fore Long Lance an' his warriors get to us, so if that's the way it goes we can set up in the timber an' hold 'em off pretty easy, that is if we keep our rifles real handy. Chenoa, I bought you a scabbard ta hang on your saddle, so that ought ta make it easier for ya."

"Yes, I saw that, Ben. And thank you. That's something I didn't think of, and would have regretted later," the French and Paiute woman said appreciatively.

"Anything else anybody wants ta talk about?"

When no other comments or thoughts were expressed, Ben continued. "If anybody gets hit, 'r if they take down an animal, call out loud an' clear, an' we'll circle up. I'd sooner lose an animal, even Captain, 'fore I'd lose any o' you."

"Indeed, Ben. Animals, no matter how much they are worth or

how close we feel to them, can always be replaced, but a friend or family member's loss will be felt forever. Now, if there is nothing else, I need to start packing my personal things. You know how we women are. We need three times as long to pack as a man, because we have to decide what we can do without, while a man only has to decide what he will need," Chenoa stated a truth most men didn't think about, and brought a laugh to not only those at the table, but the Renner's as well.

"All right, we'll meet here for grub again in the mornin' 'round six, make sure nothin's changed an' then go about what we have ta take care of 'fore dark. No offense, Jason, but I think we'll have supper at the Congress tomorrow night, an' we're having breakfast there the mornin' after as well, so we can get an early start at Salty's."

"None taken, Ben. We always 'preciate it when ya come by, but sometimes it just don't fit a body's plans. We'll make sure ya get a good feed in the mornin' though, an' that's a fact, right, Margarite?"

"Yes indeed. I might even bake an extra pie 'r two for ya ta take along, if ya can make room for a couple o' boxes ta carry 'em in."

"Margarite, that'd sure be nice, havin' somethin' ta eat 'sides corndodgers, even though I do love 'em corndodgers. But I love your apple pie just as much," Todd complimented the cook.

"Well, then you just consider it done, Todd. I'll see all you folks in the mornin' then. I need ta get back ta my kitchen," the full-bodied woman said with a slight sadness in her voice.

Ben tossed a double eagle onto the table, saying, "Let's go get a good night's rest, shall we? We'll need all the rest we can get tonight an' tomorrow night, 'cause it will be a long, hard an' fast trip ta camp, an' another long hard day after that ta finish gettin' camp set up 'fore we hit the claims."

As they stepped out into the late sunshine of a day coming to a close, Ben added one more thing before he and Chenoa climbed into the buggy. "I figure the second day we're there, we'll need ta check the monuments on both claims, maybe even stake out an' mark the claims you boys'll make. We'll have ta decide which side 'r which end ta make those claims, so nobody can slip into the same veins I found an' cut us off. Yeah, mining law says they can't do that, but how many times ya reckon it's all ready been done? See ya in the mornin', boys."

***

Stepping into the kitchen at the boarding house, Zack said, "Maybelline, ya got some coffee on still?"

"Why, ya knows ah does, Zack. Set tight an' ah'll rustle up some suppah fo' ya. Ah's jus' fixin' ta make some fer Mose anyways."

"No, we all ready ate, with Ben an' Chenoa over ta Renner's. Just coffee'll do fine."

A moment later, both Todd and Zack were sipping coffee, each looking at the other, both trying to get the other to ask Maybelline if she'd mind having Chenoa using her kitchen to make up more corndodgers. Finally, the older, black woman brought it to a head. "Awright's you two. Whut's a bothahin' yuns?"

Just then Mose walked in, "Woman, I reckon 'ey wants ta tell us they's goin' out sooner 'ey thunk 'ey'd do. Maybe even want ta have Chenoa come do some cookin' wit' ya 'fo' 'ey do. 'Et about it, boys?"

"Well, yeah. But keep it ta yourselves, if ya would. We'll be pullin' out early day after tomorrow. An' Lord knows when we'll make it back. Figured we'd pay up a couple o' months in advance ta keep our rooms," Zack said.

"An' there's somethin' else, Maybelline. We was wonderin' if ya'd mind havin' Chenoa come make up a big batch o' corndodgers for us ta take along," Todd finished filling them in.

"Why, shucks no. 'Et gal is welcome ta mah kitchen any ol' time. Ah's a bit sho't o' fixin's, sa she's gonna have ta bring whut she needs ta make 'em."

"We all ready talked about that, an' she wants ta replace what she used, an' bring enough ta make what she needs to make 'em," Zack answered. "She'll be by sometime tomorrow mornin', once she picks up the supplies."

"Any reason ta why ya's is pullin' out early?" Mose asked, determined to get to the bottom of their early departure. "On account o' Barriston an' his bunch?"

"Well, yeah, that's some of it, Mose. Ben wants ta try ta trap him, not ta mention that Ben almost always does this. He gets ta chompin' at the bit ta get after somethin' once he makes up his mind ta do it, an' I s'pose this time ain't no different. But this time he's drug us into it as well. Willingly, I might add."

***

"Chenoa, ya ain't figurin' on carryin' a whole bunch with ya, are ya? I mean, I've all ready paid in advance for your room so ya can leave all your town clothes here safe an' sound," Ben queried.

"No, Ben, I won't be taking all that much. I just want to make sure I take everything I'll need, like my camp clothing and such. I ordered some soap and a scrub board so I can at least keep our clothes clean. The one thing that I have to wonder about is water. What with so many animals grazing and using a lot of the water in the creek near camp, where will we get enough water for drinking and washing, as well as for me to clean our utensils and clothes, if the creek running through camp is dry?"

"There's a good mile o' grass along Blind Indian Crick that'll support the critters, an' what with Long Lance an' his warriors keepin' watch I don't reckon anybody'll be able ta make off with a single one o' 'em. If we keep the animals below where that second feeder crick dumps in, we ought ta have all the water we need for whatever we need it for. An' if push comes ta shove, we can always bring up a mule 'r two an' slip over the hill ta Towers Crick an' load up on water there. I thought I told ya that I ordered a pair o' barrels to store water in at camp, so ya don't have ta try ta haul it ever' day."

"Yes, you did, and I guess I had forgotten that. Still, four people can use a lot of water in a day, as that little pond created by the storm will soon dry out requiring canteen and gut bag water for your panning."

"Yeah, I figured it that way as well. The rainy season ought ta be on us any day now, an' with any luck we can get the bulk o' that dirt panned out 'fore the water comes along an' fills it back up again. An' as long as it don't move that boulder we should be just fine."

"Yes, I sense there will be many rains this season, Ben. Some will be heavy, but most will be light allowing you plenty of time and water to pan. It's just that water disappears so quickly in many of the small ponds that are not fed by a spring. There may be times when you will have to carry water, and other times when you pray for it to stop raining."

"Not much we can do about the rains, so we'll just deal with it as it comes," Ben said pulling up to the front of the hotel, and being met by Clete. "Clete, I 'preciate ya keepin' an eye out for us an' this buggy. Near as much as I 'preciate Salty lettin' us use it, an' for storin' all our gear in his barn. We sure got a bunch ta thank both o' ya for on this trip, Clete, we surely do."

Chenoa gave Clete a hug and a peck on the cheek, saying, "Yes, Clete. There is no way I'll ever be able to repay either one of you for all the help, and for the kindness you have shown me. Oh, and a word to the wise, you'd better ask Mary Ellen to marry you before I come back here. That girl loves you so much that it almost hurts her that you haven't asked her yet. Understand?"

"Yes, ma'am. It's just, well, I ain't got nothin' ta give her. I don' even have a decent place ta live ta more her inta if'n she was ta say yes."

"Clete, shame on you. She has a fine house, all hers, and would love to share it with you. She also has a job, and is not at all worried about what you can contribute. She just wants to spend the rest of her days with you. So you'd better ask her the next time you see her!"

"But Chenoa, ma'am, I can't even buy her a ring…"

Turning to Ben, Chenoa asked, "Ben, could you loan me a hundred dollars, so I can give it to Clete as a pre-wedding gift? That way he can buy a nice ring and still have a few dollars left to buy a nice suit to get married in."

"Naw, I won't do it, Chenoa. But I will give Clete two hundred dollars for takin' care o' all the things he's done for us the last few days, includin' takin' a knot on his head for guardin' our privacy. But, Clete, if you don't ask her ta marry ya, an' get it done pronto, I'll take ever' dollar I give ya out o' your hide when we get back ta town. Hear me?" Ben said as he handed Clete ten double eagles with a big smile across his face.

"I sure don' know what ta say, Ben, Chenoa. Thanks jus' don' seem ta be enough."

"Get a good night's rest, Clete, an' figure out how ta ask her. We'll see ya in the mornin'," Ben said as he took Chenoa's arm and turned her toward the lobby doors.

The pair walked silently up to their rooms, Chenoa finally breaking the silence with, "Ben, like Clete said, thanks just doesn't seem to be enough to say for all you've done for so many of us.

And the truth of it is, you didn't have to do any of it. You could have left your brothers out of the mining shares, and left me laying there on the side of that mountain to die. Barriston still wouldn't have been able to steal your wealth, so taking him down wouldn't have really affected you one way or another. James' practice will always be successful, but you have helped him become accepted in Prescott, and as a result his business is all ready growing. And, Ben, those are just for starters. I could go on and on about the wonderful things you have done for others, like Marisol, but frankly I'm getting rather sleepy, so I'll finish by saying just one more thing. Had we met under other circumstances, maybe in a different place, it would have given me great pride to call you my man, and to belong to you," she said as she gave him a hug and a soft kiss on the cheek before stepping inside her room and closing the door, not giving Ben a chance to say a word.

"Well, damn. If that don't beat all," he said shaking his head on the way to his room. Inside, he stripped down, flopped across his bed, and was asleep almost before his head hit the pillow.

***

Ben was all ready sitting in the dining room having coffee when Chenoa came tripping down the stairs, smiling a smile he had not yet seen. Seeing him sitting there, she motioned for him to join her in the lobby instead of joining him at the table for coffee.

"What's up? Ya don't want any coffee?"

"Not here, Ben. I have grown to like Margarite's coffee, and I'm also hungry. If we're going to get there by six, we'd better hurry along, don't you think?"

"Chenoa, it's just a quarter after five. I think we got plenty o' time. Now, what's really goin' on here?"

"Oh, Ben, it's going to be a lovely day. I can feel it. And there won't be a spot of trouble today, not one. I want to enjoy that, as

345

tomorrow will be a far different story. But I'll tell you about it in the buggy, where there are no big ears to listen to me."

"All right, but we've still got ta wait 'til five thirty for Salty ta open his doors. Can it wait that long?"

"Oh, yes, and I saw Clete out and about all ready this morning, just whistling and laughing to himself. I slept with my window open, and he could be heard from my room."

"Is that what I heard this mornin'? I wondered, but I didn't bother ta look out my window. Well, then, let's see if he's opened the doors yet, shall we?"

As they stepped onto the boardwalk, Clete was all ready pulling the buggy up to the front of the hotel for them. Jumping down, he doffed his hat and said, "It's a fine day ta be alive, yes it is. An' today is the day Mary Ellen comes ta pick up her horse for a ride. I ain't got no ring yet, but I'm askin' her anyway. I'll let ya know what she says next time I see ya!" He then turned and trotted back to the barn to finish his chores and get ready to pop the question.

"See, it's a wonderful day all ready!" Chenoa exclaimed as she hopped into the buggy.

At Renner's they were all ready seated and drinking coffee when the boys came in with news that Maybelline was ready for Chenoa, but needed some supplies to make corndodgers. Chenoa was even more thrilled, prompting Zack to ask, "What got inta her, Ben?"

"Oh, nothin'. She's just real happy this mornin'." Once they had eaten and filled up on coffee, they went their separate ways, agreeing to meet at the Congress at seven that night for supper.

Chenoa picked up the needed supplies, including double what she and Maybelline had all ready used, and was busy making corndodgers in Maybelline's kitchen by nine o'clock. Ben left her there until two that afternoon, while he paid a visit to each Mike and James, apprising them of their plans to leave the next day, not knowing if Muley or any of the other men had made it by, and then stopped by The Palace for a last shot or two of whiskey while he had the opportunity.

There were no problems all day long, and after he picked up Chenoa they swapped the buggy for the buckboard, and swung by Ralph's to retrieve their packsaddles, halters and lead ropes.

Cherokee Parks

Chapter Thirty-Seven

After a great dinner and a good night's rest, the foursome was more than ready to get started. Ben and Chenoa carried down their bedrolls, rifles and a bag each, packed and ready to ride, and wearing their gun belts while Zack and Todd arrived across the street with their possessions all ready packed into their packsaddles, but positioned to allow for removal and repacking after the bags of oats were loaded.

Breakfast was a much more solemn meal that the dinner the night before, which was all but celebratory. François immediately picked up on their mood, and privately asked Ben if they were leaving town. "Yeah, but keep it to yourself. We'll be pullin' out this mornin'."

"Very well, sir, and mum is the word. I'll certainly miss your group, especially the delightful Chenoa. Oh, and by the way, Mitzi has now moved on to Mr. Alvarez' son, Miguel, though I don't believe the feeling to be mutual. I understand that he has a sweetheart from down in Sonora that he is planning on bringing into the family late this year, and is just playing with Mitzi for something to do. Poor girl, if she wasn't so determined to marry money, I might actually feel sorry for her. At least her job performance has improved, as has her attendance, but that's neither her nor there. I wish you well, and may you have a safe and successful trip. Just be very careful leaving town, even outside of town as rumor has it that Barriston has somehow gotten word of your early departure and is amassing men to attack you."

"An' where did ya hear that, François?"

"A friend of mine actually works for Barriston, and often is my little bird when he is planning something sneaky. Apparently Carlton Stockdale overheard you telling his wife your plans, and after suffering the humiliation you provided him decided to betray your confidence. He definitely needed that beating, and I believe he knows it, but he is still such a terrible person that he couldn't help but try to get even somehow. Even if he is too much the coward to do it himself."

"Well, that figures, just like it figures he won't be anywhere in sight when we get ta the warehouse ta load up our supplies, at least if he knows what's good for him. Thanks, François, for the heads up. But we're ready for 'em."

"Indeed, I would say so. What with you four, the twenty rough men you have hired, and the sheriff and some of his deputies, I doubt Barriston or his men really stand a chance."

"Is there anything goin' on around this town that ya don't know about?"

"Well, I do try to keep abreast of all the activities here in Prescott as well as across as across as much of Yavapai County as possible. It helps me help my friends who stay here, like you and Chenoa, Ben. And, of course, your brothers. Oh, and just so you know and aren't surprised, it seems the assayer and your attorney will also be on the hillsides outside of town, rifles in hand. A lot of people have your best interest in mind, Ben Creed, as do I now. Now, one last thing regarding Barriston. Apparently he fancies himself some sort of military genius, though to anyone's knowledge he never served a moment in any uniform. He plans to be at a pre-determined site outside of town watching his planned battle unfold, and directing the movement of his men from his carriage. I suspect that if his plans go awry, he will try to make his escape and claim he knew nothing of what happened."

"I'll watch for him, an' no matter what it takes, he ain't gettin' away this time. He's hurt too many folks as it is, an' if I got anything to do with it them days are over. I just wish Meador was along with him."

"That snake never leaves Phoenix, to that I can attest, my

friend."

"So, you got skin in this game as well, eh, François? I might o' known. Well, I need ta get set down an' eat while I got a chance. We need ta be across the street gettin' started in the next thirty-five minutes 'r so. But I wanna thank ya for all ya done for us this trip, an' for all the information this mornin', François. See ya next time through," Ben said, shaking the man's hand, and then joining the others at the table.

"Well, well, François sure seemed ta have a lot ta say this mornin', Ben. You an' him seem ta have gotten real friendly this trip," Todd said as Ben sat down.

"Yeah, turns out he's a decent sort o' feller after all. At least since Chenoa turned him upside down an' shook all the nastiness out of him. Seems Carlton got ta Barrington an' filled him in that we were leavin' today. I reckon the heat will get turned up just 'fore we hit the top o' the hill, an' maybe run past that. Now, I may need ta drop my mules ta go after him, sa be ready ta pick up the lead rope for me if that happens. An' check your loads 'fore we leave Carlton's. An' Chenoa, you got my permission ta drop that snake if ya see him, but I don't reckon we'll see him anywhere around their warehouse this mornin'."

"Oh, if I see him, he will pay dearly, He needed that beating, and now has proven what a coward he really is. I'll even enlist Marisol to aid me in addressing his problems, and I'm certain she will be happy to lend a hand."

The rest of breakfast was quiet and filled with nervousness, each of them knowing that they were going to be riding straight into trouble. There was no lack of resolve, each of them filled with determination, and praying that they would all come through it unscathed. Once again, Ben paid for their meal and left a generous tip as they finished up and walked out to meet their destiny, starting at Salty's.

It took less time than Ben had planned, finding that the mules were so well trained that putting their headstalls on and attaching the lead ropes was made easy by their lining up in a straight line and standing absolutely still. Tossing on and attaching the packsaddles was also made easier by the cooperation the animals provided, and before long the cartridges were also packed aboard one of the mules near the front. The quartet went about saddling their mounts, and double-checking everything in their realm of responsibility. A full half hour ahead of schedule, Ben led out with his three mules an' geld, followed by Chenoa leading her Apache pony and three mules, and then Zack and his extra horse and three mules, with Todd bringing up the rear with his spare horse and three mules.

At the granary, Zack and Todd removed their personal items from their packsaddles and loaded the six sacks of oats, but not finding enough room to reload their personals. Instead, they each loaded their personals on mules they were leading, knowing that their things would need to be repositioned at least one more time, if not more. At the same time, Ben loaded the roan with three sacks, and put the last sack on one of the mules he was leading.

Gaining time at each stop, they rode up in front of Carlton's a full forty-five minutes ahead of Ben's planned schedule, which pleased him to no end. As he dismounted and walked along his string of mules, he was really happy at how well they handled, and knew they were all ready worth their wait in gold, much more than he had paid for them.

Chenoa quickly checked her animals, and then hopped up onto the boardwalk and opened the door to the warehouse. She didn't expect to be met with gunfire, bullets striking the doorframe just above and beside her head. Ben, Zack and Todd came running, but she was all ready crouched down, Colt in hand and running between the aisles toward the desk.

As she reached the end of the aisle, Chenoa peeked around the end of the goods stacked on the shelving to see that Marisol was tied to the chair behind the desk, and gagged. Carlton was crouched down behind her, trying to hide. He suddenly rose up and snapped a shot off in the direction of the front of the warehouse, exposing himself slightly. Chenoa held off taking a shot, not wanting to take any chances on hitting Marisol.

At the front of the store, Ben had jumped in behind a parallel aisle to the one Chenoa had used, drawing a shot from Carlton that struck high and wide of its mark. From the end of the aisle, he took a quick look straight down the aisle to see the same thing Chenoa had seen. Moving one more aisle to his right, Ben motioned back to the door to keep Todd or Zack from entering at the moment.

Back up front, Chenoa guessed at what Ben was doing, and decided to try distracting Carlton. "Carlton, untie Marisol and let her go, and I'll consider letting you live."

"Yeah, well, she's going to die here today, just like you will if you try anything. You and that worthless Ben Creed are going to die today along with his bastard brothers, whether it's here or out of town. And I don't even care if you kill me after what you people have done to me," Carlton said holding his pistol up to Marisol's temple.

As Chenoa took another look, she realized that Carlton wasn't certain where she was from the way he was looking at the ends of the aisles. She could also see that there was no fear in Marisol's eyes or on her features, and that one eye was slightly swollen. What she saw there instead of fear was anger and hatred.

From another aisle came Ben's voice, "Carlton, ya had that beatin' comin', but I see ya didn't learn a thing. You're just plain yellow ta the core, an' you don't deserve ta live. None o' us are gonna die today, at least not at Barriston's order 'r from your stupidity, but your wife is gonna walk away without any more marks from you. Now, ya wanna try doin' this man ta man, 'r ya gonna keep hidin' behind a woman."

Carlton jumped up slightly and snapped off another shot, his last as Chenoa fired, hitting him in the side of the head and dropping him where he stood. Running to where he laid jerking and twitching in his last movements, Chenoa flipped out one of her new knives from its sheath and cut Marisol loose.

The Mexican woman yanked off the cloth wrapped around her head and stuffed in her mouth, and then turned and kicked Carlton's now lifeless body several times before starting to cry. Turning to Chenoa, Marisol hugged her tightly, thanking the French and Paiute woman for saving her life and removing the source of her endless pain and suffering.

A moment later, Ben joined the pair, followed soon thereafter by Zack, Todd and Marshal Jim Dodson. "Jim, how'd you get here sa soon?" Ben asked.

"I was across the street when you rode up. I had heard there might be trouble here this morning, after the beating you gave Carlton, and decided it behooved me to be near by."

"Well, I reckon ya can figure out what happened, but I can tell ya this. He sure had it comin'."

"Yes, I suppose he did. Would you mind explaining what happened here from your point of view?"

Ben recited his knowledge of the events, making certain that Dodson knew Marisol had been tied and gagged with a gun pointed at her head, and that it was Chenoa who took the shot that ended the standoff. Dodson turned to look at Chenoa, and then back to Ben, "Do you think Chenoa is ready to talk to me? I mean, do you think Marisol is all right to be left alone for a moment?"

"Yeah, I reckon they're both ready. Ya notice neither one o' 'em is cryin'. But Jim, we need ta get the body out o' here so we can start loadin'. We're leavin' town as soon as we can."

"Yes, I understand, Ben. Before I came in, I asked someone to find the coroner and get him over here quickly, as I was certain there was going to be a dead body in here."

Turning to walk to where the two women stood talking, Marshal Dodson approached with caution. "Excuse me, Chenoa, could I have a word with you, please?"

"Before you take her away to speak with her, let me tell you something, Jim Dodson," Marisol said with a hint of anger in her voice. "Chenoa just saved my life. Carlton tried to beat me again this morning once we arrived at work, but I didn't take it and after I struck him twice for every time he tried to hit me, he stopped. Then he told me he had arranged for Barriston to kill them all as they left town, but that he wanted his shot before Barriston's men did the job for him.

"He pulled that pistol on me, and then forced me into that chair, " she said pointing to the chair still sitting behind the desk, "tied and gagged me, and then hid behind me waiting for Ben Creed to open the door. Instead, it was Chenoa who entered first, but he still fired twice at her, missing both times. A few minutes later, Ben also entered, and Carlton fired at him, missing. Chenoa tried to talk him out of what he was doing, but he just got angrier. Then Ben challenged him to face him like a man, he stood up, and Chenoa shot and ended it. And the only person who died is the one who wanted to kill others. Dodson, this means I'm free to live a normal life, thanks to my good friends here, and I intend to enjoy that life. Now, go talk to Chenoa, and let us get this mess cleaned up so we can take care of business."

Taking Chenoa by the arm, Marshal Dodson led her toward the front of the store, asking a few questions as they went. Stopping near the entrance, he finally said, "This is what one might call a justified shooting. You are free to go, as I know Ben wants to get out of town, but I have to wonder if this is the right time what with Barriston and his henchmen waiting outside of town the way they are."

"Jim, I hope you don't mind me calling you Jim, Barriston and those men of his are in for a real surprise, just as Carlton Stockdale got his surprise. We have quite a number of men waiting outside of town as well, not to mention that there will be men riding out in front of us as well as behind us, and we are all armed and ready. I'm sure you've learned of my prowess with weapons, so don't question Ben's allowing me to ride with them. I can handle whatever comes my way, just as I have all ready done this morning."

At that moment, Muley and the men he had assembled to load started walking in, and had to be sent back outside by the marshal as the scene had yet to be cleared by the coroner. Stepping outside to address them all at once, Dodson saw as many more men standing there waiting to enter, and could only assume that they had been hired by Marisol to aid in the loading of Ben's supplies.

The coroner weaved and squeezed his way past the crowd of men until he saw Marshal Dodson. "Jim, what the hell happened here?"

"Carlton Stockdale was killed after threatening his wife, Chenoa, Ben, Zack and Todd Creed. He's still inside, but we need to get him moved out as soon as possible. Marisol wants him out so she can conduct today's business, primarily that of loading Ben's supplies and sending him on his way."

"Well, I can't say I'm surprised. I expected her to end him some time back. I'll have him removed immediately, provided you bring me a copy of your report for my files." Turning back to face the gathered crowd, he said, "Men, I have three fellows standing behind you that need to be let in to retrieve the body. Now, unless you'd like to join that corpse, I suggest you make room for them."

The crowd parted, and within ten minutes, the body was gone, and several men were using buckets and mops to clean the blood off the floor while Marisol directed the moving of Ben and Chenoa's order to the boardwalk, where Ben supervised the loading of the packsaddles. Still well ahead of schedule, the train of animals reached the top of the hill east of town just past nine-thirty that morning. But things had already started to break loose minutes before.

Cherokee Parks

Chapter Thirty-Eight

Sending five riders out five minutes ahead of the pack train, and having five more riders lay back five minutes, as Ben figured they would have time to react whether the attack from came in front, or from the rear. He was right, but it was just enough time. Two dozen men came riding down from behind the side hill just after the high point of the road, pushing hard toward the five front riders Ben had sent out, most likely thinking they would be able to run over the five and be on the pack train before they could defend themselves.

But the five out front didn't try to stand. Instead they hunkered down tight against their mounts and turned for the trees. Half of the attacking riders followed the five, while the rest headed for the top of the hill and the pack train. Neither made it to their intended targets before what was left of them were forced to turn tail and run. As the five men hit the edge of the trees, those hiding along the edge of the timber started firing, dropping over half of the attackers with the first volley.

The dozen men riding toward Ben, Chenoa and Ben's brothers caught it from the four travellers, as well as the five men behind who came riding hard to get into the fight and a few in the trees that had been waiting near the top of the uphill slope. They, too, were diminished by half with the first round of gunfire, and turned to ride back in the direction they came. The second round from those in the trees took out two more, while Ben and Chenoa each took out one more from the group attacking them.

Eight men out of the two dozen who had brazenly tried a sneak attack were soon being chased by twice that number, using what little cover there was to try to make their getaway. Ben led the five men who had been riding out front along with six more who came riding out of the trees, while Chenoa led the five men who had been the rear guard, leaving a disappointed Zack and Todd to tend to the pack animals instead of being able to get into the fight.

As they rode north, weaving in and out of the small knobs that dotted the area, Ben caught sight of a carriage working its way northeast through a shallow draw. Motioning for Muley to take over the chase, he swung Captain in the direction he had last seen the carriage before it disappeared from view in the brush and scrub oak. As he cleared the top of the shallow draw, he caught sight of the carriage again, and gave Captain his head. Behind him, Ben could hear sporadic gunfire, and then it became nearly continuous.

But as Captain churned up the ground in pursuit of the carriage, he soon lost the sound in the distance. He was so focused on catching up to the carriage that he almost missed the glint of a barrel sticking out the rear of the carriage body. Quickly turning Captain to his left, Ben heard the sound of the rifle as it was fired in his direction, as well as the zing of the bullet as it missed behind he and his horse.

Just then, another shot rang out from south of his position, causing Ben to wonder what he had ridden into. Then he realized the shot wasn't directed at him, but rather at the carriage, meaning he had some help. Pushing on in a parallel route to that of the carriage, he suddenly realized the carriage wasn't moving, as it had either broken a wheel or dropped off into a hole.

Slowing to a walk, Ben studied the carriage for movement, not wanting to take his eyes off the conveyance to try to determine where the other shot had come from, or who had fired it. As he closed in on the carriage, he slowed Captain to a slow walk, and then dismounted and left the horse ground hitched as he approached the vehicle. One of the front wheels had broken, rendering it temporarily useless, but Ben was more concerned with where the driver had gone, as well as the team that had pulled it.

One of the pair of matched grays was having trouble standing on its right hind leg, while the other seemed to have injured his left foreleg. Looking around but seeing no sign of a driver, Ben slipped alongside the horse on the right, talking to it as he went, until he could release the harness and set the horse free. Stepping to the other side, he released the second horse, and half expected them to try to wander off a short distance. But they only hobbled a few feet and stopped, obviously in pain.

"Damn, Creed, you're as hard to kill as that stinking squaw you run with. All those men I hired couldn't get the job done, so I'll just have to do it myself. Drop that gun belt, and then step backward away from it. Now, or' Ill shoot you where you stand."

Ben slowly did as he was commanded, knowing that Barriston meant every word. But even as he unbuckled his gun belt, he was trying to find a way to stall long enough to take away the crooked lawyer's advantage. "Barriston, you're a backshootin', lyin cheat, as well as a claim jumper. You an' Meador have both gotten rich from stealin' what other folks have worked so hard for. But here's the thing, I ain't dead yet, an' I'm gonna turn around an' face you just ta see if ya got the guts ta shoot a man who's lookin' right at ya."

"Oh, my, but aren't you the brave one. Yes, Manuel and I have gotten very wealthy by being smart and taking advantage of every situation available to us, which now includes those mines of yours. Oh, and don't worry, I'll make certain your brothers get no part of it because I'll send them straight to hell to meet you, right along with that scroungy squaw and those Apaches you have guarding your place. Hurry up and face me, fool. You wouldn't be the first man I've killed, and when I do it I don't care if they're looking at me or not."

"Well, thanks for makin' sure I heard enough ta put you away for a long time, Barriston. Why, ya might have even give me enough ta arrest an' try Meador. Real careful like, set that rifle down an' shove 'em hands in the air. Ben, I see ya got yourself inta kind of a fix here," came Sheriff Jeff Walker's voice from behind Barriston.

"After I kill that sumbitch Creed, then I'll surrender, Sheriff. Might as well have something solid for you to try me on if you're going to put me away anyway," Barriston hissed, followed by a dull click.

Ben dove for his gun belt, yanking the nearest Colt from its holster and covering Barriston as the lawyer levered another round into the filthy, old Spencer. Another dull click was the result as he squeezed the trigger again, but instead of giving it up Barriston started to lever another cartridge into the firing chamber. Barriston didn't get the chance to complete the motion, as each Ben and Sheriff Jeff Walker fired into the big man's torso.

Even then, Barriston didn't go down, but turned around to face the sheriff, saying, "I'll drum you out of office for shooting me in the back. By the time I'm finished, you won't be able to a horsefly in any stable anywhere." Then turning back to face Ben, he continued, "And if you even remotely think you've gotten away from my wrath, you haven't. I'll see you in the ground, Creed, if it's the last thing I do."

The color was draining out of his face as he hissed out his last remark, then slowly sunk to his knees, and fell forward on his face wheezing out his last breath. And even then, he tried to lift himself back up off the ground, using the last of his strength, but after a few seconds he lost the battle to stay alive and slowly lowered himself back onto the ground to stay.

"Thanks, Jeff. I figured I was gonna be the one layin' there dead. Where'd ya come from, anyway?"

"Oh, when the rest lit out chasin' that pack o' dogs, I figured ol' Barriston was gonna try ta sneak off somehow. I thought about it for a few minutes, an' decided ta try ta cut him off 'fore he got back ta town. I seen him take a shot at ya, an' fired off one o' my own, but all I could tell I hit was the top o' the carriage. Sure took his time dyin', didn't he?"

"Yessir, that he did. Well, let me take a look at those grays. They look like the might o' got hurt when he wrecked that carriage," Ben said as he walked back to where the horses were still standing. Lifting the foreleg on the closest one, he checked the hoof area, taking time to dislodge a stone caught near the frog, and then put the hoof back down gently, followed by running is hand up the gelding's leg.

Standing back up, patting the gray on the neck gently, he stepped over to where their other gray stood. The horse seemed to settle down even more as Ben ran his hand down the middle of his back until he reached the hip area, when the animal flinched slightly. Speaking softly to the horse, Ben slowly ran his hand down the animal's leg, and then back up again resulting in the same flinch at the hip area.

"Whattaya think, Ben? We gonna have ta put 'em down?"

"Naw, Jeff. Nothing a little bit o' time won't cure. But they'll have ta be taken ta town real slow like, an' not for at least an hour or so o' lettin' 'em stand out here. That one," Ben said pointing to the first gray he had inspected, "...he's just got a bad stone bruise, al least that's what it looks like ta me. An' this one, muscle pull. How he'll take twice as long ta get healed up, an' then he'll need ta be worked real slow for another month at least 'fore he's ready for the harness again. I don't guess they'll go very far hurtin' like they are right now, so what say we get out o' here, go see how the rest o' 'em fared?"

"Yessir, let me go find my horse an' I'll meet ya up on the top o' the draw, Ben."

Separating again, the two men mounted up, and fifteen minutes later came back together on top of the draw looking down into the valley off to their right. The mules had been brought on over the top of the hill and were standing in a line waiting to continue the trip, while the riders and men who had hid in the trees were all milling around holding their mounts as well as many others. On the other horses, all but two men were slung over their saddles and those two were well tied and guarded.

Riding into the circle of men standing around waiting on something, Ben and Jeff made it to the center before he saw why they were all waiting. Chenoa was kneeling down, and with all the blood on her arms Ben thought at first that she had been injured. As he got closer, he could see that she was treating Muley, and both Jed and Bear Claw were lying on the ground all ready patched up.

Seth, Zack and Todd were acting as her assistants, tearing cloths and soaking them according to her directions while she cleaned the wound in Muley's right arm. "Now, Muley, this is gong to hurt. Do you want another shot of whiskey, or something to bite on?"

"No, ma'am, I'll be fine. Just do what ya got ta do."

Taking a needle and thread, Chenoa quickly put a dozen stitches in his arm, and even after Muley's insistence that he would be fine, he passed out cold. Chenoa asked for more water, and began washing the blood off her hands and arms. After several minutes, she looked up to see Ben and Jeff standing at the edge of the crowd.

"Ben, I'm so glad to see you are all right. Did you get Barrington? Is he under arrest?"

Looking at the sheriff before answering, Ben turned back to look at this amazing woman. "Well, between me an' Jeff here, he won't be botherin' nobody again. I got ta tell ya though, if it hadn't been for Jeff, he might o' got me instead. I see you made out all right, an' got his hired toughs rounded up."

364

"Yes, these men you hired were outstanding. I feel so bad that Muley, Jed and Bear Claw all got wounded, but they were so brave, Ben. You should have seen them. Oh, and I sent a man into town to borrow Salty's buckboard to carry them into the doctor's office, so they can be checked over and treated properly. You don't think he'll mind, do you?"

"No, I don't s'pose he'll mind one bit."

"Ben, Chenoa ain' a tellin' ya all o' whut happen. She took down half o' 'em buggers all by herse'f. Ah ain' nevah seen shootin' the likes o' whut she done," one of Jed's cousins spoke up.

"'Et's a nat'ral fac, Ben, it sho' is. Hell, ah'd ride wit' 'er anytime, ah sho'ly would now," another of the men stated.

"All I know, Ben, is I'm sure glad she'll be in camp with us, in case we ever need doctorin'. She's as good as most doctors I've seen. We topped the hill in time ta see a couple o' 'em shots she made, an' these fellers ain't exaggeratin' one little bit," Todd added.

"Seth, you see enough ta fill out the reports so's we can let these good folks get along on their way? I hear they got some claims ta work," Sheriff Walker asked his deputy.

"Yessir, I did. If it hadn't been for Chenoa, I might be layin' there shot up my own self. But I sure 'nough got a first hand look at what happened. Plenty ta say the Creed's and Chenoa ought ta be let go on their way," Seth replied.

"Thanks for that, Jeff, an' you're right about those claims, not ta mention we still got a long hard ride ta get there. Chenoa, Todd, Zack, ya all ready ta ride now?"

"You bet I am, Ben. We just lost all the time we gained this morning, and then some," Chenoa said sadly.

"She's sure right, brother. Let's get ta movin'," Todd added to the agreement to pull out, and Zack just nodded and started for his horse.

Ten minutes later, they were organized again, and riding toward Tuscambia Mountain, leaving Prescott to the hoots, hollers and cheers of the men Ben had hired, along with their good wishes. A mile and a half down the road, they turned into the timber, Chenoa taking the lead as planned, and thirty minutes later they saw three Apache warriors dogging their back trail. Another mile up Lynx Creek, Chenoa waved, and then a few minutes later motioned for a stop.

Ben started to question her when Long Lance rode up beside her. They spoke for about ten minutes, before she climbed down, untied the Apache pony and handed him the lead rope. The big Apache seemed sad, but not upset, something Ben was certainly thankful for. After a few more minutes, he disappeared into the timber, and Chenoa walked back to fill Ben in on their conversation.

"Long Lance agreed to take his pony back, since I seem to have gained such a fine horse. He and his warriors saw the battle from the trees, and he told me how brave he thought I was, too brave to just be any man's woman. Brave enough to be a warrior in my own right. But he still wants me to join him in his wickiup and stay with his family group. Also, they will scout the trail ahead as well as make sure we are safe from behind as we travel to our camp. Now, unless there is something else you need to know, I'll mount up and get us moving again."

"Well, that's all good to hear, an' that settles any questions I had. Lead the way, Chenoa!"

As she remounted and started to lead the way again, Ben leaned back to signal the boys that all was well, even if he was still a bit skeptical due to the exchange of the pony. Still, there were no problems, and Chenoa lead a steady move south along a slightly different route, stopping only twice to let the animals all blow. Just as the sun dropped below the horizon, and with a good amount of light left, the French and Paiute woman pulled to a halt on a nice sized meadow on the edge of Turkey Creek. The real surprise to Ben was, there was all ready a small fire burning, obviously courtesy of Long Lance and his warriors, which would allow them coffee and maybe a chance at cooking some food.

Cherokee Parks

Chapter Thirty-Nine

Chenoa was up and had coffee brewed and meat, eggs and spuds cooking when Ben and his brothers woke, most likely from the smell of food and coffee, long before light began to show in the east. Conversation was limited as they hurriedly devoured the food and drank their coffee, only dotted with details of the trip to this point.

"Danged if I can figure it out. Here we are leading a long pack train, an' makin' better them than I ever made with just Captain an' a burro. An' ta my knowledge, not a soul has seen us pass 'cept the Apache. How do you explain that, Chenoa?"

"It is the Ghost Trail, or close to it, Ben. Now finish up so we can get loaded and moving again," she responded. It didn't take long, as the decision had been made the night before to leave the packs in place, and only unsaddle their mounts, as the pack animals were showing no real signs of stress or exhaustion.

They were leaving their overnight camp in the pre-dawn light, again slightly ahead of Ben's planned schedule, and with the Apache leaving signs for Chenoa they traveled on at a good pace. By noon, they had crossed Turkey Creek again, much further upstream, and followed it until they turned almost directly south. An hour later, they stopped for a blow, and to water the animals after they cooled, at Barrel Spring on one of the northern forks of Blind Indian Creek.

"Boys, believe it 'r not, but we'll be in camp in less than an hour," Ben informed his brothers. "Looks like we'll even have time ta not only unload the animals, but get quite a bit put away. We're gonna have ta hobble some o' the mules, as I figure they'll all stick close ta each other, an' throw up a big rope corral for the horses, but that's gonna have ta be near a half mile from camp where there's plenty o' grass an' water for 'em."

"Really? We're that close?"

"Yessir, we sure are. An' that mountain just ta the southeast o' where we are right now is where the claims are. Damn, I can't wait 'til ya see 'em, an' how much ore there is. An' I just believe you're gonna really like the place where I set up a permanent camp," Ben said excitedly, wondering what they would think of the hidden storage cave.

With plenty of daylight still left, they rode into camp, left spotless by the Apache family just hours before. The only sign that anyone had been there was some resetting of the lean-to, a good supply of firewood, and a small fire still burning.

Chenoa took immediate charge of the unloading process, having Ben, Zack and Todd lead their spare horses to the mouth of the cave after removing the brush covering the mouth, and packing the bags of oats in to ensure they stayed dry and didn't spoil. That was soon followed by leading each mule up separately, and unloading what needed to be stored securely inside, starting with the cartridges. As each pack was emptied, the animal carrying it was stripped and rubbed down before being led off and tied to a tree to wait to be taken to the grass.

By the time darkness started to show, the packs had all been unloaded, and the mules led to grass, four of them being hobbled, while the rope corral to contain all their horses had been strung and the horses placed inside. By the time the men walked back to camp, Chenoa was busy cooking again, much to their pleasure.

"Boys, first thing in the mornin', you'll need ta string some tarps an' make up your own lean-tos. Chenoa will show ya the best place, as she knows even better'n me the high an' low spots here, an' the best place ta lay your bedrolls ta keep dry when the rains come. We got here in good 'nough time that once ya get that done, an' get yourselves set up ta sleep right 'til we get ready ta leave, that we can slip up an' take a good look at the claims after we eat

370

some grub at noon."

"Dang, Ben, I thought ya said we'd get a day o' rest," Zack said with his back turned to Ben, but facing Todd and winking. "Now here ya are tellin' us we got ta work first day in camp."

"Yeah, well, like Paw always said, 'Ya got ta make hay while the sun shines.' So get used to it, boys." Then he saw the smiles on both of his younger brothers faces, and knew they weren't one bit serious. "Oh, all right, so ya got me there. But," he continued on a more resolute note, "from here on out, we need ta be at it as steady as we can, weather an' such permittin'."

***

And so it went from that day forward as day after day they worked the gold claim, putting the gold into the large bags Ben had ordered for just that purpose, only checking once a week to make sure no one was snooping around the silver claim, but taking a day to stake out the boy's own claims. Light rain came at the end of the first week they were in camp, refilling the small pond, allowing them to continue panning and collecting more and more dust and flakes. Each day, while the boys were panning, Ben worked his way up to the vein and back down the dry waterbed to the pond, picking up nuggets until he could find no more.

A heavy rain came at the end of the second week, revealing still more nuggets, and washing more dust and flakes into the area just above the pond as well as along the edges of the water. Finally, at the end of the third week, they had collected all of the easily accessible gold in the draw, and decided to focus on the vein.

After drilling the first set of holes and blasting an opening to follow the vein, they spent two days carrying ore back to camp for storage. The third day of that week, Ben set off another small charge, and again they spent two days gathering chunks of gold rich ore. Day five brought the same routine, but everything came to a halt on the seventh day with another heavy rain, one that lasted most of the day and into the night. But it brought a much needed rest to all but Chenoa, who still cooked and took care of their camp.

The sole exception to her doing everything in camp was the refilling of the barrels every other day by lugging water up from the creek below, and checking on the animals as well as occasionally graining them. But this day of rest also broke the loneliness most women would have felt, and allowed Chenoa to actually talk to someone other than the Apache warriors, especially Long Lance, who dropped by almost daily while the Creed's were out.

The second day in camp, Ben had hung some candy and some tobacco from the trees as usual, deciding not to let them have all twenty pounds of each right away. That alone was the primary reason for the warriors to visit camp everyday, for all but Long Lance anyway, who still had hopes of taking Chenoa as his woman.

However, the only Apache to visit camp that long, wet and dreary day was Long Lance. As was his fashion, he arrived soundlessly, startling Zack to the point that he actually jumped out from under his and Todd's lean-to and into the rain. "Damn! Where'd you come from?"

"Zack, it is all right, this is Long Lance, but he speaks no English so I will translate for you." A moment later, after Chenoa told the Apache what Zack had said, Long Lance burst out laughing, and then spoke in his language.

Chenoa then chuckled, followed by speaking to Zack. "He asks if it is because he is so big, or so quiet, that you are startled."

"Hah! Both, I reckon."

"Ask him how the tobacco an' candy went over, will ya?" Ben called across the short distance between lean-tos.

A few moments later, Chenoa responded with, "He said the tobacco is very good, better than any he has smoked. Even the other warriors have spoken of it as being very good. And the candy has been a source of laughter as well as pleasure among the women and children as they try to guess which taste they will get, and if they can handle the heat of the special ones. He also said thank you for bringing them."

"Well, that's good. Glad he and the other warriors like the tobacco, and that his people like the candy. Next time I go to town I will bring back more for them."

Chenoa translated, and then giggled and blushed after Long Lance responded, leading Ben to believe that the Apache had suggested something she would not let them know about at any cost, so he decided to relieve her somewhat. "Ask him if he wants to sit where it is dry an' drink coffee with us?"

A couple of minutes later, she said, "No. He just wanted to stop by and tell you thanks for the candy and tobacco, but he needs to finish his hunt for a deer. He also said he does not really like coffee, although some of the women in his camp do. He wants to know if he should send them to sit with you, even stay with you until you are ready to leave."

Now Ben was a bit embarrassed, as that was the last thing he had thought about in some time. "Tell him I said no, but I appreciate the offer." Turning to look at his brothers, he decided to put the heat on them. "But maybe my brothers would like it."

Todd was the first to answer, "Damn you, Ben. I knew you'd get even with us sooner 'r later. Chenoa, tell him we, too, appreciate the offer, but we have much work to do and no time for women now."

Sensing that Ben had just played one on his brothers, Long Lance spoke, and Chenoa translated. "He says to tell the young ones that there are several very nice young women in his camp.

They are nice and round, and will keep a man warm at night, in more ways than one. You can even try one out, and if you don't like her he will send another, and another, until you have one you like."

Zack gasped, "Oh, hell, no!"

Long Lance and Chenoa nearly doubled over in laughter, soon joined by Ben and his brothers, who figured out that the Apache had just gotten them all, and good. Ben had heard that the Apache had a good sense of humor, and were great tricksters, but this was the first time he had seen it actually come into play. He hoped it wouldn't be his last time to see it.

As quietly as he had appeared, Long Lance left their camp, leaving a void in conversation for nearly half an hour. Zack stepped over into Ben's lean-to to get another cup of coffee, and asked, "Ben, how much gold ya figure we got now?"

"Hadn't really give it much thought, ta be honest about it, Zack. A lot, though, I reckon. Why?"

"Well, I was lookin' at all those sacks we filled up an' set inside the cave. Looks ta me like we got enough ta load four, maybe five mules with just dust, flakes an' nuggets. An' all the ore we got stacked up outside o' the cave will load up another five 'r six. Much more, an' we'll be leavin' quite a bit behind when we haul."

"Naw, I don't think we got quite that much, but ta tell ya the truth I ain't really looked to see how much you boys put inside the cave. Reckon I'd best do that after this rain stops."

The rain continued most of the night, but as he had said he would, Ben checked inside the cave first thing the next morning to see how many bags were there. Lighting one of the larger candles, he couldn't believe his eyes at the number of bags inside, and quickly checked the pile of ore they had hauled into camp. Zack was close to being correct; they had enough to load at least ten mules, if not eleven.

Stepping back to take his plate of food and cup of coffee being held for him by Chenoa, he sat down on his stump to eat. Between bites, he said, "Zack, I think you were pretty close on how much we got ta load all ready. Another day 'r two, an' we ought ta head for the smelter. Muley an' his men are prob'ly settin' in Mayer waitin' on us now, so we'll see what we can pull out tomorrow an' head in."

"Ben, do you wish for me to have Long Lance send another family to guard our camp when we leave?"

"Yeah, I think that'd be a good idea, don't you boys?"

Zack was the one to answer. "Yeah, real good idea. We still got a lot o' supplies here, an' if we can't load all the gold an' ore we got here in camp it'd be real smart ta have somebody watchin' over the surplus supplies as well as the gold." Todd only nodded in agreement, too busy eating to speak.

As they climbed over the big rock holding the water back, Todd was the first to see all the glitter. "Damn, there's more dust an' flakes ta be panned out. That rain must o' washed it down. Ben, ya s'pose there's more nuggets showin' up the draw as well?"

"I wouldn't be surprised, Todd. Looks like we'll be pannin' an' gatherin' for another day 'r two 'fore we can get back ta workin' the vein."

Zack and Todd spent the next two days panning while Ben scoured the draw for nuggets, each filling bag after bag with the precious metal. Back at camp the second night, they took stock of their storage of sacks after eating, deciding that they had panned enough to fully load all twelve mules as well as both spare horses, and still leave some ore behind from the pile outside the cave.

"Ben, once we're loaded, how long ya think it will take ta haul ta the smelter in Mayer?"

"Tops, five hours. If we start loadin' at first light, we should have it all in packs by noon 'r shortly after, an' be in Mayer with plenty o' daylight. Chenoa, how long ta button up camp?"

"If we do as before, leaving the lean-tos in place and only taking our bedrolls, I can take an inventory of the remaining food so I know what we'll need to replenish and be ready long before you finish loading the packs. But if we are to leave tomorrow, all of the animals will need an extra graining tonight, as well as in the morning before we leave. That will leave just fewer than five bags of oats, and I fear it might spoil before we return, as we have made no plans about that. Maybe we should let the Apache have it for their horses, but I can let the Apache family coming in know that once you decide. I will let Long Lance know we are leaving tomorrow, so he can send the family to us before we leave. My only question now would be, how long will we be gone, Ben?"

"I don't think 'em oats is gonna spoil that fast, but that's fine. It'll be a reward for keepin' their eye on our backside for the last month. Not for sure how long we'll be gone, but I s'pose at least a week, give 'r take a few days one way 'r tother. It all depends on whether we leave the ore an' go get supplies an' ride right back, 'r whether we decide ta take a few days break, maybe wait on the smelter ta melt it all down an' see what we end up with."

"Well, if I got a vote, I say we take a break an' wait ta find out what kind o' reward we are gonna end up with for all this work we done, Ben," Todd pronounced.

"An' I'm votin' with Todd on this one, brother Ben. We need ta file 'em new claims, an' I got a hankerin' ta sleep in a real bed for a few days, maybe get me a hot bath," Zack declared.

"I am all in favor of a real bed and a hot bath as well, Ben. And I would really like to eat someone else's cooking as well."

"Chenoa, me an' the boys really like your cookin', but I s'pose you doin' all the cookin' ya'd get tired o' eatin' it as well. All right, we'll take a few days off. Let the Apache know we'll be gone roughly a week, an' ta feel free ta use up the grain, but not any o' the rest o' the supplies. We'll need ta start loadin' at first light tomorrow, so let's call it a day an' sack out, shall we?"

Chapter Forty

Loading Ben, Zack and Todd's spare mounts first, knowing that they wouldn't be able to carry the same loads as the mules, Ben and Chenoa held the mules in line until the horses were moved off and tied to some trees. Then came the real work, putting the packsaddles on the mules and loading each with as much gold as the group dared. It was well past midmorning when the last mule had been loaded, and there were still seven bags of dust, flakes and nuggets left, though all the ore had been loaded.

"We leavin' them behind, Ben?"

"Naw, I can carry two o' 'em on Captain, an' if ya can each take two more, we can put the last on one Chenoa's little filly. We're this close ta takin' it all, no sense in leavin' any behind that we don't have to."

They all agreed, and once the mules were moved out of the way and lined out to trail, they each loaded their animals with the remaining bags by tying them together at the opening and flopping the sacks across behind their saddles, with Chenoa's load being reduced in size by emptying half of one bag into another sack and stuffing the half full bags into each of her saddlebag pouches. Satisfied that all of the gold would ride well, they mounted and started the short trek to Mayer.

It was midafternoon when they rode up to the smelter, met outside by two distinguished looking men. Ben asked, "Either of you Charles Tucker 'r Emmitt Browner?"

"No, sir, you'll find those gentlemen inside. I am Ted Dickerson, and this is Pádraig Lonnigan. We are the owners of Monument Mining Corporation, currently mining in the area of Tuscon and Globe. We're in this area looking for good working mines to purchase. What are you hauling in here?"

"Frankly, I don't see as that's any o' your business, at least not just yet, gentlemen. Now, if you'll excuse me, I need ta talk ta the owners o' the stamp mill an' smelter," Ben cut them off before they could get started.

"Ben, figured ya'd be 'long 'bout now. We's heah an' all ready ta keep an eye on things. An' Ms. Chenoa, my arm has all but healed up right nice. Doc said ya done a right fine job o' sewin' me up, he did. Said fo' me ta come back next week an' git 'em threads pulled."

"Well, that's good to know, Muley. Would you mind keeping an eye on these animals while I step inside with Ben?"

The mountain man reached up to take the reins as Chenoa stepped down and walked to where Ben stood at the door waiting. Stepping inside, they were greeted by the man at the desk closest to the door. "I see ya brought some ore in. Now, who might ya be?"

"Ben Creed, an' this is one o' my partners, Chenoa."

"Ah, yes, your attorney was here a month ago saying you'd be bringing us some ore. I'm Emmitt Browner, and that over there with his head in the books is Charles Tucker. Glad to meet you, Mr. Creed. Say, those two outside didn't bother you, did they? They've been hanging around trying to buy mines and claims for the last week."

"No, not at all. But I did kind o' brush 'em off on our way in," Ben said shaking the offered hand, and then Tucker's hand as he joined them.

"Oh, I suppose they're harmless, just businessmen looking to expand their holdings. But so far no one has brought in anything valuable enough to really peak their interests. So, Mr. Creed, what have you brought us today?

"Ben, please just call me Ben, will ya? We got twelve mules an' three horses loaded down heavy, half with gold ore an' the other half with dust, flakes an' nuggets."

The two men looked at each other, Tucker looking back at Ben and asking, "Did you say half of them are loaded with dust, flakes and nuggets? Or are my ears playing tricks on me?"

"No, that's exactly what I said."

"Good Lord, man. Let's get a look at this dust," Browner said, very excited. Grabbing his hat, he headed for the door, Tucker right behind him, stopping only to hold the door open for Chenoa and Ben.

Outside, Ben led them to the six mules loaded with dust, flakes and nuggets, as well as having Zack and Todd pull the sacks from their horses, Captain and Chenoa's filly. From there, the two men were shown the ore, which seemed to excite them as much as the dust.

"How long did it take you to pull this much, and how many men are working your claim, Ben?"

"Well, Mr. Tucker, we did this in just under four weeks, the three of us with Chenoa handlin' camp for us."

"Unbelievable. Absolutely unbelievable. All right, we just finished a smelting run this afternoon from ore we stamped out yesterday, so we can start smelting the dust, flakes and nuggets first thing tomorrow, and begin stamping the ore at the same time. Now then, if you'll lead the mules with the ore over to that area next to the stamp, I'll have the men start unloading it into the hoppers for you. The rest of it can be unloaded by some of our other men into those hoppers over there, right where we can start pouring it into the smelting vats as soon as we open tomorrow," Tucker said.

"One thing, gents, you saw them fellers standin' around our

mules an' horses, right?" When they both nodded yes, Ben continued. "Those men are the guards I hired ta watch over all out gold. They'll be stayin' here right alongside that gold 'til we haul it out o' here, as the last thing we need is somebody tryin' ta steal it 'r cheat us out o' what we worked hard ta get."

"And we will have guards on duty tonight as well, as we always do when we are holding or processing ore. Between them, your assets should be quite safe. Now, shall we step back inside, as there seems to be two sets of prying ears and eyes on us," Browner said, turning to indicate the building off to the side of the one they had first met.

"I assume your attorney told you our pricing, especially since he negotiated so hard on your behalf. And frankly, that is well below what we normally charge, but it is rare that we see this kind of quality, so high that much of it requires no stamping, and that which does will still be a very high yielding ore. Believe me, Ben, we will make as much off of this one load of your ore as we have made in the last year, maybe longer. I held serious doubts about the quality, let alone the quantity, of what you would be bringing in, even after seeing the samples your attorney showed us. Ben, both of you have made me a believer!"

"That goes for both of us, Ben," Tucker supported what Browner had said. "And I am certainly glad we agreed to the prices we quoted, as I would hate to have found out some other stamp and smelting processor got your business instead of us. Now, where are you staying tonight, as I assume you'll want to stay to see the early results. The first run should be ready for inspection by just before noon."

"Well, we haven't got that far, ta be honest. Is there any place decent where we can hang out hats an' board our animals?"

"We have a pasture out back where we occasionally run a few cattle, but we normally sell them off come spring and only replenish in the fall. There is plenty of water as well, as Big Bug Creek runs through it, and you can put your mules in that pasture. The only place in town for travelers to stay is Mrs. Bowman's Boarding House, but I'm not certain if she even has any rooms to let for two or three days this time of year. You are planning on staying for the entire run, aren't you?" Browner asked.

"Well, we do need ta resupply, so we figured on makin' a run ta Prescott 'fore we go back up, an' we'll need ta get more o' the men we've hired lined out ta start cuttin' timbers and creatin' shafts, but if all it'll take ta stamp an' smelt it is two 'r three days, I reckon we might as well hang around Mayer 'fore we ride for Prescott. Shoot, we might even buy a wagon an' haul the bars in ourselves."

"A wagon? That's rich, Ben. You'd better plan on two, maybe three wagons if you're going to haul the ingots all the way there yourself. Fortunately, you have the mules to use to pull the wagons, but you'd also need harness. That is unless you load the ingots into the packsaddles and haul it that way. I trust you have an agreement with someone with a large and secure safe, correct?"

"Yeah, the Bank o' Prescott."

"I suppose we were remiss in alerting your attorney to the fact that much of the gold and silver ore we run here ends up going to a Federal storage facility in Phoenix, or the one in Tuscon, or we can arrange to have it sold and shipped, and have a bank draft sent to your bank for deposit, but that does run about ten percent of the value of the precious metal," Tucker explained.

"I don't reckon I'd be too interested in givin' up ten percent ta somebody buyin what we worked sa hard to get an' all they're doin' is shippin it, an' makin' a pretty fair profit on top o' that."

"Well, that's our thinking as well, but we still feel it necessary to give our clients all the information so they can make the best decision for their circumstances."

"Well, I 'preciate it, Charles. But I reckon we'll take it ta Prescott this time. We might want ta do somethin' different next time. Now then, it's been a long day after a lot o' long days. We need ta get unloaded an' find a place ta lay our heads," Ben said now that they were outside and leading the mules to the two locations indicated by the smelter and stamp operators.

As they started to unload, with the help of the stamp and smelter workers, they heard plenty of long, low whistles and comments indicating the value of their loads. Lonnigan and Dickerson were hanging around like flies, just waiting for the moment they could land on any of the four partners. It took just over an hour before they finally led the last mule away, and then led all but the saddle horses to the pasture and turned them out.

Mounting up after getting directions to the boarding house, Ben called out to Muley. "Keep a good watch on it, Muley. There'll be some smelter guards showin' up 'fore long, so see if ya can sneak in a nap durin' the night. See ya in the morning'."

As they rode abreast toward Mrs. Bowman's, Todd asked, "Ben what if she ain't got any rooms ta let?"

"Don't guess it'll be the last time we sleep on the ground, do you?"

No one responded, they only nodded to the obvious truth of Ben's question. Riding up to the house, they saw a clean yard, a picket fence painted white, and a large porch with several rockers and a hanging swing with plenty of flowers at the base of the porch itself. Looking at each other, none of the men really wanted to step into such a pristine yard, so Chenoa was elected to the task of knocking on the door.

"Mrs. Bowman, we were sent here by Mr. Tucker and Mr. Browner at the smelter. They thought you might have rooms for myself and my three partners."

"Oh, I'm so sorry, dearie, but I only have one room available. How long did you want to stay?"

"Just two or three days, while we wait for our dust to be smelted, and our ore to be stamped and smelted."

"Are you the folks I was told had just brought in nearly pure gold, all loaded on twelve mules and some horses?"

"Yes, ma'am, that would be us."

"I tell you what, like I said, I only have the one room available, and I'd prefer it be used by you. But I do have a spacious barn where you can put your animals, and a nice haymow for your friends to use. I'll charge you two dollars a day and provide two meals a day, morning and night. The men, if they stay in the barn, I'll charge a dollar a day and feed them with the rest of my boarders. You go on out and tell them what I said, and let me know. I'm going to sit in my favorite rocker and enjoy this nice, cool evening air. I'll be right here when you decide."

"Thank you, Mrs. Bowman. I'll be back to let you know in a moment or two," Chenoa said as she stepped off the porch and walked to the gate to inform the men of what was available.

After explaining what the woman said, Todd commented that he'd rather sleep on hay as hard ground any day. Ben reached into his vest pocket and pulled out a double eagle, flipping it to Chenoa with a question. "What time do we eat in the mornin', an' does she have anything we can eat yet tonight?"

Walking back to the porch, Chenoa handed the coin to Mrs. Bowman and asked about both breakfast and supper. The reply surprised her. "Dearie, I'll gladly feed you an' those boys if you'll give me a half hour to heat something up. As far as breakfast, I serve it at seven every morning, on the dot. They can put the horses in the stalls in the barn, and feed them some of the hay. There is a horse trough out back to water the horses, along with a well and pump, and a bucket they can use to carry water. There is a wash bench on the back of the house where they can wash up, and no one sits at my table with dirty hands or faces, or wearing hats or guns, so the hardware will have to be removed along with your hats. As for you, you may use the wash pan and towels in my kitchen to wash yourself. One more thing, no, and I do mean NO nighttime visitors of the any variety. That pretty much covers all my rules, so tell your friends to take care of the stock and get washed up while I show you to your room."

Chenoa practically skipped out to let Ben and his brothers know the rules, and quickly grabbed her possibles bag and bed roll, and then hurried back to the porch, where Mrs. Bowman waited for her. Knocking the trail dust off using her hat, which she left off her head, she stepped inside to find the interior of the house was as well taken care of as the outside, and her room was spacious with a big feather bed and an armoire. Quickly changing into something clean, she walked down the hallway to find the kitchen.

Chapter Forty-One

Mrs. Bowman was all ready at the stove heating up what looked to be some sort of stew, and a pan of fried potatoes along with two pots of coffee. While the food on the stove was heating, she sliced off several slices of bread, carrying it into the next room. As soon as Chenoa had washed, she asked, "May I help you? Does the table need set, or is there anything else I can do?"

"Not a thing, dearie. Just go on and have a seat. You must be exhausted after a long day. And if I see things right, you don't belong to any of these men, and probably take care of all the cooking and camp work. Am I right?"

"Yes, ma'am, that's correct. We are all partners in the mining venture. Ben, the oldest brother, is the claim owner and holds the largest share, while his brothers Todd and Zack also have claims beside his, and I take care of camp for a small share. Actually, I didn't want anything, as Ben saved my life, but he insisted I get something out of helping him in camp both before and after his brothers came with us."

"Well, good for you, young lady. I wish I had been that resourceful in my youth, instead of marrying a gambling man who left me nearly destitute. And it sounds like these are good men, a rare find anytime. Say, I don't even know your name, dearie."

"Chenoa, Mrs. Bowman. I will be as honest as I can with you. I am half Paiute, which is where my name comes from, and half French."

"Oh, for crying out loud, I could care less about such things. Now go take a seat, as it's all but ready to eat. Where are those men?"

"Here, ma'am. I was wondering if we might bring in some water for ya, 'r some firewood."

"Not tonight, but thank you. Tomorrow, I might just take you up on it, but for now grab your brothers and come try this Mulligan stew. There's fried potatoes and fresh bread as well as homemade butter, and two pots of coffee I expect you to drink," she finished with a laugh.

As they all sat down, Mrs. Bowman lowered her head in prayer, surprising all four of her guests as she fervently prayed for the health and safety of these strangers seated at her table. As she finished, she said, "All right, get to it, travelers, before it gets cold."

And eat they did, each of the men eating three bowls of stew, while Chenoa ate only two but filled up on potatoes and fresh bread smothered in butter. When they finished, there was no more bread, potatoes, coffee or stew and their plates and bowls almost looked like they had been licked clean.

As they rose, carrying their plates, bowls, cups and utensils to the kitchen, Mrs. Bowman had a smile from ear to ear, and a question for Chenoa. "Dearie, do they always eat like that?"

"Well, yes, most of the time."

"It's a pleasure to seem men who eat well, and I am so happy they did. Most of my boarders complain about the food, or the coffee, and just about anything they can to get under my skin. If I thought I could get away with it, I'd throw the three of them out and have your men stay in the house with us. And polite, why they even carried their plates and such to the kitchen for me. Now that has never happened, not as long as I've owned this place. It will be a real pleasure to have them at my table at seven in the morning, just to show those other men what a real man eats like. Now scoot, get some rest. I've got dishes to do, and more bread to make yet tonight. Go one now, scoot," Mrs. Bowman said, gently pushing Chenoa in the direction of the hallway.

***

Barely remembering lying down on the soft bed, Chenoa's eyes popped open to bright sunlight, and she hoped she hadn't missed the seven o'clock breakfast time. Jumping out of bed, she hurriedly dressed and brushed out her hair, and then hustled down the hallway to wash up, if she was still in time.

"My, my, Chenoa, don't you look just as fresh as a daisy. You must have slept well. Wash up, and this morning I'll let you help me carry the food and coffee to the table. I overslept a bit after baking that bread last night. I made four loaves this time, thinking your men will most likely eat two of them," she said with a hearty laugh.

With six men and only Mrs. Bowman and Chenoa representing the fairer sex, the table was full. Her normal three boarders chose to sit together on one side of the table, while the two ladies sat together, Mrs. Bowman at the end. Ben sat at the other end of the table while Todd sat beside Chenoa and Zack between his brothers in sort of a faceoff.

The Creed's ate normally, a lot, as did Chenoa and the landlady, all while they carried on a polite and friendly conversation. At the same time, the three regular boarders sat silently, all acting like they were being fed slop at a table full of hogs. Ben kept a close eye on the trio, wondering what kind of men it took to live so miserably, like these three obviously did.

Almost as if on cue, the three regular boarders tossed their napkins on the table, leaving plates half full of food, stood and walked away without excusing themselves. "They always act like that, ma'am?" Todd asked.

"Yes, they do. I almost want to slap them they're so rude. And it seems like all they do is complain."

"Well, we were sure raised better'n that, ma'am," Zack responded. "By the way, 'fore we go about our business today, I noticed your firewood pile is gettin' kind o' low but ya got a lot o' wood out there ta be split. Me an' Todd will take care o' that, an' I think Ben said he was gonna make sure ya had plenty o' water in the house for whatever ya need. Now, if you'll excuse us, we'll go get started on that woodpile, ma'am," Zack said as he stood, picked up his plate, cup and utensils and started for the kitchen, followed in order by Todd and then Ben.

"And I am going to help you with the dishes, Mrs. Bowman, and I won't take no for an answer. So just sit back and enjoy another cup of that delicious coffee, all right?" Chenoa said as she started clearing the rest of the table.

An hour later, there were three buckets full of water in the kitchen, enough firewood stacked inside to last at least a couple of days, as well as enough split outside to last another week, and all of the dishes were washed, dried and put away, ready for the next meal. Mrs. Bowman was torn between being elated and tormented, as no boarder had ever done anything near what these four had done. She would be sad to see them leave, but she also knew they would only be with her for a few days, and she might never see them again.

She sat on the porch and waved to them as they rode off toward the smelter an hour before lunch, and she regretted not offering to feed them a third meal. Riding up to the front of the smelter office, they were met by Charles Tucker and one of the men they had eaten breakfast with.

"Ben, just in time. The first batch has been smelted and poured into ingots, and we just started a new batch. This is some of the purest gold we've ever had the pleasure of running. Ninety-eight percent pure. Ben, this first batch is worth nearly a hundred thousand dollars, and we've just gotten started. Oh, this is our metallurgist, Sam Dockings. He is the gent who checks the purity."

"Mr. Dockings and I have crossed paths, haven't we?"

"Ah, well, yes. At Mrs. Bowman's."

"Say, wasn't that a fine breakfast she served up? She always set a table like that?"

"Well, ah, yes, if you like that sort of food I suppose it would be considered good."

"You didn't like it? We all thought it was some o' the best next ta Renner's 'r the Congress in Prescott."

"I-I-I haven't eaten at any of them so I couldn't possibly judge. Mr. Tucker, I must get back inside and start pulling short samples from this next batch."

"I see our Sam Dockings didn't impress you any, Ben. If I could find somebody else ta take his place, I'd send him packing, even though he does a good job," Tucker said after Dockings had walked away.

"No, he didn't impress me any, not him 'r 'em other two stayin' there. Weasely fellers, all three, Charles."

"Charlie, Ben, call me Charlie. I sent your men down to a little café we got here in town to get something to eat, and kept my guards on duty until they return, which should be any time now. And just so you know, both Emmitt and I have been here since daybreak to keep an eye on things. We're going to run day and night until your ore has all been processed, and one of us will be here at all times, if not both of us. Oh, and I had my guards run Lonnigan and Dickerson off this morning. No need to have them hanging around all day, not on private property anyway. And dangit, I almost forgot. Your attorney is waiting inside, been here about an hour."

"Well, send somebody ta fetch him, will ya?"

A few minutes later, James joined them, but didn't have a lot to say, just listened.

"Why the day an' night operation, Charlie?" Ben asked.

"Frankly, the sooner we finish, the sooner you can get this someplace safe, at least safer than here, even with all the guards. Ben, with gold this pure, word is bound to get out. And when it does there will be men of all streaks of good and bad flocking here to see about this rich strike. The bad ones will just try to steal it, and the good ones will hope to pick up the droppings."

"Yeah, I s'pose that's right, Charlie. That said, we might take turns bein' here ourselves, standin' with the guards. How long 'fore this next batch will be done?"

"Give us four hours, and until we start with the stamped ore, every three to four hours should see a batch finished. We have a special room where we keep the ingots stacked to cool. Would you and your partners like to take a look at what we have so far?"

"Sure, I've never seen an ingot, an' I think I'd like ta pick one up an' hold it in my hand," Ben answered, motioning for his brothers and Chenoa to tie off their horses and follow he and James inside.

Inside the building, they were led to a large, sealed off room with only one large opening with a heavy door mounted over it. Charlie unlocked the padlock and removed one end of the chain, and then pulled the heavy door open just enough for them to slip into the room. "That's yours over there," Tucker said pointing to a stack of ingots. It was dark in the room, and the stack was nearly impossible to see until Tucker lit a coal oil lamp illuminating the room.

Chenoa gasped at the size of the stack, while Todd and Zack just shook their heads. Ben walked over, leaned down and picked up one of the gold bars, hefting it in his hand for several minutes before asking, "Tucker, what's one o' these weigh? An' what are they worth?"

"Four hundred troy ounces, Ben, or just under thirty pounds. Value comes in just over eight thousand dollars each."

"An' 'em twelve bars is worth near a hundred thousand, just out o' one batch, right?"

"Yes, that's correct."

"An' how many o' these batches ya figure just with the dust, flakes an' nuggets?"

"Well, rough guess, Ben, I'd say about ten, maybe twelve. The stamped ore won't be that many, and will take a bit longer to smelt, as they won't be anywhere near as pure. Still, I'd have to say that will make an additional six to eight clean batches."

Todd had been running the numbers in his head, and finally spoke. "Damn, that could be anywhere from sixteen ta twenty times as many o' them gold bars at eight thousand apiece. Ben, that's 'tween a million an' a half an' two million dollars. Just what we brought in on this load. An' we got a big vein ta work yet, an' that silver claim. Hot damn, Zack, big brother has made us all rich!"

"Hold it down, Todd. We still got ta get his someplace safe, an' hope nothin' goes wrong. 'Sides, these fellers have ta get paid, an' James, an' Lord only knows how many other hands will be stickin' out wantin' some. Ain't that right, James?"

"I'm afraid so, which is why I'm here, to monitor the process and keep a close count on the book tallies."

Todd knew that Ben would guard their gold like a mama bear watching over her cubs, and make sure they were all taken care of along the way. Over the next three days and nights, batch after batch was run, mostly gold but with some silver, a bit of copper and a little lead. When the final batch was run, and the final ingot poured, there were two hundred fifty-one gold bars, four silver, two of copper and one lead. Ben donated the silver, copper and lead to the owners and workers at the smelter, along with the last of the gold that wasn't quite enough to make an ingot, much to the consternation of James, but with Chenoa's blessing.

The decision was made to haul the finished gold to Prescott using the mules, and to have a celebration while they were there as well as pick up supplies and lead the men they would need to the area of the camp. Saying goodbye to Mrs. Bowman took a bit longer than expected, as the woman hated to see them go and praised their manners as well as their appetites before telling them, "You boys and Chenoa are welcome to stay here any time you're close enough to get here. And I expect that won't be often enough to suit me, but whenever you can you'll certainly be welcome."

Thanking her, and then politely telling her they had to be riding, they headed for the smelter to load up and hit the road to Prescott. The day and a half trip got started a bit later then they had anticipated, much to Ben's displeasure, was interrupted on the first night by Lonnigan and Dickerson riding in to where they decided to camp, and only then after Muley and two of his men were told to let them pass when they asked Ben about it.

"Gents, I ain't changed my mind one bit. The claims ain't for sale, not at any price. Don't believe it, ask my attorney. He's settin' right there," Ben said pointing to James, who was returning to Prescott with them.

"Very well, Mr. Creed, but should anything change, please let us know. Now, do you suppose we might camp nearby? There is nothing much out here anywhere, and, well, we don't carry weapons of any kind," Dickerson replied.

"Yeah, I s'pose ya can camp here next ta us, but we'll be rollin' out 'fore daylight."

"Oh my, well I suppose we will just have to rise with you and ride out as well," Dickerson said. "Right, Mr. Lonnigan?" Lonnigan only nodded, and walked to his horse to retrieve his bedroll.

Ben wondered why he had yet to hear Lonnigan say a word, as Dickerson seemed to do all the talking for both of them, but just decided it wasn't any of his business. Some men just didn't like to talk, while others loved to hear the sound of their own voice.

They rode into Prescott the next day around lunchtime, heading directly to the Bank of Prescott, where they unloaded every bar and carried them into the vault, much to Raymond Alvarez's pleasure, as that act alone would guarantee the health of his bank for many years to come. Taking three thousand dollars in gold coin out of is existing account, Ben and the group sent the men home and headed to the Congress after a brief stop to see Salty and board their mules, Captain, the roan and Chenoa's filly, while Todd and Zack headed for Cooper's Livery and then Brody's Boarding House after agreeing to meet at Renner's early the next morning.

As Ben entered the Congress Hotel and walked up to the desk, Claude nearly jumped out of his skin, not knowing anyone was anywhere around. "Mr. Creed! You're back! Let's get you and Chenoa checked in. Oh, and by the way, I have a telegram here for you," the desk clerk said reaching into the boxes behind the desk to retrieve a folded sheet of paper. "Here you are, sir."

Chapter Forty-Two

Ben started to unfold it, stopped to stare at it for several minutes, and then walked to a chair and sat down, fearing the worst. Every telegram he had received before this one carried bad news, usually of a death in the family. The exception was news that his brother Tommy had been sent to prison. *This could only be more bad news, an' just as we accomplished something most never thought possible.*

"Ben, what's wrong?" Chenoa said as she came to sit in the chair next to his.

"It's a telegram."

"Yes, and have you opened it and read it?"

"Nope."

"Why?"

"'Cause ever' time I get one, it brings bad news."

"Who is it from?"

"Don't know, really."

"Would you like for me to open it?"

Ben's response was to hand Chenoa the telegram, and then sit back in the chair to wait for the bad news to be read by the woman. After a couple of minutes, he turned to look at her, as she had not yet told him what it said. Finally, he had to ask. "Well, who died?"

"No one, Ben. It's from your father, or I assume so as it is from someone called Paw."

"Yeah, that's my father all right. An' nobody died? Another one o' the family get sent off ta prison?"

"No, nothing like that. Here, let me just read it so you know. *'Ben. Trouble brewing here at home. Need you to find your brothers and get here quick. Need help bad. Paw.'"*

"Aw, hell no. Well, I reckon it'll keep 'til mornin', 'cause I don't intend ta go roust 'em boys out now. All right, let's get some sleep, an' I'll deal with it tomorrow. Ya need ta know that once I leave, I won't likely be comin' back, an' neither will Todd 'r Zack. We'll go see James 'fore we pull out, an' let him handle the details on the claims staked out by the boys, as well as turn him loose on Dickerson an' Lonnigan an' see just how serious they are about buyin' the claims."

"Ben, that's why it took me a minute after reading the telegram. I thought it might mean you'd be leaving, something I feared all along. I hate to see my best friend in the world leave now, after striking it rich, but I will adjust and learn to handle your absence."

"Yeah, I kind o' hate ta go now as well, Chenoa. But if Paw says he needs help bad, it's got ta be serious. That man can handle near anything that comes up, an' 'tween him an' Maw an' my other brothers an' sisters… Let's just say they are as tough as boot leather an' if Paw says come quick it means it's real bad trouble," Ben explained as they climbed the stairs and walked down the hallway to their rooms.

Ben waited a moment to make certain Chenoa had entered her room before unlocking his door and stepping inside. Once in his room, he stripped down and sat on the edge of the bed, running various scenarios of potential trouble through his mind, before finally lying down and falling into a fitful asleep.

***

At Renner's the next morning, Ben's eyes were red and swollen, causing Todd to ask, "Ben, what's the matter? Figured ya'd be like me an' Zack, feelin' on top o the world this mornin'." Without answering, Ben handed the telegram to Todd, who in turn handed it to Zack after reading it.

397

"When we leavin', Ben?" Zack asked, while Todd sat silently.

"We got a lot ta handle, like ya get your claims filed, an' that comes after we meet with James this mornin'. I figure ta turn all the details over ta him, includin' seein' what kind of an offer them two mining fellers are willing to give us. Two, maybe three days tops, an' we'll head ta Flagstaff an' take the train home. I just hope Paw an' the others can hang on 'til we get there."

"We'll start takin' care o' our things right off, Ben, an' we'll be ready ta go whenever ya say. Damn the luck anyway. But, Paw didn't leave nothin' ta guess. An' if he says he needs help all we can do is hightail it home. Least nobody died 'r got sent ta prison."

"Yeah, that's pretty much what I thought. Hell, I had ta have Chenoa read it to me since I figured it was one 'r the other that had happened an' I didn't really want ta find out which. Let's just hope we can get there 'fore anybody does die, boys."

"Ben, if ya need us ta handle anything for ya, me an' Margarite'll be proud to lend a hand. Ya been a damn good friend ta us, an' it'd be the least we could do for ya."

"Naw, I think we pretty much got it all covered, an' it's all legal stuff now. Things only an attorney can handle. Well, James an' Chenoa anyway, 'cause what he can't handle she can, includin' any decisions regardin' the claims since she's a partner. But I want ya ta know how much we 'preciate the offer, as the two o' you is as close ta family we've had since we been here."

Once breakfast was finished, they sat for another half hour sipping coffee and talking about going home, and how they had been missing family anyway. Finally, Chenoa said, "If it weren't for all there is to do here, I'd even consider following you there, and helping, no matter what the trouble might be."

"An' I'll bet our sisters would be glad ta meet ya, young lady. Shoot, they might even adopt ya," Ben said with a slight smile.

"No doubt about it, big brother. I wouldn't even mind adoptin' her my own self," Todd added, as Zack agreed with a nodding of his head.

"And I would certainly welcome it. It would give me the greatest of pleasure to be known as a Creed. In fact, with your permission, I'd love to add Creed behind my name, and become Chenoa Creed."

"Well, you just go right ahead an' have James start workin' on it, an' let us know when it becomes official. We'll be in Colorado City, Texas, though I don't know how long any of us will stay there. Now, James ought ta be gettin' to his office. Let's get out o' here an' get all this business taken care of so we can get for home," Ben said, taking a last sip of coffee.

Filling James in on what they wanted done, and what they needed to do before leaving town, James informed the boys on how to handle their claim filings, to follow the same pattern as used by Ben. And he had no trouble requesting a name change for Chenoa through the local courts. His problem was in the details of dealing with the sale of the claims.

"Well, all right, James. How 'bout this, I find Dickerson an' Lonnigan myself an' see what I can negotiate, an' you handle the rest o' the sale an' transfer from there? Oh, an' I'll want ta sign off a legal transfer o' powers. Whattaya call that?"

"That will be fine, Ben, and it's called a power of attorney. Now then, just let me know the proper details and I'll take care of the paperwork, all right?"

"Good. I reckon the next stop is ta see Ray at the bank, let him know what's happenin', and see about gettin' us some travelin' money. An' I s'pose it's time ta have a long talk with Salty, that an' make some arrangements at the hotel. I reckon you boys'll be havin' a similar talk with Mose and Maybelline, an' with Mack Cooper as well. An' I s'pose I ought ta go see Marisol, Ralph an'

Nick, if nothin' else but ta let 'em know how well what we bought worked out for us."

"Ben, you should also speak to François. He'll be terribly hurt if you don't."

"François? Hurt? Well, if you say so. An' I reckon we should have our last supper here in Prescott at the Congress, kind of a celebration of sorts along with a farewell. Now then, I s'pose we better get movin'. See you boys over ta Renner's again, less'n ya plan on headin' ta the bank with us. After all, you both got plenty o' money there that's yours, an' you'll have ta decide how ya want ta handle it. As in leave it there, 'r take all of it, 'r just leave some of it there an' transfer the rest ta home."

"I reckon that pretty much settles it, Ben. We got no choice but ta go with ya. Me, I figure ta have all mine sent home, as I don't plan on comin' back this way any time soon," Zack replied.

"Same here, Ben. Oh, I s'pose I might drift through here again sometime, but I got no plans on it now."

"Then let's get ta movin'. James, I reckon we'll be back sometime this afternoon, once we get all the pieces sorted out."

"I'll be here, going over the smelter reports as well as computing the final splits on what you hauled to the Bank of Prescott. And I'll let Ray Alvarez know exactly what those splits are so he can adjust the account totals properly, and after I arrange to settle up with the smelter, as I assume they have not been paid as yet. As to the power of attorney, I'll include the handling of your bank accounts as well as paying any bills left behind after you leave in it. Ben, Todd, Zack, I really hate to see the three of you leave. And not just because you have made me a lot of money in a very short period of time, but because I consider you all to be good friends. One more person you might think about stopping to see before you leave town is Mike Hutchison, as he thinks of you as good friends as well, not to mention Seth and Sheriff Walker, and

Marshal Dodson, and the twenty men you hired to help you. You men have made a lot of very good friends here, and you will be sorely missed."

"Reckon that's right, James. We'll see how many we can get to in the time we have left in town, but we sure 'nough need ta get ta home pronto. Any that we miss, just let 'em know we ran out o' time, will ya?"

"Yes, I certainly will," James nodded as he answered.

The quartet rose almost simultaneously and stepped out of his office and into the foyer, and then through the outer door and to the buggy and the boys' mounts. Fifteen minutes later, they were inside the bank, speaking with Raymond Alvarez about the handling of their tremendous wealth.

After explaining that he was leaving town, along with his brothers, and why, as well as the fact that he would be giving James Whitaker power of attorney over all his local dealings, Ben said, "Ray, I figure ta leave half o' my share here, at least for the time bein', but I'll have ta let ya know the details o' where I want that half sent once I know for sure. But for now, I'm gonna need about five thousand for travelin' money. An' I need twenty thousand ta take care o' the men I hired ta watch out for us, since I promised 'em plenty o' work once we got ta rollin' an' if we get the claims sold I'm don't know that they'll get hired ta do the same things. Got that much on hand in gold coin?"

"Yes, of course, Ben. You still have over ten thousand in your account, not counting any of the gold you just brought in yesterday, and I'll gladly make certain you have the twenty-five thousand in coin, but you'll need to give me a day to arrange for that much coin."

"No problem, Ray. As long as I have it by noon tomorrow, that'll be fine." Several other details were discussed, and their meeting only lasted another few minutes before Ben said they needed to keep moving if they were to get home in time to help.

From the bank, the boys headed to the courthouse to file their claims and pay a visit to both Seth and the sheriff while they were in the courthouse, while Chenoa and Ben drove the buggy to Salty's. They hadn't seen Clete that morning, and Salty had another client waiting so they didn't have time to talk.

Pulling up to the front of the barn, Clete came trotting out to greet them. "Howdy, you two! Glad ta see ya made it back 'fore me an' Mary Ellen tied the knot. Next week, by golly. Yessir, by Thursday o' next week, I'll be married ta one o' the purtiest gals in all o' Yavapai County!"

"Clete, is Salty in?"

"Yeah, back in the office. Why?" the stableman asked, sensing that there might be something serious on Ben's mind.

"Come on back with us, an' I'll let ya know."

Clete helped Chenoa down, and then followed the couple back to Salty's office. "Salty, I need ta tell ya somethin', an' ask ya ta do a big favor for me."

The stableman looked back to see who it was, and then turned in his chair to face them. "Sit down an' tell me what's goin' on, Ben. I swear, I ain't ever seen ya look so serious in all the time I've known ya."

"Paw sent me a telegram tellin' me he needed me an' the boys ta home pronto. We'll be pullin' out as soon as we can get everything handled here in Prescott, an' ride ta Flagstaff an' catch a train home. I figure we'll be leavin' day after tomorrow. Now then, I'm gonna need ya ta sell 'em mules an' all the tack includin' the packsaddles, halters an' lead ropes, an' all the money ya get for 'em goes ta Chenoa here 'cept for the ten percent you keep for handlin' the sale."

"Ben, that's pretty generous, but I got an offer ta make ya first, 'fore ya turn me loose with 'em mules. I'll pay ya three thousand cash, lock, stock an' barrel for the mules an' all the tack. I can rent them mules out with tack, or ta pull wagons, or for ridin', an' get my money back in no time at all. Whattaya think, Ben?"

"Done. It's all yours. I'll have James make out a bill o' sale for ya, an' I'll sign it 'fore I leave. That work for you?"

"All day long. 'Preciate it, Ben. I truly do."

"Good, then I'll have James make the paperwork out this afternoon when we get back ta see him," Ben said shaking Salty's hand before turning to face Clete. "An' Clete, congratulations. Sorry, but me an' the boys'll be long gone by next week. But I'm sure Chenoa will gladly be there, since she was the one told ya ta ask in the first place."

"Yeah, she was. Chenoa, you'll be there, right?"

"Oh yes, Clete, with bells on! I'm so happy for you two," she said giving Clete a hug. "Ben, we'd best get moving again, as we have many stops to make yet before this day is over."

Ben nodded, took Chenoa by the elbow and guided her out of Salty's office and through the breezeway to the buggy, where they climbed aboard and turned back in the direction they came. "You seemed kind o' anxious ta get out o' there, so whattaya got in mind?"

"I was just trying to help you, because if I have learned anything about Salty and Clete, you could stay there all day talking about nothing in particular and everything in general. Shall we go see Nick, while we have time?"

"Sure, why not," Ben said as he headed toward Loshkarev's shop. From there, they made their way to Porter's Saddlery, and then on to Stockdale's Mercantile, where a thankful Marisol made it hard for them to leave. But they finally excused themselves, and left for the Congress, mostly to see François, but also for some badly needed coffee.

Ben thought for a moment that François was going to cry, until he found out that Chenoa was going to stay on at the hotel. At the front desk, Ben let Claude know that any money left over from his paying for his room in advance should be transferred to Chenoa's room charges after he checked out, even though Chenoa objected.

Silver, Gold and Blood In Arizona

405

Chapter Forty-Three

As Ben turned to leave, none other than Dickerson and Lonnigan appeared in the lobby. "Gents, there's been kind of a change in plans. What say we set down and discuss the sale o' my claims over coffee?"

Eagerly joining Ben and Chenoa in the dining room, Dickerson opened the conversation. "So, Mr. Creed, you have decided to sell out after all. Might we inquire as to why?"

"Not really, but I'll tell ya this much. It's a family crisis ta home in Texas, an' if things don't work out I'll most like turn operation o' the digs over ta Chenoa an' the attorney. So, that said, what were you thinkin' on offerin'?"

"We have considered it carefully, and feel that half a million dollars would be fair," Dickerson said, with Lonnigan nodding in agreement.

"Yeah, well I guess we're all done here," Ben said as he started to stand.

"Now hold on there. That's not how negotiations normally work, Mr. Creed."

"Yeah, well I don't hold with all that nonsense an' I got no time ta spend a week dickerin' back an' forth, so here's what comes next. You deal with Chenoa, 'r you're likely ta raise my hackles an' get yourselves shot." Turning to Chenoa, he said, "I'm goin' upstairs for a bit, sort out some o' my things an' start packin'."

"No wait a minute, does she have the power to complete any deal made?"

"Not really, but I got things ta do an' she'll put up with your nonsense where as I won't. The attorney is gonna have power of attorney, an' if we don't have a deal 'fore I leave ya can deal with him based on Chenoa's recommendations. Chenoa, I'll be back down in half an hour 'r so, an' ya can let me know if there's gonna be a deal 'r not," Ben said leaving the table and walking back out into the lobby.

"Gentlemen, I believe you have insulted my partner and friend with a ridiculously low offer. Why, we took out nearly twice that much in less than a month, and only opened the vein a few feet. All the dust, flake and nugget material was picked up off the ground or panned in less than three hundred feet of the draw where the vein is located. Not to mention that a heavy rain washed more of the nuggets, flakes and dust into plain sight, easily picked up off the ground. Now, how about a serious offer, or do I walk away also?"

The two men looked at each other, but said nothing. After a few minutes, Lonnigan spoke, for the first time Chenoa could remember after meeting the two men. In a heavy Irish brogue, he said, "Ms. Chenoa, me partner here seems ta think the best way ta do a deal is ta try ta steal it, an' when that doesn't work he tries ta talk hisself inta a deal that's still less than outright theft. But I can see neither you nor Mr. Creed are the type o' people we normally deal with. So, instead o' me wastin' my breath, why don' ya just tell me how much ya want?"

"For all the claims, or just the two owned by my partner?"

"An' what do ya mean by 'all the claims', ma'am?"

"Ben Creed owns the primary claims, one of gold, which has been worked only slightly, and one of silver, which has yet to be worked. His brothers each have claims positioned in what appears to be in the general directions of each claim based on the veins. Ben and his brothers want to sell all six claims, not just the two."

"I see. Well, that certainly adds ta the value, but not too much as none o' the claims but the one have actually produced a lick."

"Still, the way they are positioned keeps another operation from squeezing you off or taking over the vein somewhere along its path. Not to mention that they also give you more access to the main claims for ingress and egress."

"My, but aren't ya just a smart little lass. Now I see why Mr. Creed has left ya ta deal with us. All right then, we'll offer two million dollars for all the claims ta include all rights now an' in the future. Do ya think that will interest Mr. Creed then?"

"Yes, and I believe he would say that we are certainly getting closer, but still aren't there."

"An' just what is it goin' ta take ta get there, miss?"

"Two million for the two main claims, half a million for the additional four claims, and a guarantee that the twenty men Mr. Creed has lined up to work as both lumberjacks to cut the timbers used to create the mines and miners to work the tunnels will be not only hired, but kept on as long as either mine is in operation. Oh, and shutting it down for six months and then reopening to avoid keeping them on will not be allowed. In the event the mines are closed for any reason, these twenty men must be the first hired back, and for as long as they wish to work there. And there is one more thing. The land around the mines, as well as any roads brought in to remove any ore, must protect the land as much as possible so as to keep the integrity of the area, its trees, with the exception of those removed, and the Apache and Yavapai, as well as all animals who live there."

"An' so what you're sayin' is that ya want ta control who we hire ta work for us, preserve the landscape as much as we can, an' not do anything ta disrupt the animals an' people who live there any more than necessary, correct?" Lonnigan asked.

"I suppose you could put it that way, but I promise the men are good men and very hard workers as well as being as honest as any man can be, and that if you don't take care of the land and the animals there the Apache and Yavapai who live in the Bradshaw

Mountains will cause you so much grief you will never recover," Chenoa said.

"That may very well be, but we still prefer to hire our own people, and use our proven leaders and performers to open any mines, and we secure our timbers from a firm in Tuscon, not cut and provided locally," Dickerson injected.

"Then I believe we are done here. If you'll excuse me," Chenoa said as she started to stand.

"Ms. Chenoa, forgive my pushy friend here. He isn't suited well for this type o' negotiation, ya see. He's a bit too pushy, doncha know. Now then, is there any chance I could meet these men? Well, that, an' talk to them before we finalize this deal?"

"I'm not completely positive of it, but I think I might be able to arrange it for tomorrow afternoon, provided you will be available and your partner won't, that is. I dare say I believe he would not do well speaking to them," Chenoa said looking directly at Dickerson. "In fact, I can guarantee it. Lord knows, they would take offence the moment he opened his mouth and shoot him or hang him from the nearest tree, not to mention what Mr. Creed and his brothers, even I, might do. He would most assuredly make a fine target, and I'm sure you've learned enough about us to know of our profiency with firearms."

"Oh, believe me, I know of what ya speak. I've been tempted ta shoot him more than once meself. Yes, I'll be available tomorrow right after lunch, an' I'll make sure I'm alone. Shall we meet here at the Congress? How will that be?"

"I think we'd be better off meeting at Renner's Café, as this is a bit, shall we say, high-toned for our friends. But if we are going to meet there, I think two o'clock would be better, as the café is still quite busy at one."

"An' where is this Renner's? Oh, never mind. If we intend ta do this deal, I need ta be smart enough ta find it on me own. Now, as far as the numbers, I don't see that as any problem, really, except for the claims with no proven results, that is."

"And what do you propose then?"

"Let's say a hundred thousand total for the additional, unproven claims," Lonnigan stated.

"And two million for the two claims owned by Ben, even though only the gold claim has been truly proven?"

"Yes, that's what I wanted ta offer Mr. Creed ta begin with, but Dickerson there thought we could get them for much less, seein' as how ya all ready pulled such a large amount out o' the gold claim. That is with the exception o' the men ta be hired an' all the land care an' protection o' the animals. An' I'll be honest about the other claims. We visited the courthouse just before we came ta the hotel, an' knew o' them all ready. Sorry if I was being deceptive, I truly am, ma'am."

"I sensed that, but accepted that as a part of your ploy to get the claims at a reduced price. Ah, here comes Ben now. I'll inform him of our agreement, and make certain it is acceptable."

"Chenoa, are ya ready ta get out o' here? We need ta get ta our next meetin'."

"Yes, Ben. And we have reached a tentative agreement. At least Mr. Lonnigan and I have, and I'm quite certain Mr. Dickerson will gladly go along, although he won't be involved in any further negotiations. But I'll fill you in on the way," Chenoa said, following Ben's lead, though she knew of no other meeting scheduled just yet.

After telling Ben about the negotiations, and Lonnigan's willingness to meet the men, Ben sat quietly in the buggy in front of Renner's for several minutes before speaking. Finally, he said, "We'll need ta run this past the boys, make sure they don't have any problems with it. An' that was a good call, makin' it all hinge on hirin' the men an' keepin' my promise ta Long Lance. But I reckon we'll most likely take the deal even if they don't hire all of 'em. That's part o' why I plan on givin' 'em each a thousand dollars. That'll last 'em quite a while, an' likely be as much as they'd make in a full season workin' timber 'r minin'. After we get some lunch, we need ta pay a visit ta James an' let him know what we're lookin' at, an' I need ta get word ta Muley ta have all o' the men here tomorrow at two. We prob'ly need ta let Jason an' Margarite know that we'll be havin' a meetin' here as well. Then there's lettin' the boys know so they don't make other plans, but I reckon they'll be here 'fore long so we can let 'em know about the offer an' possible deal then. After we meet with James, we ought ta pay a visit ta Mike, an' Jim Dodson, an' Jeff Walker. Let's go get some coffee, shall we?"

Ben and Chenoa had no more than taken a seat and had their cups filled when the brothers came walking in and joined them at the table. "Well, I think we got most o' the things we needed ta handle done with. You makin' any headway?"

"Yes, Chenoa has worked out a possible deal for us, but she needs ta know if it'll work 'fore we set James ta work on it. Girl, go on an' tell 'em what ya did."

Over the next twenty minutes, Chenoa informed the boys of the details of the deal and answered their questions about the reasoning behind it all. Finally, after sitting silently for another ten minutes after the last question had been asked, Todd said, "Well, that suits me. Zack, how 'bout you?"

"Hah! I was waitin' on ya ta say somethin' first. I'm good with it, 'specially takin' care o' the land an' all the critters, as well as the Apache an' Yavapai. An' that bunch o' men. If it wasn't for them, we might not o' made it ta Ben's claims, let alone staked out our own 'r pulled all that gold out. Shoot, we might not o' made it out o' town alive without 'em. An' Ben, that's right generous o' ya ta take care o' 'em all with a grand each. Todd an' me talked about it, an' we'd sooner ya take it out o' the total, not just your share. So we need ta let James know that 'fore the agreed to split takes place, an' let him lay it out for the banker instead o' us doin' all that."

"I agree, Ben, and would like to have it come in an equal split from my share as well,' Chenoa added.

"Well then, I reckon we'd best get movin' an' get over ta James' office pronto, 'fore he closes up for the day. Tell ya what, an' no arguin' about it. Let's have supper at the Congress tonight, go over all the details an' see what else there is ta be done, as I'm sure James will give us some work ta do 'fore we can pull out. An' try all ya want ta share, but I'm buyin', hear me?"

They all laughed, and then went on their way to James' office after letting Jason and Margarite know about the meeting scheduled for two in the afternoon the next day. "Ben, we'll make sure ta run the rest o' the customers out by five 'til, an' give ya the run o' the place for your meetin'. That way there won't be no false tales an' details o' your business goin' 'round town. Agreed, Mother?" Jason Renner asked his co-owner and wife.

"Agreed, Papa. An' good thinkin'."

James was thrilled at the idea of making certain the land, animals and Indians were all taken care of, as well as the men, but he didn't offer to be included in the payments to them. No one questioned it, as James' share of the gold was the least of the amounts involved. They were all glued to their seats as he went through the final numbers with them after figuring out how much the added offer from the Tuscon miners came out as in the previously agreed to splits.

"All right, let's start with the add on claims at a hundred thousand. Since two are Todd's, and two are Zack's, that works out to twenty-five thousand each claim, and fifty thousand to each man before the splits. The splits are, then, twenty-five thousand five hundred dollars to each Todd and Zack, forty-three thousand to Ben, five thousand to Chenoa, and I get a thousand. Now for Ben's gold and silver claims at two million, Ben will receive a million twenty thousand, each Todd and Zack will receive four hundred thirty thousand, Chenoa gets a hundred thousand, and I get twenty thousand.

"The total on deposit at the bank is two million seventy-five thousand two hundred sixty-eight dollars, of which thirty thousand one hundred twenty-five dollars goes to the smelter. Deducting that leaves the dividable total at two million forty-five thousand one hundred forty three dollars, and after taking the twenty thousand out for the men the new total comes out to two million twenty-five thousand one hundred forty-three dollars. Ben's share is one million thirty thousand eight hundred twenty-three dollars, Todd and Zack each get four hundred thirty-five thousand four hundred five dollars, while Chenoa gets one hundred one thousand two hundred fifty seven dollars, and I get twenty thousand two hundred fifty dollars.

"So, let's total those so everyone knows the total amount they will receive overall, shall we? Ben, your full total comes out to one million seventy-three thousand eight hundred twenty-three dollars. Zack and Todd will each receive eight hundred ninety thousand nine hundred five dollars, Chenoa's total will be two hundred six thousand two hundred fifty-seven dollars, and I will receive for my services a total of forty-one thousand two hundred fifty dollars. Are these totals acceptable?"

"James, they sound fine ta me. Right Todd, Zack, Chenoa?"

The three others all nodded, all thinking they would never have seen that much money that belonged to them if it hadn't been for the generosity of Ben Creed, even though each of them worked hard for their share. But only Chenoa could find the words to express what they were all feeling. "Ben, thank you for this life changing gift. I don't really feel I deserve it, though, since it means absolutely nothing compared to what I owe you for saving my life in the first place. I will always owe you more than I can ever repay, and yet here you are sharing your wealth with me, and the rest of us." Standing, she leaned over to kiss him on the cheek and hug him before leaving the room dabbing at her eyes.

"Ben, though Chenoa's eloquence is unmatchable, I will offer my humble attempt at thanking you for hiring me as your attorney, and for aiding me in growing my business as a result. Not to mention the money I am receiving from just being your attorney and representing you in all your legal dealings. I owe you so much that if you ever need an attorney for any reason, anywhere, or anytime, all you need do is reach out to me and I'll be there just as quickly as I can. And Ben, there will never be another charge for my services."

"Ben, as your brother, an' that bein' the only reason either one o' us is settin' here as rich men, there is never gonna be anything we can do ta repay ya. As for me, an' I reckon Zack will go along with it, whatever, whenever an' wherever ya want us, we'll be there, an' we'll also do all we can ta help out the family, no matter what they need. Right, Zack?"

"Spot on, Todd. Ben, if nobody ever says it, now is sure the time for me ta say it, and do so for the rest of the family. You are a credit ta the name Creed, an' make me proud ta share the name with ya."

Silver, Gold and Blood In Arizona

Chapter Forty-Four

Leaving James Whitaker's office that afternoon, Ben remained stoic, too stunned at the accolades given him by his partners to respond, but determined to live up to what the others felt and said about him. Helping Chenoa into the buggy and then climbing in after her, he headed the buggy toward town with the full intent of stopping at the bank with the power of attorney handed him by James as they left his office, as well as to visit Mike in his office, Jim Dodson in his office, and the sheriff at the courthouse. What he didn't expect was to have James ride up behind them at the bank.

"Ben, I didn't want to waste a moment in getting this information to Mr. Alvarez, as he will need it once the money comes in from Lonnigan and Dickerson, and long before you reach home in Colorado City. I hope you don't think I'm rushing things."

"Not at all, James. In fact, I'm glad ta see ya takin' care o' business so promptly. I 'preciate it more'n ya know. That an' ya bein' here, we can take care o' bringin' Ray up ta date on what's happenin', since he's gonna be the one ta handle gettin' the money sent ta the bank in Colorado City when I let 'em know it's comin', as well as make sure the smelter gets paid, an' that the payment is made proper by Dickerson an' Lonnigan. We don't even know how they intend ta make payment yet, let alone make sure the payment is good."

"Indeed. I'm sure it will require their attorney and myself meet at some point, unless they happen to be carrying a bank draft with them. Now that would be fortuitous, to say the least. Well, shall we see about Mr. Alvarez?"

Inside the bank, things went smoothly and quickly, as Ray Alvarez was not only expecting them, but also had prepared all the documents he anticipated they might need, as well as having the twenty-five thousand ready for Ben. As they finished and shook hands all around, Ben commented, "Well, that puts us one step closer ta home, an' helpin' Paw with his trouble. 'Preciate it, Ray, James. Oh, an' James, I want ta make sure you'll be there at the meetin' tomorrow at two, right?"

"Yes, of course, Ben. And I'll be prepared to meet with Lonnigan and Dickerson after as well. In fact, I plan on having all the necessary documents there and ready for signature, with the conditions of payment all laid out to ensure they cannot start any operation on the claims until all payment has been received."

"Ben, you have got yourself one fine attorney here. And if you don't mind, I'd like to be there as well. Who knows, some of those men might want to open accounts with us, not to mention that these buyers will need a local bank to deal with going forward."

"Glad ta have ya there, Ray. The more the merrier. Well, if we're all done here, me an' Chenoa got a few more stops ta make 'fore folks start lockin' their doors," Ben said as they wrapped things up.

Following that statement, James, Ben and Chenoa left the bank, James headed to his office to work on more of the Creed's paperwork, and Ben and Chenoa across the street to the courthouse. Chenoa stayed outside, informing Ruth Bishop of the current changes, while Ben said thanks and goodbye to Jeff Walker, who all ready knew he was leaving having spoken to the brothers. Well wishes went with Ben, from both the sheriff and Mrs. Bishop, as he left and slowly walked down the steps of the courthouse and climbed back into the buggy.

The next stop was Mike Hutchison's office, where Mike voiced his appreciation for Ben and his brothers, as well as the connection with James Whitaker, establishing the honesty and trustworthiness of his assay office, which had all ready begun to pay off with additional customers. And when Ben tried to brush it off as nothing, Hutchison insisted that if Ben ever needed anything else assayed, no matter when or where, he would personally see to it that the assay office it was taken to did the right thing and treated Ben's assays with the utmost respect. Once again, Ben was speechless as they headed back downtown to find Jim Dodson.

"Jim, I s'pose ya all ready heard, me an' the boys will be leavin' town, most likely day after tomorrow. Damn sure gonna miss ya, as ya been a good friend, an' I consider ya ta be one o' the best law dog's in the entire territory. You, an' Jeff Walker as well, are as honest as the day is long, an' there ain't any way in the world either one o' ya could be bought."

"Ben, I really hate to see you all go, even though it will definitely reduce the amount of paperwork in my office by double," Dodson said with a smile and an extended hand. "But at least Chenoa will still be around to sort out the bad hombres and help Jeff and I keep them under control."

"Well, Jim, keep this ta yourself, but I think Jeff is all but done. I don't believe he'll be runnin' again."

"Now that's a shame, Ben. It truly is, as Jeff is a man I've tried to emulate, both in action and thought. He's made me a better lawman as a result. I only hope the city and its residents decide to keep me in place for a long time to come, and that I can withstand any attempts to remove me by using violence. It might help if you were to leave me your draw as a departing gift…"

"Not likely, though I sincerely hope I don't need ta use it any more than necessary ta stay alive. Still, we're headin' back ta Colorado City to help Paw, an' Lord only knows what kind o' trouble is stirrin' there that would cause Paw ta send for all three of us. Well, I'd best get out o' here, as I know ya still got things ta do an' I'm keepin' ya from 'em," Ben finished, shaking hands with still another respected lawman, thinking to himself that if ever he needed to wear a badge, these two men were ones to copy in enforcement and attitude both.

Outside, climbing into the buggy again, he said to Chenoa, "Damned if I don't hate ta leave, an' for more reasons than just the claims. If I don't get the chance ta tell ya, I'm gonna miss you. You've taught me a lot, about people of all colors an' upbringin', animals an' business dealin's. Things I all ready thought I knew, an' would never have changed my mind about 'til ya showed me better. Now, don't say nothin', just accept that you've been a great friend, an' a fine teacher. Now, it's near time ta meet the boys at the Congress, an' we need ta get cleaned up 'fore supper. An' damned if I know when 'r where we're gonna find Muley an' still give him time ta pass the word ta have all the men meet us at Renner's tomorrow afternoon."

"I think we can handle that on the way to the hotel, Ben. It's about this time of day that Muley and some of the others get together at Renner's for coffee, according to what Margarite told me earlier. I also told her that we would need to see them there tomorrow at two, just in case we missed them this afternoon," Chenoa said as they headed toward the hotel.

"An' when did ya manage ta tell her without me knowin' it?"

"While Jason was talking, just before he asked her about having the meeting there and making sure we had the café to ourselves."

"Well, I reckon Muley will be waitin' at the Congress for us when we get there, 'r if he ain't he'll be along 'fore we finish eatin' supper. No need ta turn an' head for Renner's then, is there?"

"No, I suppose not, Ben. Let's see if he is waiting on us, and if not we'll just get ready to eat and see him then."

As suspected, Muley was sitting on one of the two benches Salty kept in front of the barn, waiting for them to show up with the buggy. Seeing Muley, Bear Claw and Jed sitting there, instead of stopping in front of the hotel and turning the buggy over to either Salty or Clete, Ben pulled up in front of the barn.

"Fellers, good ta see ya again. Glad you're here, as I need ta talk to ya, an' I got a favor ta ask of ya as well."

"What is it, Ben?" Muley asked. "We heared ya was a leavin' town real short like, an' takin' your brothers wit' ya."

"Yeah, got a wire from home. Paw asked us all ta get home ta help with some trouble there, an' it didn't leave much room not ta get there as soon as we could. But that's only a part of it. Since we got ta go an' got no idea how long we'll be there, 'r if we'll ever be back this way, we decided ta sell out. Chenoa has negotiated a pretty fair deal for us, but there's some details we want ta meet with ya on an' get your approval 'fore we finalize the deal."

"Margarite said somethin' 'bout a meetin' we needed ta be at tomorrow at two at their place. That when ya wanna talk ta us? All twenty men?" Bear Claw asked.

"That's it, Bear Claw. We'll have James Whitaker there along with the banker Alvarez, an' one o' the partners o' the company buyin' the claims, Lonnigan, as well as Chenoa an' my brothers. That way you'll all know all the details an' can ask any questions that come ta mind."

"Fair 'nough, Ben. We'll see to it 'et ever'body is 'ere whut needs ta be. Sho' hate ta see you fellers leave. Ya been right fair wit' us, fo' sho', an' al'ays treated us as good as a body can be expected ta," Jed said, standing up to shake Ben's hand. "But whut 'bout Ms. Chenoa heah? Ya takin' her 'long as well?"

"No, Jed, I'll be staying here in Prescott, although I may need someone to go out into the timber with me for a day or two now and then, and I can't think of anyone better to accompany me than any of you twenty men," Chenoa answered for herself. "You have all gained the respect of the Apache and Yavapai who still live in the Bradshaw Mountains, and will each be accepted among them as I travel out to visit them."

"Mighty good ta know 'et, ma'am. An' ah reckons 'ere ain' a man 'mong us whut wouldn' be right proud ta ride wit' ya no matter whar it happens ta be. Ain' 'et right, Muley?"

"Yessir, ol' Jed sho' got it right. Why, ah reckon ah'd ride into the fires o' hell wit' ya if'n ya ask," Bear Claw said before Muley could respond.

"I s'pose that's right, Ms. Chenoa. Ain' a man what rode wit' ya tothah day whut wouldn' ride through hell wit' ya if'n ya jus' ask, startin' wit' me, ma'am," Muley said, hat in hand and head bent.

"Oh, my," Chenoa said as she hugged each man. Then turning to Ben, she said, again dabbing at her eyes, "Ben, we'd better get across the street and get cleaned up before they send out a search party for us." Then, turning back to the men, her eyes dry, she said, "You men have no idea how much that means to me, to know you all respect me so much. You will always have a special place in my heart, and I'll look upon each of you as a close friend." She quickly turned away, taking Ben's arm as he escorted her across the street and into the hotel, leaving these men of the mountain standing there in awe of her spirit and humility.

Ben and Chenoa quickly washed up and changed clothes, and then hustled downstairs and into the dining room to wait for Zack and Todd. It was only five minutes before the pair walked into the dining room and joined Ben and Chenoa at their table. They all sat without speaking very often, except to order their meals and ask for more coffee, until the meal was finished, and even then none of them had much to say.

Finally, Chenoa spoke more words in a few sentences that they had said combined. "Gentlemen, I'm sure you've figured out by now just how much each of you will be missed after you've gone. And not just by me. Everyone you know, and a good many you have never met here in Prescott, even across Yavapai County, will miss you desperately. Surely no one more than me, though, as I have come to look upon you as the brothers I have never had. That is precisely why I will be so proud to carry the Creed name as soon as James can fix it for me, to honor you and your family's name."

"Chenoa, I think I speak for my brothers, an' for the whole family if they could meet ya, when I say you are the one ta be honored for addin' a quality ta our family name that none o' us are likely to have ever reached. An' I'm damned proud ta call ya sister," Todd said, to which Ben and Zack quickly agreed.

They decided to have a drink in celebration of adding a new sister to the family, and for Chenoa to finally have some brothers, so a bottle of good wine was ordered. Taking their time drinking the bottle, slowly sipping the wine over the next hour, they finally finished the bottle and agreed it was time to call it an evening.

Chapter Forty-Five

After early morning coffee and pastries, Ben and Chenoa agreed to spend the morning resting, but Ben's real reason was to spend time packing and getting ready to head for home, including slipping out of the hotel to buy some luggage in which to pack his clothing. Settling for a trunk, he had it carried up to his room and began filling it. Opting to carry his weapons and some of the ammo with him, he finally decided that he had stuffed everything he wanted to into the trunk and slipped back downstairs.

"Claude, I need a favor. I got that trunk filled ta the brink, an' I need ta get it shipped ta home. Can ya take care o' gettin' it out o' my room an' sent while we're out this afternoon?"

"Yes, yes, of course. Do you have an preferred method for shipping?"

"Prob'ly Wells Fargo is the safest an' fastest, so let's go with them. Here's sixty dollars ta handle the cost, an' if that ain't enough let me know. Just take care of it, will ya?" Ben said as he plopped down three double eagles, turned and walked away, and then climbed the stairs and walked down the hallway to his room to finish getting ready for their lunch and two o'clock meeting.

Ben was still sitting on the edge of his bed, wondering what trouble he and his brothers were heading into that was so bad that their father and family in Colorado City couldn't handle it without them, when a light tap came on the door. "Ben, are you ready? We should be going," came Chenoa's soft but strong voice through the door.

"Yes, ma'am, I am," Ben responded as he stood up, grabbed his hat, fastened his gun belt and stepped to the door. A few minutes later, he and Chenoa were standing together in front of Salty's waiting on Clete to bring the buggy up for the last time for the two of them.

Fifteen minutes later, they climbed out of the buggy in the lot next to Renner's Café and walked to the door. Inside, they faced another packed room, but trusted that there would be a table near the back. The table usually used by Jason and Margarite, where the Creed's and Chenoa were always welcome. A few minutes later, Todd and Zack, who were apparently hungrier than normal considering how much they ordered to eat, joined them at the table.

Lunch took a considerable amount of time, as the café stayed busy until one thirty when Margarite started saying the kitchen was closed until five, and refused to take any more orders. By ten minutes until two, the place had all but emptied out, the exception being those who had arrived early for the meeting. And by two everyone else had shown up, including Lonnigan, Alvarez and Whitaker.

When Ben told Jason that everyone was there, Jason locked the door and hung the closed sign in the front window. Tapping his spoon on his cup to get everyone's attention, Ben waited until it was quiet before starting to speak. "Men, I 'preciate ya all bein' here. Muley, you an' Jed an' Bear Claw tell 'em why we're meetin' here today?"

After Muley responded that they had, Ben continued. "Good. Sorry this happened, but I don' reckon there's a man among ya that wouldn't head for home if your paw called, so I know ya understand. Now, here's what I need from ya. Mr. Lonnigan there in that fancy suit is here representin' the buyers, an' the deal hinges on ya all gettin' hired to work the timber an' the mines by Lonnigan and his partner. He wants ta speak with ya on account o' that, an' see if they can make that work. An' ya can thank Chenoa for addin' that condition ta the deal. Now then, Mr. Lonnigan, the floor is yours."

"Good afternoon, everyone. An' thank ya Mr. Creed for the

introduction. An' let me thank the Renner's for lettin' us use their café for this meetin'. I hate it that they might be missin' out on some food sales, so here's what I'll do for 'em. If Mrs. Renner will be so good as ta take the orders o' anyone who wants ta eat 'r have somethin' ta drink, I'll pick up the tab. Now I have ta warn ya, if ya take a job with me, I won't be buyin' your meals anytime soon."

That brought a quick laugh to the room before Lonnigan continued. "All right then, me name is Pádraig Lonnigan, but me friends call me Paddy, an' I'd just as soon all o' ya did the same as I'd like ta think I'm among friends here today. Me partner, Ted Dickerson, is not as friendly a man as me, an' is the bankin' end o' our partnership while I'm the miner. An' I've done me share o' cuttin' timber as well. So let me explain a few things ta ya, startin' off with the fact that we rarely use local timber as we have a supplier in Tuscon. However, after lookin' at the maps o' the area, an' considerin' the distance, we'll be changin' that fact here if the deal works out. An' any man that cuts timber for us will be given the opportunity to move inta the mines if he so chooses. Any questions so far?"

"Yeah, Paddy, what are ya payin' for workin' in the timber 'r in the mines later?"

"Aye, an' now there's a fine question, an' one of great importance ta any workin' man. An' along with it should be the question o' how many hours an' days do we expect ya ta work, right?"

Looking around the café to see how his question was received, Paddy took a moment before answering. "We like ta give our men one day a week off, Sunday, an' we only like ya ta work a twelve hour day, not the sixteen hours most employers demand. An' for that, an' again we don't normally hire men ta work in the timber 'r lumber industry, we're prepared ta pay twenty dollars a week for miners, though we'll also pay that for those working timber for us. Further, we'll pay our foremen twenty-five dollars a week, so those of ya that can be a leader an' have your crews meet our production requirements, an' most of ya all ready know who ya are, you'll also earn bonuses above that, as will your crews. Next question?"

"What about this heah Dickerson, he gonna go 'long wit' this? I knowed a Dickerson back in the coal mines in Pennsyvany, an' if'n this heah is the same feller 'r related ta 'et'n, ya sho' gonna have yo'self some troubles heah."

"Mr. Dickerson's family is from Pennsylvania, to be sure, but most o' me family is as well. An' me family has also worked in the coal an' iron mines in Ireland, England an' all across Europe as well as here in America. I have also worked the mines in this country, especially those coalmines in Pennsylvania managed, operated an' owned by the Dickerson's. An' I promise ya this, none of the bad things that went on there are goin' ta happen under me watch, or in a single one o' me mines. I'll not have it. An' ya can ask any man workin' in any mine I own 'r operate if that isn't so," Lonnigan stated firmly.

"Ya any kin ta a feller whut called hisse'f Conor Lonnigan?"

"Yes, that would be me uncle, an' me father was Liam. I lost them both in the Fairmont Field in Monongalia County, West Virginia, back in '68 along with three cousins, an' two uncles on me dear sainted mother's side," Lonnigan said crossing himself.

"An' whut was the othah uncles names?"

"Micheál an' Cormac Sweeney. Why, did ya know them?"

"Hell, ah knowed 'em all, worked the same mines wit' 'em 'til '67 when ah pulled out wit my wife an' baby an' settled here in Arizona Territory. 'Ey was ever' one good men, an' it'd be a damned shame if'n ya was ta not be like 'em. Why, ah reckon ah'd

427

haf ta take ya ta task for it, Paddy. Fellers, ah reckon if'n Paddy says it's true, it is, an' his word is good 'nough for me," Jed Smith said.

"Aye, an' ya have me word that I'll make sure ever one o' ya is well taken care of if ya come ta work for me."

At that point, the men were all satisfied, based on Jed's say so, and began ordering food, lots of food, and plenty of coffee. Lonnigan joined them in eating and drinking coffee as well, until finally he joined the Creed's and Chenoa at their table. "I hope ya don't mind me joinin' ya, but I saw Mr. an' Mrs. Renner settin' here as well an' wanted ta meet 'em. How do ya do, I'm Pádraig Lonnigan, an' I believe we'll be seein' a lot o' each other in the future. But call me Paddy, please."

"Paddy, I'm Jason Renner, an' this here is my wife Margarite. Pleased ta know ya."

"An' I ta know you as well, Mr. Renner, an' you, too, Mrs. Renner," Lonnigan said kissing Margarite's hand.

"None o' that now. If we're ta call you Paddy, then call me Jason an' my wife Margarite. I trust you were tellin' 'em men the truth, Paddy, 'cause if ya weren't then the Bradshaw's will be the death o' ya. An' any one o' 'em men can see to it. They're as hard an' tough as any men I ever had the pleasure ta know, but they'll give ya the shirt off their back if ya do 'em right."

"Aye, an' that is my intention, ta do them as good as I possibly can, an' ta get all I can in the way o' work from them as I can get. An' I'll pay them every penny they're worth, because the more they make me the more I'll see to it they get paid. An' speakin' o' gettin' paid, I believe I owe ya some money," Paddy said as he carefully counted out seven double eagles on the tabletop. "That should take care o' the bill, an' the rest is yours, Margarite. Oh, an' I'll be in tomorrow for breakfast, providin' you're open by seven."

428

"Hah! We're open by six ever' day but Sunday, the only day we're closed. Now then, if you'll excuse us, I believe me an' the Creed brothers, an' o' course the lovely Chenoa, have some business ta handle."

"Not quite yet, Paddy. I need ta meet with each man at the door as they leave," Ben said, standing up to walk to the door and get the men's attention before they started leaving. Standing at the door, Benn called out to the men. "Men, we need ta start clearin' the café so the Renner's can get it cleaned up an' ready to reopen for their supper customers, but I want ta see each o' ya right here at the door on your way out."

As the men finished their food and drinks, one by one and a few in pairs and groups of three and four, they stepped up to Ben, who handed each of them a thousand dollars, saying, "This is just in case things don't work out with Monument Mining Company, an' in appreciation for all ya done for me, Chenoa an' my brothers."

Repeating the same thing to each man, they all thanked him profusely, pledging to do their best to honor the Creed brothers as well as to honor and protect Chenoa as long as she or they livid in the Prescott area.

Once the men had left and Ben rejoined the table, Paddy opened the conversation with, "So, Ben Creed, have we met your expectations? And those of yours, Chenoa? An' let me tell ya somethin' ya most likely all ready know, Mr. Creed. Chenoa is as tough ta deal with as any businessman I have ever met, an' far tougher than most."

"Didn't take ya long ta learn that, I take it, Paddy. An' ya can call me Ben, that's my brother Zack, an' the other one is Todd. Over there is James Whitaker, who I believe ya all ready met, an' Raymond Alvarez, president of the Bank o' Prescott."

"Good ta meet ya all, gentlemen. It took longer than it should have ta figure out I was dealin' with a hard woman, an' I always considered meself a fast learner, I did. Until I met this one, that is, an' I near took too long ta learn it an' almost lost the whole deal on account o' bein' so slow. Now then, have we got ourselves a deal?"

Looking across the table to Todd and Zack for their approval, Ben turned back to Paddy with a smile. "Yessir, I believe we do, but we do have a couple o' questions we'll need ta have answers to first. I know James here would likely ask ya if I didn't so, how do ya intend ta make payment an' when?"

"I'm carryin' several bank drafts on the First Bank of Tuscon right here in me pocket. Among them I've got two for a million each, an' another pair for a hundred thousand each. That should meet the agreed upon price, an' I can pick up Dickerson an' we can sign the paperwork yet today if that would suit ya. Oh, an' I'll make certain Dickerson keeps his trap shut, 'cause frankly he tends ta get on me nerves a bit as well," Paddy said with a big smile.

"James, shall we move this ta your office an' get it all behind us? Ray, mind comin' along, an' you can take possession o' the bank drafts when we're done," Ben said more as a directive than a question, but Alvarez nodded that he would do so. Two hours later, Lonnigan and Dickerson and the Monument Mining Corporation owned the Creed claims on Tuscambia Mountain, freeing Ben, Todd and Zack Creed to leave for Texas and meet whatever trouble their father was facing.

Epilogue

Goodbyes were said over supper at the Congress Hotel that night, as Ben insisted that the Renner's join them for an evening out, along with James Whitaker, Mike Hutchison and Ray Alvarez and his wife and two children. Mitzi had a great deal of trouble keeping her wits about her as she served them as Miguel Alvarez kept teasing her, much to his mother's displeasure and his father's enjoyment.

Chenoa was at times happy and at others very sad, not really wanting any of the Creed brothers to leave, but understanding that they must, while being thrilled that they kept referring to her as their sister. What happened that no one saw coming, least of all Chenoa, was that she and James grew closer and closer as the evening wore on. Much to the disappointment of her other suitors, as well as those who wished they were, like Sergei, that closeness grew into something much deeper, ending with them being married the following June. None of the Creed brothers were able to attend, but they all made sure she knew they were thinking of her by sending plenty of flowers and several wonderful, and expensive, gifts.

Ray, James and Mike also grew closer as friends and businessmen, and their association continued to grow for many years to come. Some of it was fostered by Mike, James and Chenoa becoming major investors as well as board members, and the trio eventually purchased the bank by buying out the rest of the owners.

After the others had all drifted off, Ben, Chenoa, Todd and Zack were left alone to chat about how the deal had gone as well as the amount of money they now had, and what they would use it for. Only Ben was without plans for his money, as the others, like most people, had all ready found dreams to fulfill long before they actually had any money to begin with.

Then the time came to say goodnight, and in the case of Chenoa, goodbye. Chenoa wept, gained control of her tears, and then wept again, while the men pretended that they weren't crying while dabbing their eyes. Todd and Zack each held the French and Paiute woman in tight hugs for several minutes before letting go and using made up excuses to leave the hotel. Chenoa stood at the table watching as each left the dining room, staring after them for several minutes.

Finally, Ben said that he had to get a few hours of sleep and that he needed to get to bed. Chenoa hugged him tightly, and then picked up her handbag and took his arm to be led upstairs. At the door to her room, she cried even more, holding on tightly to Ben with her arms wrapped around his waist refusing to let go. And then suddenly she turned loose and hurriedly entered her room with only a quick goodbye.

Ben was exhausted, as well as relieved the deal was done and they could be on their way to Texas with only a few strings still tying them to Prescott, and Arizona Territory. Yet sleep came slowly, mostly because of Chenoa and how close they had all become over the last few weeks.

Still, morning came early as his eyes popped open well before dawn. He dressed, packed the last of his few possessions, picked up his sougan and left in his room at the Congress Hotel and drifted down the stairs to the lobby. Without stopping or looking back, he made his way across the street to Salty's to find his horse still in the stall and ready to saddle. He said his goodbyes to Salty and Clete, and then headed to the stall holding Captain.

Slipping on the headstall and then leading Captain out into the breezeway, something seemed different, out of order, but he couldn't figure out what as he tossed the saddle blanket and then the saddle. He tied on his sougan and tossed his saddlebags onto the horse and then put the headstall and lead rope on the blue roan and led it out, dallying the lead rope to the saddlehorn. Looking around the barn one last time, he stepped into the stirrups, and then walked Captain outside to find his brothers waiting, along with Chenoa.

"I'm sorry, Ben, but I decided in the middle of the night that I was going to ride as far as the top of the hill with you, and then watch you ride out of sight from there. Oh, and Maybelline and I managed to sneak around and make a sackful of these for your trip," Chenoa said as she lifted a large flour sack filled to the brim with corndodgers. Sitting the sack on her lap, she reached inside and pulled one out and started munching on it as they rode.

Ben and his brothers also grabbed one, and then another, and still another as they rode out of town and up the hill to the east of Prescott. At the top of the hill, Chenoa begrudgingly surrendered the sack of corndodgers, but only after taking several out to eat as she watched the Creed brothers ride away. However, she decided at the last minute to continue riding east with them just a bit further and galloped her filly to catch up with them. All too soon, they had ridden another four miles and she still wasn't ready to watch them go, but let them go she must.

They stopped, shook hands again, and then let Chenoa take a few more corndodgers to stuff into her saddlebags. As they turned to the north-northeast, Chenoa suddenly felt very alone as she sat on her filly watching them ride out of her day-to-day life. She held onto her tears until they were at least a quarter mile away, and then had no choice but to let them flow, and flow they did, for a long time as she watched until they finally were too hard to make out against the landscape.

Ben had decided to take a shorter route, though a bit less traveled and a lot rougher, riding just north of Cleopatra Hill and then east through the red rock country, where they would camp the first night. The following day they would continue to push hard, and be in Flagstaff by the next night, maybe in time to get their animals loaded into a stock car and start their six hundred fifty plus mile, three day rail trip.

Ben's plan worked, saving them nearly a full day on their long trip home thus allowing them to reach Colorado City just six days after leaving Prescott, much to the pleasure of his mother and father as well as their siblings. Trouble had all ready dug in its heels at Colorado City, forcing the three brothers to enter the fray the next day after they arrived. Fortunately for everyone involved, as well as many others in the town and surrounding area, their arrival was just in time to start bringing that trouble to a sliding halt, but not without several people being injured, and a few losing their lives.

You can read about the next steps taken by these three brothers and their family in the book *No Town for Outlaws*, where violence surrounds the entire Creed family and those they know, forcing them all to fight for their very lives and their entire way of life.

The End

Printed in Great Britain
by Amazon